STRAYBECK RISING

By Michael James Lynch

First published in Great Britain 2018
Published by Solodog Publishing

Copyright © Michael Lynch 2018

Michael Lynch has asserted his right under the Copyright, Designs and Patents Act 1988 to be identified as the sole author of this work.

All rights reserved. No parts of this publication may be reproduced, stored or transmitted in any form by any means, electronic, mechanical, photocopying or otherwise without the prior written permission of the publisher.

This is a work of fiction and any resemblance to actual persons living or dead is purely coincidental.

ISBN 978-1-9999150-6-3 - Paperback
ISBN 978-1-9999150-7-0 - Epub
ISBN 978-1-9999150-8-7 - Mobi

For more details visit MichaelJamesLynch.com

Close your eyes, my darling,
close your little eyes.
Say goodnight, and sleep tight,
close your eyes, 'til tomorrow.

And if you dream, my darling,
say you'll dream of me.
And all the things that we can do,
tomorrow, you and me.

For James and Alanna
This book is for you.

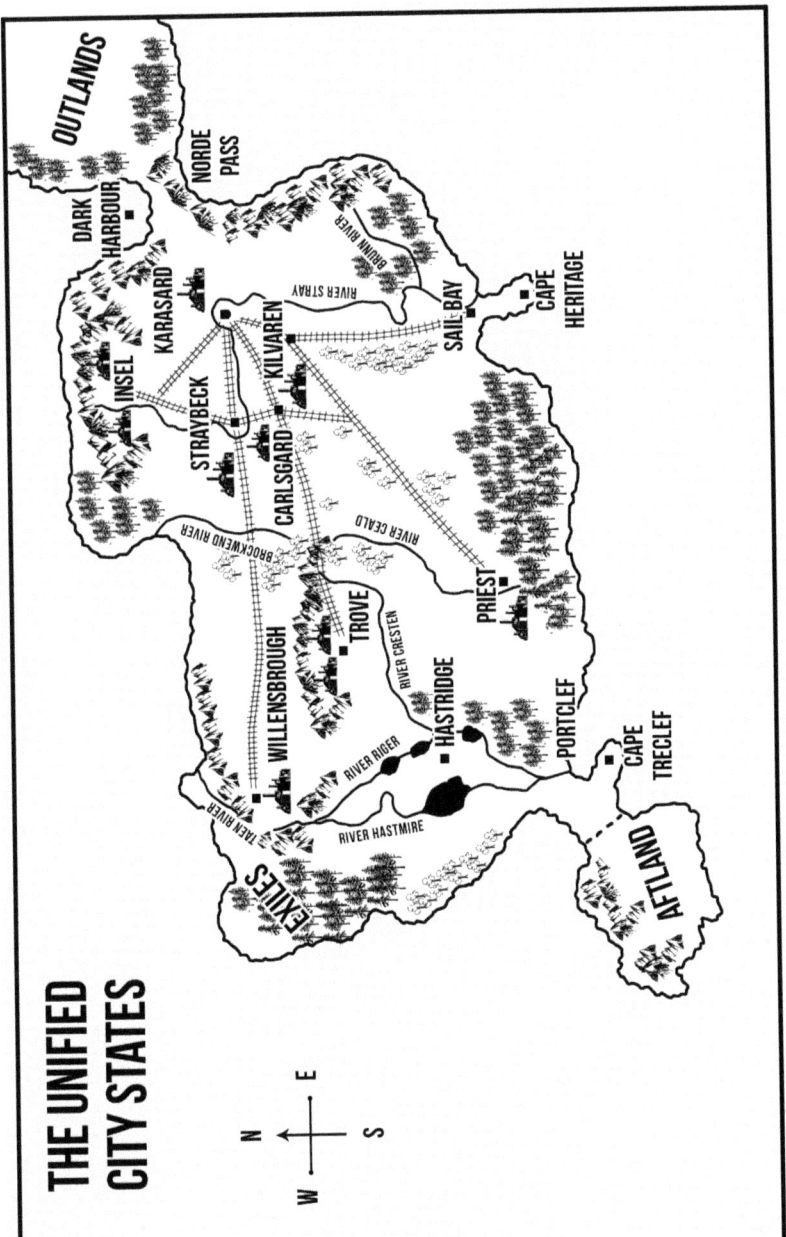

CHAPTER 1

He had once been an angry young man. Then they strung him up in the arches of The Cathedral and broke his body. Thirty-three years later, at two in the morning, Robb was lying awake, praying for his son. The curfew bell had struck hours ago and he knew the gunnermen were always looking for an easy arrest. Robb pulled back the blankets and limped towards the window, knees flaring with pain and his breath frosting in the cold.

The house was cloaked in darkness, so he peeled back the curtains and searched the street. It was a tomb. Ignoring the flashes of pain in his legs, he knelt before the window and waited. Eventually Robb saw what he had been hoping for. A silhouette drifting down the road. Coming home.

For a moment he allowed his anxiety to fade, until the figure outside suddenly stopped and sank back into the shadows. Robb held his breath, turning an ear to the window. The sound of an engine was quiet, but undeniable.

He watched the patrol car cruise into view at the top of the road where it waited for a few moments before cutting its engine and lights. Using the slope of the hill, it ghosted forwards, barely a whisper escaping the tyres.

Out on the street, Robb's son darted across the road like a startled hare. Then he was off through the gardens while a gunnerman jumped from the passenger seat to pursue on foot. The patrol car roared into life, sped to the end of the road and turned out of sight.

Robb was at the bedroom door in an instant, grabbing his clothes.

"Wait."

He pulled on his trousers and fumbled beneath the bed for his shoes.

"Robb. Please." It was Eliza. For the first time in memory he heard emotion in her voice. "The curfew. They'd lock you up."

"I can't just leave him," he said.

When he turned, Robb saw the fear on his own face mirrored in his wife's.

"They wouldn't let you out. Not again."

"I can't leave him," he hissed.

"You have another son."

Robb's shoulders sank because he knew she was right. With a hopeless sigh, he suppressed the feelings of anger and fear that constantly simmered beneath his skin.

Hours later, the front door clicked open and footsteps crept softly upstairs. Eliza was dozing quietly, but Robb hadn't slept. Not for a moment. He looked at the clock and saw it was nearly five. Two hours since he'd heard the patrol car make its last circuit.

He waited for the house to settle before crossing the hallway to Ryan's room. His son was fully clothed lying on top of the covers. Unhurt. Unaware. Robb closed his eyes and felt the worry fade, to be replaced by a deep resentment. From bitter experience he knew that Straybeck was a city without mercy. His son's recklessness risked everything.

He returned to his room and perched at the foot of the bed. There was no chance of finding sleep now so he slipped out of his bedclothes and dressed for work

"Is he back?" Eliza whispered.

"Yes." Despite the darkness, he instinctively turned away and covered the scars on his chest. "Go back to sleep," he breathed.

She rolled over without a word and Robb dressed in the dark. Downstairs, he lit one ring on the hob and flexed his fingers over the flickering blue flames. Then he ran a cloudy glass of water from the sink and listened to the world sleeping around him.

It was earlier than usual when Robb stepped outside and the sunlight was still struggling against the gloom. He made his way to the train station beneath a pale blue sky, while the wind bit around his face and neck. His legs were stiff and ached with every step, but Robb knew that the only answer was to move through the pain. By the time he reached the station, his strides had evened out and he was almost able to ignore the grinding at his knees.

He passed through the gunnerman checkpoint, finding as usual that the guard was dozing. Robb didn't wake him. If he was stopped later, he knew he had clearance to ride the trains to the city.

An enormous banner of Talis hung above the station entrance and the Premier's disapproving glare followed Robb down the platform. On the wall beside him, plastered at regular intervals, was a poster depicting another Gabbler invasion. It was the usual type of image. Thousands of the monstrous creatures swarming through a mountain pass, only to be repelled by a handful of noble gunnermen.

Robb walked on, head down. He took a seat on one of the metal benches and waited. Flecks of rain were illuminated in the dirty yellow lights hanging from the gantries. Somewhere in the distance Robb heard the hush and shunt of an approaching train and as he rose, both knees gave an angry crack of pain. The old train clattered to a stop and threw open its doors allowing Robb to step into the empty carriage and take his usual seat. The doors slid together with a hiss and the train jolted forwards, carrying him back to the factories. Back to Karasard.

Ryan woke after just three hours sleep. He took off his mud stained clothes from the night before and dressed quickly. His whole body was covered in bumps and bruises after his escape from the gunnermen.

He'd been talking with Brynne until way past curfew. Just before he left, the old man passed over one of the political pamphlets he handed out around the city.

You know what will happen if you're caught with this?

Ryan had nodded and promised to keep it safe.

Back in his bedroom he examined the puncture marks on the heel of each hand. He had scaled the wall into someone's back garden, only to find it topped with razor wire. The narrow cuts were quite deep, but they had scabbed over in the night.

Reaching under his pillow, he found the pamphlet that Brynne had given him and flicked to the first polemic.

We must give everything to the cause. We must forsake family and friends as they will be used against us. The revolutionary is a doomed man.

Ryan felt the hairs on his neck stand up. *Revolutionary*. He turned to the mirror straight-backed and raised his chin. Seventeen-years-old and already fighting the Government. Already making a difference.

Ryan placed the pamphlet back beneath his pillow. He'd find a better hiding place later, but right now he needed to go downstairs before his mum left for work. She was staring vacantly at the hall mirror, running a brush through her hair. Ryan watched her right hand, just three fingers and a thumb, gripped around the handle. The skin around the knuckle of her fourth finger was twisted into an ugly stump.

"You were back late," she said quietly, taking him by surprise.

Ryan felt guilty when he lied to his mum, so as usual he told her a half-truth. "I was at a friend's. I lost track of time."

Her eyes flicked up to meet his, but she didn't push any further. Maybe she didn't want to hear him lie. Ryan noticed that her handbag was on the hall table and he waited nearby for a chance to take some money.

His mum finished brushing her hair and turned towards the kitchen. Then, as an afterthought, she unfastened the zip on her handbag and left it unattended, almost like she was giving him permission. The idea made him feel even more ashamed than he already did.

We must forsake family and friends as they will be used against us.

He dipped into her purse and took a handful of bronze and coppers from within. It wasn't like he was spending it on himself. Not really. Brynne had arranged for him to get a counterfeit ID. He'd been begging and stealing the money for weeks and today he was finally meeting the forger. If it could get him past the checkpoints, it would be worth all the dishonesty.

Behind him, his younger brother John was halfway down the stairs, still in his pyjamas. John didn't say anything, just stood with a hand on either bannister, swinging his feet back and forth.

Ryan looked at his watch and then swore quietly.

"What's up?"

As usual John looked at Ryan with eyes of total devotion. It was an exhausting standard to maintain and the main reason why Ryan had begun to distance himself from his younger brother. It was easier than trying to explain the life that he led now. The way that Straybeck really was.

"Nothing's wrong," he said. "Except I'm late." Ryan grabbed his coat from the hook in the hallway and then returned to the kitchen to grab the last chunk of bread. In the fridge he found a wedge of cheese and took that too.

"Bye Mum," he said quietly, but there was no answer.

"Where are you going?" John said.

"Out. I'm meeting someone."

"But it's still early. Who's going to walk me to school?"

"You're twelve, I think you'll be alright." Ryan opened the door and a blast of cold air blew through the house. "Just stick to the main roads." As an afterthought he broke the lump of cheese in half and tore a chunk from the bread. "Here. Breakfast."

John grabbed them and hungrily popped the cheese into his mouth. "Dad will be angry if you don't take me."

"Well he knows where he can find me," Ryan said, slamming the front door as he left.

For the past two days he'd gone through the same checkpoint, so today he took a different route. Brynne said that the gunnermen tracked ID scans, so he tried to keep them guessing.

He felt bad for not walking John to school, but it couldn't be helped. He was already late for the meeting with the forger. He ran as far as the stone pillars at the park entrance and then walked along the muddy path trying to catch his breath.

The perimeter of trees thinned out and the path opened onto a huge playing field. Ryan crossed the open grass and traipsed up the hill at the far side. As he reached the playground, he saw the bench where he was supposed to meet the forger. It was empty. Ryan checked his watch again. He wasn't more than a couple of minutes late, so he sat down on the cracked wooden slats and waited while grey clouds coasted through the sky.

From his vantage point at the top of the hill, Ryan had an unobstructed view of the park in three directions. In front and behind there was open parkland. To the left there was a steep slope followed by a thick ribbon of water. It was the River Stray, or at least an offshoot of the main thing that began all the way up in the mountains of Insel.

Beyond the river, a high wall marked the boundary to the sprawling Worker District. Above the wall, dirty chimneys stabbed skyward forming a bleak horizon over Straybeck. It was only to his right that Ryan's view was obstructed by a wide strip of woodland, old as Straybeck itself. As Ryan glanced at the tangled trees, his attention was drawn to a movement beneath the boughs of an oak tree. He squinted at the swaying branches where there was the unmistakable shape of a man. A stab of nerves twisted his stomach and he waited, wide-eyed and unsure what to do. The figure in the trees took a step forwards and gave an urgent twitch of his hand, beckoning Ryan closer.

They were supposed to meet on the bench, so either he'd decided to wait out of sight, or it was a gunnerman trap. Seconds passed while Ryan considered running. The figure stepped fully into the daylight revealing a skinny guy with a pale face. He gave another urgent wave to Ryan before jumping back into the shadows.

Ryan pushed himself from the bench and jogged warily towards the trees. As he came closer, the man moved deeper into the tangle of brambles and branches.

"What's your name?" he said.

"Depends," Ryan answered. "Who are you?"

"Premier Talis." The skinny guy gave a withering look. "I don't have time for this. Just tell me your name."

"Ryan Calloway."

His eyes went wide. "Just like that," he almost shouted. "Ryan Calloway. As easy as that." He turned and stalked away through the trees.

"Wait," Ryan called. "Where are you going?"

"I'm out," the guy said. "Tell your man I don't deal with amateurs."

"But I've got your money," Ryan called desperately. "Ask Brynne."

The guy span round so fast, Ryan thought he was going to attack him.

"Will you shut your mouth," he hissed. He glanced over his shoulder as though the forest might be listening.

"I'm sorry," Ryan said. "I've not done this before."

"No kidding. Word of advice, if you live long enough to do it again…which I very much doubt…try to be just a little more cautious."

"Okay, okay. But what do I do now? Aren't you the guy that Bry…that he sent me to meet?" The forger didn't answer, but he didn't walk away either, so Ryan pressed on. "Have you got the ID?"

"Of course I haven't," he hissed, clearly trying hard to hold his temper. "How do you think it would look if I was searched and they found someone else's ID card? But I can show you where it is." Suddenly, he froze.

"What?" Ryan whispered.

The man silenced him with a finger in the air, cocking his head to listen more intently. That was when Ryan heard it too. Footsteps scrunching nearby and the choked panting of a dog.

"Get away from me," the man growled, running deeper into the trees. "You've been followed."

Ryan said nothing. He was out of his depth and he knew it. He tried to make off in the other direction, but after three steps a voice called out, sharp as a punch.

"After 'em lad."

He heard the crash of broken branches and then a huge black dog burst into view, muzzle drawn back in a snarl. It moved through the undergrowth with long, high bounds, sighting for its prey. Ryan dropped to the floor, pressing his face into dead leaves.

If he'd had time, he would have warned the forger. Called out to him and told him to stay quiet. But there hadn't been time and now Ryan heard a growl of excitement from the dog as it locked onto the retreating figure. It was followed by heavy boots running past Ryan's hiding place, crunching over fallen branches.

"Stand still. Hands in the air." It was the same deep, angry voice.

Ryan didn't wait to see if the forger had stopped. He jumped to his feet and sprinted through the trees in the opposite direction. A shout went up, and he saw another gunnerman closing in. Ryan dipped his head and charged down the steep slope and towards the river. He lost his footing and slipped down the sodden grass on his backside. Scrambling up, he risked a glance over one shoulder only to see two gunnermen in pursuit with a dog. The River Stray was wide and fast flowing, swollen by rain. It frothed and churned beneath the lip of the embankment, leaving a barrier nearly thirty feet across.

"Stop," one of the gunnermen shouted.

Ryan backed up a few paces.

"Stand still," the command came, louder this time.

Ryan charged forwards and leapt high in the air, tensed for the crack of gunfire. As he plunged into the icy water, the current pulled him under and thrust him downstream. He kicked upwards, breaching every few moments to snatch a lungful of air before he was dragged back beneath the surface. Rocks pummelled his body each time the water tumbled him over.

A turn in the river created a natural eddy where the pace of water momentarily slowed. Ryan was able to find his footing amongst the loose stones and waded closer to shore. His boots sank into the muddy embankment at the far side and he pulled up handfuls of grass as he clambered up the slope.

Glancing back, he saw a gunnerman levelling his rifle

to take aim. Ryan sprinted for the park wall, scaling halfway before a gunshot split the air. It blasted out a chunk of brick, showering his face in grit. As the volley resonated across the park, Ryan scrambled onwards, wet clothes clinging to his body. He dragged himself over the lip of the wall and landed heavily on the paving stones. He was trembling with fear and adrenalin but forced himself to jump up and sprint for the factory walls ahead. Hopefully he could lose the gunnermen in the narrow streets of the Worker District. If not, he'd be in The Cathedral by nightfall.

CHAPTER 2

JOHN HAD BEEN in bed an hour when the first gunshots sounded. He crept down the ladder of his bunk and sat by the window to watch flashing red lights split the Worker District. The faint wail of a gunnerman siren reached him through the glass.

"John?" His dad was silhouetted at the door. "Go back to bed. It's not safe."

John let the curtains fall back into place and padded across the room. "What are they shooting at?"

"Nothing. It's just fireworks."

He pulled the duvet to his chin while his dad stretched the cracks from the curtains.

"Night," John whispered. He waited for a hand on his head or a comforting word. There was neither and his dad shut the room into darkness.

He was woken some time later by a muffled thud at the other side of the room. John shot upright and saw someone shadowed at the end of his bed. The figure was standing on a chair and reaching into the loft hatch. John gave a quiet whimper and the figure spun around dropping a small booklet onto the floor.

"Go to sleep."

John recognised his brother's voice and watched as he balanced back on the chair and hid the booklet in the roof space.

"What time is it?" he whispered.

"Late." Ryan threw himself onto the lower bunk and kicked off his shoes. Within seconds, his breathing levelled out and John knew his brother was asleep.

The next day, he dressed quietly and came downstairs to sit with his dad. The radio was playing in the kitchen and the newsreader was describing a training exercise in the Worker District. He said that shots had been fired, but it was just the gunnermen testing their night-time defences.

John took a bite from his crust of bread and chewed it thoughtfully. "You told me it was fireworks."

"I was wrong." His dad left the table and limped into the hallway where he tugged on his coat.

"Where are you going?"

"To buy a paper."

"Can I come?"

Without waiting for an answer John jumped up from the table and grabbed his own coat. His dad sighed, but held the door for him. It was cold outside and John pulled his sleeves over both hands. When the first checkpoint came into view, he stepped close to his dad.

"I've got my card," he whispered. "For the paper."

"Good lad."

"Will they search you?"

"They always do."

Robb's legs were hurting more than usual this morning, but he kept his pace brisk, refusing to let John see how much they pained him. There were two checkpoints between their house and the Trade District, one at each railway station. Years ago, Robb would never have taken the train for a journey like this, but even short trips were becoming hard lately. There was no chance he could walk the forty minutes across town and back.

He let John pass through the first checkpoint ahead of him, hoping that his son wouldn't see the list of previous convictions that were going to flash up on screen. Robb knew he couldn't hide his past forever. John was twelve and more curious that was good for him, but he still hoped for one more year before his youngest boy looked at him the way Ryan did.

As it went, the gunnerman on duty recognised him and waved Robb through without scanning. It was a minor offence - for both of them - but Robb reasoned that he was safe enough. An old offender like him wasn't their priority anymore.

The train took almost half an hour to reach the centre of Straybeck and the gunnermen at Municipal Station were not so lenient. When they scanned his ID and the warning markers flashed up on screen, two gunnermen gripped Robb by the arms and shoved him against the station wall.

"Take it easy," Robb said calmly. "That's my son watching."

The response was a gloved palm that pinned his face against the bricks. Once they had searched him though, they relaxed a little and sent Robb through to the Trade District.

John walked solemnly ahead, saying nothing about the checkpoint and eventually waited for him on the high kerb of Market Street. They stood a while watching the wagons make their deliveries until an army truck rolled past, lurching from side to side on the uneven cobbles. The driver gave them a hard stare and Robb lowered his eyes as he took John by the hand. "Come on. Let's go."

The nearest buyall store was a couple of blocks away. They moved through the busy streets, cutting between bakery lines and pushing through the thin crowds. There were gunnermen on every street and as he walked, Robb *tap-tapped* at his front pocket feeling for the reassuring shape of his ID card.

"Do you want me to buy the paper?" John whispered. "So you don't have to scan?"

Robb gave him a sideways glance and then nodded. "But if they ask who it's for?"

"It's for me. And I won't pass it on to anyone else."

"Good lad."

While John queued up, Robb waited outside the buyall. Not wanting to raise suspicions by standing idle though, he walked a short distance up the street and browsed the butcher's window. It was important to appear busy in Straybeck. Anyone seen standing idle risked coming to the attention of the gunnermen. All they needed was an excuse.

As Robb glanced over the collection of meats in the shop window, he wondered exactly when they had accepted fear as part of their lives. Straybeck hadn't always been like this. *He* hadn't always been like this.

Thirty-three years ago, Robb had been a swaggering young man of eighteen. Back then he was living in the capital city of Karasard and he remembered walking through the Royal Gardens with Eliza. Of course, it wasn't actually called the Royal Gardens by then. Almost six years had passed since The Liberation War when Talis overthrew the King. Any trace of the royal family had been stripped away; their statues torn down and melted for munitions.

Robb and Eliza hadn't been seeing each other for long.

Even so, he knew that he loved her and recalled with wonder the thrill he had felt with each touch. That day when he wrapped his arm around her shoulder, she tilted her head and they shared a long slow kiss. Robb had grinned like a buffoon, carrying his happiness too freely, never suspecting it would run out.

Eliza had laced her fingers through his, a simple act, but one that in a few months' time, she would never allow again. They settled on a bench and stared down at what had once been the king's palace. It was now the party headquarters.

"I liked it better before," Robb said.

Eliza glanced nervously around her. "Robb," she whispered.

"What? It's not illegal to talk about the past." Which it wasn't, but it wasn't a good idea either.

During The Liberation War, the palace had been bombed into submission. As a boy, Robb watched it burn through the worst night of shelling the city had ever seen. Premier Talis built his party headquarters above the foundations. It glared over Karasard; all concrete and hard lines. An unspoken threat. Robb remembered how gunnermen had patrolled the gardens back then and one walked purposefully towards them. The sky was bright and from the bench Robb squinted up at him.

"What are you up to?"

"Nothing," Robb said.

"What are you doing here?"

"Just enjoying the day. Is there a problem?"

The gunnerman scanned the park, still not making eye-contact. "Maybe," he said. "Why did you point at the Party Headquarters?"

"We didn't."

"Yes you did."

The eighteen-year-old Robb knew nothing of pain or suffering. Maybe that was why his first reaction was anger instead of fear. "Listen, we're just sitting on a bench, enjoying the weather. If we pointed, it was probably to say how ugly the thing is." He stood up and took hold of Eliza's hand. "Come on, let's go."

"I've not finished yet."

"Well we have," Robb said as he shouldered past the gunnerman's outstretched arm, pulling Eliza with him.

"Oi," the gunnerman called, striding forwards.

Robb remembered that he had been ready to fight the gunnerman, if it had come to that. He and Eliza walked quickly to the gates and out into Karasard. For some reason, the gunnermen didn't pursue them and now it was just a memory. The truth was though, that day in the gardens had been the last time he ever back-talked a gunnerman. The thought of doing it now made his insides run cold.

He shook his head and moved away from the butcher's window, making his way down Market Street and towards the buyall. John appeared soon after, proudly showing him the newspaper.

"Keep a tight hold of it," Robb said automatically.

He knew that spies patrolled the markets watching for anyone that passed on restricted items. Halfway up the road, they saw a patrol car and Robb instinctively kept his eyes to the ground while his fingers *tap-tapped* on the ID card in his front pocket. All they needed was an excuse. When the car had passed by, he gave a sad shake of his head, mourning the loss of the man he had once been.

When they returned from town, John gave the paper to his dad and went into the kitchen. All morning his mind had run back to the image of his brother searching through the loft hatch last night. John guessed that he had something hidden there but couldn't risk looking while Ryan was still in the house.

His mum was sitting at the table with her head resting on one hand. She looked tired and sad, but that wasn't unusual.

"Where's Ryan?"

"He went out," she didn't look at him and her voice was flat.

"Where did he go?"

She gave a small shrug and he guessed that it was the only answer he was going to receive. Filled with excitement, John bounded upstairs and cautiously pushed open his bedroom door. A cool breeze hit him from an open window and a faint trace of smoke hung in the air. Ryan's blankets were heaped up at the end of his bunk, the only evidence that he even lived in that room.

As John pulled the window shut, he noticed an old woman looking at him from the house opposite. He smiled at her, but she glared back, hard-faced. Against his better judgement, John drew the curtains and hoped that she wasn't an informer. His dad said that people were always informing on their neighbours. He said that all they needed was an excuse.

The room dipped into darkness and John pulled the chair out from beneath the desk. He reached up on tiptoes and pushed at the wooden loft hatch. It slid to one side and John pushed his hand through the gap, feeling around in the roof space. He didn't exactly know what he was looking for, but when his fingers felt paper, he pulled a magazine into view.

It sent a shower of grit into the room that left him blinking dust. He stepped down from the chair and perched on the edge of the lower bunk.

John thumbed through the magazine and with each page his stomach clenched tighter. Thick black text jumped out at him, broken by pictures of a war-torn city. Some showed the gunnermen beating workers and others showed piles of bodies rotting in the street. One of the captions read:

Troops murder protesters in Karasard

John shut the magazine, afraid to read on.

"John?" His dad pushed open the door and then stared in horror at the closed curtains.

"What are you doing?" he limped across the room and yanked them open. "You've got to think, John." That was when he caught sight of the magazine and held out one hand. John looked at the outstretched fingers, glimpsing the burned and discoloured skin at the edge of his shirt sleeve.

"It's not mine," John said. "It's Ryan's"

His dad's face drained of colour as he scanned the front cover. He leant forward and spoke with icy threat. "You never saw this."

John nodded.

"Get downstairs."

As he ran from the room, he heard the creak of Ryan's chair, followed by a shallow grunt of effort. He knew his dad was searching inside the loft space and just prayed that Ryan would forgive him.

CHAPTER 3

At the end of the road Ryan dropped the stub of his cigarette to the pavement and ground it flat with one foot. As usual, he grew angry when his house came into sight. He had accepted that his dad was a spineless traitor, but he hated that people would think he was like that too. As far as Ryan was concerned, they shared a roof and a second name. That was all.

He approached the front door and predicted a fight with his dad about breaking curfew. Ryan had practised his response.

I'm seventeen years old. I can come home when I fucking want.

But his dad wasn't in the kitchen or in the lounge. In fact, he could only find John who was waiting on the sofa with a guilty expression on his face.

"What's up with you?"

"Nothing."

An odd pang of sadness twisted his stomach.

We must forsake family and friends for they will be used against us.

Ryan knew that his brother was the only one anchoring him here. The only person he really cared for anymore. But he also knew that he no longer had the luxury of those feelings. Brynne had made it clear that he needed to shut his family out if he was to keep them safe.

In spite of himself though, he gave his little brother a smile and shoved him gently on the arm. John rocked back and forth like a pendulum, finally coming to rest on Ryan who grabbed him in a playful headlock.

"Ryan." Their mum came to the doorway while they were both grinning. For a moment - just for a moment - it felt like the old days.

"Dad wants to speak to you, love."

He locked his smile back inside. "Why?"

"I don't know." It was a lie. Her eyes flicked to the carpet because she could never look him in the face when she lied. "He's waiting in your room. He's been there all morning."

She retreated to the kitchen and Ryan took a deep breath before heading for the stairs. At the bottom step, a small voice called him back.

"Ryan?" It was John. "I found a magazine. In the roof."

Ryan sprinted upstairs, two at a time. The bedroom door was open and his father was sitting on the lower bunk. At the sound of footsteps he twisted round, his jaw clenched tight. Ryan felt a flutter in his stomach but pushed it aside.

"What are you doing in my room?"

"Don't start," he said, rising slowly from the chair. "You're in enough trouble as it is."

"Why? What have I done?"

"What about bringing a…" he paused, biting back his temper, "a pamphlet. An anti-government pamphlet into my house." He took a long deep breath, his fists slowly clenching and unclenching.

"You shouldn't have gone through my things."

"I wish I'd done it sooner. I wish I'd been the one to find it. But it was your brother. Your twelve-year old brother." His dad's temper flared again. "What do you think would have happened if he'd shown it to his friends? What if he'd taken it to school?"

"Well he didn't, did he?" Ryan pushed past and sat at the desk. "And, I'm giving it back later anyway. So you don't have to worry."

"You're kidding, right?" His dad scoffed. "You actually think you're getting it back?"

"I need it," Ryan said, the pitch of his own voice rising. "I've promised."

"Well you can just un-promise. Or better yet, tell me who gave it to you and let me deal with them."

"I bet you'd love that," Ryan sneered. There was no way he'd let his dad inform on Brynne. Never. "Where's the pamphlet?" he demanded.

"I burned it," his dad said with a shrug.

"You what?"

"I burned it."

Ryan was furious. He had promised Brynne he'd look after it. He'd never trust him now.

"Why do you have to be such a…" he struggled for the words, "such a fucking sell-out?"

His dad's eyes narrowed and he spoke with a voice that was low and full of threat. "I'm trying very hard to stay calm now, Ryan. More than you'll ever know. But keep pushing me and you'll not like what you find."

Ryan gave a short laugh. "Doesn't matter," he said. "I can get another. You can't watch me all the time."

"Can't you see what you're doing to this family?" his dad said, rubbing one hand over his scalp. "To your mother? To John? Do you ever think of anyone but yourself?"

"A revolutionary must forsake his family and friends or they will be used against him," Ryan quoted proudly.

"A *revolutionary?* Do you have any idea how ridiculous you sound?"

"*I'm* ridiculous?" Ryan fired back, refusing to be cowed. "Take a look at yourself, you cripple." That hit the mark. His dad thrust one hand into Ryan's chest, knocking him backwards.

"What is wrong with you? Who's filling your head with all this?"

"Don't touch me." Ryan shoved back, putting his whole body behind it. Both of them shouting now.

"Who is it? Who's twisted you up like this?"

"No one."

"Who gave you the pamphlet?"

"No one."

"Who gave it to you?"

When he refused to answer, his dad stepped closer, less than a hands width between their faces. Ryan's next words were out before he'd even thought them.

"Fuck you."

Ryan felt two large hands grab him round the neck and slam him against the wall. As he struggled against the grip, he felt his dad's leg buckle beneath their combined weight. Quickly Ryan kicked out at the weakened knee, sending them sprawling to the floor. His dad struggled up, breathing hard and Ryan braced himself for the punch he felt sure was coming. Instead his dad tore at the buttons of his own shirt, his voice raw with emotion.

"Is this what you want? To see *this* when you look in the mirror"

The open shirt revealed a mass of disfigured flesh. His stomach was lumped and stitched like old clothes, crisscrossed with angry red scars. Large burns had healed into shiny patches of soft tissue and the flesh across the left side of his chest was sagged and melted like candle wax.

Ryan's stomach heaved and he dragged his eyes away. He ran from the room, taking the stairs in twos and threes. He saw John in the hallway, white-faced and frozen to the spot. He shouldered past and slammed the door behind him.

CHAPTER 4

As his heart slowed and his breathing grew steady, Ryan stared at the surrounding houses. There were faces in the windows but he didn't care. He tilted his chin and glared back until they looked away. He tried to light a cigarette, but his hands were still trembling from the confrontation with his dad. He shoved them back in his pockets before hawking a mouthful of spit onto the road. He only had one place he could go now and Ryan set off at a run for the Worker District.

He had wanted to visit Brynne ever since the gunnermen chased him at the park, but the old man had made his thoughts crystal clear about that. If ever he was compromised, he should wait at least three days before making contact. Standard gunnermen procedure was to keep a seventy-two hour surveillance on every snatch target. After that time, you were either in the clear or The Cathedral. As he walked, Ryan counted the days off on his fingers. It had been five days since he'd tried to buy the ID card. Even for Brynne that should be enough.

At the first checkpoint he showed his card. The gunnerman wasn't much older than Ryan and had craters in his cheeks from acne scars. He snatched it from Ryan's hand and scanned it into the machine. *No restrictions* blipped up on screen but the gunnerman wasn't satisfied. He glared at the photograph and thumbed at the side of the card, looking for a join.

It was genuine though and, when he couldn't prove otherwise, he passed it back. As Ryan tried to grab it, the gunnerman tossed it to the floor and walked back into booth laughing.

Beyond the checkpoint Ryan found himself walking the narrow streets, surrounded by terraced slum-houses where rubbish piled up in the alleyways. He cupped his hands and blew a stream of hot air through them before taking a left onto Carragon Road.

This stretch of town was always eerily silent. On one side it had a long, high wall that ran the length of the street. On the other side stood a row of buildings that had been destroyed by gunfire. The brickwork fronts were pockmarked by bullet holes and Ryan ran his fingers in and out of the ridges. There was one building that had completely crumbled leaving only a skeleton frame of jagged masonry. As always, Ryan felt his eyes drawn to the whitewashed wall opposite.

Brynne had once shown him a picture of this exact spot from over thirty years ago. He remembered holding the faded, black and white image in his hands, the hairs on his forearms standing on end as he stared at a mound of corpses. That same day, Brynne had taken him to Carragon Road and stood him at that very spot. Even now it was possible to see the faint outline of a word that was written beneath the whitewash.

JUSTICE?

On the path ahead, a small chunk of brick had dropped from one house. Ryan kicked it across the road and watched it rebound against the wall with a satisfying thud. He turned his thoughts back to the argument with his father, replaying it again and again. When the image of his ruined chest and melted skin came to mind, Ryan squeezed his eyes shut and forced it away.

Years ago, he used to stick up for his dad. He would fight other kids when they called him the son of a traitor. If his dad asked why his clothes were ripped, or his lip bloodied, he would make up some excuse, desperate to spare him the hurt.

That was before Brynne had told him the truth though.

When he turned off Carragon Road, he moved quickly through a maze of back alleyways until he found himself outside an abandoned chapel. It looked derelict from the outside, but so did everything else round there. He gave one last check to make sure that no one was following before pushing open the door.

Ryan waited for the gloom to clear from his eyes and took a few cautious steps into the chapel. The wooden door, swollen with age, scraped over the sandstone floor with a groan. Even something as mundane as that sounded exciting here. Brynne was everything his dad would never be. A living legend, leading a secret life deep in the heart of the Worker District.

Inside the chapel it was even more ramshackle. The few remaining pews showed scorch marks from an old fire and had now begun to rot with damp. Although the vaulted archways were still intact, the roof they supported was collapsing so that rain and sunshine fell through to the chamber below. Whatever fire and time had left, the looters had taken.

Ryan made his way towards the chancel at the back of the church. His nerves were still jangled from the argument and it was a relief when he saw Brynne appear in the side archway behind the altar. As always, the old man's presence was reassuring. He had a strong face, broad shoulders and a temperament like deep water. Instead of the usual relaxed smile though, right now it looked like he had seen a ghost. It lasted barely a moment though until he was smiling.

"Ryan, my boy," he offered his hand. "I'd expected you days ago. You gave me a start."

They shook hands. "I've been staying away," he said. "There were gunnermen."

Brynne glanced at the back of the church as though he expected them to burst in.

"Come on," he said. "Let's talk downstairs."

The old man turned towards a moth-eaten tapestry at the back of the altar. He drew it to one side revealing a staircase that led down into the tombs below the main chapel. That was where Brynne had made his home.

At the bottom of the steps there was a gas lamp flickering and blowing in the drafts. The small flame shifted silhouettes across the cellar wall and as usual Ryan scanned the clippings and pictures that were fastened to the stones. They told the true history of Straybeck over the past thirty-five years. A sordid tale of greed and oppression by Premier Talis and his gunnermen since the Liberation Wars. It was illegal to even read these articles, but anyone found with a collection like this would live a short and painful life inside The Cathedral.

"So?" Brynne asked, sitting on the chair and gesturing for Ryan to take a seat opposite. "What happened?"

"I went to the park like you said and the forger was there in the trees. But as soon as we started to talk, the gunnermen turned up. They had dogs"

Brynne leaned back in the chair, his face suddenly

shadowed. "Were you followed?" His voice was low, the hint of an accusation showing.

"No, I swear I wasn't. It must have been him they were watching because the gunnermen were already waiting when I got there."

"How many?"

"Three. I think. And maybe two dogs. One of them shot at me while I was running away, but I climbed the park wall and hid in the Worker District."

"And Caylin? The forger?"

"I think they took him."

A sudden scraping cut through the quiet.

"What was that?" Ryan said, spinning round in search of the noise. There was a recessed archway at the back of the cellar, but it was shrouded in darkness and the door looked old and unused.

When Ryan turned back, a cold, angry expression had settled over Brynne's face.

"Did you actually see him snatched?"

"Well no, not exactly. He was running and the dogs were right behind him. But he might have got away. I guess."

"No," Brynne said quietly. "No he didn't."

Beside his chair there was a narrow gap in the wall and the old man reached inside. He drew out a pistol, never breaking his gaze from Ryan.

"Caylin couldn't have got away. He was always book smart, but he couldn't escape a snatch team. Not in a hundred years."

Ryan's heart was racing, his stomach clenched tight. His eyes flicked back and forth between Brynne and the pistol he had now rested on his lap.

"I need you to understand this," the old man said. "The test of a true revolutionary is in making hard choices, regardless of personal feelings."

"What's happening?" Ryan's voice was barely a whisper.

Brynne raised the gun and moved forwards while Ryan shrank further into his chair. In a few quick strides though, Brynne had swept past him and was poised in the archway at the end of the room. The old wooden door was studded with thick iron bolts, but Brynne wrenched it open in one quick movement.

There was a sudden cry of alarm and through the gloom, Ryan made out the shape of a mattress and some blankets heaped untidily on the floor. There was a man there too, scrambling to his feet and shielding his eyes from the sudden burst of light.

It was the forger, although Ryan barely recognised him. He was barefoot, wearing dirty, dishevelled clothes and his hair was sticking out at all angles. Even his mannerisms seemed wild, like a caged animal, hunched over and frightened by the light. As soon as his eyes adjusted, they fixed on Ryan.

"Here?" he shouted. "You brought him here?"

The forger rounded on Brynne, not realising for a few moments that there was a gun levelled at him. "What's this?"

"You should have stayed away Caylin. You shouldn't have brought this to my doorstep."

"What?" the forger spluttered, a look of incomprehension on his face. Then his eyes cleared as though he had suddenly grasped the answer to a problem. "You," he said to Brynne. "You…"

A deafening impact burst through the vault as the bullet ripped into Caylin's chest and dropped him back to the mattress. Ryan cried out in shock, pushing away from the terrible scene. As the echo of gunfire faded, Brynne knelt beside the forger, listening to him breathe ragged gulps of air and cough out globs of blood.

"Sorry old friend," Brynne whispered.

Caylin looked up with hatred in his eyes and scraped for his final breaths.

Ryan didn't know whether he should stay or run. His eyes strayed to the crumpled body once more and his stomach lurched. He doubled up and puked onto the stone floor. Brynne rose and half-closed the heavy wooden door so that only a pair of legs showed through the gap.

"Why did you do that?" Ryan groaned, wiping strings of saliva from his mouth.

Brynne returned to his seat and hid the gun back within the wall. He reached onto the shelf beside him and took hold of a whisky bottle. There were two small tumblers beside it and he took them down, blowing the dust from them before pouring a generous measure of whisky into each. He offered one to Ryan who took it and sank numbly into the chair opposite.

"He came to me three nights ago," Brynne said quietly. "He reckoned that the gunnermen had taken you but he'd managed to escape. Told me this great sob story about how he'd slept rough for two nights before coming to me for shelter. And like a fool I believed him."

"But what if," Ryan stopped, feeling his stomach fall again. "What if it was the truth? What if he did get away?"

Brynne shook his head. "You think he outran a snatch squad? *Him*? You said it yourself Ryan, the hounds were right behind him."

"But what if I was wrong? What if I missed something?"

"It wasn't just that. His story didn't add up. He couldn't tell me anything about where he'd been the past two days. Two days Ryan. Doesn't that seem odd to you? Because if I worked at The Cathedral, I reckon two days would be plenty of time to break a guy like Caylin."

"You think he was working for *them*? For the gunnermen?"

"I think part of me knew it as soon as he turned up at the door. I just didn't want it to be true." Brynne leaned forwards, his expression more intense than Ryan had ever seen. "This is the reality of what we do. These are the sacrifices we have to make."

Ryan took a sip of whisky, the burning liquid almost making him gag a second time. He searched Brynne's eyes, waiting for something that could take away the awful emptiness he felt.

"I'm sorry," the old man said, his face softening. "I've tried so hard to shield you from this side of it all."

"How can you do it?" Ryan said, his voice rough and quiet. He forced himself to look away from the forger's body at the end of the room. Brynne took a sip of his own drink, nursing the liquid round his gums.

"The first time I killed a man I was two years older than you. I was crying when I did it, if you can believe that." He gave an empty laugh. "I've no idea how many people I've killed since. But it gets easier. It gets...*normal*."

The silence dragged out between them.

"I fought with my dad today," Ryan said eventually. It almost made him laugh just saying the words aloud. "He found the pamphlet you gave me. Tried to make me tell him who I got it from." He chanced a look at Brynne, but the old man's expression was unreadable.

"He pinned me up against the wall. Then showed me all the…" Ryan pointed a hand over his own chest, "scars and stuff. You know."

Brynne nodded.

"It was the worst thing I've ever seen…until now."

"He's concerned for you," Brynne said. "He's always given in to the Government. So when he sees you full of fight and fire, it scares him."

"I'm not like him. I won't swear allegiance." In ten months it would be his eighteenth birthday. Like everyone else they'd expect him to take the oath.

"You know, it's no small thing to face The Cathedral," Brynne said.

"I'm not going to change my mind."

There seemed very little worth saying after that and when Ryan stood to leave, he gave no explanation. At the bottom of the steps, he paused, half-turning towards Brynne.

"I didn't tell him. Where I got the pamphlet from."

"I know."

Ryan nodded and climbed back to the streets of Straybeck.

CHAPTER 5

ALIA TURNER WALKED through the schoolyard alone. Overhead, the skyline was as grey and gloomy as her mood. Three girls were whispering at the main doors and as she drew closer, laughter erupted from the group and they ran inside. A year ago, they had been her friends. A year ago, things had been very different.

"Miss Turner?" It was Mr Kinley, the head-teacher. He walked across the yard and the wind flipped his tie over one shoulder. "Alia?" She had been going back into school, but Mr Kinley beckoned her out onto the yard again. "I need to talk to you. About…things," he said.

Her stomach sank. Since she started at Straybeck Academy, she had only spoken to Mr Kinley twice. The first time was last year, when he had looked at her with big sad eyes, made bigger and sadder by his thick glasses. He told her how sorry he was.

"Your Father and I were friends. He was a good man. But don't worry, at least your future here is secure."

The first time was last year. The second was today.

"There's been an error with the admissions this term," Mr Kinley said. "I know that when we spoke about your place last year, we came to an understanding. I told you that it was my intention to keep you at the school as long as a place existed for you."

Alia nodded through the lie.

"Unfortunately, a place has been promised to a student this term despite our classes being full. The parents of this child are very important to us. Very important. I'm sure you understand the situation this puts me in?"

"I'm sorry, I don't understand, Sir." She refused to make this easy for him.

Mr Kinley cleared his throat. "What I'm trying to say is that it would be impossible for me to turn this child away. Especially when we have a non-fee paying student in the school. The Governors simply wouldn't allow it. I'm very sorry, but I can't keep your place open any longer."

"What about my exams, Sir?"

Mr Kinley handed her a piece of paper. "Ah. Now. That is the good news. You see, I've pulled a few strings with a friend of mine at Straybeck Central."

Alia's eyes closed and she made an involuntary groan.

"I know what you're thinking," Mr Kinley said quickly. "But the school has improved dramatically over the past few years and there really is no reason why a hard-working student can't graduate with above average grades. The qualifications will no longer exempt you from the factories of course, but there's no reason why you wouldn't be assigned to low level management or even a secretarial position after graduation."

She took the slip of paper from him and unfolded it to see the crest of Straybeck Central. Beneath the crest was a lesson timetable for the next term. "What about here? What about my coursework? My books?"

Mr Kinley shifted his stance uneasily. He stared at the school gates behind her. "We'll post them on," he said. "I'm sorry, but there really is no point in dragging this out any longer."

Without another word, he turned his back on her and Alia walked out through the main gate. The old security guard smiled at her from his kiosk. She passed her ID card beneath the glass, but he shook his head and slid it back to her.

"Couldn't forget a face like yours," he said. It was the same joke he used most days, but she managed a weak smile and set off through Old Straybeck and towards the Slum District.

The next morning, despite having no school, Alia still woke at first light. The house was silent and she opened her eyes to the familiar ache of hunger. It was a cold morning and as she plodded downstairs, her breath frosted the air. Her mum was sitting in the lounge, shivering as she listened to the radio.

"What are you doing down here?"

With dull, swollen eyes her mother turned to the voice, but showed no recognition. Her hair was unwashed and unbrushed, like she hadn't slept in a week.

"Have you been to bed yet?" Alia said, not expecting an answer. She stooped to kiss her mum and wrapped a blanket around her. With a sigh she picked up a small bottle of antidepressants, noting that it was empty.

Alia went through to the kitchen and ignited the hob beneath a saucepan of water. It was a black and battered thing left behind by the previous occupants. She remembered the gleaming kitchen at her old house, kept spotless by a cook and two scullery maids. It was all gone now of course. Auctioned off to settle her father's impossible debt.

Alia opened the fridge and the stench of rotten food made her jolt backwards. There was nothing edible and she shut the door, resting her head on the cold metal. She waited there for several minutes feeling drained and empty. Eventually, the kettle set up a shrill whistle, demanding her attention and Alia steadied herself for the day ahead.

"Here you go," she said a few minutes later. With a forced smile she carried two mugs of tea into the lounge. Her Mum took hold of one and brought it to her chest. Alia sat down and let their shoulders rest against each other. Even this small touch was comforting. "I'm going out for a bit, Mum. For food."

There was no reply.

"I'll have to take some jewellery, but it's just in case. Don't worry."

They sat in silence while Alia finished her tea. Her mum didn't drink and Alia knew she would just hold it to her chest until the mug grew cold. There was a noise upstairs that made her flinch. Her mum heard it too and lowered her head while the mug trembled in her hands.

"It's okay, Mum," she said. "I'll sort it."

An hour later, she stepped out into a bitterly cold Straybeck morning. Alia fastened her coat as she walked away from their rented house. It was a squalid, damp-ridden place in the Slum District. Outside the front yard was a metal skip, overflowing with bags of refuse and remnants of broken furniture. It had become the official dumping ground for the entire street and Alia held her breath as she walked by.

The further she travelled from home, the wider the streets grew and the larger the houses. Before long she was moving between the offices and smaller factories of the Worker

District. Alia considered crossing the checkpoint into Old Straybeck, but quickly dismissed the thought. She no longer had the strength to face whispered comments and scornful looks from people that used to be friends with her father.

Instead, she went to the Trade District and begged the buyall staff for credit. She told them the truth about her circumstances and when that didn't work, she told them lies. She tried to barter with the jewellery but knew how it must look. A young girl with a handful of rings and necklaces. In their position she'd have thought it was a set-up too.

The fourth store she tried was small and the shelves stacked high with tins. Alia walked past a row of crates that were full of fruit and vegetables and ran her finger along their tops. She waited at the newsstand, holding a copy of The Straybeck Times as if she were going to buy it. When the other customers left, she dropped the paper and approached the counter.

Behind it was a short, wiry man who was writing notes with the stub of a pencil. His sleeves were rolled up and he leant one elbow on the counter to stare at Alia. When she didn't speak right away, he shook his head and chuckled to himself. It was a mocking laugh as if she was the punchline to a joke.

"Do you let people have goods?" Alia said. "You know, on tab?" She was already sure of the answer.

The shopkeeper put the pencil behind his ear. "I knew you were one of them the moment you walked in here."

Alia dropped her eyes. "I don't usually do this," she said, "I promise I'll pay you back next week. It's just that my mum's not well and she's been out of work. And my dad, well he's…"

"Yeah, yeah, I'm sure it's terribly sad. But you're the third one today. I've had all the sob stories I can take thank you." He took down the pencil and resumed his writing.

Already burnt by the response at the other shops, Alia broached her next question carefully. "Maybe I could pay you some other way," she said and reached into her pocket for the small cloth that contained her mother's jewellery.

The shopkeeper put the stub of his pencil between his teeth. "I think maybe you could."

Alia heard the suggestion in his voice and tried to hide her revulsion. She picked a ring from the cloth and held it out towards the shopkeeper. It was a gold ring with a blue stone set on top. "Would this pay for two weeks food?"

The shopkeeper snorted in reply and took the ring off her, taking care to slide his fingers over hers as he did so. He looked closely at the stone and then tossed the ring onto the counter. "It's fake."

"No it isn't, it's my mum's."

"That won't buy you two days."

"It's worth at least a week."

The shopkeeper leaned across the counter and beckoned Alia closer. Reluctantly she stepped towards him. "I tell you what," he said. "How about I give you a week of food for that ring."

Alia said nothing.

"But after that, no more jewellery. I want a different payment. You understand me?" He gave her a lingering smile.

Alia nodded her head, unable to form an answer. Leaving the ring on the counter, she grabbed as much food as the shopkeeper would allow and then ran from the shop.

As she carried the bags of food back through Straybeck, she checked her watch giving a start when she saw it was almost midday. The workers would be loose from the factories at any moment. Up ahead, she saw a gang of them already knotted around the doorway of a bar, blocking half of the pavement. Alia crossed the road between the slow-moving traffic and hurried down the other side. One of the workers called out, but she didn't turn around. They whistled a second time and shouted after her, the voices sounding closer now.

A gunnerman truck idled towards her and she could tell from the driver's face that he'd zoned in on the workers. Relief breathed through her. She turned back to them and saw that they had lost interest in her and were re-forming their circle outside the bar. With a vindictiveness she would have found unthinkable a year ago, she flagged down the truck and waited for the gunnerman to unwind his window.

"What?"

"I just thought you should know," she said quietly. "I heard one of them talking about a gun. The tall one there. I think he passed something to one of the others."

"Right," the gunnerman said. He didn't even want details. Just an excuse to lay into them and she hoped that they got what they deserved.

When she rounded the corner of her street, Alia unconsciously slowed her pace, prolonging her return for as long as possible. At the end of the yard she waited with her key in hand, feeling a sudden anxiety spread through her body. Her heart began to hammer, hands tingling with pins and needles. She fell against the wall and sank to her knees, unable to fight the throbbing in her head and chest.

She knew she was going to die. Her heart was beating too fast and her breathing had grown rapid and shallow. The certainty of death was in itself quite soothing though and as the seconds dragged on, Alia's breathing levelled out. The house bricks were damp and cooled her face. As her thoughts cleared, she realised it was not death, but simply another panic attack. The fifth in just over a week.

Her fingers closed around the pills she had bought for her mother. They were opiates, bought from the pushers for the cost of a silver necklace. Now, with shaking hands, she unscrewed the lid and poured one of the speckled white tablets into her mouth.

She waited, breathing in and breathing out. The wind bit keenly round her neck while the afternoon sun glared into her eyes. She focused on these sensations as she waited for the tightness to ease in her chest. It was almost ten minutes before she felt well enough to stand. Alia gathered up the shopping bags and was about to go into her house when she heard the sound of footsteps. She span round quickly and saw a worker sprinting towards her.

CHAPTER 6

IT HAD BEEN weeks since John found the pamphlet in his brother's room. Weeks since that terrible fight and the fall-out it had left. Ryan walked round like he was charged with electricity, while his dad became a ghost to them. John found himself chattering about anything and nothing, so long as it brought noise back to the house.

Today he was listening to an old war story on the radio and retelling the best bits to his dad in the kitchen. Suddenly the sound turned to static and the radio powered down. John flicked it on and off at the wall but it didn't help. Not even when he banged on the top with his hand. In the kitchen his dad was washing the dishes, staring out of the window.

"Dad," John said. "The radio's broken."

His dad dropped the plate into soapy water and leaned heavily on the sink. "It's not broken. I've already told you our district's on savings today."

"Did you? I don't remember. What should I do now?"

"I don't know, John," he sighed. "Read a book." He shook the suds off his fingers before walking quietly upstairs.

John paced around the downstairs, trying to imagine where they might keep some books. Then he remembered the restrictions on his Dad's ID card and stopped looking. Suddenly Ryan jogged down the stairs and grabbed his coat off the hook. John hadn't realised he was still here.

"Where are you going?"

"Out," the thump of the front door put an end to further questions.

John waited a few moments before following. By the time he had grabbed his own jacket and sneaked from the house, his brother was already at the corner and heading towards the checkpoints.

John had never been to the Worker District without his dad before and even then they had stuck to the main routes. He recognised Carragon Road, but after that the route became confusing and John grew worried. Just when he was about to turn back, his brother veered off the main road and towards a burnt out old chapel nestled between smaller shops and houses.

John hid in the alleyway opposite, peering from behind a stack of bricks and rubble. It was bitterly cold and he scrunched his toes up to stop them going numb. He waited for maybe half an hour as his breath come out like dragon smoke.

Eventually, Ryan emerged from the chapel and back onto the street. He was holding a bundle of papers that had been rolled into a tube. John watched him trap them under one arm as he fished around in his coat pocket and brought out a pack of cigarettes and box of matches. He lit up, dropped the match onto the wet road and then set off towards the factories.

John crept from the alleyway and followed at a distance. The streets were empty though and it was difficult to stay hidden while Ryan was continually checking over his shoulder. The further his brother moved from the broken-down chapel though, the less he checked and John was soon able to walk with more confidence.

A sevener plodded slowly down the pavement towards him. They were the police in Straybeck who kept everyone in order. Danny Saunders at school said they were all related to giants and never grew old and had super human strength. He also said he'd found one of their secret tunnels that went under the city. John remembered how half the class had followed him after school to a dark staircase that led below an old factory. None of them dared to go down though, not even Danny Saunders.

As the sevener loomed closer, John gawped upwards, spellbound by the figure who was easily a foot taller than his dad. The officer's blue tunic was buttoned smartly to his chin and as he passed by, he put one finger to the brim of his helmet, a wry smile on his face.

John hurried to the end of the road and saw his brother waiting at the edge of the factories, glancing warily in all directions. He jumped into the nearest doorway, pressing close to the walls as he peeped around the edge of the metal doorframe. He needn't have worried though. Ryan seemed completely unaware as he pulled out another cigarette, lighting it between cupped hands before heading onto Foundry Lane. The heart of the Worker District.

John kept moving too and found himself on a long, cobbled road that stretched into the distance. Even from his position at the end of the street, John was stunned by the cacophony of noise that pushed against him. There were dozens of gigantic mills and factories, each housing enormous machines whose combined movement seemed to shake the ground beneath his feet.

Opposite the factories, and running the length of the

street, stood the gunnermen walkway. John eyed the wall of red bricks and saw two gunnermen standing near a watch hut. Ahead of him, Ryan was oblivious to the scene and hardly broke stride as he approached the first factory. From inside his jacket, he produced the roll of papers and what looked like a can of spray paint. He took a cursory glance at the gunnermen and then shook the can up and down and sprayed its contents onto the factory wall. It made a messy Z shape and Ryan slapped one of the posters on top, smoothing out the creases with his sleeve.

From his hiding place, John felt his stomach twist into knots. He watched helpless as Ryan went to more factories and glued more posters onto the filthy black bricks. He checked his wristwatch and saw that it was nearly midday. He knew the factories would stop for lunch and the street would soon fill with workers. He wanted desperately to go home, but knew he couldn't leave his brother.

While Ryan had his back turned, John ran to the first factory and read one of the posters. His jaw fell open in shock when he saw the stark black and white image. It was a cartoon of Premier Talis with his pants down, taking a shit over Straybeck.

The dinner horns echoed up and down the row of factories. John ducked for cover behind a rusty set of stairs that climbed up the side wall of a factory. Workers poured onto the street, laughing and shouting at their friends. He lost Ryan in the sea of dirty overalls while the workers searched for a ledge to perch against while they ate their sandwiches. He caught an occasional glimpse of his brother's black jacket moving in between the workers. Unbelievably he was handing out the posters as he moved along the street.

Most of the workers paid no attention to either Ryan or the picture. Some crumpled it up while others rolled their eyes and dropped it to the floor. Occasionally, John would hear a bark of laughter and see Ryan slapped on the back as he walked past. As he reached the centre of the crowd though, it all went terribly wrong.

"Hey," a young worker shouted. "Hey you." At first his words were drowned out by the general din, but John saw his brother's stride quicken in response.

"Hey," the man shouted again. More workers broke off from their conversations and turned to the noise. They saw Ryan retreating through the crowd and then saw the young worker waving one of the posters like a flag. "Someone stop him," he yelled, gesturing for the gunnermen now and pointing after Ryan.

John stared up at the walkway. The two gunnermen at their watch-hut had stopped talking and were unhooking their rifles as they moved towards the steps.

"Stay where you are," one called.

For a moment Ryan seemed to obey as he came to a stop and stared up at them. A moment later he broke free of the crowd and sprinted back up Foundry Lane. He passed alongside John's hiding place and then ran out of sight. The gunnermen were down at street level in an instant and barrelling through the crowd of workers in pursuit.

CHAPTER 7

STILL RECOVERING FROM her panic attack, Alia gathered the fallen bags of shopping and retreated closer to her house. The footsteps grew louder and she looked up to see the worker sprinting towards her like his life depended on it. She thought back to the gang outside the bar and wondered if one of them was coming to take his revenge.

As he drew closer, she saw that he was older than her, maybe eighteen, and he was carrying a fistful of rolled up papers. She braced herself for an attack, but he barely glanced at her as he ran past.

Ahead of him lay a vast industrial estate with open plots that offered no obvious hiding place. The worker looked exhausted and stopped beside the skip at the end of Alia's yard. He walked in a tight circle looking first at the industrial estate and then back up the narrow road. Eventually his eyes lighted on the skip and, as he grabbed hold of the metal rim, he looked directly at Alia.

"If the gunnermen come," he said, "tell them I kept running." Then he hoisted himself into the skip and burrowed beneath the bags of rotten food.

Seconds later Alia heard more footsteps and watched a

thick-set gunnerman lope around the corner of the road. He was blowing hard by the time he reached her house and his rifle was hanging at one hip. Another gunnerman appeared at the top of the street.

"Go round," the first one shouted, gesturing for him to circle behind the houses. Then he walked past Alia and scanned the empty industrial site ahead.

"If you're looking for the worker," Alia blurted out, "he went that way."

She pointed across the wasteland, to the nearest collection of buildings, not knowing what had made her say it. The gunnerman waited in silence, trying to judge whether or not the worker had been that far ahead.

Although his expression was full of suspicion, he gave a terse nod and began jogging across the industrial estate. Alia leant back against her wall, shocked at what she'd just done. She was an accessory now. What if the gunnerman came back and looked in the skip? He'd know that she had lied and she'd be arrested. What would happen to her mum?

As the gravity of the situation hit her, Alia dropped her shopping bags and ran forwards, delving into the stinking bags of rubbish. The worker's face suddenly appeared, squinting against the burst of light. From his frightened expression it was clear he had been expecting the gunnerman.

"Get up. Quick." He rolled awkwardly to his feet and peered above the side of the skip. "Hurry," Alia said. "If he comes back he'll know I lied for you." While the worker climbed onto the road, she ran back to her house, relieved to be rid of him.

"Wait."

To her horror, Alia turned to see him running into the yard. "What are you doing?" she hissed.

"He's turned back. If I go on the road, he'll see me."

Alia couldn't believe this was happening. She grabbed the key that she wore around her neck, rammed it into the lock and rushed into the hallway. The worker followed behind her and they bundled into the kitchen together. Standing in silence, Alia saw his eyes flick over the cramped space and shabby cupboards. Suddenly she was embarrassed and hoped that her mum stayed shut away in the lounge.

"I'm Ryan," he whispered.

"Alia," she said in spite of herself.

"Thanks for helping me."

She shrugged, still angry at herself for doing something so stupid.

"Shall I go out the back door?"

"You can't. There was another one that went that way." She crept over to the back window and searched the alleyway running behind the house. It looked empty, but she couldn't see further than a couple of houses in either direction. "Why was that gunnerman after you?"

Ryan unfolded the roll of papers he was carrying and handed the top sheet to Alia. It showed a picture of the Premier with his trousers down, squatting over Straybeck. She gasped and turned to Ryan, one hand over her mouth. The reaction made him smile and in spite of herself she realised that she liked that. He had a warm smile.

"Why have you got those?"

"It's just a picture," he said.

She looked back at the poster and a nervous laugh burst out. It was a fairly accurate reflection of her life over the past year. A bump sounded from somewhere overhead, followed by a soft moaning. Ryan frowned up at the ceiling.

"What's that?"

"Nothing. Just the neighbours I think." Alia turned back to the window to hide the blush creeping up her face. "Are you from a factory?"

"No."

"Have you ever worked in one?"

"Briefly. Why?"

"Where do you work?"

"You ask a lot of questions," Ryan said with a bemused smile. "What about you?" he said. "Where do you work?"

"I'm still at school."

"Straybeck Central?"

"Kind of."

"Kind of?"

But before she could explain, three loud knocks rattled the front door. They both froze and Ryan crept into the hallway, his face drained white. Through the frosted panel the outline of a gunnerman was clearly visible. The knocking sounded again, louder and longer this time.

"Shit," Ryan jumped backwards, colliding with Alia in the doorway to the kitchen.

"That way," she hissed, snatching the key for the back door from the counter. "Just a minute." she called in as calm a voice as she could muster.

Ryan took the key from her, unlocked the door and tugged it open. He ducked beneath the washing line, scanned the alleyway in both directions and then was gone. Alia closed the door and leant her back against the old wood, heart racing. A moment later she was pushed across the floor as Ryan reappeared in the doorway.

"Hi. Sorry."

"What are you doing?"

"Can I see you again?"

She couldn't believe he'd risked capture to come back and ask her that. "Are you insane?" The knocking came again, even louder but Ryan made no attempt to move. "Okay. Yes. I'll see you again."

He grinned and then bolted out of sight.

CHAPTER 8

WHEN HE SAW the gunnermen chasing his brother, John scrambled out from his hiding place and went after them. He'd barely reached the end of Foundry Lane before he lost sight though. He kept running, guessing at their route, but soon grew tired.

The streets were deserted and John glanced nervously in all directions. Up ahead, he saw the huge Straybeck library. It was boarded up at every window, but he could see that the bottom of the door had been kicked through. As he stepped closer, he heard the clatter of wood and shrank against a wall. One of the gunnermen emerged through the broken doorway, crouching low and shuffling into the sunlight. Then he set of at a jog towards the Slum District.

John took another look at the broken doorway and listened for signs of life. Had Ryan gone in there to hide? He walked slowly up the stone steps and knelt before the splintered frame.

"Ryan?" he hissed. "Ryan? It's me."

There was no reply, so he ducked beneath the remains of the door and into a musty darkness. He waited and listened.

"Ryan?"

He found himself in a narrow entrance hall where timbers from the roof had fallen to the ground, partially blocking the passageway. John crept between the broken beams and pushed open a second set of wooden doors, slipping into the central atrium. He stared up through an enormous circular staircase that had left a column of empty space the full height of the library. It reached up to a domed ceiling that was topped with a stained-glass window. As the light passed down, it diffused into a wide shaft of colours that fell upon John's face, painting him in soft reds and blues. He crossed the atrium and climbed the circular staircase

"Ryan?" he said as loud as he dared. Somewhere overhead, a bird started at the noise and flapped across the stairwell until it found a perch nearby. The hairs on his neck were tingling but he continued to climb until he reached a large stone archway. It was the first-floor balcony that ran in a long, lazy circle, finally emerging from a second archway behind him. A plaque on the stone wall read: *History. Politics.*

John crept slowly onto the balcony and peered through the doorway of each room he passed. Inside were huge bookcases lying on their sides, surrounded by charred piles of books. The stone walls were soot-stained and where the fire had burned hottest, the roof was missing to reveal blackened timbers.

John didn't dare go inside and had soon completed a full circuit of the balcony before finding the staircase to the second floor. As the steps levelled out, he rubbed the grime away from the wall plaque.

Fiction.

The books up here were dusty and neglected, but otherwise untouched by the fire. John stole between the shelves, running his fingers along the old leather spines. A soft light drifted into the chamber allowing him to squint at the titles. John thought back to his own house and how they'd never owned any books. He toured the shelves, choosing the most amazing titles and carrying them under one arm.

As he came to the final bookcase, he noticed a small stone archway sunk into the back of the room. John twisted the black metal handle until the latch clunked. He pushed forwards and the door creaked open

As his eyes grew accustomed to the gloom, he saw that the walls were lined from floor to ceiling with shelves. Each one was stacked full of newspapers and journals, all piled neatly together. Cobwebs covered the papers, and he wiped them away with both hands. Years of dust and dead insects stuck to his fingers.

John had only ever known one newspaper, *The Straybeck Times*. The names on the shelves left him confused though. *The Truth*, *The Chronicle* and a small pamphlet called *Workers Union Paper*.

He hefted down a stack of *Straybeck Times'* that were dated from years before he was born. The headlines were incredible. Tales of plots and arrests, kidnappings and murders. They talked about political parties that fought against the old King. A man named Willem who threw himself under the royal carriage. John recognised one name in amongst the muddle, *The Workers Party*. That was Premier Talis's party.

The papers mentioned it often, but they told the story differently. John struggled through the text but didn't recognise any of his heroes from school. They kept calling the Premier *General* Talis and said he was leading a group of rebel fighters.

They called him a traitor to the crown and said that he was wanted for treason.

When he hefted down another stack of papers, the tone of writing was different. A large headline said "Victory" and the picture below showed Premier Talis, still young, still strong, sitting on an enormous tank in the city square.

John sifted through three more stacks of the paper. He read the headlines and scanned some of the articles before casting them across the floor. Eventually, he took hold of the final copy, dated over thirty years ago. John took a breath and smudged the butt of his hand across the front page. Through the gloom of the windowless room a stark black headline yelled up from the carpet.

Assassination of Premier stopped by gunnermen.

John quickly scanned the text below, wanting to know the whole story before he had read it. Snapshots flickered up at him, "One gunnerman in hospital…shot in the chest…arrests made… Alistair Argyle, David Farren, Robbert…"

He froze.

Robbert Calloway.

John's stomach dropped and he closed his eyes while the name Robbert Calloway coursed through his head. Why had his dad tried to kill the Premier?

CHAPTER 9

Robb sat at the kitchen table clenching his fists. When it was cold like today, it was the only way to stop his knuckles aching. There was a noise behind him and he turned to see John standing in the doorway holding a small parcel in one hand.

"What's the matter?"

John passed it over and he found himself holding a tightly folded sheet of newspaper. He opened it slowly, already guessing it was about him. Another reminder of a past he could never escape.

Assassination of Premier stopped by gunnermen.

They were only words, but his chest swelled and hardened like armour. He gazed into John's unblinking eyes.

"Was it you?" John whispered.

Robb sank back against the table top, still holding the piece of paper. He thought about lying, or not answering at all, but he had done that with Ryan for seventeen years. He didn't have the strength to endure the hatred of both his boys.

"Sit down," he said quietly. "We need to talk."

An eighteen-year-old Robb Calloway slipped quickly through the streets of Karasard. The capital city was quiet tonight and he stayed instinctively close to the shadows. The fake ID in his jacket pocket was an expensive one, so the prospect of meeting a gunnerman patrol was not the reason he was so nervous. Right now, he was more concerned about the woman who'd been following him for three streets. It was only three streets, so it could be nothing. Or everything.

In a few days they were attacking the palace. In a few days they would be heroes.

At the end of the road, Robb paused as if unsure of his direction. He glanced at the reflection from the windows opposite and saw the woman break stride too. That was all the confirmation he needed. Calmly he turned left into Tower Street before sprinting flat out for a hundred yards and turning back onto the estate. He ran down a series of alleyways that eventually brought him back out on Tower Street, but half a mile further down.

If the woman had just been out for a walk, then he'd given himself a bit of exercise and a longer route back. If she was an agent though, then Robb hoped she was chasing shadows through the estate. It was not unheard of for gunnermen to make random follows, but this was the second time in a month. He set off in the opposite direction. Robb knew that he should have just gone home. Even so, he slipped the static checkpoint and found a looping route that took him back to the safe house.

When he checked his watch it was almost nine. Robb picked up his pace, knowing that Alistair and Farren would be waiting. Soon enough, he arrived at a deserted street where every window and door were either boarded up or kicked in. At a house no different from any other, Robb ducked into the rear yard and moved quickly out of sight.

Instead of a back door, the safe house had a wooden board fastened over the opening. Robb reached below the chipboard and pulled it towards him. It had been hinged at the middle and the lower half swung up just enough to let Robb pass under and out of sight.

He crawled through to the kitchen and saw a man silhouetted in the doorway of the front room. His face was covered by a black scarf and he stared at Robb wide-eyed. Slowly, he tugged the material down and shook his head.

"Robb," he sighed. "Ya bastard."

Alistair lowered the gun clenched in his right hand while Robb grinned at him through the gloom.

"Sorry, did I make you jump?"

"Jump? I nearly shite myself. Were you followed?" he said quickly.

Robb thought about not telling him. Alistair would only talk to the Colonel and that would mean yet another delay. They were so close now.

"Maybe," he said. "I'm not certain."

"That's two now." Alistair rubbed one palm across the back of his neck, no doubt trying to decide what the Colonel would do. "We'll have to clear out."

"Oh come on," Robb said impatiently. As he moved through the kitchen, the smell of chemicals almost made him gag. There was an old cloth on the cooker and he held it over his nose. "I left her on the Tower Estate," he said with a muffled voice. "There's no way she could have tracked me here."

The staircase rose steeply at his side, dividing the front room from the kitchen. At the top of the stairs Robb heard a bang as Farren threw open the bedroom door and stepped into view. He was wearing a face mask and goggles like a scientist. On his hands he had heavy-duty gloves that he tore off while erupting into a violent fit of coughing. When it subsided, he pulled the mask down and slid the goggles up onto his forehead.

"I need a break," Farren croaked, launching the gloves downstairs. "Alright mate," he added, noticing Robb for the first time. Robb gave him a nod and picked the gloves up with one hand, the other still holding the rag over his nose.

"Robb was followed," Alistair said suddenly.

"What?" Farren jogged downstairs to join them in the kitchen. "When?"

Robb glared at Alistair. "I *think* I was followed. I'm not certain."

"What happened?"

"Some woman," he said, leading them into the front room where the fumes weren't so bad. Although the windows were boarded here, a faint light crept in around the edge of the boards. There was an old decorator's lantern burning away merrily and Alistair had obviously been studying the plans of the palace while Robb was away.

"I saw her when I passed the first checkpoint," he continued. "Then I lost her at the tower estate."

Farren broke into more coughing and brought up a gob of phlegm. His face soured and he ran over to the back door. Crouching by the wooden board he pushed open the lower half so that he could spit into the yard.

"That's better," he said, lowering it gently. "Have you told the Colonel?"

"He's out," Alistair said. "Not sure where. But we can't wait. Let's get this place broken down."

"Whoa, whoa, whoa, whoa," Farren said, his hands in the air. "We've spent the past week mixing that stuff up there."

"And it might have been a random follow," Robb said, turning to Farren for support.

"Yeah," his friend agreed. "He doesn't even know for certain that he was followed. Do you Robb?"

Robb shook his head, even though it wasn't true.

"Come on," Farren continued. "At least wait until the Colonel gets back. Let him decide."

Alistair was cautious by nature. He planned and prepared where Farren jumped in without looking. Even so, with a reluctant nod, he agreed to hold off until Colonel Stephens returned.

"Who's up next then?" Farren said with that cocky grin of his. He held up the goggles and face mask.

Alistair leant over his plans of the Premier's palace, tracing his finger across the lines as though deep in thought. No one liked mixing chemicals and Robb reluctantly took the goggles and mask from Farren.

"One hour," he said before heading for the stairs.

"Before you go," Farren said. He rummaged through some clothing in one corner of the room and produced a black and green gunnerman's uniform. It looked just like the real thing.

"Where'd you steal that from?" Robb said.

"Made it with my own fair hands," Farren said.

"You mean *we* made it," Alistair added, leaning up from the plans. "And there are still two more to make."

Farren rolled his eyes. "Okay, okay." Then to Robb, "but what do you think?"

He felt the fabric between finger and thumb and gave Farren a nod of approval. "It'll do the job." Which it would, because once they had blown up half the wall, who would stop three gunnermen running through the Premier's palace?

Farren re-folded the uniform and placed it in the corner. With an exaggerated sigh Robb pulled on the goggles and headed for the stairs. They were mixing the chemicals in the front bedroom and the fumes were overpowering. It wouldn't have been so bad if they could just open a window, but the colonel said it was too risky. If a gunnerman or a neighbour were to smell the chemicals, then they would all be sent straight to The Cathedral.

"Good luck," Farren laughed. It quickly turned into another fit of coughing and he raced past Robb towards the back door. He pushed back the wooden board and hawked into the back yard. Suddenly there was a quiet *fizz* and, without warning, a chunk of plaster jumped away from the wall behind him. Farren dropped to his backside, letting the board swing into place with a bang. He turned to Robb, wide-eyed.

"What?"

"Move!" Alistair strode into the kitchen, gun in hand.

A moment later Farren was on his feet and bundling Robb towards the lounge.

An almighty crash shook the house and the wooden boards splintered away from the back door, covering the kitchen in debris. Alistair fired three quick shots, but a volley of gunfire came back at him. The bullets caught him in the chest and shoulder, throwing him off his feet and against the wall.

At the same instant, a tremendous impact sounded from the front door and Robb watched in horror as it buffeted forwards, the flimsy boards about to give way.

"Come on," Farren shouted and together they raced up the narrow staircase.

A shout from the kitchen rang through the house. "Dogs loose."

Savage growls resonated upstairs as the first dog sprinted inside. The snarls quickly mixed with Alistair's screams. A second hound skidded into view, its claws scratching for grip on the wooden flooring. It scented Robb and Farren at the top step and barrelled up the stairs towards them.

Farren broke right and slammed the bathroom door shut while Robb went for the mixing room. As he shut the door, the dog's massive head squeezed through the gap. It snapped at his legs, but its body was thick with muscle and couldn't fit through. Robb shouldered his weight to the door and felt the dog's neck crush against the frame. It shrieked in pain and withdrew to set up a furious barking outside.

He ran across the bedroom and kicked at the window board. Three sharp blows made the wood crack and he was able to tear it from the wall by hand. The dog was still clawing at the wood and then a gunnerman's voice called out.

"Koba. Get 'ere. Koba."

Robb leaned through the window and looked down to the pavement twenty feet below him. The height jolted his stomach and he stepped back, cursing quietly. Behind him there were more footsteps and angry shouting. As the door banged open, he ducked his head to the sound of gunshots.

When the first gunnerman stepped inside, Robb leapt into clean, cold air.

The drop was long and he landed badly. Both his legs cracked, forcing a scream from his throat. He rolled onto his back with one hand hovering at his left leg, not daring to touch it. He took a deep breath and tried to limp away. As his leg took the weight though, his shin buckled at a sickening angle and Robb dropped to the concrete screaming.

A solitary gunshot fired above him and the pavement dusted by his face. He rolled over and saw a gunnerman grinning down the barrel of his rifle. Another one joined him and Robb closed his eyes to their laughter. With a massive effort he tried to crawl away, barely making it a few feet through the splintered wood that had fallen with him. He rolled over, staring at a narrow path that ran between the houses opposite.

"No," he screamed. "Go. Just go."

"We're not going anywhere, you dumb bastard."

A gunnerman had been waiting on the street for any runners. When Robb turned, a boot stamped down on his face.

When he regained consciousness, he was on the shores of Lake Stretten. Pain thumped across his head and his vision was swimming. His clothes were soaked with sweat and felt cold against his skin. Robb shivered, sending a spasm of pain through his legs.

He realised he was caged in the back of a military van. The outer door was open, but the inner one was still locked. Through its steel mesh he could see the gunnermen smoking and sharing stories. Behind them was the water and beyond that - dark and oppressive - The Cathedral. One of the gunnermen gave a quiet laugh and flicked his cigarette into the lake. It was the one who had tried to drag him from the pavement by his ankles. Robb had felt the bones click apart just before he passed out.

"Here we go," the gunnerman said, nodding at the lake. Robb followed his gaze and saw the boatman of Lake Stretten gliding through the darkness.

"Move," the second one said, opening the cage door.

"I can't."

The one from the safe house stepped forwards. "Stupid bastard jumped from a first-floor window."

The gunnermen waited for him to shuffle to the edge of the van. When they grew bored, they took an arm each and carried him to the small boat. The water was black and still and Robb tumbled to the bottom of the boat. The gunnermen clambered in after him and stood with a hand on their rifles and their feet braced apart.

The boatman was a thick-shouldered man in ragged clothes. He stood at the prow, watching his passengers without interest. He too was a prisoner here and wore heavy iron bracelets on each ankle with a rusted chain curled between them. Reaching below the side of the boat, he pulled a thick rope from the water that was slick and dripping with algae. He gave a grunt of effort, hefted on the chain and then sent the little boat lurching across the water.

"Careful," one gunnerman growled as he fought for balance.

The boatman muttered something that may have been an apology. Robb rolled sideways and bit down on his wrist. Flashes of pain lanced through both legs which were crooked and swollen to a grotesque size. His knuckles drained white as he bit down on the scream in his throat. The boatman drew them ever closer to The Cathedral.

"Take off my boots," Robb hissed, his words forced between gritted teeth. "Please."

"Best thing you can do is leave them on. Stops the swelling."

The boat shunted to a stop and the gunnermen lifted him from deck with a hand under each armpit. As they jumped to shore, Robb banged his legs against the shale slope and almost lost consciousness again. Somehow though, he made it to the steps of The Cathedral.

There were two gibbets protruding from the wall on either side of the main doorway. Each one held a coffin-shaped cage in which Robb could see the rotting corpse of some unfortunate prisoner. As one slowly twisted at the end of its chain, he saw that the man's face had been pecked and eaten by birds.

The gunnermen left him lying on the steps while one approached the main door and knocked loudly. Almost immediately a metal hatch slid open and he exchanged some words with the face on the other side. The hatch slammed shut and then they were left waiting for several minutes until the door creaked inwards on rusty hinges. In spite of the pain, Robb propped himself on one elbow so he could see what was coming. It was a small and unassuming man who emerged from the gloom, wearing glasses and a suit. Even so, the gunnermen appeared nervous as they gathered him up and dragged him towards the doorway.

"Why are you carrying him?"

"His legs are broke," the first gunnerman said.

"Jumped out a window," the other added.

"Really?" The man stepped forwards and smiled at Robb.

He placed one hand on his shoulder like they were old friends. Robb saw the smile, saw the slight raise of an eyebrow, but completely missed the knee that thumped into his shattered leg.

Thirty-three years later, he and John were standing silently in the rear yard. The whole story hung between them. From the shores of Lake Stretten right into the bowels of The Cathedral. Robb reflected how those days had shaped the rest of his life. How the choices in his past had imprisoned him more than any cell.

"I shouldn't have told you," he said eventually.

John looked up and gave a solemn shrug.

"It was selfish of me," Robb said. "I'm sorry."

He stretched out his hand but then withdrew it, afraid his son would shrink away. John swallowed and there were tears in his eyes.

"I just don't get it. The Premier's good, so why would you want to kill him? And the gunnermen protect us, so why were they horrible to you? And The Cathedral is for the worst people in Karasard, but…but you're my Dad."

Robb smiled sadly. "It was a long time ago. Things were different then."

"Why didn't you tell Premier Talis? He would have stopped that man hurting you. He stands against cruelty and injustice."

Robb winced at the party line but didn't correct his son. "Sometimes real life doesn't work out the way they say it will at school."

John nodded slowly as if he understood. "They must have kept you a secret. The Premier can't know everything."

Robb laughed but without any humour. He was tired of seeing his family so sad. "That's probably it."

"Does Ryan know?"

"No."

"You should tell him."

A fine rain fell around them and Robb stepped gingerly towards the back door, always wary on the slippery wet stones. John took hold of his arm as they walked. Instinctively, he wanted to push him away, insulted by the offer of help. With an effort he fought back the sting of pride and allowed his son to help. At the very least he owed him that.

"It's Saintsday next week," Robb said, once inside. "How would you like to go to the parade this year?"

John beamed. "All of us? Ryan too?"

"Yes. If he'll come."

As if on cue, the front door thrust open and footsteps stomped through the hallway.

"Ryan!" John called like he hadn't seen him in a week. He ran towards his big brother, but reading the scowl on his face, stopped short of hugging him.

"What?"

"Nothing," John said. "Just glad to see you."

Ryan's expression was as suspicious as ever. "Whatever. I'm going upstairs."

When he was halfway up John called out again. "Dad says he'll take us to the Saintsday Parade this year. There's a bonfire and fireworks and a band."

"I'm busy."

John followed him up the stairs. "Oh come on, it'll be brilliant. Don't you remember the last time we went?"

Robb continued to eavesdrop from the hallway and found

himself smiling. It had been eight years since they last went to Saintsday and he doubted John could even remember it.

"I'm not going anywhere with *him*."

That knocked the smile from Robb's face. Even so, he intervened for John's sake and went to the bottom step. "What do you say Ryan? It might not be so bad. I know John would like it." He tried to adopt an air of good humour despite the undisguised anger on Ryan's face.

"Pleeeeeease," John said. His hands were locked together as if in prayer. Ryan glared at them both and then went into his room, slamming the door behind him. Even so, John came downstairs smiling.

"He didn't say no."

CHAPTER 10

IT WAS THE day before Saintsday. John knew he should have been giddy with excitement, but he couldn't shift the weight of fear in his stomach. Only a few days ago he had watched his brother flee from the gunnermen. He had hoped Ryan would be too scared to try anything again. Yet here they were - back in the Worker District - moving quickly though the same checkpoints. Ryan in front, completely unaware. John trailing behind, watching for both of them.

He waited for his brother to turn the corner of the street before showing his own card to the gunnerman. *No Convictions* flashed up on screen and the computer chirped to say he had clearance to pass through. Making sure he remained hidden, John closed the gap between them and followed Ryan towards the factories. At the last moment though, they turned away from Foundry Lane and skirted around the enormous smokestacks and chimneys. John gave a slow exhale of breath. At least they weren't going back there again.

Without exactly realising how, John found himself back in the Trade District where his dad bought his paper. As the streets grew busier, John was able to reel in the distance between them. When they were separated by only a few house lengths, Ryan suddenly turned a corner forcing John to scurry after him.

Cautiously, he peeped around the edge of the building, but instead of seeing his brother, found himself on a long and empty road. Lining the pavements on either side were crumbling terraced houses, sandwiched between a series of derelict workshops. These had once been Straybeck's cottage industries. Small businesses that were owned by individual families and run from their homes. When Talis built the factories though, the time, attention and detail shown by the family businesses were no longer profitable and they quickly went out of business.

If Ryan had gone inside one of these buildings, John couldn't see a way to find him. He wandered down the street a short way, searching the pavements in both directions. That was when he noticed the rusted archway that was spanning a wide break between the buildings. The metal in the arch had been wrought into lettering which read *Manufacturing Station*. John had never heard of it before, but as he drew nearer, he saw the opening in the ground that he guessed led down to an underground platform. He never knew that Straybeck had an underground.

John understood how Ryan had disappeared so quickly now. He peered nervously down the steep flight of steps, but the curve of the roof prevented him having any view of the station below. After a moment's hesitation John made his choice and began the slow descent into the tunnels beneath Straybeck.

He guessed that the tiled walls and decorative mosaics would at one time have looked as grand as those on the overland. These ones were covered in thick layers of dirt and dust though. Even so, John recognised the familiar outline of Premier Talis in many of the images.

At the bottom step he found himself in a short tunnel that formed a T-shape with the train track running across its path. Most of the lights were out and John moved cautiously through the darkness. Where the tunnel opened out, he peered around the edge of the wall, first left and then right. There was only one light and it buzzed and flickered in the roof, washing the tunnel in a yellow glow.

John froze when he caught sight of the two figures hunched at the far end of the platform. One of them was Ryan, but the other was a much older man that he had never seen before. He was maybe fifty years old, and although he was in shadow, John could tell that he was powerfully built, with a broad chest and shoulders.

His brother moved over to a bench and fished out a bag from underneath. As he looked inside, the old man went to the very back of the platform where it met the tunnel. John gasped as he suddenly dropped down onto the track and disappeared from view. Unbelievably Ryan followed him.

John waited for what seemed like an age before he crept down the platform after them. There was no sound from the track in either direction and the air inside was heavy and stale. Cautiously he moved closer to the bench where Ryan had been talking but then the sound of scuffed footstep echoed up the tunnel towards him. John bolted for the safety of his earlier hiding place in the entrance tunnel, just in time to see the old man climbing back onto the platform.

He was alone.

John's stomach clenched tight. What had he done with Ryan? There was no time for him to worry though as the old man was striding forwards, closing the gap between them. John sprinted back up the passageway, abandoning any pretence of concealment. If he didn't go now, there was no way he would make it back to the surface.

He wasn't sure if he'd made it up without being seen, but there was no shouting and no footsteps in pursuit. With a sudden thrill he left the stifled atmosphere of the underground behind and was once again breathing the cold Straybeck air.

John waited out of sight in a small alleyway until he saw the old man appear on the street. With barely a glance around, he set off towards the main road, directly past John's hiding place. The man seemed oblivious to the world around him and moved with his head down and hands stuffed into his pockets.

John counted to twenty and then – just to make sure – counted again. That gave the old man plenty of time to disappear. He'd probably be halfway to the checkpoint by now. As he crept out of his hiding place though, John was dragged across the pavement and pinned to the wall.

His head snapped against the bricks and for a moment he sank to the ground as everything blurred around him. The attacker momentarily loosened his grip and John tried to scramble out of reach as he gathered his senses. It was useless though. The same big hands hauled him to his feet and pinned him against the wall a second time. When John stopped struggling he found himself face to face with the old man from the tunnels.

"Okay lad," he said, in a low voice. "What're you up to?" John had expected him to shout but somehow the controlled tightness of his voice was even more frightening.

"I'm just...nothing."

"Don't lie to me," his voice flared. "You were in the station just now, weren't you?"

"I wasn't."

One hand moved to John's throat and slowly tightened.

"I know Ryan," John gasped. The man said nothing, his hand locked firm. "I go to school with him. I'm one of his friends." John's eyes flicked frantically around him searching for a way to escape.

"Are you alone?" the man said quietly. John didn't know which answer was safest. "You know," he continued, "children in Straybeck disappear all the time."

A tuneless whistling drifted towards them from the end of the street. John twisted his head to the sound and his heart soared when a sevener appeared. He summoned all the breath in his lungs knowing that this would be his one chance to escape.

"Help me."

The old man snarled, losing all composure and gripping John's neck so hard that he thought the bones would crack.

"If you follow me again," he hissed, "I'll kill you."

"Oi."

That was the sevener, his deep voice thundering ahead of him. The old man released John and was away with startling speed up the street. The long legs of the sevener swept past John as he lay gasping for air on the pavement. It was maybe a minute before he reappeared and judging by the scowl on his face, he hadn't found the older man.

"Right son, what just happened?"

The sevener peered down and John could feel his bottom lip pulling as tears brimmed in his eyes. He wanted to answer but knew his voice would crack.

"Who was that?" the sevener asked.

His dad had always said that you could trust the seveners and John desperately wanted to tell someone what had happened. He couldn't think what to say though without landing Ryan into trouble. All he managed was a sad shrug of his shoulders. The sevener sighed, all sternness dropping from his face as he knelt beside him and removed his hat.

"Come on, what happened?" John shrugged again. "Why was he hurting you?"

John looked down, searching the floor by his feet. "Don't know."

"Are you in a street gang?"

"No." He said it with such indignation that it made the sevener smile.

"No. I don't reckon you are." He stood up and replaced his hat. "What's your name?"

"John."

"John what?"

"Calloway."

"Okay John Calloway, I'm Constable Rutledge." They shook hands with mock formality and the sevener's palm wrapped fully around John's hand and wrist. "Shall we get you home?"

John felt helpless. He needed to check that Ryan was alright but could see no way to do it without alerting the sevener. He swallowed down the rising sense of panic that threatened to overwhelm him. The only choice he had was to hope that Ryan's luck would stay with him a little while longer.

CHAPTER 11

RYAN HAD HIS back to the wall in the crypt beneath Brynne's Chapel. He was waiting for the gunnermen to close in, his whole body shaking with cold and fear. Up at street level he could hear the patrol cars, their sirens rising and falling as they circled the streets.

You've been trained for this he berated himself, attempting to stand. His body was sluggish though as if he had been drugged. The best he could do was slide his back up the lumpy stone wall and wait for his focus to return.

Ryan looked down and was surprised to see a gun in his hand. He tried to grip it, but his arm was tingling and all the strength had gone. That was when he saw blood falling from his fingertips and rebounding against the stone floor. Ryan reached inside his jacket and found that his shirt was soaked through and the material clung to his skin. The realisation that he'd been shot sapped his remaining strength and he slipped back to the floor.

He knew he was going to die in the tombs and the thought sent a shiver through his body while black spots appeared in the periphery of his vision. From the top of the stairs, Ryan heard the soft tread of someone moving closer and saw a faint light taking the edge from the shadows. He held his breath and pointed his gun at the sound. The footsteps grew louder, but the light was not from a gunnerman torch. It was the secret whisper of a candle coming to find him. *Brynne.* It had to be.

"I'm in here." Ryan could only manage a low moan.

It was not his mentor who appeared in the doorway though. The figure was smaller than Brynne and seemed to shuffle forwards on unsteady feet. One of his arms hung deadweight at his side, while the other was carrying a small candle which had melted to the stub.

The soft light revealed a face disfigured by trauma. The left eye was missing and smoke drifted up through the blackened socket. Behind that, the top of its skull had been blown outwards and skin was sticking up like a tuft of hair. Ryan stared in horror as he recognised Caylin, the forger, standing before him.

"Get back," he shouted. "You're dead." Caylin's corpse said nothing, but shuffled forward while thick, black blood dripped from his eye-socket. "What do you want?"

Caylin glared from his one good eye. "I want you."

Ryan awoke gasping for breath with his heart drumming noisily in each ear. He reached for the glass of water at his bedside and took a steadying gulp. It was the third time he'd dreamt about the forger and each time it left him with the same feelings of nausea and despair that he had experienced first time around. Ryan lay back on the bed but was unwilling to close his eyes for fear of dreaming once again. He lay awake for a long time before sleep came for him. Then, as the full weight of dawn fell upon the windows, Ryan rolled from his bed and slowly began to dress.

It was mid-morning when he finally left the house for his meeting with Brynne. He travelled quickly to the Worker District, his mind still drifting back to the dream. The fear that lingered since he had witnessed the forger's murder was almost tangible. Ryan squeezed his eyes shut and pushed the images away. It cleared his mind for a moment, but he knew it was only a matter of time before they returned.

In this distracted state, he skirted the main factories and found himself outside the abandoned underground station just outside the old Manufacturing District. Long before Ryan was born, he guessed it would have been the thriving heart of Straybeck. As he stepped beneath the rusty metal arch though, it was hard to imagine it being anything but what it was now. A forgotten underground station that linked the mining towns of Insel with the foundries and factories of Karasard. Throughout the night, thousands of tonnes of metal ore rolled through its tunnels, headed for the capital city.

Ryan descended the cracked and moss-covered steps and found himself on a long narrow platform. There was only one light still working in the roof, but it was bright enough to see Brynne already waiting at the far end of the tunnel. He was propped against the wall, still as stone. Ryan felt his stomach flip over while he contemplated why the old man had requested that they meet here.

"How're you?" Brynne said.

"I'm okay." He didn't mention the nightmares or his own growing sense of unease.

"Safe journey?" Which was Brynne's way of asking if he'd been followed.

"All fine," Ryan said quickly. Although when he thought back, he could barely remember the walk across town.

"So, I bet you're wondering why I dragged you out here." When Ryan said nothing, he gestured at the bench beside him. "Take a seat. Check the rucksack."

Ryan sat down and followed Brynne's gaze to an old bag that had been tucked beneath the seat. He rummaged inside to find two spray-cans and a piece of black material. It turned out to be a balaclava and he gave Brynne a quizzical look.

"There's a list of buildings I want you to tag. Little and often, that's the key. In the next few days and weeks it'll look like the whole city's rising up." Ryan didn't know what to say. After the hours he'd spent worrying about the task he'd be given, the idea of graffiti left him cold.

"What will I be writing?"

Brynne smiled indulgently. "That's up to you my friend. Anything that gets the hackles rising. Anything that tells the truth."

"But I wouldn't know what to put."

"You'll figure it out. You've always had a natural instinct for this kind of thing. You've always seen past the bullshit and found the truth in this city. Find a way to hold a mirror to the Government. They can't ignore us forever."

Ryan nodded, but still hadn't the faintest idea what he would write. "Are you coming with me?"

"Not this time. There's somewhere else I've got to be."

Brynne must have seen the disappointment on his face for his next words carried extra bite. "We've no time for egos, Ryan. We're close to something big now. Really big. I can't say too much, but I promise I'll explain it all soon. Just know that when it comes, we're going to need all the workers to be ready."

Ryan nodded, shouldered his rucksack and turned to the stairs.

"Not that way." Brynne moved further into the shadows at the back of the platform and suddenly dropped onto the tracks, disappearing from sight.

"Brynne?" Ryan called. He glanced up the track in the opposite direction although there was nothing he could do even if a train were to appear. Cautiously, he edged to the lip of the platform and peered over the track. Brynne was unhurt and waiting patiently for Ryan to join him. After a final check for approaching trains he clambered down onto the rails.

"Where are we going?" he said. Brynne didn't answer straight away, but walked him further into the tunnels as though he had perfect night vision. He stopped and reached into a cavity in the wall where he retrieved an old gas lantern. A moment later it flared into life and a breathy flame glared out at the tunnel, lighting their path.

"There are tunnels all over Straybeck. Some are smuggler routes, some known only to the gunnermen agents." Brynne pointed at a larger opening just up ahead. "This one though… I hear this one was carved out by the seveners centuries ago."

"The seveners? Where does it go?"

Brynne pulled a torch from his pocket and handed it to Ryan. "Follow it until the tunnel splits three ways. Make sure you take the left route. After about half a mile, you'll find yourself at the bottom of some steps that lead up to Foundry Lane. No checkpoints. No gunnermen."

"Foundry Lane? But that's impossible." Ryan was

dumbstruck although Brynne's face remained impassive. "Do I come back this way afterwards?"

"No," the old man said quickly. "Never use these tunnels unless I'm here, okay? You're only ever one turn from the gunnermen."

"But if I try to come back through the checkpoints, they'll search me."

"Then stash the bag, blockhead. And meet back at mine when you're done. Like I said, I've got somewhere to be today, but if I'm not back, use the place as your own."

Ryan nodded, proud at the trust that Brynne was placing in him. He took hold of the lantern and made his first tentative steps through the tunnels below Straybeck.

CHAPTER 12

IT WAS LATE afternoon when Ryan finally returned to the abandoned Chapel. He thumped down the cellar steps and dropped into a chair. There was no telling when Brynne might be back, but he was still buzzing from the mission and couldn't face going home yet. Also, he wanted Brynne to know how hard he'd worked. He wanted the old man to be proud of him and remembered what he had said in the tunnel earlier that day.

Use the place as your own.

So, Ryan went to the bottle of whisky and poured himself a glass. While it warmed his insides, he moved slowly around the cellar, flicking through the shelves of anti-government magazines. He picked two at random and placed them in his coat pocket.

Ryan had never been alone in Brynne's cellar before and the urge to explore was overwhelming. He checked in a mysterious wooden box beside Brynne's chair, but was disappointed to find it filled with nothing more than musty newspapers. Below them was a messy tangle of wires that relaxed into the room as soon as the papers were removed.

There was a tiny camera lens too and Ryan guessed it

was a spy camera. He spent the next few minutes trying to repack the box and place it back in the same position beside Brynne's chair.

He circled the cellar for a second time, avoiding the door at the back corner where a dark stain still crept over the stones. Ryan squeezed his eyes shut as the memory of Caylin's ruined face appeared in his mind. He steadied himself against the bookshelf, breathing deeply before continuing his tour of the cellar. Finally, he stopped alongside a projector and box of reels. The top one had a marker-pen label that read *Insel uprising*.

The mining camps at Insel were notorious for their riots and pitched battles with the gunnermen. The reprisals by the authorities were equally famous for their swiftness and brutality. There was already a reel on the take-up spool, so before he set the motor running, Ryan detached that wheel and placed the film on top of the box. When he read the label though, he was left staring open-mouthed.

R Calloway.

Why did Brynne have a tape with his name on it?

He flicked on the machine and a square of white light shone on the far wall. Ryan re-attached the film onto the feeder spool and watched as a rush of numbers sped past. When the image cleared, it showed a man sitting in the centre of a grey room. He was in his early twenties, wearing a loose-fit jumper and staring directly at the camera. Behind him, two gunnermen were standing to attention and on the wall between them hung a banner of Premier Talis.

One other thing. The man in the chair was Ryan's father.

The film had been magnetically layered with sound and Ryan heard a young woman's voice speaking from somewhere off camera.

"What of the threat to Our Leader? What else has been planned?"

His father replied with a voice that was so familiar and yet seemed totally alien to Ryan. "I don't know of any future plans at this point," the young Robb said. "Except for those I've already described." When he looked into the camera, Ryan was surprised to catch a flash of anger in his eyes, but it was soon replaced by the all too familiar look of shame.

"While Colonel Stevens remains free," he continued, "there will always be a threat to Our Leader. Unless immediate actions are taken by the Government, the Colonel's group will only grow in its organisation and ambition."

"The group that you were formerly a part of."

"That's right."

"And that you are now helping to eliminate."

The young man's jaw clenched tight.

"That's correct."

There was the sound of paper turning over, as though the interviewer were reading from a script. "Can you confirm once and for all Mr Calloway? Where do your loyalties lie?"

Robb's voice was calm and still.

"With the Government. With Premier Talis."

The screen held on Robb's face while - back in the cellar - Brynne strode quickly across the room and jabbed at the power button with one finger. Silence descended on the room.

"I hadn't wanted you to see that," he murmured eventually.

"I don't..." Ryan began, but then realised he had no words to use. He turned away, afraid that his emotions would spill out. "I'm sorry."

Brynne removed his jacket and dropped it onto his chair. For a moment he seemed distracted by the old wooden box and shifted it a fraction with one foot. He reached for the whisky bottle and poured himself a generous measure before topping up Ryan's glass.

"I'm the one who should be sorry," he said eventually. "I haven't watched that footage in years. But recently…well I've found myself thinking about the past more. Much more than I'd care to."

"Did you know my dad before he did that?"

Brynne nodded, looking suddenly old and worn out. He opened his mouth to speak but when no words came, he drained the glass of whisky, allowing a slight grimace to twist one side of his face.

"Ah, but these secrets are killing me," he said. "I suppose it's being with you these past few months, it's churned up some old memories. Things I'd buried a long time ago. Certainly nothing I'd wanted you to find out about."

"I always knew what he was," Ryan said quietly. "I knew what he'd done. But seeing it on screen like that…what could make him do that?"

Brynne took a seat, reached for the whisky and re-filled his glass. "Pain?" he said. "Fear? *Money?* Everyone's got their limits."

Ryan felt sick in his stomach. "Are you saying he did that for money?"

Brynne screwed his face up, apparently troubled by the question. "I don't know. It's more complicated than that. I don't blame your father for what he did. Honestly, I don't. You beat a man bad enough and then offer him the world… well as I said, everyone has a limit."

"Was he always working for them?"

"I don't know. Maybe. It was a lifetime ago."

Ryan was ashamed. Even here, in this place where he had proved his worth over and again, the shadow of that bastard was still upon him.

"You shouldn't feel responsible Ryan," the old man said. "It's not your debt."

He knew it was true but it didn't hurt any less. Ryan left the chapel soon afterwards and they shook hands before he went. He supposed it was meant to show that nothing had changed, but it only emphasised the gulf that had opened between them.

It was raining hard when he stepped out into the Worker District and his clothes were soon drenched through. When he approached the checkpoint on the edge of the Worker District, he zipped his jacket to the top and pushed his chin into the collar. He wondered if the soldier that chased him would remember his face. Then - not for the first time - his thoughts fell back to the girl that had helped him escape. Ryan had planned to visit her the next day but didn't want to risk the checkpoints. After that, the prospect had become more daunting with each passing day.

Ryan stopped; the rain and whisky making him reckless. He knew that changing direction in sight of a checkpoint was asking for trouble, especially with a pamphlet hidden down each sleeve. Ryan made a play of searching his pockets, pretending he had forgotten something. The gunnerman gave a disinterested glance and then turned back to the booth while Ryan headed for the Slum District.

It took him several minutes to find the exact street, but eventually he was standing beside the metal skip where he had hidden from the gunnermen. The rain had backed up at this end of the street and Alia's front yard was covered by a shallow moat. Undeterred, Ryan picked his steps through the water and knocked on the door.

"Hi, remember me?" he practised. Then in a deeper voice, "Hey, remember me?" Through the frosted glass he saw someone approaching. Ryan ran a hand through his sopping hair and tried to act natural. To his surprise, an older woman opened the door and waited with a vacant expression on her face. She stared silently over Ryan's shoulder.

"Err, hi," he said. He followed her stare and checked that no one was standing behind him. "Is Alia home?" Through the doorway he saw her trot downstairs. He smiled as they made eye-contact but she rushed to the door and pulled the woman back inside. The front door slammed shut.

"Okay," Ryan said quietly. He waited a few moments and then stepped back into the water and towards the road. Suddenly the door opened again and Alia reappeared.

"Hi." Her voice was low and she wouldn't make eye contact.

"Hi."

"I thought the gunnermen must have got you."

"No. I got away." He looked up at the swollen grey clouds. "Can I come in?"

Alia didn't answer. She looked inside the house and then back to Ryan. "I'm sorry, it's just…."

Ryan bluffed a smile. "It's alright. I was just passing by and thought I'd say thanks for last week." He took a step back to the pavement.

"Ryan wait." She quickly disappeared from view but left the front door wide open. A moment later she was out and running through the ankle-deep water like it was hot coals. Her coat was on but unfastened and as the water kicked up she started laughing. "We can't go inside," she said, "but I can still come out."

"What about the rain?"

Alia looked down at her jeans that were already soaking to the knees. "It won't kill me."

They walked across the industrial estate at the side of Alia's house. The one where she had told the gunnerman to search for Ryan. They took shelter in an old warehouse and he offered Alia a cigarette. She shook her head, so he took one for himself and then leaned back against the wall. As they chatted, he angled an occasional plume of smoke towards the doorway.

"Was that your Mum?"

Alia withdrew, her face suddenly serious. "Yes, but…she's not well."

"I didn't mean anything."

Alia reached over and snatched the cigarette from his lips with a smile. "Give me that." She took a quick drag and then broke out in a fit of coughing.

"Regular smoker then?"

"Oh yes," she said hoarsely. "All the time."

Her hair was almost black with rain and she had dimples when she smiled. For a time, Ryan forgot about Brynne and the gunnermen and even his father. The floor was littered with gravel and loose stones which they pitched out the doorway as they spoke. Ryan felt the weight gradually lifting from his shoulders, but it wasn't long before Alia glanced at her watch and her face dropped.

"What's up?"

"I've been gone an hour. I'd better get back."

"An hour? It can't be. Come on, you can stay out a bit longer. Let's go for a drink."

She smiled but stood up anyway. "I can't. Not today. But you can take me out another time, if you like?"

Ryan felt a flutter in his chest. "How about Friday?"

"Sure, what shall we do?"

"It's Saintsday," he said and then cursed inwardly as he remembered that John had already asked him to go.

"What's the matter?"

"Nothing. It's just my little brother. He wants me to go with him. But don't worry, I'll tell him I can't make it."

"No," Alia said sharply. "You mustn't do that. Not for me."

"How about afterwards then? We could go for a drink?"

"I'd like that."

He walked her back to the house, pausing at the big metal skip outside her yard.

"Fancy a quick dip?" Alia grinned. "For old times' sake?"

"Oddly enough, I think I'm okay."

As her eyes lighted on the front door though, Alia's expression turned serious and her shoulders dipped. Ryan put a hand to her arm.

"So, I'll see you at the parade?"

She flinched but forced a smile. "Definitely. Can't wait." Then she sloshed back through the dirty water and into her house.

The sun was falling on the way back through Straybeck and as the sky grew darker, Ryan's mood followed suit. He was regretting his choice of venue for meeting Alia. The whole idea of Saintsday went against everything he believed in. Brynne had made him go last year. Said that he needed to see the truth of the city with his own eyes. When the prisoners were lined up behind the fire though, Ryan knew he had seen enough.

His thoughts fell back to the video of his father and how

he had watched him betray the group he was involved in. The more he thought about it, the angrier he became and by the time he had reached the front door, he was ready for a fight. Ryan waited in the hallway for longer than was necessary, silently daring his dad to say something. No one spoke though and the house remained silent.

Ryan went upstairs and slammed his bedroom door. At the far side of the room was a loose floorboard and he went to it now, coaxing it upwards with one fingernail. He placed the pamphlets from Brynne into the space and then drew out a black notebook which he had got from a buyall months ago. He knew Brynne would be furious if he found out, but Ryan had been using it as a journal, writing down his most intimate thoughts. He replaced the floorboard and sat on the bed to read through the first few pages.

He had begun with such thought and care. Then, as the weeks passed and the need to exorcise his thoughts grew, the writing transformed into a barely legible scrawl of angry words. When he reached the description of Caylin's death, Ryan quickly flicked past. He found a pen and on a fresh sheet of paper began to write.

Today I saw the triumph of greed over loyalty. My own father betrayed his friends for money and sold them to the Government.

As usual, once the first lines were written, the words flowed quickly. He recounted all he had seen on the footage, writing until his hand cramped. When he was finished, a furious black text shouted back at him. He read it through, feeling satisfied by the anger. With a nod of his head, Ryan closed the book and placed it back beneath the floorboards.

CHAPTER 13

THERE WERE ONLY ten minutes left of Alia's first week at Straybeck Central. The school was identical to her old one, in as much as there were buildings and teachers. Apart from that, it was different in every way imaginable. At Straybeck Academy she would have had three years of schooling ahead of her. Only then would the law firms, financiers and secretarial colleges send their reps to fight for the best scholars. That dream had drifted out of reach like smoke from a window. The best she could hope for now, was an apprenticeship with one of the lesser traders, or to be taken on as a lady's maid for a family in Old Straybeck. The sort of family she had once been part of.

She was sitting in the main hall surrounded by the five hundred or so seniors; pupils from the top two years at school. They were rude and rough, and it was fair to say that Alia hated them already. The girls were wild and flirted shamelessly with the boys who, in turn, swaggered through the corridors like they were on the factory floor. They shouted and swore and fought in the yards while the teachers did nothing about it.

The headmistress, Mrs Reaton, suddenly appeared and

Alia was pleased to see that she at least inspired some fear in the students. Upon her arrival, a hush settled over the hall and people seemed to sink down in their seats.

"Good afternoon students," Mrs Reaton said. She was a bullish lady with a face like a lump of clay. Her hair was sparse and hung in an unruly mess from her head, further adding to the fearsome appearance.

"Today I will be talking about a truly remarkable story from our country's history. I'm sure you all know of what I'm speaking," she said, raising one eyebrow doubtfully. "It is, of course, forty years since Our Leader became the hero of the Outland Wars."

Without thinking, Alia began to applaud and was mortified to hear her solitary claps echo around the hall. It would have been the expected response at Straybeck Academy. The other students would have raced to be the first one clapping. Here though, all heads swivelled in their seats to find the culprit and a mocking laughter rippled through the students. Alia's face turned bright red while Mrs Reaton screeched for silence.

"As I was saying," she swept her hair to one side with a well-practiced flick, "after taking the fight to our enemies in the Northern Mountains, Our Leader found himself outnumbered by a force of those ruthless half-breeds. Instead of retreat, he seized command from the cowardly generals and - under his inspired leadership - the gunnermen rallied once more. Together they secured the safety of our lands from the Gabblers for a generation to come." Reaton surveyed the hall while everyone did their best to avoid her gaze.

"I think the Premier's bravery and heroism is a lesson to us all. We will never encounter challenges as significant as those faced by him in that battle. However, if we remember his bravery and selflessness when making our own decisions, then his wisdom will help us to choose the right path."

The students were thoroughly uninspired by the headmistress's speech and a numb silence hung over the hall. Reaton seemed blissfully unaware of their boredom though and continued without pause.

"In other matters, I'm pleased to announce that the refurbished Informer Station has been a huge success. We have already made more referrals than this time last year and earlier this week I received a letter from the head of the Investigation Section in Karasard."

Mrs Reaton produced an envelope from the inside pocket of her suit jacket. She read a short and bland missive from the Investigations Section which Alia remembered Mr Kinley reading out in assembly the week before she had left Straybeck Academy. It thanked the school for continuing their patriotic duty in rooting out anti-Government behaviour in Straybeck and Karasard. Any pride she had felt upon first hearing the words was washed away by the knowledge that it had probably gone to all the schools in the city.

For Mrs Reaton though, there was evidently nothing that could surpass the letter's importance because as soon as it was read, she ended the assembly. They recited the school prayer, thanking God and Premier Talis for their health, wealth and the world around them. Alia mumbled through the words as best she could and then found herself filing out behind the other children. As she made her way towards the front office, two boys from the assembly bundled past her.

"New girl," one of them called while the other slapped the back of her head.

"Hey," she shouted, but no one cared so she plodded on towards the main office. The window hatch was closed when she got there, so Alia pressed her head up against the glass to look inside. The receptionists already had their coats on, and one was stacking up the diaries and registers while another secured some coins into a safe. Alia tapped one knuckle on the window and saw a blurry shape walk towards her.

"Yes," the woman snapped as she slid the window open. She glanced at the emblem on Alia's jumper and a momentary flicker of recognition seemed to pass over her face.

"Hi. I'm Alia Turner. I've just transferred schools this week." She paused, expecting a welcome, but the receptionist stared back, stone-faced.

"I was told to come here and sort out some uniform. I've only got the stuff from my old school." She gestured to the sweater she was wearing.

The receptionist gave her an appraising look, her eye settling once again on the *Aspire to Greatness* badge that was sewn into Alia's sweater. She gave a short, unpleasant laugh but decided not to share the joke. "Your old school may have been able to provide free uniforms, but we don't do that here."

"I don't need much," Alia said quietly, hating that she even had to ask. "But my tutor said there may be some lost property or something? Just to get me started for this week."

The receptionist gave a shrill laugh and turned to the other woman in the office.

"Just to get her started," she repeated mockingly. "How the mighty have fallen, ay? Well there isn't any lost property and you'll just have to buy your uniform like everyone else."

When she tried to slide the glass shut, Alia blocked it

with her fingers. She leaned in close to make sure that no one else could hear.

"I don't have any money."

The receptionist's face was full of scorn and she too dropped her voice to a whisper. "Your family made its fortune while the rest of us broke our backs in the factories. You'll get no handouts from me."

She slammed the partition shut, leaving Alia in a state of stunned silence. She couldn't believe that a complete stranger could be so angry with her. Tears prickled in the corner of each eye, but Alia pushed them away with the back of her hand. She shouldered her rucksack once again and walked back through school towards the knife gates.

In the junior buildings, John's lesson was also coming to an end. As the bell rang, his teacher sank into her chair and the students piled out of the classroom.

"Stack your chairs," she called wearily.

John bumped back against the tide and lifted his chair onto the desk. No one else had bothered so he gave the teacher a quick smile and then ran back through the door. His friend, Danny Saunders, was waiting out of sight and clipped his heels when he ran past. John went sprawling into the crowd of children.

"Enjoy your trip?" Danny laughed.

"Funny." They fell into step and John counted off the time in his head. Less than four hours to go until Saintsday. "How big do you think the fire will be?"

Danny shrugged irritably. "Stop going on about it. It'll be shit anyway."

He'd been like that all day. Usually he'd be saying how

the parade was going to be the biggest and best ever. But now that John was going, Danny had decided the whole event was going to be a waste of time.

"Where are you going to stand?"

"At the front," Danny bragged, "but don't you try it. Last year they put the ropes too close and someone got burns all over their face. You wouldn't be able to stand it."

"Yes I could," John said.

"How do you know, you've never been."

"Yes I have."

"When? About ten years ago? Big deal. I bet they didn't even have any convicts to kill when you were there."

"Yes they did, they had loads." Although as soon as he said it, John realised he'd totally forgotten about that part of the parade. He had a sudden memory of the fireworks exploding overhead while firelight danced across a line of gaunt, emaciated faces.

Putting it from his mind, John jostled down the corridor until he reached a knot of children waiting outside the detention rooms. He caught a momentary glimpse of a black jumper in amongst the sea of blue and craned his neck for a better view.

"It's her," he said, knocking Danny on the arm. "That girl."

They had first spotted her two days ago from the science lab window. Her uniform was the same colour as the Academy kids, and she had a way about her that seemed out of place. Even now, she was like a tourist as she passed through the packed corridor.

"Watch this," Danny said, sticking his fingers in his mouth. He blew a shrill whistle that pierced the clamour and caused a sudden silence to settle around them.

Mr Matthews bristled from the doorway of his classroom. "Who was that?" he shouted. The silence continued and John filed past with his eyes on the floor. "The next one to speak, stays an hour." Mr Matthews called, eyeballing anyone who dared to lookup.

Danny waited until they rounded the corner. "Well?"

"Well what?"

"Did she look round?"

"I don't know."

Up ahead a jam had formed at the knife gates and they joined the queuing students. John squeezed forwards between two seniors and chuckled as the gap closed before Danny could get through. He shuffled forwards a few more paces and saw the black-jumper girl struggling to move through the crowd. He ducked low and gained a few more places until he was standing beside her. They inched forwards and John felt his arm pressing against hers. Out the corner of his eye he saw that she might only be a year older than him.

She reached the gates before him, clutching her rucksack in front like a shield. John watched the other students push her aside. When it was his turn to go through, he braced his feet and bent his back to the crowd, waving her into the gap. She scurried under the knife gate, holding her ID to the school guard who nodded irritably.

John was shoved in the back of his head for holding up the queue, but managed to dodge through the gate before he received any real payback. On the other side, the girl had waited for him.

"Thanks," she said.

He shrugged, suddenly tongue-tied. "No problem."

They walked towards the main road, moving past the

small pocket of students that were waiting outside a sleek black building. It was a perfect cube and appeared to have risen from the ground rather than been built.

"Is that the Informer Station?" the girl said.

John nodded and dropped his voice. "Last year someone informed on a teacher and they got dragged out of school by the gunnermen."

"How awful."

"Shh," he warned. They walked in silence until they were clear of the Informer Station. Eventually John pointed at the strange crest on the girl's jumper. "Why are you wearing that?"

"It's my old school," she said. "I've only just moved here."

"Where from?"

Before she could answer, John felt a weight on his back and fell to the ground as Danny jumped on top of him. The girl drifted away while John struggled to his feet and rubbed the mud from his knees. "What did you do that for?"

"Ooh," Danny cooed. "What's the matter? Did I embarrass you in front of your girlfriend?"

"Shut up."

John turned around to let her know that he hadn't said anything about her being his girlfriend, but she had already moved away and disappeared beyond the school gate.

A few hours later, John was back home and sitting on his bed, sulking. "You said you were going to come with us."

Ryan was lying on the bottom bunk with his fingers laced behind his head and a hard expression on his face. "So? You can still go without me."

"But you promised. And now it's nearly seven o'clock. We're going to the miss the fire being lit."

"So, go then. I'm not stopping you."

"I'm not going without you. It won't be the same." He had known something like this would happen. Everything had been going too well for it to last.

"It's not because of you," Ryan sighed. "I just don't like Saintsday anymore. Besides, I don't want to be seen anywhere with *him*."

"He's not as bad as you think," John said quietly. The image of his dad lying on the pavement, both legs broken, hadn't been far from his thoughts lately.

Ryan just laughed though. "Trust me. You don't know everything I know."

John was confused by that. Because if Ryan knew about the raid at the safe house and how their dad was tortured, why would he still be angry? To his surprise, his brother gave a deep sigh and pushed himself off the bed.

"Fine. But I'm only staying an hour."

"An hour? They won't even have done the fireworks by then."

"Do you want me to come or not?" he snapped. "I'll stop until the fire's lit and then I'm meeting someone."

John froze. He knew the only person Ryan could be meeting at that time of night was the man from the underground station. The one that had threatened to kill him.

"Don't meet him, Ryan. Stay with us."

"Who says it's a he?" He took his ID and some copper coins from the desk before grabbing John by the ankles and dragging him down the bed.

"Get off you big goon," he laughed. Ryan kept pulling until he was hanging by his fingertips to the top rung of the ladder.

"Goon am I?" Ryan teased.

"Ryan pleeease," he squealed, his whole body suspended five feet in the air.

"Ryan's not here. It's just a big goon."

"You're not a goon," John squealed.

"Who is then?"

"It's me. I'm a goon."

Ryan lowered his brother's legs to the safety of the ladder. John was immediately running for the stairs. "Goon."

By the time they had wrestled their way to the hallway, both were laughing and Ryan was back to his old self. Then their dad appeared and the room went cold.

"You two ready?"

"Yep."

Ryan didn't answer. He snatched his jacket from the banister and opened the front door. John sneaked a look at his dad in the mirror. His face was old and sad.

"I'll lock up," Eliza said quietly as she appeared beside him. Out on the street, Ryan had already set off towards the park. John waited on the edge of the pavement, torn between his parents and his brother.

"Go on," Robb said. "We'll catch up."

He grinned and ran after Ryan.

CHAPTER 14

THE FLASH BANGS of homemade rockets were bursting over the city. Except for the Government, it was illegal for anyone to use fireworks in Straybeck, but that rule didn't apply on Saintsday. Robb walked side by side with Eliza, but neither tried to talk or hold hands. She was tucked away in a scarf and coat, her hands dug into deep pockets. As they moved towards the centre of Straybeck they joined with other families all making their way to the park.

Robb knew that the Saintsday parade was a sham. A muddle of ideas brought together over thirty years ago after Premier Talis assumed power. Back then, the City States had been deeply divided by the Liberation Wars. Saintsday was manufactured by Talis as a show of strength and unity from the new Government. Only with hindsight could Robb fully appreciate how shrewd the Premier had been in those early years.

Three months into his reign, he paraded hundreds of nobles and aristocrats through the streets of Karasard. The masters of the old regime shuffled along the cobbled roads, stripped of their uniform and finery. The Premier revelled in their humiliation as they marched towards the gallows he'd built in the city square.

Any workers that turned out for the spectacle were rewarded with ale and freshly baked bread. The starving crowds of post-war Straybeck couldn't afford to pass up such an opportunity. He was ashamed to admit that in his youth he had watched the executions and taken the food like everyone else.

The gunnermen no longer gave out free bread and the prisoners were no longer hanged. Instead they were paraded before a huge bonfire while fireworks erupted overhead and the crowd sang songs. Then they were escorted back to their prison cells for a more secluded death.

As Robb and Eliza turned onto Park Road, they saw a bottleneck of people filing through the main gates. Beyond that thousands more were on the grassy slopes, waiting for the parade to begin.

Robb could see a circle of gunnerman that formed a cordon around the enormous pyre. He had forgotten how many were drafted in from the outlying regions on Saintsday. It was the one occasion each year when checkpoints were un-manned and the ID cards un-scanned.

The last time Robb came to the parade was eight years ago. He hadn't wanted to go, but back then he hadn't long been off curfew and knew that it was wise to appear patriotic. He remembered seeing a group of workers getting too close to the fire. The gunnerman told them to move back, but no one listened and they weren't in the mood for asking twice. Four of them waded in with fists and rifle butts, knocking the workers backwards. Ryan was only nine at the time, but Robb would never forget the horror on his face as the violence closed in around them.

As he and Eliza approached the main gates, Robb offered

up a silent prayer for the parade to pass them by without incident. Then he searched the crowd ahead for any sign of his boys. To his left, a gunnerman shoved out when somebody strayed too close. The worker made some comment, a half-hearted protest that got him dragged from the crowd by the front of his coat. Like everyone else, Robb kept moving with his head down.

His boys were waiting on the path up ahead, one scanning the crowd with a smile on his face; the other eye-balling a column of gunnermen that stood nearby. Robb moved forwards, deliberately blocking Ryan's line of sight.

"Where shall we stand?" he said with a cheeriness he didn't feel.

John pointed halfway up the slopes. "Just there. That's the best view." Without waiting for an answer, he weaved through the crowd, dragging his mum by the hand. Ryan was planted to the spot though, staring at the gunnermen by the gate.

"Hey," Robb said.

"What?"

"Cut it out."

"What?

"You know what," Robb hissed.

"So it's illegal to look around, is it?"

"If they want it to be. Yes." All they needed was an excuse.

Ryan stalked up the slope, half an argument eating away at him. Robb limped after him and eventually they found the place where John and Eliza were waiting. Down below at the bottom of the hill, the fire marshals were dousing petrol onto the huge stack of wood.

Robb looked around, checking for potential problems or anyone that looked out of place. His eyes settled on the enormous figures waiting at the very top of the slopes. Standing at regular intervals, they seemed like huge monoliths, guarding the celebration. Robb was comforted to know that the seveners were out in force tonight. He checked his watch. Seven-thirty. From across the park, a steady drumming struck up to mark the beginning of the parade. A line of torches flared into life and moved slowly through the crowd. The brass band walked behind them and the first of their Saintsday anthems rang brightly across the park. The procession split in half so that one section circled either side of the bonfire. It had been timed perfectly so that when the band finished its first song, the circle was complete. There was a moments silence and then applause rippled through the crowd.

Robb watched his youngest son clapping and cheering while the other stared mutely ahead, jaw clenched tight. Following his gaze, Robb saw two gunnermen shouldering their way through the crowd. They weren't close enough to notice the stares of one angry youth, but even so, Robb's pulse quickened.

The prisoners appeared at the edge of the trees in a carefully planned piece of theatre. The Premier used these doomed men to reinforce his same message each year. Dissent will not be tolerated. They were chained together to prevent escape and the chains were kept short so that each prisoner was forced to shuffle with stooped shoulders. Talis intended everyone to see them as a pitiful sight; never to be mistaken for heroes. It was a spectacle repeated throughout the City States, from Dark Harbour to Aftland.

As far as Robb could see, there were maybe forty prisoners this year, corralled by two lines of gunnermen. They would be forced to wait at the edge of the trees until the fireworks had finished. Sensing their arrival, certain sections of the crowd broke into an enthusiastic applause. The hypocrisy made Robb's lip curl with disgust. Somewhere amid the cheers though, another sound took hold, mirroring the thoughts in Robb's head. He heard boos and jeers piercing the applause and the mood of the crowd began to subtly shift.

At some unseen signal, a hail of bottles, stones and coins rained down upon the procession. When Robb saw a gunnerman stagger backwards clutching one eye, he knew they had to get out of there. There was a sudden shout behind him and Robb turned to see Ryan launching a stone into the air.

"No." He grabbed hold of his arm, but it was too late.

At the bottom of the slope, gunnermen were forming up for a sortie into the crowd. At the top of the hill, Robb saw a half dozen giants drifting down towards them.

"Get off me." Ryan dragged his arm away and squared up.

For a moment Robb felt his temper bubble over and he grabbed Ryan by the jacket, shoving him backwards. "Enough."

But Ryan wouldn't be subdued. He bounced back at his father, chest out and arms wide. "Come on then," he said. "Do it."

Robb's blood rose and his hands balled into fists.

"Stop," John screamed, his voice shrill with fear.

Before either of them could act, a sudden *wumph* of air and burst of flame signalled the lighting of the fire. Over a dozen gunnermen were fighting with a nearby group of workers. Oblivious, the band began their second song just as two immense forms lumbered past and the seveners waded in. Only they had enough sway with both sides to stop the violence escalating further. The shock of their arrival gave Robb the breathing space he needed to snuff his anger.

"What's happened to you?"

"What's happened to me? What's happened to you, you fucking traitor."

"Shut your mouth," Robb warned. Already people around them were staring. *Traitor* was not a word to be used idly in Straybeck. Ryan had lost all reason though and wouldn't let it drop.

"I've seen it you know," he shouted. "Your confession. How you betrayed everyone."

With a growl of anger, Robb spun away. He knew that if he didn't leave, Ryan would talk them both into a cell, or he'd have to shut him up some other way. As he limped towards the main gates, the sound of fighting reached a crescendo beside him. That was when he heard Eliza scream.

CHAPTER 15

Robb wheeled round expecting to see Ryan coming at him. Instead, his son was moving in the opposite direction, straight towards the melee of workers and gunnermen. Eliza had hold of his arms trying to pull him back, but he shrugged out of his jacket and continued forwards.

Robb ran towards them, slipping on the muddy slope and cursing the stabs of pain in his legs. The clash had drawn in more fighters on both sides. The nearest gunnerman had his back to Ryan and was swiping viciously at those around him with a steel asp. Robb watched in horror as his son charged in, shoulder first, sending the gunnerman to the floor. A pack of workers set upon him with fists and feet while Ryan jumped skittishly back and forth, searching for another target. Robb grabbed him round the neck with one arm and spun him away from the fight.

"Go home," he yelled.

Ryan twisted out of the grip, swinging his arms wildly. His fist caught Robb in the mouth and rocked him backwards. He responded without thinking and dropped Ryan with a solid slap of his right hand. His son hit the mud with a wet smack and they stared at each other, regret and shame meeting shock and contempt.

Ryan was up in an instant and then sprinted away. Robb called his name, but before he could follow there was a crunching blow to his back. He fell to his knees and twisted round to see a gunnerman with his asp raised, ready to strike again.

Robb curled up in a ball and felt the second blow strike on the meat of his shoulder. Somewhere in the distance he heard a scream but couldn't tell if it was Eliza or John. Slowly he crawled towards them as the metal bar fell across him again. No attempt was made to arrest him though; this attack was for punishment only. Once Robb had reached the safety of the crowd, the gunnerman re-joined the skirmish.

Eliza and John, both crying, helped him to his feet. He cradled his right side and took a few deep breaths. There wasn't the same snagging that he'd felt the last time his ribs were broken, so maybe he'd been lucky. In any case, that was something to worry about later. He put one arm around Eliza's shoulder and lurched unsteadily towards home.

Ryan had angry tears in his eyes as he shoved through the crowd. He hated his dad so much. Even more than that, he was ashamed and humiliated that he'd allowed the old bastard to knock him down. Ryan checked his watch. It was still too early to meet Alia, which was probably a good thing. He needed to calm down before then.

At the south gate of the park he saw the lights from a food stall and made his way towards it. He looked over his shoulder, but no one had followed. He'd half expected to see John running behind, begging him to come back. It would be just like him to side with their dad.

The stall was busy and when he reached the front of the queue, there was a man and woman sweating hard, surrounded by grills and hotplates full of meat. "What do you want?" the woman snapped.

"Burger."

"Two coppers."

Ryan passed her the coins and bit into the junk meat. It tasted good and he waited in the shadows, chewing robotically while he gathered his thoughts. Over where his family had been, the fighting seemed to have blown itself out and he could see a handful of seveners positioned like human shields between the gunnermen and the workers.

By the time he had finished his burger, both sides had dispersed and all eyes were back on the bonfire waiting for the fireworks. Accompanied by a gasp of excitement, the first sortie fizzed into the air with a sound like tracer fire. The rockets soared skywards and a huge explosion illuminated the park in reds and golds. Ryan moved to the edge of the pyre where he had arranged to meet Alia. The fire was at its worst there and even though the searing heat hurt his skin, Ryan refused to step back, staring down the hungry flames.

There was a tap on his shoulder and he turned to find Alia smiling nervously and shielding her face with one hand. She was wearing a woolly hat pulled down over her ears and dark brown hair poked out from underneath. She had big, bright eyes and looked beautiful.

"Hi," she said.

"Hi." More rockets burst overhead and they both craned their necks to stare at the sky.

"Did your brother enjoy the parade?" She spoke the words into his ear and he felt her cheek brushing his own. The nearness sent a thrill into his belly. When he remembered the fight with his dad though he let out a humourless laugh.

"What's up?"

"Doesn't matter," Ryan said. "When did you get here?"

"I got here nice and early," Alia said with a cheeky smile. "I think I was a bit nervous."

Ryan liked that. "Me too," he said, surprising himself with an honest answer. "I've been looking forward to seeing you again."

Alia ducked her head with another smile but then caught sight of the lump on Ryan's face and gasped. "What happened?"

He prodded at his cheek with one finger, noticing for the first time how swollen it was. He didn't want to go back over it though. He knew it would only make him angrier. "It was just a bit of a scuffle. Nothing serious." Once the words were out, he loved how cavalier it made him sound.

"It doesn't look like nothing,"

Ryan shrugged. "Do you want to walk for a bit?"

He steered a path through the crowd and felt another jolt in his stomach as Alia took his hand in hers. They weaved between several families, some with small children riding high on their parents' shoulders. Others were waving their sparklers at the band as if conducting the music. Ryan circled slowly around the fire, enjoying the touch of his fingers entwined with Alia's. They found a small break on the far side of the cordon where the fire hadn't caught as well. Together they stood by the rope and watched the flames in silence. As the heat prickled at his face, Ryan's thoughts predictably turned back to the fight.

"Do you get on with your family?" he said after a while.

Alia didn't answer right away and when he turned he

found that the smile had gone from her face and been replaced by the familiar look of sadness. It was an expression he noticed all too regularly on her face.

"My family's complicated," she said. "My dad…he's dead…and my mum's not coping."

"I'm sorry." Ryan closed his eyes, angry at himself for asking.

The fire distracted them with a loud crack and golden embers shot skywards. The fireworks had ended and over the chatter of the crowd, Ryan heard the bandleader count to four and then the trumpets blared out the opening bars of their last song. The music sent a chill down Ryan's back. It was *A Song for the Damned* which meant the prisoners had run out of time.

From the woods to his right two columns of gunnermen appeared; each one about thirty strong. As they approached the fire, Ryan saw that they were flanking the sorriest group of men and women he had ever seen. It was a collection of the condemned, victims of the Premier's law, shortly to pay the ultimate price. They wore chains at their ankles and wrists, while a long length of rope looped them together at the waist.

Ryan realised that he and Alia were standing directly in their path and he was suddenly seized by the urge to do something. He gazed at the prisoners with their ragged clothes and gaunt faces, knowing that he could no longer ignore them. Instead he stared down the first gunnermen, chest tensed, fists ready. He remembered the shame of his father's confession and a flash of anger gave him all the courage he needed.

CHAPTER 16

ALIA HAD BEEN watching Ryan with sly, sideways glances. Her appraising look studied every part of him, from the set of his lean but broad shoulders, to the beginnings of stubble that showed on his face. He was – she decided – very handsome. As soon as she acknowledged the thought, she realised how close they were standing and that sent a shiver of excitement through her spine. It was a new feeling, one that scared and excited her in equal amounts.

Then the procession appeared from the woods and Alia slid out the way like everyone else. Only when it was too late did she realise that Ryan was not with her. She glanced back and saw a solitary figure standing before the approaching column.

"Clear the fucking way!" The lead gunnerman yelled, breaking step and going straight for him. Ryan never flinched, even as one gloved hand grabbed him round the throat, and the other struck the side of his head.

Alia saw him brace his legs and for a moment he stood firm against the older man. Then the gunnermen yanked Ryan's head down, meeting it with a solid knee. He managed to turn his face at the last moment, but then another gunnermen waded in and threw Ryan to the floor.

Alia flung herself between them using her body as a shield. A boot thumped into her head and the world tipped sideways. She heard screaming, although she couldn't be certain if it was her or someone else. Clambering to her knees, she reached out for Ryan, only to be knocked down a second time.

As the procession passed them by, the gunnermen evidently felt they had made their point and re-joined the column. Ryan pushed to his knees, blood dripping from a gash on his forehead, and dragged Alia up too. He cut a path through the crowd until they were within sight of the prisoners who were standing meekly on a platform behind the bonfire.

Alia's head was still spinning and she held onto Ryan for support. His whole body seemed to resonate with anger and through his jacket she could feel the tension in his muscles. He was staring up at the prisoners, his mouth curled into a snarl.

"Fuck," he yelled, drawing wary glances from those around them.

"Ryan," she placed her fingers onto his cheek, trying to steer his face back to hers.

"Why aren't we stopping them?" He stomped away and Alia couldn't tell if the comment was aimed at himself, or her, or the thousands of people gathered around them. She ran after him, scared of what he might do next. When she finally caught him at the very edge of the crowd, he was still cursing the gunnermen.

"Why can't they see it? If we all stood up together, they wouldn't be able to stop us. We'd be rid of them forever."

Alia wiped at the blood on his face, knowing it should convince her of the truth in his words. But it didn't. Instead she recalled the moment he had stood before that column of gunnermen. He had only got hurt because he chose to defy them.

"We can't carry on like this," he said. "Surely they must see that."

And although she knew it would be better to say nothing, Alia couldn't help herself. "They're just doing their job."

"What?"

"We need them," she said. "Who else can control the workers?" The gunnermen were cruel and brutal, but the alternative was unthinkable. If people got hurt because they broke the rules, then Alia would lose no sleep over it. She wouldn't make the mistake her father had. Ryan's face twisted like she was speaking gibberish.

"Control them? They don't *need* controlling."

"Ryan, they're animals. They go to work, they get drunk and then they fight. We need the gunnermen to protect us."

"You're unbelievable. How can *this*," he pointed to the swelling on his face. "How can this be right?"

"It's not," she shouted back. "But back there at the fire. Why provoke them? Why stand in their way?"

"Because no one else was." Ryan spun her by the shoulders so that they were facing the raised platform. "Those people are going to die tonight and no one is stopping it."

Alia had no answer for him. She felt a twinge of pride at the passion in his words, but she couldn't share them. She couldn't unlearn what life had taught her. "You've no idea why they're up there and neither do I. Maybe they deserve it."

The silence dragged out between them until eventually Ryan gave a derisive snort. "Whatever. I'm done."

He stalked away through the crowd and all the righteous anger that Alia had felt suddenly drained away like bathwater. She called his name, but any reply was drowned out by a fresh volley of fireworks. It was all part of the mock execution and the prisoners cringed away from the raised rifles of the gunnermen. The crowd gasped and then laughed at the scene playing out before them.

Despite the heat from the fire, Alia felt a familiar numbness seep through her bones. An hour ago, she thought it had shaken loose but that had been a dream. She realised now that she'd never be free of it. Her fingers toyed once again with the bottle of opiates in her pocket and without a second thought she tipped one out and swallowed it down.

CHAPTER 17

THE SAFE HOUSE was gone and the mission over. Alistair was dead, Farren captured or killed, and when Robb awoke, he found himself strung up in an archway at the top of The Cathedral. It was open to the sky and squalling winds threw rain against his bare chest. Both wrists were chained, and his legs were bound in tight bandages and set with splints.

Footsteps echoed behind him and Robb strained to see over one shoulder. He couldn't see anyone, but he knew he was being watched. Long seconds passed until the footsteps sounded up again, retreating back the way they had come.

Before long, two more people entered the stone cell. Robb twisted round again and saw a small figure step into view. His stomach sank when he recognised the man that had been waiting for him off the boat.

"Hello," the figure said amiably. "My name is Ashgate. I asked them to fetch me when you woke up." He looked hospital clean surrounded by the damp stone cell. "I'm the caretaker for The Cathedral."

Robb gave no reply. Just blinked through the silence.

"You have been declared an *enemy of the people*," Ashgate said. "Imagine that." He moved like an aristocrat across the stone archway, hands pushed into the pockets of his suit jacket. "That, unfortunately, has made you my concern." He reached up to test the strength of the chains that attached Robb's arm to the stonework. Together they stared from the high window and considered the swollen grey skies over Karasard.

"Why did you bind my legs?" Robb said.

"You want to open with the questions, do you? Well why not." Ashgate smiled as an indulgent uncle might do to a child. "It's because I need you to be conscious while I question you." He pointed at the bandages that stretched from thigh to foot. "It's just a temporary measure and I don't think you'll ever walk again."

Somewhere, far off, Robb heard a scream.

"Now my turn," Ashgate said. "What's your name?" He allowed a few seconds before stepping closer. "Hmm?"

Silence.

Tensing did nothing to dull the impact of a gloved fist as it barrelled into Robb's back. He grunted at the impact and flopped forwards. The chains at his wrists jangled in reply while the guard stepped back to the shadows. Ashgate held an ID card in front of Robb's face. He couldn't focus on the picture, but he presumed it was the fake one from his wallet.

"Simon Puller," Ashgate said. "214 Crester Way."

"Why ask me," Robb said, breathing hard. "If you already knew?"

Ashgate didn't rise to that. "How long have you lived there, Simon?"

"Three years," he said.

A second punch landed in his back and the chains took his weight while Robb sprawled forwards, all the wind knocked out of him.

"Give me some credit," Ashgate said. "It might get you past a checkpoint or two, but it won't work here." He tossed the card through the archway and they watched it sail above Lake Stretten towards the city. On the wind Robb heard another scream.

"What's your name?" When there was no answer Ashgate shook his head. "Oh dear. You're going to find it very difficult here."

Ashgate was true to his word. He had known about the plan to attack The Palace well before Robb arrived at The Cathedral. It didn't stop him asking questions though and punishing the lies. Lately they had all been for the Colonel. *Where would he meet you? What were his plans? Where is he now?*

Ashgate made himself a bystander while the guard meted out the physical pain. Robb was knocked to the floor and punched and kicked, but never in the face. They were very particular about that. Sometimes his chains were unfastened and he was dragged to the centre of the cell. There the guard would work him just until the pain dulled. The precision was frightening. On the second day, a huge right-handed punch was delivered to his midriff and Robb felt his ribs give way. As he rolled on the ground, cradling his side, a heavy black boot crunched down on his fingers fracturing the last two so that they bent at near right-angles.

And so it went.

Hours later, Robb was back at the archway staring over Karasard. Each breath he drew was a struggle and made a low whistle in his chest. The guard had a cane in one hand. The outside was wood, but Robb guessed that a vein of metal had been threaded through its spine. The first blow that lashed across his back had him clenching his jaw and pulling at the chains. On the second Robb gave up any show of control and sent his screams through the stone archway to mix with the howling wind over Karasard.

It was hard to know how long the pain had stopped for. Time had little meaning in The Cathedral. Robb dangled limply from the ceiling and could hear quiet voices from somewhere in the cell. He didn't even realise that Ashgate had left the room until he heard those clipped footsteps returning and watched him appear with a knowing smile on his face.

"Well Robbert," he said. "It seems our position has changed. Objectives have been *redefined*." Outside there were more footsteps. Two people dragging a third. "It certainly puts you in an unfortunate position. Yes it does."

Ashgate reached up and unfastened one bracelet. Robb dangled by his left arm, his weight naturally spinning him towards the door. Outside he saw two guards dragging a battered and bleeding body between them. It was Farren.

"Hey," Robb yelled, pulling against the chain with all his strength. "Hey."

Farren turned back, eyes brimming with tears as he struggled to reach his friend. "Robb," he yelled. The guards dragged him away.

"Farren," he shouted.

"Robb," the voice grew fainter. "They said you were dead."

Robb awoke in the darkness with a cry caught in his chest. Thirty-three years had past since they'd held him in The Cathedral. The nightmare was so realistic though, that for a few moments he believed himself still to be a captive. When the initial wave of panic subsided, his senses confirmed that he was lying in his own bed and that sweat - not blood - soaked his back.

Using the handrail, Robb hauled himself upright, only then remembering the injuries from last night's fight. A sudden rush of pain stabbed through his body, forcing a quiet groan to escape his lips.

"It's okay," Eliza whispered, "he's home. I checked."

"Thank you," Robb grimaced. "I hadn't meant to sleep."

He didn't bother to tell her about the dream. She had heard it all so many times anyway. Like hands beneath the water, these memories had pulled at him for a lifetime.

He unbuttoned his bed-shirt and slowly peeled the damp material from his back. His ribs gave another shout of complaint, but he was able to suppress the pain. It was four-fifteen. Too early to get up and too late for him to sleep. Robb lay back down and waited in the darkness, trying desperately to escape his thoughts.

CHAPTER 18

Saintsday had been the worst night that John could remember in a long time. They had walked back in silence while his dad nursed his injured ribs. Ryan hadn't reappeared and John had stayed awake for hours, waiting. It was the early hours before he recognised his brother's footsteps creeping upstairs. The bedroom door opened and Ryan slipped quietly out of his clothes and into bed. Within minutes his breathing slowed and drew deeper until John knew that he was asleep.

An hour after that he heard his mum treading softly across the landing and watched her face appear at a crack in the door. Although he pretended to be asleep, it was then that John made a promise to himself. He would protect his brother and keep him safe, no matter the cost. Within minutes his eyes became heavy and at last sleep found him.

The next morning the bang of the front door woke him with a start. Fearing he was too late, John scrambled over the bed and peered through the window, but it was only his dad limping down their path in the darkness. It seemed strange that after last night, he could just wake up and go to work as though nothing had happened. John clambered down the ladder and crept past his brother who was still sleeping with his back turned. He went downstairs and raided the kitchen for a hunk of bread and a small apple. He ate the first and put the second in his coat which was hanging by the door. After readying his shoes at the bottom step, he waited quietly and ordered his thoughts.

It wasn't too long until he heard his mother descend and she came into the kitchen ready for her shift at the hospital. She flicked on the light and gasped when she saw John staring back at her. "You scared me," she said. "What are you doing awake?"

"Nothing. I just couldn't sleep."

She leaned over and kissed his forehead. "It'll be okay. You'll see."

"I know Mum. Don't worry."

She kissed him again and then picked up her bag from the chair. "I haven't time for breakfast," she said. "But I'll see you tonight. We can have a talk if you like."

"Okay Mum."

The door closed and John listened to her shoes clipping down the pavement. It was another hour before Ryan surfaced. John stared with wide-eyes at his brother's face. The left eye was badly swollen and there was dried blood in his hairline.

"What happened?"

"Nothing." The tone of his voice invited no further questions and John watched him scavenge through the cupboards for something edible. He settled on the bag of oats and poured some into a pan with water.

"You want some?"

"Yes please."

They said nothing more until he had sat down with two

bowls of thin, yellow porridge. Ryan opened his mouth for the first spoonful and winced in pain.

"Does it hurt?"

"A bit." Ryan pressed his finger to the puffy swollen skin on his face. "I'm sorry you saw all that last night."

"It's okay."

"Has he gone to work?"

"About two hours ago."

They ate in silence, the only sound coming from the clang and scrape of their spoons. Eventually, Ryan cleared his dish and rinsed out the last of the food beneath the sink. "What are you doing today?"

I'm going to follow you and make sure you don't get into any more trouble.

"I don't know." John said. Then with a hopeful smile, "why don't we go to the wreck?" It was an old bomb site they used to climb as kids. Ryan seemed to at least give it some consideration until his eyes hardened.

"I can't. I've got somewhere I need to be."

He was up and gone soon after and John watched his progress up the road from the lounge window. Grabbing his coat and shoes he waited until his brother was out of sight and then dashed up the road in pursuit.

He trailed his brother in this stop-start manner until they reached the heart of the Worker District. When he went down Carragon Road, John guessed they were headed to that old chapel again. He recognised some of the buildings from when he had followed Ryan last month.

His brother made one last check over his shoulder before approaching the large stone building and pushing open its stout wooden door. As he had done the first time, John took up position in the alleyway opposite. While he waited, he chewed thoughtfully on the apple he'd stashed at breakfast. It was soft and brown in parts, but it satisfied John's rumbling stomach for the moment. Several times he considered sneaking closer, but decided it would be too dangerous. The best thing he could do was wait for Ryan to leave and then take a look afterwards.

Eventually, when John's fingers and feet were numb with cold, the chapel door inched open and Ryan emerged into daylight. His brother squinted against the bright autumn sun and John noted that he wasn't carrying any bags or posters like last time. Part of him wanted to follow Ryan, but he knew that this chapel was key to keeping him safe. Curiosity got the better of him and he scampered across the road, pushed on the wooden door and slipped inside.

It was dark and dusty and John gripped the first pew while his eyes adjusted to the low light. When he could make out the gloomy outline of the main chamber, he moved with more confidence between the benches, surveying what was left of the building. He went as far as the altar where a moth-eaten tapestry hung from one side of the chancel.

This far up the church, the stone floor was littered with debris that had crumbled away from the ceiling. John kicked at a fist-sized rock, instantly regretting it when the thump and echo filled each corner of the building. Footsteps reached him through the darkness. Quiet, sneaking steps from the tombs beneath. John froze, his heart thumping. The footsteps came closer, rising from the belly of the chapel. He ran halfway down the aisle and then dived beneath one of the pews, squashing himself against the rotten timbers, trying to slow his breathing.

"Who's there?"

John recognised the voice immediately and his stomach turned to water. It was the man from the underground station. The one who had threatened to kill him. He shrank further into the shadows while slow, deliberate steps approached.

A few rows ahead of him, there was a sudden crack of splintered wood as the first bench was ripped aside. John stifled a cry against the sleeve of his coat and waited for the echoes to fall away. Then the gentle scrape of the door sounded at the rear of the chapel. New footsteps thumped slowly towards him.

"Problem?"

John prayed it was a sevener drawn by the noise.

"It's nothing." That was the man from the underground station. "I thought I heard something, that's all."

The figure at the door walked closer and John twisted his head to peer through a gap in the wood. He saw a pair of gunnermen fatigues and heavy black boots clump past.

"You're early," that was the first man again.

"What's the matter?" the gunnerman replied. "Got one of your pups here, Brynne?"

"No. But keep to the arranged time in future. I can't have you seen here."

"You worry too much."

They walked back to the altar where it sounded like a curtain was drawn back. Their voices faded away and silence once again smothered the church. A judder of fear rocked down John's spine. He rolled out from beneath the bench and slowly shuffled to the edge of the pew. The church was empty, but John saw that the tapestry beside the altar was now drawn to one side revealing a narrow stone archway.

"Brynne," John whispered the name, storing it away. Then he crouched low and ran for the safety of the street.

When he got home, the house was empty and John rubbed the dirt and dust from his trousers. He went to his bedroom and took a notebook from under his pillow. The first couple of pages were filled with a description of what happened last week when he followed Ryan to the underground. He found the place where he wrote about being threatened. John scrawled *Brynne* into the margin in capital letters.

He turned to a fresh page and wrote the date and time. Beneath that he wrote about the chapel and how Brynne was hiding in the tombs below. He wrote about the secret room behind the tapestry and how the gunnerman had turned up. If Ryan couldn't see the danger he was in, then he was going to have to show him.

CHAPTER 19

Even though Brynne had finally given him the all clear to use the sevener tunnel again, Ryan still had to dodge a checkpoint before returning to the chapel. The spray-cans he had been using were poor quality and now his fingers were stained with red and blue paint. If that wasn't suspicious enough, he also had a fantastic collection of bruises from the parade last night.

Ryan pulled his hood up and mulled over the day's work. Brynne had asked him to keep painting the city with slogans and messages for the people. Last week, that thought had left him paralysed by indecision. He had no idea what he should be writing or what the workers needed to see to enflame their hearts. Then last night, as he wandered the streets smouldering with a fierce resentment, the answer spilled out of him.

Fuck them!

It wasn't poetic, but at least it was honest and Ryan had felt pride while writing it. He leant his shoulder to the chapel door for the second time that day and found Brynne sitting in one of the pews, deep in thought. He started at Ryan's sudden appearance, but it was only a moment before the usual smile returned.

"How did it go?" he said quietly. "No trouble?"

"None. Except these," Ryan wiggled his paint-covered fingers.

"Get yourself downstairs then. I've some turps beneath the sink."

Ryan nodded and walked to the tapestry behind the altar. It was already drawn back to reveal the hidden staircase and he descended to the tombs where Brynne had made his home. Ryan smiled. It was good to be somewhere safe. All day he'd been watching over one shoulder, expecting gunnermen to appear. At least now he could relax. Brynne followed him into the cellar and poured out two tumblers of whisky.

"That's coming up a treat," he said, pointing at the shining bruise around Ryan's eye.

He had already told him about the fight on Saintsday. Brynne had listened in silence to the whole thing, offering no comment until he was certain that the story was complete. Ryan couldn't remember his dad ever showing that much interest in what he had to say.

"Have you decided what you're going to do about Alia?"

He blushed at the mention of her name. Then his face grew dark as he remembered their argument. "I don't see how it can work, if that's what she really thinks."

"And is it? What she really thinks?"

"Brynne, she looked me in the eye and said the gunnermen were right." The old man nodded, a thoughtful expression on his face. Ryan waited for his answer, but none was forthcoming. "I mean, I know she'd just been knocked over in the fighting. And she was probably scared, but even so…" He took another sip of whisky and thought about it some more. "You think I should give her another chance?"

Brynne chuckled. "I'm not going to advise you one way or the other. But what I will say is that we've all done things we don't mean when we're scared, or angry, or hurting. God knows I have." Ryan watched the old man take a drink of his whisky. He always had a way of stripping complicated ideas down to their bare bones. With Brynne, everything was so simple.

"I don't know anything about this girl," Brynne continued, "except that she's got big blue eyes and laughs at your jokes and makes you smile more than I've seen in months."

Ryan's ears burned.

"You're both products of your past. Both forged in this shithole of a city. Neither one of you is perfect. You have your own views. She has hers. They come from where you've been and what you've seen."

"But how can we ever get past that?"

"You'll have to teach her. Explain to her, the way I explained to you. Your eyes are open now Ryan. You see this city for what it is. Alia doesn't have that yet. She's still lost in the fog of lies and bullshit."

Brynne pointed at the newspaper clippings that littered his walls. "She's blind to all of this, but if she likes you as much as you like her, then maybe you can make her see."

Ryan took another sip of whisky and leaned back in his chair. "Even if I wanted to, I don't think she'll give me a second chance after last night."

Brynne smiled. "She'll be fine. Take her some flowers."

"Flowers? Isn't that a bit…you know?"

"Old fashioned?" he laughed. "You wait and see. I didn't get to this ripe old age without learning how to impress the ladies."

Ryan tried to imagine Brynne at his age, but it was impossible. Before he left though, the old man handed him a few copper coins.

"Remember those flowers," he said.

Ryan smiled and then raced up the steps and out of the chapel, happier than he had been in days. Even though it was early evening, he couldn't face going home yet and found himself at a bar two streets away. He and Brynne had been there a few times and it was sufficiently seedy to attract no attention from the authorities.

Ryan ordered a beer and took a seat on one of the back tables. There were two other people in there and Ryan looked them over while he drank. In one corner was an old man with blotchy red skin. He was hunched over a tall glass of spirits staring at the bottom of his glass. His eyes were a watery blue, diluted by alcohol and old age.

The other man was enormous and dwarfed the table he was sitting at. He had a thick, peppery beard and even out of uniform, it was obvious he was a sevener. As though sensing that he was being watched, the giant flicked his eyes up and then turns away without comment.

Ryan sat in the shadows watching time slip by. Suddenly, the heavy wooden door banged open and his heart sank. Three gunnermen pushed into the bar, full of their own importance. They were off duty and didn't look much older than him, but they were big, with stocky shoulders and loud voices. Two of them were still wearing their green camo-trousers and they horsed around, playing up the tallest of the group. He had a broad, bony face with hair so short that it was barely a shadow across his scalp.

He ordered three beers and handed them out to his

friends before scanning the rest of the bar. Ryan pretended to be lost in his own thoughts, staring at the far wall. He absently turned his pint glass on the table and watched the three gunnermen sit at a nearby table. Leaning further into his chair, he stretched his legs out, trying to seem confident. It would be stupid to get up and leave straightaway, but he wasn't going to hang around too long. After a few minutes, the gunnermen went quiet and Ryan knew they were watching him. The skinhead pulled out a packet of cigarettes and leaned across the tables.

"You got a light mate?" He had the cigarette between his lips and mimed striking a lighter in his empty hands.

"Sure." Ryan fished inside his pocket and brought out a box of matches which he tossed over.

Skinhead lit his cigarette and put the matchbox in his pocket. Ryan guessed it was meant to provoke him, but he'd been taught better than that. When he said nothing, Skinhead leaned over a second time. "What happened to your face?"

"This?" Ryan hesitated, searching for a plausible lie. "Just an argument that got out of hand."

"There were quite a few people who lost arguments yesterday. Pissed up and fighting at the parade were you."

It looked like he was just making small talk, but Ryan knew better than that. He shook his head. "Just an argument. I wasn't at the parade."

Skinhead held Ryan's gaze, a tight grin on his face. "I don't believe you. I think you were there." The camo-boys stopped drinking and twisted round in their chairs to look at Ryan. "One of our lot did that to you, didn't they?" Skinhead said. "What happened? Had too much to drink and thought you could take on the big boys?"

The barman glanced over, sensing a change in atmosphere from across the room. A chair scraped out and the sevener ambled slowly towards them. For a moment, Ryan thought he was going to intervene, but he moved straight past and into the toilets. Skinhead suddenly broke into an amiable grin.

"Never mind. We don't hold grudges, do we lads?"

The camo-boys shook their heads. "Gives us a bit of sport," one said. "You lot have always got something to moan about."

"I've noticed that," the other chimed in. "First they complain there's no work. Then they moan the job's too hard."

"You should try a tour in the Outlands. That'd stop you complaining." Then they laughed. Except for Skinhead who simply watched through narrowed eyes.

"We've got friends up there you know," he said. "Killing Gabblers to protect you ungrateful bastards." This was ever the justification for gunnermen violence. They had to keep order to stop the Gabblers overrunning the City States.

Ryan said nothing, just toyed nervously with his beer. He gulped down the last third of his glass and felt it slop over the side of his mouth and pour down the front of his shirt. The gunnermen roared with laughter, pushing each other and pointing. Ryan shook his head and smiled weakly before crossing the room to put his glass on the bar. He headed for the toilets and stood before the sink wiping at his beer-stained shirt. A few seconds later, the door opened and Skinhead walked up to the urinal.

"We were only fooling back there," he said. Ryan could see his back in the mirror and when he didn't answer, Skinhead turned to face him. "Did you hear me?"

"What? Yeah. Don't worry about it." Ryan said.

"I'm not worried." He zipped up his jeans and pushed in front of the sink.

With a sigh, Ryan went for the door, but it opened before he could get there. It was the camo-boys and at an unseen signal, Ryan was shoved against the wall with a forearm at his throat.

"Card," Skinhead demanded.

"Get off me."

He slapped Ryan across the face while his pals closed in on either side. "Give me your card, worker."

A hand grabbed the wallet from Ryan's back pocket. He tried to block it, but Skinhead pinned his arm to the wall. They both watched as one of the camo-boys rifled through his cards and money.

"What's his name?"

"Ryan Calloway."

"Calloway? Sounds like a gypsy name."

One of the camo-boys laughed. "I fucking hate gypsies."

He sent a vicious jab into Ryan's stomach, doubling him over and then hauled him back up, ready for the next blow. Before he could throw the punch though, a toilet flushed in the cubicle beside them. The door rattled open and out stepped the sevener, apparently oblivious to what was happening around him. He plodded to the sink, washed his hands and smoothed his beard on both sides. Finally, he turned to face the gunnermen.

"Are we finished?" he said.

The camo-boys lost their bravado immediately and looked to their friend. Skinhead still had his hand at Ryan's throat and wasn't ready to back down yet. "This has got nothing to do with you," he said. "We've no problem with the seveners."

The giant pushed off the sink, filling the room. "I disagree."

Camo-boys shrank towards the door. "Come on," one said. "Let's just leave it."

Skinhead wouldn't back down though. "I am a gunnerman of the City Garrison," he said. "I'm ordering you to walk away."

"Well I'm a big bastard who was trying to take a shit," the sevener said. "And I don't really follow orders. Let the kid go, or I'll break your face."

Skinhead unclamped his hand from around Ryan's neck, but couldn't resist a final dig. "You'll keep," he said, jabbing two fingers into his chest.

Before he could say another word, a huge hand scooped up his face and threw it against the cubicle door. It smacked open and Skinhead clattered to the tiles. He scrambled up clutching his nose, both knees wet with piss from the floor.

"Anything else?" the sevener asked.

Skinhead slid past without a word followed by his two friends. As they left, Ryan grabbed his wallet and card.

"Thanks."

"No problem." They returned to the bar and through the window saw the gunnermen striding towards the nearest checkpoint.

"I wouldn't hang around lad. They'll be back soon. And with backup."

Ryan nodded and grabbed his coat from the back of the chair.

"Shall I take you past the checkpoint?" the sevener rumbled.

"I'll be alright," he said. "But thanks."

As he was leaving, the sevener shouted over. "Are you really Ryan Calloway?"

He nodded.

"Robb Calloway's boy?"

The video from Brynne's cellar re-played itself in his head.

Where do your loyalties lie?

With the Government. With Premier Talis.

The sevener didn't wait for an answer. "Tell him Kellie Downs sends his regards."

Then he ordered another beer and sat back in his seat.

CHAPTER 20

ALIA GHOSTED THROUGH the Worker District, enjoying a new sense of calm. The school day had gone in a giddy haze that she could barely remember. Although she had physically been in the lessons, her thoughts had drifted far and away from the classrooms and corridors of Straybeck Central. The worries of her old life no longer held sway in this altered perspective and even when she thought back to the fight with Ryan, it no longer had the cruel sting that it once had.

As she walked now, her finger closed around the bottle of opiates. There were still enough pills to last until tomorrow, but Alia wondered if she should turn back and find one of the pushers now. The only concern that held any real meaning was the idea of losing these tablets.

She decided to fetch more tablets now and headed home where she could recover the last of her mother's jewellery. When she reached the end of her street though, Ryan was waiting for her, leaning against the metal skip and holding a bunch of bright red flowers. Her heart snagged with the memory of their Saintsday argument, but it was only an echo of what it had been. Alia realised he was talking quietly to himself, completely unaware that she had arrived.

"Hi…Hiya…Hello," he said and mimed offering the bouquet. "I brought you some flowers as an apology." He changed to a brighter more relaxed voice. "Hi. I brought you some flowers. As a bit of an apology."

Alia cleared her throat and hid the smile from her face when Ryan spun round. His face suddenly beamed as red as the flowers. "You made me jump."

She pointed at the flowers behind him. "Are those for me?"

Slowly, he drew them out and offered them to her. "If you'll have them."

"They're lovely."

"I acted like an idiot the other night," he said. "I'd argued with my dad and then the gunnermen came and I couldn't do anything about it. And, it's not an excuse…well I guess it is…but I just wanted to say I'm sorry. I know we have different views on some things…"

"Come on," she said, sparing him further embarrassment. She led him towards the front door and marvelled that it held no fear for her. A few days ago, she would have been ashamed to invite someone into her house. Now it seemed trivial. A single grey cloud in an otherwise blue sky.

Alia took the loop of string from around her neck where she kept her key and unlocked the door. There were clothes and crockery strewn throughout the hallway and she doubted that the rest of the house was any better. "Just give me a minute," she said serenely and closed the door on Ryan.

As she stooped to tidy the clutter, she called out to her mum. There was no answer. The kitchen and lounge were empty, so she quickly tidied the dirty pots and kicked the worst of the mess out of sight. Alia could tell that her mum had surfaced briefly during the day but guessed that she was back in bed now. She ran upstairs and found her lying on top of the blankets. On the bedside table was an open box of tablets, with a few loose ones scattered next to the half-empty glass of water.

Tucking her hair behind one ear Alia bent down to her mum's pillow. She could hear slow but steady breathing and felt a surge of relief pass through her. Without thinking she scooped up one of the tablets and swallowed it with a gulp of water.

In the hallway she paused outside the spare room. After a deep breath she pushed the door so that it brushed slowly over the carpet. The room was quiet and still so Alia crept back to the landing. She went downstairs and invited Ryan into the house.

"Sorry about that, would you like a drink?" He nodded and they went to the kitchen where the tap grumbled and shook before releasing a burst of cloudy water. "It always takes a couple of minutes to run clear."

She grabbed two glasses and filled them up before leading him through to the lounge where they sat side by side on the sofa. Ryan sipped his drink and scanned the room. Alia followed his eyes over the tatty wallpaper and worn out carpet.

"I'm sorry about the house," she said. "We've not rented long."

Ryan frowned. "It's not that different to mine, really."

"I doubt that." They lapsed into silence.

"You go to Straybeck Central, right?" he said.

"Yes."

"You don't wear their uniform though?"

Alia scoffed. "It's not through choice. But they won't give me any at the school and I can't afford to buy any." Part of her couldn't believe she'd just admitted that, but the other part was liberated by the tablet-induced calm.

"Where were you before?" Ryan said with a frown. "The technical?"

"Straybeck Academy," Alia said quietly.

Ryan laughed, but when she didn't join in, he gave a low whistle. "The Academy? I thought you had to be super rich to go there though."

Alia put her glass down and then pulled Ryan up from the sofa. "Come on, I want to show you something."

When she had said they were going to Old Straybeck, Alia wasn't sure if Ryan would come. It was an understandable reaction. Getting through a checkpoint was one thing, but unless you had been born to it, Old Straybeck was always out of reach.

"Please, just trust me," she said. "I have to show you something."

They reached the checkpoint and Alia presented her card to the gunnerman. Gone was the stooped shoulders and sad face from the past few days. This was now an Alia filled with self-confidence and an unswerving sense of her own belonging.

The gunnerman who took her card had worked on the checkpoint for years. He gave her a quick nod of recognition, barely glancing at the picture before passing her card back and pressing the gate-release. Once through she waited for Ryan pass his card over. The gunnerman studied the picture and then stared at his bruised and swollen face before scanning it.

"No convictions?"

"That's what it says," Ryan answered.

The gunnerman paused then reached for the radio in his booth. "Delta four-one."

There was a static hiss and then a monotone voice transmitted back. "Control, go ahead."

"Nominal check," the gunnerman said. "Surname Calloway, first name Ryan." He relayed Ryan's date of birth and the three of them waited in silence.

"Ryan Calloway is known on the system. Not wanted, not missing and no convictions. If he's in company with a Robbert Calloway, stop and search."

Still not satisfied, he stared again at Ryan's photograph. "What's your business here?"

"My own."

The gunnerman stepped out of the booth and stood in front of Ryan. "Cut the attitude lad. I've not seen you at this checkpoint before and you're not getting through unless I say so. Now what's your business?"

"He's with me," Alia said curtly. "You know I'm from Old Straybeck and he's a friend of mine."

The gunnerman weighed up her answer, deciding if it was worth the hassle of upsetting a girl who would no doubt have important and influential parents. "Alright Miss," he said. "But I suggest you choose your company more carefully." He leaned into the booth and pressed the gate release.

"Thank you," she said when Ryan was through. "But the company I keep is absolutely no concern of yours." She linked her arm through Ryan's and they walked up the street. A few steps later, he unhooked his arm and Alia could tell he was silently fuming.

"Sorry," she said.

Ryan took a breath. "Do you see what I mean now? How

can it be right for him to talk to me like that? I've done nothing wrong. I should be allowed to go wherever I want."

"It isn't right," she said. "But it's how it's always been." Ryan bridled at the comment and she put her hands up to pacify him. "Wait, just hear me out. That's why I've brought you here."

They walked in silence down the wide-open streets of Old Straybeck. She wondered if Ryan had ever been here before. From the way he gawped up at the rows of grand, whitewashed houses, she doubted it. This place was closed to anyone but the elite. Here lived the families who collectively controlled the political, economic and military power in the city; all residing within a few square miles of each other.

In a place where she had always been so comfortable, Alia suddenly felt like a beggar. The people here dressed expensively and strolled without purpose, confident of their place in the world. It was a far cry from her ramshackle, filthy street in the Slum District, where the workers beetled from door to factory under cover of darkness.

Eventually, Alia stopped outside an enormous double-fronted building. It was set back from the road with carefully landscaped gardens and topiaries. Its door was framed by two bulging stone pillars and the huge windows were criss-crossed with lead mullions.

"That's my house," she said.

"What?"

"Until just over a year ago, I lived there." She pointed up at the top-right window. "That was my bedroom." She could tell by his face that Ryan didn't believe her.

"I suppose you had servants too?"

"We had people that worked on the estate. And I had

a nanny. But we didn't treat them like servants. They were more like family."

There was an ornate metal bench nearby and Ryan sat straight-backed, staring at the façade. "I don't understand. I've been to your house. How could you have lived here?"

She took a seat beside him. "My dad used to own a factory in the worker district. It was one of the biggest in Straybeck." She could feel his eyes fixed upon her, but she continued the story. "My dad was not an evil man Ryan, and he was never cruel to his workers. Do you remember the strikes ten years ago? Well his was the only factory not burnt out. That means something, doesn't it?"

She didn't wait for an answer. "A couple of years ago, he hired two new foremen. They were starving and needed work and because of that he hired them over more qualified people. But pretty soon, problems started in the factory. Machinery broke and money went missing. The rest of the workers, who had never concerned themselves with politics, were suddenly holding meetings and calling for strikes.

"Slander and lies about my father spread though the work force. People said that he was going to lay off half the staff so that he could pay the rest lower wages and work them longer hours. By the time he figured out who was to blame, it was too late. The foremen he had hired out of pity had turned the entire factory against him." Tears swelled to the corner of her eyes and she blinked them onto her cheeks.

"They forced the lock to my father's office and beat him unconscious. They carried him down to the factory floor and tied a rope round his neck. Then they hooked it over one of the rafters and took it in turns to pull him in the air and let go. It was nearly half an hour before the seveners broke through and carried him to a hospital."

When Ryan put his arm around her shoulders, she leaned into him, burying her face in her hands. Despite the numbing effect of the tablets, the tears wouldn't stop. She wiped them away with the cuff of her jacket and straightened up.

"You think the gunnermen are evil and the workers are all victims. You think that, because it's all you've ever known. Well that's not my life. They're not victims. Not to me." Ryan hunched forward, his chin on his hands, silently studying the pavement below.

"What a mess," he said eventually, allowing a deep breath to escape.

"What?"

"All of it. This whole city."

CHAPTER 21

YEARS AGO, THERE had been an idea that the Government could eliminate unemployment throughout the City States. They spent millions regenerating the Worker Districts, creating enormous new factories and power plants. Thousands of unemployed were relocated and drafted into work in a move that Premier Talis hailed as the end of their economic depression.

The reality wasn't quite like that though. The huge fall in unemployment was only achieved by offering the workers a stark choice. Work or starve. While lines of desperate young men came to the factory gates, the bosses rubbed their hands and dropped wages a little more each day. People who had no business being on the factory floor, those with broken bodies or broken minds, were forced to toil for endless hours at the machine face.

After he was released from The Cathedral, Robb almost starved in the months it took to recuperate. Eliza earned a pittance as a trainee nurse and she couldn't support them indefinitely. So as soon as he could walk, Robb went to the factory like everyone else. He stood straight and tall while the foreman spoke to him and then he was given a job at the busiest munitions plant in Karasard.

He struggled for as long as his body would hold out, working without breaks just so he could keep up with the other machinists. On the third day though, exhausted and dehydrated, his legs gave way and he collapsed beneath a stack of aluminium sheeting. Blood streamed from a gash on his arm, but he doggedly got to his feet and began restacking the fallen metal.

The foreman ran over, yelling and cursing at Robb while the other workers kept their heads down. It was actually the floor supervisor, a quiet man called Don Wyatt, who intervened on Robb's behalf and stopped the foreman from throwing him out. He was one of those rare people, respected throughout the factory by both the workers and the management. Although he rarely spoke, his words were carefully considered and carried all the more weight as a result.

"That's enough," he said, one hand resting on Robb's shoulder, the other removing a sheet of metal from his grip. The foreman fumed quietly at his side but knew better than to challenge Wyatt. Robb allowed himself to be led from the factory floor where he sank dejectedly onto an empty pallet by the huge roller shutters in the loading bay. Wyatt gave him a crisp white handkerchief to staunch the bleeding and he gingerly dabbed it against the cut.

"Don't just pet it," Wyatt grumbled and pressed his hand down firmly on top of Robb's.

A man in his fifties strode past with an impossibly large coil of wire balanced on one shoulder. He pulled up short when he saw the blood on Robb's arm.

"He alright Don?"

"Aye. Looks worse than it is."

The man nodded and then hoisted his load back into

place before continuing across the work bay. Robb had the feeling that Wyatt had something else he wanted to talk about.

"I've been watching you the last few days," he eventually said. "You must have known someone would be. A past like yours."

Robb glanced up. He had a fair idea where this was going.

"Relax. I could get rid of you for a lot less than dropping some bloody scrap metal." The supervisor lowered his voice. "So, The Cathedral huh? You were lucky to come out of there at all. I've known many that didn't."

Robb was immediately on his guard although he could sense no hidden agenda. Besides, there would be no purpose for this man to entrap him in a conversation. The gunnermen could snatch him away at any moment and he'd be simply one more disappeared worker.

"Can I be honest with you?" Wyatt said and then continued without waiting for an answer. "You're not strong enough or fast enough to be a factory hand. You've flogged yourself half to death for three days and could barely keep pace with the other lads."

Robb was stung by the words, but knew they were true.

"How long do you think you can do that for? A week? A month? Sooner or later accidents are going to happen and someone's going to get hurt."

"You're telling me," Robb said as he drew back the bloodied handkerchief.

Wyatt was unimpressed though and his forehead creased into a deep frown. "I mean seriously hurt. Or worse."

"I know that," Robb said wearily. "But what am I supposed to do? I can't eat if I don't have money."

"I've always been a believer in second chances. God

knows I've needed a few in my time." Wyatt took a seat on the wooden pallet and unwrapped a paper bag filled with sugar sweets. "So, what I'm asking myself is can I use you for something else? You got a head for figures? Money and such?"

Robb caught his meaning. "I've done exams and I helped run the books for a builder's firm last year. Before…"

"Before you were otherwise employed?" Wyatt suggested.

"Yes. Something like that."

"Well it so happens - as of next week – that I'm short a member of staff on the corridor."

The corridor referred to a row of offices that housed all the finance and administrative staff. Almost thirty feet in the air, it ran along the upper edge of the factory wall. There they sat, like bird's nests, overseeing the factory floor with an interconnecting balcony that allowed the admin staff to move around without ever stepping foot among the workers. They had a place that fell somewhere between management and labourers and were welcomed by neither side.

For Robb though, there was no choice to be made. He had just publicly renounced all the ideals he ever held close. So taking a job where people avoided him was irrelevant. That same day he found himself climbing the circular staircase that took him off the factory floor. His uneven footsteps left the metal stairs ringing and when he reached the top he was sweating and panting for breath. There he stayed, while thirty years slipped through his hands and Robb found he was still working on the same corridor of the same factory.

Don Wyatt was long since dead. A heart attack claimed him four years after he gave that second chance. Staff came and went and Robb eventually became the old-timer. New workers stopped hearing about his past, while the older ones simply stopped caring.

The end product was a tired and worn out man, nursing his bandaged ribs the day after Saintsday. In a gloomy corner of the office he sat and balanced the books, filed reports and ran production figures. It had been over a quarter of a century since he left The Cathedral, but Robb finally realised this had been the real punishment.

Across the room, the corner speaker was transmitting government broadcasts that played continuously through their factory network. Very occasionally, it allowed censor-approved songs to be played and Robb glanced up as the opening bars of a song crept into the office.

It was an old one, from when he had been young. A lifetime ago. The soft lilting voice prickled his memory and set his hairs standing on end. Try as he might though, he couldn't quite place the tune. Each time a certain refrain played through, he almost glimpsed it. Without thinking he stood up and limped over to the radio. The other clerks stopped their tasks one by one and stared as he went past. In the silence left by the absence of chatter, Robb let music fill their space and a voice carry him away.

He remembered it all. A night out in Karasard before The Cathedral. Before he had been transformed into this twisted wreck of a man. A chance encounter after too much beer. The first time he had heard that song.

Back then, there were the state-owned bars and the cooperatives. These were back-alley pubs where people brewed their own drink and sold it off cheap. The gunnermen - for a small fee - were persuaded to turn a blind eye; the brewers made a profit; and half a city got drunk very cheaply.

Robb and Farren had been in one of the cooperatives all day, drinking through their weekly wage. Fuelled by too much beer, they decided to see how the other half lived and swaggered across town until they found a glass-fronted bar in the Trade District. They found a table in the centre of the room and waited for someone to take their order.

"I reckon I fit in round here," Farren said surveying the other patrons. "Two glasses of the house beer please," he called imperiously to the waitress.

"And two for me," Robb added, setting them both off laughing.

She returned a few minutes later, carrying the drinks on a circular silver tray. She ignored their attempts to catch her eye and left their drinks without a word. Farren whistled softly as she circled the room clearing away empty glasses.

"Very nice," he said.

Robb took a sip from his glass and nodded. Over the next couple of hours, the restaurant cleared out leaving just the two of them. Farren stumbled to the toilet and Robb sank into his chair, feeling hopelessly drunk. He watched the pretty waitress cleaning while music played from speakers above the bar. The song was an old ballad from years back, but Robb felt it suited the mood in the bar perfectly. For the briefest of moments, he was sobered by the beauty in the music and his eyes cleared.

Seized by a sudden impulse, he rose unsteadily and approached the waitress who was wiping down tables with her back to him. Before he could speak though, Farren returned from the toilet, seized her by the hands and dragged her into a space between the tables.

"How about a dance?" He slurred and tried to twirl her around like a gypsy girl.

"That's enough now," she said but Farren didn't stop and stumbled against her before dipping her at the waist and forcing a kiss on her lips. She broke away, raising her voice. "That's enough. Go now or I'll get the manager."

Farren flashed her that cocky grin of his, but Robb quickly apologised for them both. "You're right," he said. "We're drunk."

"It was just a bit of fun," Farren said. "Don't be so serious."

Robb ushered his friend towards the door, walking backwards as he apologised again. "No, it's okay, we're leaving. Sorry." He never saw the barstool that tangled his legs and put him flat on his backside. Farren doubled up with laughter and even the waitress smiled in spite of herself. Once they had left, she locked the door and changed the sign from *open* to *closed*. Robb made it as far as the first checkpoint before turning back.

"No way," Farren called after him. "You're ditching me for the waitress?"

"I'll see you tomorrow," Robb shouted as he ran through the Trade District towards the bar. The lights were out when he got there and Robb peered through the windows, trying to catch his breath. He saw movement at the very back of the bar and banged loudly on the glass. The waitress peered back, already wrapped in a thick coat.

"What?" she mouthed impatiently through the glass.

"I just wanted to say goodnight," Robb shouted back. "And sorry for the way my friend behaved. And for falling over."

She leaned closer to the window and glanced up and down the street. Apparently satisfied that he was alone and not planning to rob the place, the frown dropped from her face. "Don't worry about it," her voice was muted by the glass, but she gave him a tired smile. "It's been a long night though."

"Sure, yeah," he shouted back and then waited in silence, trying to think of something else to say. "I'm Robb."

"Hi."

"I could make sure you get home safe, if you like?" At which point he wobbled forwards and hit his forehead on the window with a dull *thunk*.

"Are you sure about that?"

He rubbed his head and stared accusingly at the glass. The waitress smiled.

"Tell you what. Why don't you go home, sober up, and if you can remember my name in the morning, come back and see me."

"It's a deal," he said and staggered away from the window. He made it about three steps before turning back to see her waiting with a sly grin on her face. "You haven't told me your name yet, have you?"

She shook her head. "It's Eliza."

"I'm Robb."

"You said."

"I'll see you tomorrow, *Eliza*." Robb tapped the side of his head knowingly and then stumbled home.

That was the first time he met Eliza. The next night he went back at closing time and asked her out. He knew she was too good for him, but somehow, she never realised. Or if she did, she was kind enough not to say.

Back in the office, the song trailed away and Robb was left standing in silence with his hand still on the speaker. He muttered an apology, to no one in particular, and went back to his desk. Immediately the chatter resumed as though nothing of great importance had just happened.

CHAPTER 22

It had been two days since Ryan last saw Alia but in that time she had never been far from his thoughts. Her story was a hard one to make peace with. Born into the elite of Straybeck society, only to be dissected and discarded from it. It felt like he should resent her for her past. But if she was guilty by association to her father's wealth and privilege, then what did that say for him? The thoughts circled his head, inevitably reaching the same conclusion. She was hurting and needed help. He wanted to be the person that helped her.

He knew there was nothing he could do about her father's death, or about her living in the worst part of the Slum District. After two days of replaying their conversation though, he struck upon the one thing he could do to help.

Which was how he found himself crossing the checkpoints with a bag of school uniform. He had found an old tie and two jumpers and bundled them up with a couple of blank jotters and some pens. It wasn't much, but they were in pretty good shape and better than nothing. His mum had been saving the clothes for John, but another year in his old things wouldn't do any harm. Ryan hoped they made Alia smile. If only for a little bit.

He had nothing to hide today, so he took the more direct route through the Trade Quarter. It was only as he reached the first checkpoint that he realised it was the anniversary of Talis's inauguration today. He gave an irritable sigh. A few years ago, they had made a really big deal when it was the thirtieth anniversary and forced the schools and factories to sit through hours of footage from the original ceremony.

At least he was spared all that today. Instead, the Government were blasting the Premier's speech from the speakers above each checkpoint. Ryan had heard it dozens of times and it almost made him feel sorry for the gunnermen who were working the checkpoints.

As he passed through each one, he saw people gathering in awkward groups around the speakers. So ingrained was their fear of the Premier that they felt obliged to stand and listen, unsure how long they should stay to show the appropriate level of respect.

Ryan did not wait with them. Instead he pushed through the small gatherings, carrying his bag of clothes like a plunder ball. And at each checkpoint he watched with a tight jaw as the gunnermen upended the bag and sifted through its contents.

In this way, he reached Alia's street and as he walked up the path, ran one hand over his hair, flattening any tufts. He gave a confident knock and waited. No one came, so he tried again. There was a thud like something had been knocked over and then the sound of floorboards creaking as footsteps approached. A shadow fell over the small panel of frosted glass but instead of Alia, it was her mum who pulled open the door. She squeezed her face into the narrowest of openings and stared at him.

"Are you from the doctors?"

"Err, no. I'm a friend of Alia's. Is she in?"

"I haven't the faintest idea," she grumbled. "Now if you'll excuse me." The door was slammed in his face.

Ryan waited a few seconds and then knocked again. When it opened this time, he stepped forwards and wedged his foot into the door. "Mrs Turner?" he said.

"Yes? Who are you?"

"My name's Ryan. I'm a friend…" but before he could finish, she tried to slam the door again.

"I don't know anyone called Ryan at the doctors."

"I'm not from the doctors, Mrs Turner. I just want to speak to Alia."

"I'm sure I have no idea what you're talking about? Kindly remove your foot from my doorway or I'll call for Mr Turner and have you thrown out."

Ryan wriggled his foot free and watched the door close for a second time. With a sigh, he reached inside the bag and retrieved one of the notebooks and a pencil. On the front sheet he wrote *From Ryan* and beneath that wrote down his address. Then he placed it at the top of the bag and left it on the doorstep.

An hour later he was in the cellar beneath Brynne's chapel learning how to use a covert camera. The old man had fixed it to the inside of his jacket and was explaining how it worked. A muddle of wires connected the camera to a chunky monitor and as Ryan turned his body this way and that, the image on screen panned around the room.

When it settled on Brynne he shielded his face and scowled. "Turn the other way."

He was sending Ryan out to get footage of the gunnermen mistreating workers. They had made a small hole in the collar of his coat and then poked the camera lens through that.

"Hold still," the old man grumbled as he fiddled with the controls on the battery pack. The image suddenly sharpened on screen. "How's that?"

"Spot on."

"Okay, it's very simple to operate," Brynne said. "To record…push this switch left." He mimed the action because it was already recording. "And to switch off…"

"Move it to the right?" Ryan said with a smile.

"Quite the wit, aren't we?" He turned it off and removed the TV line making the screen snap to black.

"Brynne?"

"Hmm?"

"When do I get to meet the others?"

The old man stared back with the same expression he had worn moments before he shot Caylin. "Why do you ask that?"

Suddenly nervous, Ryan studied the inside of his jacket and toyed with the fastening of the camera. "I was just wondering. That's all."

"People don't just wonder, Ryan. There's always a reason they ask things in my experience." It was a heavy silence that followed.

"It's just," he began, "I've put up posters and spray-painted slogans, but the next day they're always torn down or washed away. It feels like there are real people getting hurt, or worse, and I'm not doing anything about it."

"So what exactly is it you'd like to do?" Brynne said, making no attempt to hide the disappointment and anger in his voice. "Shoot a few gunnermen? Plant a bomb in the factories? Maybe you're after storming the Premier's palace?"

"No of course not. It's just that I look at all your old pictures and the clippings. I hear about the things you used to do. You had marches and demonstrations and strikes."

"We did," Brynne nodded. "And look where it got us. Tortured or killed or squatting down in some rat's nest of a cellar. I told you Ryan, we need to be smarter than that. If those years taught me anything at all, it's that you can't beat the Government in a direct conflict. Not yet. We need the support of the people and the only way to get that is to change the way they think."

It was unusually cold in the cellar and Brynne knelt beside the fireplace to load it with knots of paper and a small stack of kindling. He gave three small squirts with the lighter fluid and struck a match. It flared bright and then settled, but instead of throwing it onto the fire, Brynne paused.

"Turn out the lamp and come over here. I want you to look at this."

"Turn it out?"

"All the way."

Frowning, Ryan twisted the collar of the gas lamp until its flame sputtered and died. Then, in the meagre light offered by Brynne's match, he shuffled across the cellar and knelt beside the old man. Together they stared at the tiny flame that was creeping closer to his fingertips.

"What do you see?" the old man asked.

"A match?"

"No," he shook his head. "This isn't a match. This is you. Right now."

The flame flickered around Brynne's thumb and finger.

He never flinched and a moment later it burnt out leaving the cellar in total darkness.

"You're burning bright Ryan, but you've no idea what to do with it."

There was a sudden scratch of sparks as the old man lit another match. This time he held it at arm's length, illuminating the large fireplace. "What do you see now?"

Ryan shrugged, unsure what he wanted to hear. "I don't know."

"This is Straybeck."

He dropped the match and Ryan watched the small lick of flame burn through the lighter fluid and quickly consume the bundles of paper. From there it took hold of the kindling and soon the flames were strong enough to load on a thicker block of wood.

"You are the spark, Ryan. I have no doubt about it. But I'm the one building a fire. So when I tell you to do a job, it's not to side-line you or keep you from the action. It's because when those workers leave the factories, I need them to see one of us with a pamphlet in our hand. When they leave the bars and buyalls, they need to see your slogans ten feet high before them. It's only when they're ready to hear us that we can light the fire. Do you understand?"

Ryan nodded solemnly. "Show me how to use the camera again. Tomorrow I'll get your footage."

CHAPTER 23

THE RADIO HAD been playing the Premier's inauguration speech all day. Commentators recounted the momentous occasion that took place thirty-five years ago. They described each moment in its finest detail. They told of the thousands of gunnermen who marched through the streets and how ten thousand workers lined the route to the palace. Cheers echoed between the buildings as the Premier drove past in a golden carriage.

As Robb listened to the speech, it seemed like the Premier was blessed with almost mystical powers of prediction. Somehow, in that inauguration speech, he managed to foretell the major changes that would befall the City States for years to come. He hinted at troubles with the Aftlanders, sea-raiders off the coast of Cape Heritage and even a temporary truce with the Gabblers.

The footsteps of the past he said *would be wiped away and together they would stride towards the future.* When he tried to leave the stage, the crowd clamoured for more, refusing to let him leave. Robb had once seen a film reel that accompanied the commentary. It showed Talis unveiling a huge bronze likeness of himself gazing majestically skyward. A monstrous thing that was still standing in Liberation Square outside the Party Headquarters.

The footage was so entrenched in the general consciousness of the City States that very few people would now say it happened any differently. Robb had been at the palace that day though and he hadn't forgotten. The speech had been re-written many times over the past thirty years and they'd re-filmed the entire day to erase what happened the first time around.

The inauguration took place a year after Talis defeated the old King. It had taken that long for tensions in the capital to ebb away. The Premier had shelled the King's army into submission and Karasard was still a ruin in places. By the time of the inauguration, the palace had been rebuilt. It was now a monstrous building freshly released from the scaffolding and rebranded as the official Party Headquarters. Robb and Farren had taken their place amongst a crowd of thousands that were penned into the main courtyard.

"It's a pretty big turnout," Robb said appreciatively.

"I wonder why that is," Farren said, chewing on a mouthful of *freedom loaf* that had been given to all those who attended.

Robb studied the crowd and saw lots of tired and hungry people. A band was trumpeting out the victory march and a few moments before, hundreds of birds had been released from behind the podium. Farren laughed as they shit on the heads of those around him.

A regiment of gunnermen marched into view, signalling the arrival of Talis. As they stopped and turned with a stamp of their feet, the crowd fell silent. The Premier appeared at the steps of the podium. Robb was amazed at the sheer size of the man. He towered head and shoulders above the gunnermen who waited stiff backed.

The people were slow to react, but a gentle applause soon gathered momentum. Farren joined in with some slow, sarcastic claps and then made a gun with his fingers, aiming it at the Premier's head. Robb quickly dragged his hands down.

"Are you trying to get us arrested?"

He just smiled back with that cocky grin of his. Up on stage, Talis began his speech and although the crowd cheered in all the right places it was fairly uninspiring. Robb shook his head. These were the same people that roped their trousers over empty bellies and cursed the Government to their family each night. Yet here they were, cap in hand, waiting for a glimpse of the Premier.

As Talis reached the climax of his speech, he turned to the edge of the stage where something was covered beneath an enormous blue drape. The hidden object stood at least twenty feet high and jutted out at irregular angles. Robb presumed it was a statue, although of exactly what, he had no idea.

"I'll come clean. It's a statue of me shagging your mum," Farren said helpfully.

Back on stage, the Premier held up his hands expectantly, but nothing happened. The crowd fell silent, waiting for the grand unveiling. On the far side of the stage, two aides were dragging frantically on a length of rope, trying to free the statue. Talis fixed them with an icy stare and they dropped the rope and set about pulling the drape itself.

Murmurs rippled through the crowd while the Premier's cold stare bored into the two men. By now some of the gunnermen had joined the struggle and took hold of the material, but it had caught fast on the point of the statue and both sides were dragging with equal enthusiasm so that it simply stretched and jerked the fabric.

Talis strode forward, ordering them to stand aside. He grasped the drape in both hands and wrenched backwards with all his might. The material ripped down the middle where it had caught on the statues outstretched hand. Talis fell backwards and the heavy drape pinned him to the floor. The gunnermen rushed back on stage to free him, but the damage had already been done.

Despite all the lies that had been told about that day, Robb knew he would never forget the sound of ten thousand workers laughing while their Premier stormed from the stage.

John had been sitting at the kitchen table sharing a comfortable silence with his dad. The radio was droning in the background and the familiar cadence of the Premier's coronation speech broke through his thoughts. It was the really famous part where he talked about wiping away the footsteps of the past and striding for the future.

"They've already played this today."

"I know," his dad said quietly.

"How long has the Premier been in charge?"

"Thirty-six years, give or take."

"Were you there when he came to power?"

For a moment he thought he caught half a smile on his dad's face but the sound of Ryan's footsteps clomping downstairs soon made it vanish. From the kitchen. John watched his brother lace up his boots on the bottom step. He had a large paper bag with him that looked like it was stuffed with clothing.

"Dad?" John said quickly. "Shall I buy you a paper?"

His dad was immediately suspicious and then glanced at Ryan in the hallway. "What's going on?"

"Nothing. I'm just bored."

With a weary sigh, Robb leaned to one side and dug a hand into his pocket. He brought out two coppers and flicked them towards John. He caught the first and dropped the second.

"Stick to the main roads."

"I will."

As Ryan left the house with his bag under one arm, John rushed into the hallway to gather his own shoes and jacket. He gave a slow count to ten before quietly slipping outside and onto the street.

Tailing Ryan to the first checkpoint was easy, but instead of taking the usual winding route towards the old chapel, they ended up walking across the centre of Straybeck. Ryan didn't seem to be avoiding any of the checkpoints and it was as if he no longer cared whether the gunnermen stopped him.

After half an hour like this, John found himself in the Slum District. His brother walked down a narrow street lined with terraced houses, stopping at the very end house which had a metal skip dumped outside it. By crouching in a nearby yard, he was able to watch his brother and still remain hidden.

Ryan banged sharply on the door and John tried to remember the pattern, wondering if it was a code. The door eventually opened, but he couldn't see the person inside. Moments later it slammed shut and there was more knocking. When it opened this time, his brother stepped into the doorway and continued to talk.

He glimpsed a woman, dressed in loose-fitting clothes.

She seemed angry and soon slammed the door for a second time. Ryan had no idea what his brother was trying to get rid of, but the woman clearly didn't want it. In the end, he dropped the bag on the doorstep and walked away.

John tucked himself behind the wall until his brother had passed by. He considered sneaking up to the house to check in the bag, but knew it was too risky. Besides, he had already been gone too long and if he didn't get back soon, his dad would be suspicious. Reluctantly John turned back the way he had come.

Although John had never been to the Slum District before, he found his way back to the Trade District without too much trouble. He scanned both sides of the street for a newsstand or a buyall and was stunned to see a familiar figure on the opposite pavement. She wasn't wearing her uniform, but John immediately recognised the new girl from school. He closed the distance between them and crossed the road. It had to be fate that he had found her here, especially when she stopped outside a buyall.

John hung back and saw her take a small handkerchief from her pocket, spreading the corners to count something inside. Whatever it was, the contents seemed to disappoint her, and the girl already looked defeated when she walked into the shop. John followed her in, justifying it to himself that he would always have chosen this buyall to get the newspaper. He walked past the barrows of fruit and tucked himself behind the news rack. She went straight to the counter where a collection of jewellery and watches were displayed behind glass cabinets.

"Just a minute." That was the shopkeeper. He wore a surly expression on his face as though warning against timewasters.

When he saw the girl at the counter though, his frown suddenly melted into a sly grin. He scanned the shop, not seeing John who was tucked behind the tall stand of papers. He leaned forwards, resting on his elbows.

"Hello again young lady. I wondered when you'd be back."

John immediately disliked the man, although he wasn't sure exactly why. He strained his ears to hear what they were saying as the girl placed her handkerchief onto the counter. Her voice was barely above a whisper.

"I thought I could swap some more jewellery."

The man shook his head, the smile never leaving his face. "And I thought we had an arrangement."

She picked out some of the jewellery and held it closer to him. "These earrings are pearl. On their own, they're worth twice what I took last time."

The man behind the counter shrugged his shoulders. "If you can sell them somewhere else then you're welcome to try. But we both know you wouldn't be here if you could."

"It's not stolen, if that's what you're thinking. No one's going to come looking. Not the seveners or the gunnermen."

"I wouldn't care if they did. All I need is *an honest held belief* as they say." He puffed out his chest smugly. "If I were to call a gunnerman right now though," he wagged one stubby finger towards the girl. "I don't believe you'd find the law quite so forgiving."

"I just want to sell my jewellery and buy some food."

"*Your* jewellery? I doubt it. Do you know what they do to pretty little thieves like you?"

He brushed his fingers down her cheek and as she pulled away, he grasped her neck tightly. The girl tensed up and with an effort wriggled out of his grip. At that moment a man with grey hair and glasses stepped into the store banging a shopping cart against the doorframe. The storeman was instantly alert and busied himself behind the counter while the girl snatched up her jewellery and practically ran for the door. John followed her without thinking, side-stepping the old man's shopping cart as he left the store.

He found her leaning in the alleyway beside the buyall. Her face had taken on a greyish tinge and she was gasping for breath. Slowly she sank to one knee and leant her forehead against the dirty bricks in the alley.

"Are you okay?" John asked.

The girl didn't look up. Instead, her hands worked away at the lid of a small bottle. A single white tablet fell into her hand and the girl swallowed it down. Then she sank fully to the ground and wrapped her arms around her knees. People walked by the alleyway, but no one stopped. John knelt beside her with no idea what to do.

"Shall I get someone?" he said.

Slowly her breathing levelled out and she shook her head, eyes closed. "No, I'll be fine. Will you help me up?"

John put a hand beneath her armpit and gripped her wrist with the other. She let him support most of her weight and haul her upwards. "Are you sure you're alright? You don't look well."

"I'm fine. It happens sometimes."

"Have you been to a doctor?"

The girl gave an unhappy laugh. "Do you know any free doctors round here?"

"Well my mum's a nurse. I'm sure she would help."

She looked at him then as if she had only just realised he

was there. John reddened up beneath her stare. "I know you from somewhere, don't I?"

"We go to the same school. I helped you through the knife gate?"

"That's it," she said, a sudden brightness to her face. A moment later it had slipped away to be replaced by a deep sadness. "God what must I look like. Don't tell anyone at school about this will you?"

"Of course not," John said earnestly. "I never would."

She tried to walk out of the alleyway but immediately stumbled, only staying upright when John steadied her. "Come on," he said. "You're not well. Let me get my mum to look at you."

"That's not what I need. The only things that can make me better were in this." She held up the empty bottle.

"Are they pills? How can you get them if you don't see a doctor though?"

"It's not that hard. But I'll need your help."

John glanced at his watch. He was already late and the thought of being told off by his dad was churning at his insides. Even so, the decision was an easy one to make. "Of course I'll help."

"Thank you."

She assured him that it was only a few streets away and looped her arm through his for support as they walked. They moved off the main street and into narrower roads. Natural light was filtered out here by the imposing three-storey slum housing and John swallowed down his fear and forced himself onwards.

So distracted was he by the shadowy figures and half-hidden doorways that he never saw the patrol car crawling slowly up the street behind them. He never heard the engine cut out and certainly didn't see the gunnerman follow them into the alleyway. Which was why he never imagined that he would soon be staring down the muzzle of a gun.

CHAPTER 24

"I'm Alia by the way."

"John."

"Pleased to meet you," she said with mock formality. "So how old are you John?"

"I'm fourteen," he lied. "How about you?"

"Sixteen."

Although she seemed more surefooted now, Alia's arm was still looped through his. John had scarcely dared to move it in case she suddenly remembered. They took a left and then a right off the main street and that was when she slowed down and disentangled herself. She brought out the handkerchief of jewellery and picked out the pearl earrings. The rest of the bundle she placed back in her pocket.

"What's that for?" John said. "I thought the man wouldn't let you use it."

Alia scowled. "He's not a man. He's a vile excuse for a human. Do *you* think I look like a thief?"

"Of course not. You look…normal." John realised how lame that had sounded but Alia didn't seem to notice.

"It's the next street," she said. "But you should stay here."

"What's the next street? What are we doing here?"

"I'm going to buy some more tablets. I need them."

John looked doubtfully at their surroundings. "This doesn't look like the kind of place you'd find a doctor."

"No it doesn't. But these are the people who sell what I need."

She turned the corner and moved out of sight. John wondered if he should follow, but buying drugs from the back streets of the Trade District didn't sound like anything he wanted a part of. He wished his dad were here; he'd have known what to do.

After a few moments, he peered around the edge of the building and saw that Alia was approaching a short, stocky teenager. The youth stared with hard eyes as Alia spoke to him. John was too far away to hear their words, but he saw her presenting the earrings.

Behind him, there was the sudden crunch of footsteps and when he span around there was a gunnerman not ten paces away. They both froze until the gunnerman reached for his sidearm. "Stay where you are."

Until that moment, John had not thought of fleeing, but as soon as the idea was there, he could think of nothing else. Like a startled rabbit he tore round the corner, blundering into Alia and the pusher.

"Gunnerman," John called.

The youth gave three sharp smacks of warning on a metal shutter beside him and then pulled a neat black handgun from his belt.

"Did you do this?" he growled, pointing the muzzle at Alia.

Before she could answer, the gunnerman ran into view. He stepped back when faced with the youth and his pistol, quickly levelling his own weapon. Holding it at shoulder height with a straight arm, he stalked forwards.

"Drop it."

"Fuck off."

The youth squeezed off three shots in quick succession while the gunnerman dropped to one knee and returned fire. Alia threw herself against the wall, but John wasn't prepared to stay there any longer. Ducking low, he grabbed her wrist and dragged her out of the crossfire. Alia quickly found her feet and together they raced out of the alley.

Behind them, they heard more gunfire followed by a grunt of pain and the wet smack of someone hitting the ground. A heartbeat of quiet followed until the clatter of a bike engine reverberated between the narrow streets.

It growled through the gears and more shots were fired. John gave an involuntary duck of his head with each recoil, but neither he nor Alia stopped running until they were across Main Street and safely out the Trade District.

Back home, Robb pulled the plug from the wall and the radio cut to silence. He paced the length of the kitchen biting down his anger. It was becoming harder to lock it in these days. Harder to keep the rage from bubbling over. Beside him, Eliza was slicing vegetables, her knife clipping rhythmically against the wooden chopping board.

"Was I too hard on him?"

She shrugged, sweeping tiny discs of carrot to one side and then reached into the sink for another. He leaned against the worktop with his arms folded and watched the nub of Eliza's fourth finger rest on the knife.

"All they need is an excuse," he said. "Just one little thing."

"He knows that. He was trying to explain. If you had listened to him properly, you'd see it too."

"I did listen," his voice gave an involuntary rise in volume and immediately he sensed Eliza shutting down. "At least I tried to. It's just that when he was away so long, I knew he was... I knew *something*."

That part was true. He had watched John follow his brother from the house and it had prompted a churning sense of dread inside him. By the time three hours had passed, that feeling had gnawed away at any thread of self-control he still possessed. So when John finally appeared, wearing a wide-eyed look of guilt, all Robb could do was tear into him.

"I should never have let him go on his own."

"It could have happened just as easily if we were there."

He heard the truth in her words. Worse still, he also knew that part of him had wanted this to happen. He had lived in fear of someone noticing his family for so long now, that he almost welcomed the certainty that the gunnermen had finally proved him right. All John's excuses had been swatted away without any concern for how scared he had been. It hadn't even been about him at that point. So when John fled upstairs, blinking back tears, Robb had paced the lounge, swearing in his own disbelief and shouting himself to a standstill.

"Maybe you should try to talk to him," Eliza said. "He's not Ryan. He'll still listen." Before he could feel the unintended sting behind that comment, she suddenly gasped and the knife clattered to the floor. Eliza ran to the sink, suckling at her finger, squeezing lines of pain into the corner of each eye.

"You okay?" Robb said, standing beside her and reaching

for her hand. He was surprised when she let him guide her fingers below the jet of cold water. It had been so long since they touched that even this small contact was strangely intimate.

The knife had opened a clean slice across the pad of her middle finger. Eliza winced at the sting but held it there until the blood had washed from the cut. When she pulled it from the tap, fresh blood quickly swelled up.

"We don't have any plasters," Robb said, taking a cloth from the kitchen drawer and wrapping it round her finger. "I'm sorry. I was distracting you."

For a moment, he withdrew, a natural reaction to the number of times she had retreated from his touch in the past. To his surprise though her hands sought his out. "No," she said quickly. "I wasn't paying attention."

"I'm still sorry," he said quietly.

"Why?"

"Where do I begin?" His anger had receded, leaving a void that suddenly pitched with emotion. He tried to speak again, but his voice cracked, and he simply shook his head. Eliza breathed deeply, closing her eyes as she brought Robb's hand to her lips.

"We're okay. Go and speak to John. He needs you now."

CHAPTER 25

ONE OF JOHN's earliest memories was going to the Trade District with his dad. He had only been four or five at the time, chattering away to the gunnermen at each checkpoint. In his mind's eye, the sun had been shining fiercely that day making everyone red-faced and short-tempered. Even so, his dad had worn trousers and a long-sleeved shirt which was buttoned all the way to the top. It was only when he grew older that John understood the significance of that. Only after seeing the scars.

That day – maybe eight years ago – there had been a long queue at the buyall. They waited in line, shuffling forward a few steps at a time as people paid and left. His dad picked up a newspaper and placed his ID card on top. The electronic ones had only just been released and John remembered how special it had seemed to own a shiny plastic card with your face on it.

When they reached the counter though, John's dad was sweating worse than before. He kept checking over his shoulder at the dozen or so people who were now waiting in line. Reluctantly he passed across his ID card. As soon as it was scanned, a high-pitched alarm sounded on the terminal and the storekeeper tensed up. John watched him reading through the list of words that cascaded down his screen. He didn't know at the time, but they were a list of his dad's previous convictions, the first of which read *Treason*.

"Get out," the storekeeper said, his entire body trembling with anger and fear.

"It's okay," his dad said calmly. "Check your screen. I have permission to buy this."

"Out of my shop, now. Or I'll call the gunnermen."

"Please. I've queued for ten minutes. Just let me buy the paper."

"Get out," the storekeeper fumbled with the latch on the counter flap. The high-pitched alarm was still sounding, and John felt the mood in the shop change. The other customers stepped back, leaving a circle of empty space around them. He remembered placing one hand inside his dad's.

"What's happening?"

"Nothing son. We're leaving."

Despite the fear he had felt at the time, John knew now that it hadn't been so bad. No gunnermen arrived and no one had been hurt. He knew for certain that the damage to his family on Saintsday was much worse. Even so, that day with his dad in the buyall had been the first time he felt truly afraid. He had hated the ID cards for a long time after that and had always found reasons to stop his dad from scanning his.

It was true that he had been elated when his own card arrived last year. It just wasn't for the reason that his parents believed. The wonder at having his face on a card had left him forever that day in the store. Owning one himself though, meant that he would never have to watch his dad be shamed like that again.

As if on cue, the bedroom door opened and his dad gave three quiet knocks. "John. Have you got a minute?"

He was lying face down on the top bunk and quickly rubbed away the tears from his face as the door creaked further open. John's dad limped into the room and leant against the rails of the top bunk.

"I didn't handle things very well earlier, did I?"

"No, you didn't."

"You were trying to tell me what happened, but I just shouted at you."

"Yes, you did."

"I'm sorry." John couldn't remember a time his dad had apologised to him for anything. "I just got so worried. You were only supposed to be gone half an hour and then…" as he went over it again, his voice began to rise. He took a deep breath. "I'm trying hard to listen now. Tell me what happened."

John slid to the back of the bed and held a pillow in front of him. It was a difficult day to explain. He didn't want to get Ryan or Alia in trouble, but his head was spinning from everything he'd seen. Since the first time he followed his brother, so much had happened and it was just too big for a twelve-year-old boy. Any words he had to explain it though suddenly felt trapped in his throat and instead hot tears pooled in each eye and his bottom lip shook.

"Hey? What is it?"

A sob broke from deep inside him and John squeezed the pillow even tighter, letting his tears flow while his dad waited in silence.

"Are you in trouble?" he said eventually.

John shook his head.

"Hurt?"

"No."

"Is it someone else then?"

He nodded, but sensing his dad's frustration, forced himself to speak. "It's Ryan."

Immediately, his dad's jaw clenched tight. "Go on."

"I think he's in trouble and I don't know what to do."

"What's he done?"

"First, you've got to promise not to say any of this to him. He can't know that I've spoken to you about it." His dad nodded, never actually saying the words. "No, you've got to promise. Do you promise?"

"I promise," he snapped. "Now tell me. What's wrong?"

He explained how he had been following Ryan for weeks. That he had seen him handing out posters at the factory gates and then later watched him run from the gunnermen. He described the man from the abandoned chapel who had threatened to kill him. Finally, he told him about why he had really volunteered to get a newspaper today, so that he could find out where Ryan was going. When he got as far as the buyall his dad interrupted.

"Who's Alia?"

"Just a girl I know. When she went to the counter to pay I saw…"

"Know her how?"

"From school. She's only been there a few weeks. She was trying to buy some food, but the man there wouldn't take any of her jewellery. He kept trying to touch her face and whisper to her so she left the store. Then she was in the alleyway outside and it looked like she was having a heart attack or something."

"John," his dad groaned. "Why do you get mixed up in these things?"

"It wasn't like I tried to. But how was I supposed to leave her when she asked for my help."

"What did she ask you for?"

"To help buy her pills."

"Pills?" he near shouted.

"You're doing it again," John cried, meeting the volume of his dad's voice. "You never listen."

His dad bit back a comment and his hands balled up into fists. The next words were much softer. "Okay. Go on."

"I told Alia she should go and see a doctor if she was ill, but she said she didn't have enough money. Then she went to this man who was behind the Trade District. She asked me to wait for her around the corner while she spoke to him, but a gunnerman had followed us."

His dad folded his arms but remained silent.

"He told me to stand still but I didn't listen. I ran around the corner and the man that was selling the pills suddenly pulled out a gun. They started firing at each other and I think one of them got shot. Me and Alia were already running though and we hid for ages in a building site until the sirens had gone. She left after that and I came home." A small tremor passed up his back when he finished the story. An aftershock of the adrenaline.

"Did they see your face?" his dad said quietly. "The gunnerman or the pusher?"

"Pusher? No Dad, he was just someone that sells pills. Like a doctor for people that don't have money."

"Did they see your face?"

"Maybe, just for a second. But I don't think they'd remember me."

"We'll need to get rid of your coat," his dad murmured, grabbing it from the floor. He limped to the window and scanned the street in both directions. "And I want you to stay away from this girl, Alia. You're forbidden from seeing her now. In school or out."

"But Dad…"

"I don't know her, and I don't trust her. She could be an informer or a spy for all you know."

"She's not. She's just a girl."

"Enough," he growled. "These are my conditions. Until I find out more."

"What are you going to do? Go into school?"

"No, nothing like that. And you don't need to know anyway. If we're lucky, you were just in the wrong place at the wrong time. Keep your head down and stay away from the Trade District. You understand." John nodded. "You don't want to get noticed by the gunnermen. All they need is an excuse."

"What about the other stuff I told you? What about Ryan and that man?"

"Leave all that alone now too. You've done well looking out for him. But let me handle it for now."

"You won't tell him that I said anything will you?"

"He'll hear nothing from me. But no more following, okay?"

He nodded and wiped his nose with the back of his hand. His dad walked past the bed, but then halted in the doorway. Hesitantly he placed one hand on John's arm. "I love you, you know." John didn't know what to say and rebuked by the silence, his dad quickly left the room.

CHAPTER 26

IT WAS MAYBE a year before his time in The Cathedral that Robb met Kellie Downs for the first time. He and Farren had been drinking steadily all day, working their way through the week's wage. Back then they were working as unskilled labourers, the kind of graft that left them bone-weary at the end of each day. It was Robb's first day off in weeks, but his body seemed even more worn-out than usual. With the combined effect of too much beer and too little sleep, he was slumped in the chair, supporting his head on one hand.

"Cheer up you miserable fucker," Farren said, draining the last of his beer. "It's the weekend, remember." They were sitting in a packed bar in a rough part of Karasard. The room was thick with smoke and the rowdy banter of workers who had been drinking all day under a high sun.

"I'm knackered. I don't know about you, but I can't keep this up forever." They'd been clearing rubble heaps from the capital's Trade District, making room for the architects and builders to begin. Even though they'd been at it for months, the supply of war-damaged buildings still seemed endless.

"Give over. We're in the prime of our lives." Farren collected their glasses. "Same again?"

Robb nodded and watched his friend swagger to the bar. Behind him, the door pushed open and a momentary hush fell over the punters. Robb turned, curious as to what would make a room full of drunkards stop their chatter. An enormous figure parted the crowd, moving like a galleon towards the bar.

He was at least a foot taller than Robb, with an impressive beard, powerful shoulders and a heavy paunch. At the table next to him, Robb saw another man paying keen attention too. This one had a scar running from eye to jaw that made the left side of his face twist up in a snarl. Scar-eye straightened up, a look of obvious recognition passing over his face. From the expression he gave, Robb guessed it was not a fond remembrance.

The newcomer, clearly an off duty sevener, picked his spot at the bar, inadvertently bumping Farren to one side as he did so. Robb grinned as his friend did a double take at the giant who had taken his place. Not to be outdone, Farren clambered onto a chair so that he was of equal height with the sevener.

"Can me and my mate get some service please? We've been patrolling all day." It got a few chuckles from the other customers and - to Robb's surprise - the sevener put one massive arm around Farren's shoulders so that they stood like a double act.

"Get down," the wrinkle-faced landlady shrieked. "Both of you." That brought fresh laughter from Farren.

"Yeah, come on, get down," he scolded the sevener.

Realising her mistake, the landlady scowled and threw her dishcloth which landed on Farren's face with a wet smack. It didn't take long for him to charm his way back into her good graces though and he soon returned to the table with a pint in each hand. The sevener moved to the far corner of the room and found a quiet spot to drink.

Robb and Farren chatted idly for a while, but he could tell that his friend's mind was elsewhere. After the third time he lost the conversation, Robb gave up and followed his gaze to a group of three couples who were standing at the bar.

"I might have known. Go on then, which one is it?"

"What?"

"Which one are you after?"

"I don't know what you mean."

Robb looked them over and found they were a strange mix. The men had broken away into a trio of their own and were entertaining themselves with jokes and stories. Next to them, two of the women were conspiring across their drinks and making no effort to include the third in their conversation. It was this woman who had clearly caught Farren's eye. She had long blonde hair and a handsome face that was wearing a thoroughly bored expression. She must have been late thirties or early forties and as she locked eyes with Robb, the hint of a smile turned the corner of her mouth. He spun round quickly.

"She's old enough to be your mum."

"You can't buy experience."

As he watched her lips lingering on the edge of her glass though, Robb guessed that you probably could in this case. Just then, his attention was taken by a stirring of the crowd beside them. It was the huge sevener who had lumbered up for a refill.

"There's your mate," Robb said.

"I don't think this lot are too keen though." Farren had also noticed the stares from Scar-eye and his friends at the next table. In truth they weren't being subtle about it or keeping their voices low as they berated the seveners in general. If their words carried to the big man across the crowded bar however, he made no acknowledgement.

"Hey," this time Scar-eye's voice was too loud to ignore and a small circle of people turned to him. "Hey, I'm talking to you, you big fucking lump."

The sevener took a long slow taste of his beer and seemed oblivious to the space that was now clearing behind him. Scar-eye would not be ignored though. "What? You forgot me?" He slurred the words slightly. "You forgot giving me this?"

Robb thought he wouldn't answer, but eventually the sevener spoke, his voice low and even. "I remember just fine. And I also remember *why* I got called that day, Mulloy."

He stepped towards the table and the discomfort of Mulloy and his three friends was clear for all to see. "Speak to me again and it'll be more than a scar you're worried about. Besides, I know you don't want everyone to know what you were doing that day." There was no reply and the sevener raised his glass. "Enjoy your drinks." Then he returned to his corner where he drank in silence. In his wake, normal conversation resumed at the bar and Mulloy, who was momentarily lost for words, took a long, fierce drink and stared angrily at the table.

Farren tapped the side of his head. "How mental have you got to be to pick a fight with a sevener?"

Robb shook his head, but as the evening wore on, realised that Mulloy was not a rational man. Time and again he recounted the injustices visited upon him by the seveners. He described how three of them had come into his home unannounced. How they'd held him down and sliced his face with a knife.

"Me and my missus were arguing about the kids," Mulloy slurred. "Nothing serious. But one of my neighbours must have done us in. Fuckin informers. Anyway, those bastards…" he jabbed a finger towards the sevener. "They believed every word she said just cos the girl was crying about something. Left me with half a fuckin face. Well I've not forgotten what they did to me. I've not forgotten."

And on it went, until everyone in earshot was sick of it. As stories went, Robb thought it fairly unlikely. It was rare nowadays to see even two seveners patrolling. He couldn't imagine three of them turning out to anything short of a riot. Mulloy was a vicious looking individual, but he was all bone and sinew. A sevener would have little difficulty subduing him if it came to it. When the bell for last orders rang out, Mulloy leaned across the table so he could speak to the others without being overheard.

"They're up to something," Robb said.

Farren shrugged. "Whatever it is, it can't be worse than listening to another of his stories."

With a scrape of their chairs, all four of them were up while Mulloy fired one last glare at the sevener. The big man made no acknowledgement and they left the bar. The room had already thinned out as the more sensible workers staggered back home. A fog of cigarette smoke filled the empty spaces they had left and each table was littered with pint pots.

"One more?" Robb said.

Farren rose unsteadily to his feet, knocking the table as he did so. "It's alright mate, I've got it."

Robb looked at him suspiciously. "In two years, I've never known you to buy a round out of turn. What's going on?"

"Nothing. I just thought I'd get my mate a drink." Robb turned to the bar and saw that the blonde was now standing alone and unashamedly beckoning Farren towards her.

Robb shook his head incredulously. "She's not shy, is she? Go on then, good luck."

"Cheers mate." In a flash he was at the bar and flirting outrageously. For her part, the blonde was more than accommodating as she leaned in close, touching her hands to his arm and chest. The two women she was with seemed to have completely disowned her now and on a nearby table, her man was still deep in discussion with his two friends. Robb reasoned that a guy like that, so completely unaware, deserved whatever he got.

Across the room, the sevener unpacked himself from the corner table and carried a prolific stack of glasses to the bar. Farren reappeared at the table and plonked two more full pints in front of Robb. "I'm just going for some air mate," he whispered. Behind him, the blonde strode outside without a backward glance.

"You're a bad man."

Farren gave him a wink and then gestured to the trio of men she had been with. "Keep an eye out, will you?"

Robb nodded wearily and watched him scamper for the door. As it opened though, he saw Mulloy and his three friends skulking back towards the pub, each one carrying a metal scaffolding pole. The door swung shut, leaving Robb in no doubt who their intended victim was. Even a sevener would come a poor second against four men armed with iron bars.

CHAPTER 27

THE SEVENER PLACED his stack of glasses on the bar and left without a word. Robb took a gulp of ale and watched his huge silhouette drift past the window. He drummed his fingers restlessly on the table.

"Nothing to do with me," he murmured and raised his glass again. Before he could take a drink though he slapped it down and strode outside. A chill breeze hit him immediately lending Robb a moment of clarity. There was no need for any heroics. He would catch up with the sevener, warn him about Mulloy, then return to the warmth of the pub and finish his drink.

It was a clear night with black skies and bright stars that showed the sevener maybe a hundred yards ahead. Robb was about to call him when someone else shouted up. It was a faint cry, but clearly that of someone in distress. The sevener heard it too and left the well-lit street to investigate. Three dark shapes emerged from a doorway opposite and silently followed him.

Robb jogged closer but before he'd made it halfway, he heard a deep grunt of pain and then the steady *whump* of those metal bars hitting something solid. He sprinted into the alleyway and saw the sevener laid out on the floor while four men rained blows down upon him. From the shadows to his left, a face appeared and Robb instinctively grabbed the figure by the throat and shoved him backwards.

"Robb? What the fuck?"

Farren stared indignantly up at him. His trousers were round his ankles and the blonde from the bar was perched on a rusted cooling vent with her skirt hitched up to her waist. She jumped up with a shriek and ran back to the road, pulling her clothes back into place as she went.

"Come on," Robb shouted. Then he grabbed a plank of wood from the floor and ran at Mulloy and his gang. "Leave him alone."

The four attackers rounded on him immediately and Robb could see they'd lost all reason. Mulloy delivered a vicious kick to the prone sevener while the other three advanced, their metal bars held like clubs.

"Come on lads," Farren hovered at Robb's shoulder, quickly re-buttoning his trousers. "There's no need for this. You've made your point. Let's go back and get a drink." They showed no sign of hearing him though and continued to move forwards. Robb felt Farren's hand on his chest, trying to guide him back to the road. "We've no fight with you," he continued, keeping his voice reasonable. "Come on, let's get back inside and find some girls." He backed slowly away. "Better to get your dick warm in there, than freeze your arse off out here."

Robb hadn't moved an inch. Not since his hand first gripped that wooden plank. With each step that the attackers took towards him, a strange heat spread through his body. His vision had tunnelled so that Mulloy was the whole world.

Robb's anger turned to hatred and sank deep into his bones. It flooded him with a strength he'd never imagined. It was intoxicating. He was no longer fighting to protect the sevener, it was just because they were in his way.

The nearest man took one more step and Robb swung the plank like a mace trying to cave his face in. He raised his metal pole to deflect the force, but still the wood splintered in half and dropped him to the ground.

The second man rushed in, swinging his bar in a high arc. Robb jumped aside and threw the now useless chunk of wood at him. The man swung again, but Robb ducked beneath it and delivered an uppercut to his chin which clattered his teeth together and sent him toppling sideways. Farren ran forward, grabbing at the metal pole while Robb faced the last two men.

Mulloy was tall and wiry, while his friend was short and stocky. They both had a few years on Robb and knew better than to charge in. Instead they trod a slow circle around him, splitting his attention.

Robb shifted stance, holding his hands up like a boxer but leaving the fists loose. He knew he'd have to grab one of their bars when it came close enough. The longer they waited though, the more his resolve faltered. The initial fury was ebbing away and Robb experienced his first flicker of fear. Behind him, he could hear Farren struggling with someone but he had no idea who had the upper hand. Sensing his doubt, Mulloy's scarred face twisted into a grin.

"You're a dead man."

Before he could make good on his threat, a hulking shadow rose up behind him. As soon as Mulloy turned, an enormous hand grasped his neck and drove him backwards. The sevener let out a savage cry, thrusting Mulloy into the air and against the wall. His eyes bulged and fingers scratched uselessly at the iron grip around his throat. He gave a feeble swipe with the metal bar, but it bounced off the sevener's arm and then fell to the ground with a hollow ring. Mulloy was dropped beside it like a rag-doll and left in a heap. His friends cowered away and then ran for the street.

That had been the first time he ever met Kellie Downs. They began a friendship that night that was to last even beyond his time in The Cathedral. Robb had always believed their loyalty to each other was unswerving. As it turned out, there were limits to the friendship though. He had paid a heavy price finding that out.

Right now though, Robb had no one else he could turn to and he figured the sevener still had a debt to pay. Which was how he found himself on the steps of the police station with a scrap of paper held tightly in his fist.

Town Hall. Tomorrow. 12:15pm.

He placed it below his ID card and limped up the stone steps. The atmosphere inside the station was always eerie, even when it was full like today. A few faces turned to view the new arrival, and some gave a terse nod of recognition while others quickly looked away.

Robb joined the back of the queue and scanned the large, church-like waiting room. It hadn't changed in the past thirty-three years and he saw no evidence that it had changed in the hundred years before that. He wondered how many generations of seveners had worked in this city, always keeping the peace; holding that line between right and wrong.

At the front of the queue was a low stone wall which formed a barrier between the seveners and the public. Beyond that were a dozen sturdy, wooden desks in perfect straight lines. In and around them trudged the seveners, moving like monks going about their orders. The ceilings back there were higher than in the waiting area and Robb wondered if it had always been designed that way to accommodate the massive size of its inhabitants. It all added to the church-like atmosphere and pious detachment of the seveners.

Robb had been coming here since he was released from The Cathedral. It was supposed to be a process of Government rehabilitation. He would turn up at the station each week to declare that he was a loyal citizen who posed no threat to society. After five years he was allowed to come every month. Ten years after that they said he could do it every three months and now it was just an annual formality.

He was a month early for his sign-on date this year, but he doubted that anyone would notice. As he waited in line, he scanned the station and eventually caught sight of Kellie Downs speaking with another officer. He didn't look a day older than he had in that alleyway fighting with Mulloy. He still had wide, powerful shoulders and a thick, black beard with only the merest hint of grey around the chin.

They made eye-contact and if Robb didn't know better, he could have sworn that a grin appeared on the big man's lips. A moment later it was gone and Robb inclined his head just a fraction, enough to get his attention, but hopefully unnoticed by everyone else.

Kellie ended his conversation with the other sevener and paced slowly to the counter where he gazed absently over the line of people. He leaned towards the officer who was at the desk, speaking quietly into his ear. The younger man nodded, gave the briefest of glances towards Robb and then walked away from the counter so that Kellie could take his place.

"Next," his deep voice rumbled.

Robb stepped forwards offering his ID card, the note pressed firmly underneath. "I think you need to see this," he said quietly.

Kellie took the card and turned it over. He stared at the picture and then scanned the barcode, watching the pre-cons roll down his screen. "You're a little early this year," he said then took a clipboard from beneath the counter and scanned down a list of names, marking a box alongside *Robbert Calloway*.

"Thank you." He limped out of the building and down the steep, stone steps. He hadn't believed in God for many years but as he left, Robb offered up a silent prayer that Kellie was still one of the good guys.

CHAPTER 28

"Okay, we've got camera, adapter, battery pack," Brynne tapped them off one at a time like he was checking items on a shopping list. "Go on then, let's see how it looks."

Ryan fastened his coat and tried to stand naturally, despite the very unnatural feel of a bulky battery pack wedged into his waistband. "Does it show?" he said, craning his head to look down.

"No. You're good to go. I'll ride with you as far as the factories, but then you're on your own I'm afraid. My face is on too many watch-lists."

"Okay."

"Remember, we want footage of the gunnermen mistreating workers. But don't go overboard. The last thing I want is you getting arrested."

They backtracked to the Trade District of Straybeck and joined the overground there. For most of the journey they travelled in silence along with half a dozen other commuters. There were men and women of all ages, bundled up in mismatched clothing and staring from the windows with vacant eyes. Every time he rode the trains, Ryan saw people just like them. They were the migrant poor of Straybeck and Karasard, unsuitable for work - usually addicts - who travelled to the boroughs and back again each day simply staying warm. The train rolled into a station and two of them shuffled towards the platform.

"There goes your army," Brynne whispered. "Folk who are disillusioned and cast aside, just waiting for a cause."

Ryan nodded, but had to wonder at the courage of someone who lived like that. It seemed like putting one foot in front of the other was enough of a challenge for them. How could they be expected to face down the gunnermen?

"Remember Ryan, a man with nothing to lose is a man without fear."

The train rolled on, collecting a steady trickle of commuters, all making their way to Karasard. They passed through the farmlands of Kirsk and Alderton, eventually leaving the last belt of greenery behind them as they entered the outer suburbs of the capital city. Ryan gazed from the window and saw in the distance a skyline of towering chimneys that would have dwarfed the factories in Straybeck and above it all swirled an oppressive bank of smog. As the train gathered momentum, the track banked sharply downwards and they entered the underground tunnels of Karasard.

They disembarked at the heart of the Worker District and were immediately swallowed into the bustle of city life. Commuters from the other boroughs fell in alongside them at the main concourse and Ryan found himself herded towards the checkpoints. Dozens of gunnermen were waiting with scanners, dragging people at random who they felt were suspicious enough to warrant searching. Brynne put a reassuring hand on Ryan's elbow.

"Get your card ready lad. Look them in the eyes."

The sevener at the gate wasn't interested though and scanned him through with barely a glance. Ryan stepped into the vast arena of Central Station and sighed with relief. Around him were hundreds of people all rushing to the next destination, each focused on their own tasks. The sheer numbers alone would act like camouflage for him.

A queue had formed at the nearest food cart and the smell of grilled meat gave the air a sweet tang of flavour. Ryan scanned the faces of those around him and found that they were mostly local workers. Karasard men had a style all of their own, with thick padded shirts buttoned to the chin and faces always kept clean of stubble. Mixed in amongst them were the immigrant workers from the large Midland states of Trove and Willensbrough. They were easy to spot from their dark skin and loose clothes. The women never cut their hair and kept them in long plaits. These were covered up with bright headscarves, which cut a stark contrast to the drab clothes worn by Karasard women.

Two men in suits strode purposefully through the crowd, an air of arrogance radiating from them that instantly made Ryan bristle. Behind them trailed a porter who was sweating and struggling to control a trolley stacked high with wooden crates. Ryan and Brynne broke step so that he could cut in front without changing path. The porter smiled gratefully but had no time to stop.

In and amongst the workers were gunnermen too, each one carrying a rifle slung across his shoulder and portable radio strapped to their chest. Ryan wondered how long it would be before these personal radios were given to the gunnermen in Straybeck too. That could make it harder to get past a roaming patrol. As he watched the crowds of people moving around him though, another more unpleasant thought occurred to him. Absolutely any of them could be an informer.

Suddenly, the hidden camera seemed ludicrously bulky and he self-consciously pulled at his coat, checking that the battery was still hidden. The movement dragged at the wire running up his back and pulled it tight which then tugged at the camera lens. Ryan fumbled with the small hole they had made in his coat and pressed the lens back into place.

"Keep your hands by your side." The warning in Brynne's voice was completely at odds with the easy smile he wore. "Just remember our story and act natural."

Easier said than done. They always had a cover story for travelling to the city so that if the gunnermen stopped them, they could at least withstand cursory questions without tripping each other up. The usual script was that he was looking for work in the factories and Brynne – a family friend – was introducing him to some foremen he knew. Simple and believable.

Ryan steadied his pace and felt his arms loosen up. Up ahead he could hear the sound of a kalelo drifting through the open archway of the station. The hunched musician was twisting the most complex melodies from the four-stringed instrument, never once looking up from the pavement. Brynne flipped a copper into his hat as they moved by but didn't pause to listen. It was only when they had cleared the station by a few streets that the old man decided it was safe to stop. He rolled a cigarette and passed it to Ryan before rolling a second.

"This is where I leave you," he said. "My face is too well known around the factories."

"What are you going to do?"

"Well boss, I was thinking of getting a coffee if that's alright?" Brynne smiled. "But after that, I've got people to see."

Ever since their conversation in the chapel, Ryan knew better than to press Brynne about details. If he was to prove himself loyal to the cause, then he needed to accept without question what the old man told him. So he said his goodbyes and set off towards the Worker District. It was past midday when he crested the main road to behold dozens of huge factories standing shoulder to shoulder. Swarming through the cobbled road were thousands of workers who buzzed and chatted while waiting in the cool air. Just like Foundry Lane in Straybeck, the workers were hemmed in by a gunnerman walkway that rose twenty feet above the cobbles and stretched the entire length of the seemingly endless street.

Ryan pulled nervously at the back of his jacket, making sure the battery pack was fully concealed. He switched the camera on and then cut a path through the workers, turning his chest to their faces as he went. They were grimy and exhausted, but most were chatting in lively bursts as they chewed on the last few crusts of bread they had brought. Some were drinking hot tea from small tin flasks and others had roll-ups hanging out the corner of their mouths. Their clothes were often torn and dirty but even so, it was hardly the stark and damning footage that Ryan had hoped for.

He moved through the crowd, suddenly feeling out of place in his clothes that had never seen a factory floor. He glanced warily up to the watch huts on the walkway. The gunnermen were all the way up there and the workers were on the street. Neither side seemed to acknowledge the other. The only link between them were the stone steps that led from the watch huts to the cobbles Ryan plonked himself down at the foot of one of these and considered his options. In front of him a group of three workers were chatting and smoking.

One of them, a leather-faced veteran of the factories, looked first at Ryan and then up at the walkway.

"You new here?" he said. He didn't wait for an answer and Ryan guessed that the blank face and clean clothes gave all the confirmation he needed. "Well I wouldn't sit there too long, lad."

Ryan followed his gaze up to the watch hut where two gunnermen were chatting idly. Neither one seemed to have the slightest interest in what was happening below them. "I'm not doing any harm," he said.

The worker shrugged. "Your choice. But you're likely to get a kick up the backside."

Before he could respond, a series of air-horns bellowed out from the factories sending a jolt of activity through the crowd. The old worker grumbled, then took a final fierce drag on his cigarette. Like a flock of birds, the other workers migrated back to their factories and within minutes Ryan was the only one left on the street. It seemed pointless waiting there, but before he had chance to move on, he felt a sharp kick on his shoulder.

"Move." The shout was accompanied by a second kick to the base of his spine. It connected squarely with the battery pack and the corners dug into his body.

"Hey."

"They're for climbing, not sitting." The gunnerman had descended to the bottom few steps.

"You only had to ask," Ryan said testily.

With a flash of panic, he realised that the fastenings had snapped on the battery pack. He put his hand to his hip like it was hurting, but in reality it was simply to stop the camera from falling out the bottom of his jacket.

"Talk back to me again, worker, and you'll have more than a sore back." He dropped down a step. "I suggest you go back inside with the other shit-heels."

Ryan swallowed his pride and walked away. He'd have to get the footage another time. If he didn't sort the battery pack soon, it was likely to scatter to the cobbles at any moment. Only when he was level with the last factory did he chance a look back. The gunnerman was back up on the walkway and there was no one else nearby. Ryan unzipped his coat and surveyed the damage to Brynne's camera.

"Shit," he whispered. The entire unit had cracked apart revealing a small green circuit board and some loose wires. Ryan clamped it back together and shoved the whole thing into the waistband of his trousers. Karasard would have to wait for another day; right now, he needed to get the camera back to Straybeck.

He spent the next half hour finding a new route to the station that dodged the main checkpoints. He had a general idea of where he should be heading, but when he stepped off the main roads Ryan found Karasard's Worker District to be a twisting labyrinth of passageways and back alleys. More than once he came up against a chain-link fence or solid wall that forced him to double back and find a new route. It was a relief when at last he reached the station and fell into step with the rest of the workers. Every instinct in his body was telling Ryan to dump the camera before he went inside, but the thought of disappointing Brynne again steeled his nerves. With a knot in his stomach he joined the platform for Straybeck and prayed that the gunnermen would wave him through.

CHAPTER 29

Inside the munitions factory the clock on the wall said it was almost twelve. Robb folded up his ledger, placed it in the top drawer and grabbed his jacket. His desk was hidden behind a grey filing cabinet that dominated Robb's side of the office. He enjoyed the solitude it offered, especially as most days people forgot that he was even in the office. The clock ticked slowly round, but he didn't dare go yet. Not until the air horn had blown.

When the single blast died away, Robb pushed out of his seat and limped through the office. His co-workers momentarily broke off from their ledgers to watch him pass. "I'm going out for lunch," he said quietly. No one answered but it was likely that one of them would make a note he had left.

Robb clanged along the high metal balcony where all the admin offices were housed. He glanced down to the shop floor and saw hundreds of workers already streaming towards the main gates. His joints were aching today and that made his descent to the bottom of the spiral staircase even harder. Eventually, when both his legs were throbbing with pain, he reached the factory floor and made his way onto the cobbles outside.

It was exactly 12:15 when he reached Karasard's city square. Robb scanned the town hall steps but couldn't see Kellie Downs. He crossed the wide-open space purposefully avoiding the two metal slabs that were bolted to the floor. Robb remembered the deep pits that Premier Talis had built there over thirty years ago. Hundreds of people had suffered a slow public death there. One of them he couldn't bear to think on and closed his eyes to the memory.

Robb clambered up the high stone steps of the town hall and had to lean against the bulging stone pillars when he finally reached the top. He was suddenly glad that the sevener hadn't appeared yet. It would take another few minutes to bring his breathing under control and he didn't want Kellie to see him like that. Not after all these years. The city square itself was huge and uninspiring. Robb guessed it had once been used for the markets and fayres, but those days were long since past. When he was a young man, there had been marches and processions that gathered there, but now the only gathering allowed was the Government's annual show of strength. For the past five years, on the first day of summer, Talis had filled the space with thousands of gunnermen marching in unison, flanked by row after row of gleaming army trucks and armoured cars. Crowds lined the streets in all directions to see them march past and the message it sent was crystal clear.

Today though, it was all but deserted. Two women and a man, dressed like simple clerks were heading towards a law firm at the other end of the square. In each corner Robb could see the checkpoints and a single gunnerman who guarded each one. He wondered from which direction Kellie would appear and then checked his watch. It was twenty past twelve now. Maybe he wouldn't even come. Just then, someone coughed and he turned to see the huge policeman standing behind him. Robb smiled.

"You're light on your feet, for a big guy."

"You're just getting deaf in your old age."

They hadn't spoken for many years and Robb was momentarily stuck for words. He offered his hand and the giant shook it with an iron grip. "It's good to see you again, Kellie."

"You too. But I'm guessing this isn't a social call." As always, the sevener was straight to business.

"I don't know where to start really…I just need your advice."

"You must be desperate," he said. "What's happened?"

"What do you know about a derelict chapel in Straybeck?"

"There are a lot of derelict chapels in Straybeck. Any particular one?"

John hadn't been able to tell him the name of the street, just a rough location. "It's at the edge of the Worker District. A few blocks down from Carragon Road. I can't be more specific I'm afraid."

Kellie blew his cheeks, weighing up the information. "Are you caught up in something?"

"I'm a bit long in the tooth for all that now." He paused, not sure how much he should tell him. "It's not me. But it's someone close to me."

Kellie nodded, his face a mask. "What is it you're looking for?" he said.

"Anything you've got on the man that lives there. His name's Brynne." For a moment Robb wondered if the name had struck a chord with the sevener, but he had always been hard to read.

"Brynne?" he said. "I'll ask around. See what I can find

out. But don't come to the station again. I'll come to you." He walked down the steps and paused alongside the two slabs of metal covering the pits. Just like Robb, he seemed unwilling to look down. "I'm glad you could still come to me for help."

Robb watched him go, then he hunched his shoulders against the cold and limped back towards the factory.

Ryan had never been so relieved to see the familiar outline of Brynne's chapel. On the return train journey from Karasard, two gunnermen had been patrolling the carriages. They demanded to see his ID card and quizzed him about where he had been. Ryan was certain they were going to search him, but they seemed satisfied with his story.

With safety just half a street away, Ryan picked up the pace and jogged towards the chapel. As he drew closer though, the distant revving of a car engine caught his attention. He stopped. It didn't sound like the deep grumble of an army truck, but it was so unusual to see any other cars on the road, especially in this part of the city.

The sound was drawing closer and Ryan quickly darted from the road and crouched behind a low wall. The car trundled past his hiding place and parked up opposite the Chapel returning the street to silence. Ryan flattened himself against the wall but raised his head a few inches so that he could peer above the top row of bricks.

He studied the car, a dark coupe with narrow running boards. It was the type of car you'd see in Old Straybeck or taxiing around the Trade District. There was nothing particularly unusual about it, except the fact that it was here and waiting outside Brynne's house. The driver climbed out and Ryan saw that he was in his late twenties, wearing ragged trousers and the dark, round-collared shirt of a factory worker. His jacket was old and battered and from the front seat he retrieved a black cap identical to the ones worn by so many of the workers. Ryan noted however that not many of those workers stood with such straight backs or had ever sat in a motorcar.

The driver strolled towards the chapel, offering a lazy scrutiny of the street as he went. He knocked and waited with his hands in his pockets. It was all very casual. Far too casual. Ryan felt certain this man was not who he appeared to be. But if not a worker, then who was he? As he thought it, his fingers curled around a half-brick that was lying on the ground at his knees.

The chapel door opened a few inches and he thought he saw Brynne's face appear. There was a brief conversation and then the door swung inwards and both figures moved out of sight. Warily, Ryan surfaced from his hiding place and crossed the street. He knew that Brynne had fixed metal plates against the grimy arched windows, so it was pointless trying to peer through the glass. The only way to see what was happening in that chapel was through the front door. Ryan wasn't expected until much later though and Brynne had made it very clear how he hated unscheduled visits.

In an instant Ryan's fear turned to excitement. If Brynne had allowed this man inside, then it meant he was another member of their group. A second spark for the fire. That would explain the car and the clothes and why they'd seemed so out of place. The driver was no more a factory worker than Ryan was. He moved towards the door, knowing that Brynne would forgive his early return if he showed the broken battery pack. Once inside though, there would be no reason not to introduce him to the other operative.

Quietly Ryan inched open the chapel door and stepped inside. A moment later he felt the press of cold metal at the base of his skull. His breath caught fast and instinctively he raised both hands away from his body. The gun nudged him further inside where Brynne waited, a grave expression on his face. The seconds dragged on until the old man gave a quick shake of his head. The gun was lowered and when Ryan slowly turned, he saw the driver placing it back into a shoulder strap beneath his jacket.

"What are you doing here?" Brynne's voice held no emotion.

"I had to come back. The camera…" The old man hissed a warning and Ryan stopped.

"I take it he's one of yours then?" That was the driver. Brynne said nothing, but the look that passed between them did not suggest friendship.

"You need to leave," Brynne said. Ryan turned to the driver, but it took a few second to realise that the words were meant for him. They bit colder than the muzzle of the gun had just moments before.

In the silence that followed, there was the faintest burst of radio chatter and the driver's face blanched. Ryan tracked to the sound and saw a small black circle, no bigger than a pea, fixed inside the driver's ear. It was a covert earpiece and in that instant Ryan saw him for what he was. A gunnerman agent.

He looked at Brynne and slowly raised one hand to his own ear. Those sharp blue eyes were as inscrutable as ever though and Ryan had no way of knowing if he had understood the meaning. Left with no other option, he emerged from the chapel to find the sun hanging low in the sky and long shadows stretching across the street.

CHAPTER 30

"Silence."

A familiar voice bellowed from the back of the classroom signalling the entrance of their Truths and Histories teacher. Mr Matthews eyeballed each row of students in turn to ensure their full attention. John's stomach churned as the gaze momentarily fell upon him, but Mr Matthews seemed content to dump all forty of their writing books on his desk.

"Calloway. Distribute." While John quietly handed the books out, Mr Matthews attacked the board with his usual ferocity. He spoke the words he was writing in a slow and deliberate voice. "What…factors," he said, "enabled… Premier Talis…to defeat…the King?"

He paced the gap between his desk and the classroom like a gunnerman, gently tossing a piece of chalk up and down. "Well?" he said. "How did the Premier come to power?"

Jenny Sears tentatively raised her hand. "Because the king was bad?" she said.

Mr Matthews sighed and rubbed the bridge of his nose between finger and thumb, momentarily displacing his glasses. "Yes," he said. "We know the King was bad and we know Premier Talis is good. But I'm looking for something a little more incisive." Everyone was too scared to speak but their silence only made him more impatient. "Why would people think the King was bad? What was he doing?"

"He killed people," someone said behind John.

"Good," Mr Matthews said. He turns to the board and wrote *Executions*. "What else?"

"Torture," someone else shouted out.

"Yes, that's right." Up it went in big chalk letters. "What about the economy? Did people have jobs?" A few of them shook their heads which was enough for him to write *Unemployment* on the board. After several minutes of wringing these ideas from the class, there were a dozen more words that described the bad things that happened before Premier Talis came to power. John wrote them in his exercise book while Mr Matthews continued speaking.

"Of course, we all know that the Premier succeeded because it had been pre-determined by God." Mr Matthews said this often, but as usual, John sensed little conviction in the words. "However, as historians, as *Truth seekers*, you can see that it was all of these," he waved one hand in front of the blackboard, "that made the people of the City States desperate for a change in government? Premier Talis arrived and they - *we* - welcomed him with open arms."

He picked out a couple of words from the list and calls them out. "*Unemployment*," he said. "Since the Premier came to power, everyone who is able to work has been given a job. *Law and Order*. There are patrol cars and checkpoints on every street corner. It is the Premier's ability to keep the people safe that makes him such a popular leader."

"What about torture?" John said suddenly.

Mr Matthews' gaze caught him like a lighthouse beam. "What's that Calloway?"

His mouth went dry and he sank closer to his desk. He had been thinking about his dad in The Cathedral, but now desperately wished he had kept his mouth shut. "There was still torture," he said quietly. "After the Premier came to power. I think."

He was suddenly aware of the silence in class and then watched Mr Matthews launch a piece of chalk at a child in the back row. "Concentrate," he barked. The rest of the class snapped to attention and Mr Matthews continued the lesson without breaking stride.

"Ah. You mean the gypsies. Very good Calloway. It is true that the people asked Premier Talis to clear out the campsites so that gypsies could be set to work. Some of the old travelling families called this torture, but the Premier correctly saw it as a *re-education* of an underprivileged class. Now," he said, changing tack, "turn to page fifty-eight in your textbooks." He dropped a stack of them at the end of each row. When he reached John's table, he leaned forwards and spoke in a whisper. "Careful lad." Then he was away and speaking to the whole class as if the words had never been uttered. "I want you to work through questions one to ten." A collective groan escaped the class but as he reached for another piece of chalk, everyone dropped their heads and busied themselves in work.

After the lesson, John found himself scuffing across the schoolyard on his own. There were some older boys kicking a football around and beyond that a group of girls huddled in the corner smoking. Danny Saunders had been kept in, so he didn't have anyone to talk to and he plodded aimlessly with his head down. There was a sudden sharp smack against his face that almost knocked him off his feet.

"Sorry kid," one of the older boys shouted. Then he pointed at the football. "Kick it back then." The ball had managed to hit his cheek and nose at the same time. John felt tears tingling at the corners of his eyes but had enough pride to hold them back. He kicked the ball and it landed reasonably close to where he had aimed. The older boys resumed their game and John scuttled away.

There were some steps at the entrance to the lower school and his stomach turned a somersault when he saw Alia sitting there. She had a forlorn look in her eyes and seemed paler and thinner than when they'd last met. John moved alongside her and cleared his throat. She squinted up into the low sunshine and shielded her eyes with the flat of one hand.

"John," she said happily and her face broke into a genuine smile.

As overwhelmed as he was by that response, John couldn't help but notice the bottle of pills that she quickly hid inside her pocket. Alia gave him a wan smile but said nothing. "How come you're sitting here on your own?"

She shrugged. "You know. New girl, new school. People don't exactly go out of their way to be friendly."

"I know what you mean."

"How about you?" she said. "Not with that mate of yours?"

"Danny? No, he's in detention with Mr Matthews. We're not even that good mates really. He's just someone to talk to."

She shifted along the step and patted the cold stone beside her. "Well how about we sit on our own together?" John plonked himself on the step in a heartbeat and she pushed her shoulder against his in a playful sort of way. "What happened to your face?" she said, pointing at the red mark.

"I got hit with a football." Alia pinched her lips together, trying not to laugh. "It's not funny. They kicked it really hard. I could have lost an eye."

She laughed out loud then which gave John butterflies in his stomach. He wished they weren't sitting in such a hidden away corner. He wanted everyone to know that he was spending his break time with Alia Turner and that she had just laughed at his joke. She helped him wipe the mud off his face and they chatted until the bell rang. Begrudgingly, John got to his feet.

"Where are you now?" she said.

"Upper school."

"I'm down this end. Thanks for the company though." She flashed him one last perfect smile and went inside.

At home that night, John stayed at the kitchen table after tea and took out the homework that Mr Matthews had given them. His dad was sitting across from him, reading his paper and listening to the drone of the radio.

"What's up?" he asked.

John realised he had been staring into space. "What? Nothing. I just don't know what to do." He propped his elbows on the table grumpily.

"What are you learning about?" his dad said, folding his newspaper on the table

"How Premier Talis overthrew the King. I've already answered question one," he passed his dad the book, "but the rest are really hard."

He scanned over the answer and looked genuinely impressed. "It's very good. Did you answer this on your own?"

"Mr Matthews helped with some of it," John said quietly. Although in reality, most of the first answer had been copied from the blackboard.

"Steve Matthews?" his dad said, a strange smile on his face.

"I don't know. We just call him Mr Matthews." John had never known anyone smile when they talked about Mr Matthews before. "Dad? Were you alive when the King was in power?"

His dad laughed. "You make it sound like the dark ages. But yes, I was."

"Was it really bad back then?"

He took a deep breath and then checked the doorway as though he expected a gunnerman to storm in. "Honestly? Things weren't that different from how they are now. The old King was no more cruel or corrupt than Talis. But prices were rising, people were going hungry and the Gabblers had been raiding further inland than ever before. People were afraid, and in those conditions, it was easy for a man like Talis to seize power."

"But if he was just trying to make things better, why did you want to kill him?" The words hung between them and John wondered if his dad would answer.

"Even if Talis began with good intentions, he didn't keep them long. He used fear to divide the people. Turned friends against friends, even families against one another. I think it was the fear, more than anything else, that I was fighting against. I didn't want to live…" he stopped and gave a quiet laugh as he looked around the room. "I guess I didn't want to live like this. That was why I tried to kill him."

No one ever talked to John about this stuff, but it seemed to make sense. At least more than the version he had read at school. "Mr Matthews is as old as you. Why doesn't he tell us what it was really like?"

His dad shrugged. "He probably wants to. But it's not always safe to say what you think. I shouldn't really be talking to you like this. And you must never repeat our conversations to anyone. All they need is an excuse."

"I know Dad."

"You just need to be careful."

"God, you sound like Mr Matthews."

"What?"

"In class today, he told me to be careful."

"Why?"

"He was talking about how life had changed since the old King. He said that everything was better now, but I said that it wasn't."

"John," his dad said with a groan.

"I was just thinking about you," he said defensively. "Mr Matthews said that it was all different now, but I said people still got tortured after Talis came to power." John's dad closed his eyes and exhaled slowly. "It's okay," John said quickly. "He thought I was talking about something else. About the gypsies. He said it was a good answer. But when he was handing out the textbooks, he said that I should be careful." His dad still said nothing. "Will I get in trouble?"

"I don't think so. But you've got to think about what you're saying. The things I've told you about my past. They can't leave these four walls. It's too dangerous to drag it all up again."

The front door suddenly clattered open and they heard

Ryan bustle into the hallway. John quickly leant across the table. "Have you spoken to him yet? About what I told you?"

His dad put one finger to his lips. "Don't worry about that anymore. I've said I'll deal with it." They both turned to see Ryan watching them. John grabbed his schoolbooks and squeezed past his brother, unable to mask the guilty expression on his face.

"And John," his dad called. "You listen to Steve Matthews. He's a good man."

John nodded and ran upstairs. He threw his homework onto the top bunk and then clambered up after it. From inside the pillowcase he grabbed the notebook that he'd been using to keep track of Ryan. This time he needed it for an altogether different reason. He turned to the centre pages, creased the book down its spine and with a nervous hand put pen to paper.

Dear Alia...

CHAPTER 31

Ryan had felt miserable since Brynne sent him away from the chapel. In the heat of his anger he'd thought about dumping the camera on the steps outside but knew he couldn't do that to Brynne. So instead, he had made the journey across town and decided to stash it at home until it was safe to go back.

When he arrived, his dad and brother were talking in the kitchen. Judging by how quickly the conversation stopped and then the guilty look on John's face, Ryan guessed they'd been talking about him. He stared accusingly at his dad while John squeezed by, but the coward wouldn't even meet his eyes. With a snort of disgust Ryan walked away.

"Have you got a minute?"

There was nothing his dad could say that Ryan wanted to hear. Even so, he found himself dragging out a chair and sitting side on at the table. He said nothing, waiting for his dad to break the silence.

"When did you quit the factory?"

Ryan sighed. "Does it matter?"

"Only if you want to earn money. Only if you want to stay clear of the gunnermen."

"Whatever."

"You should have told me. I had to vouch for you to get that job."

Ryan gave a cruel laugh. As if the word of that old has-been made the slightest bit of difference in the biggest factory in Karasard. The truth was, he quit because the work was dull and physically relentless. There was no way Ryan was going to throw half a lifetime into a hole like that.

It was actually Brynne who gave him the way out. He had got Ryan's details on a fake work card so that he wasn't red flagged by the employment department. He even gave him money each week like an allowance. It wasn't much, but what else did he actually need? A true revolutionary should be able to leave at a moment's notice with just the clothes on his back. It was the only way to be self-sufficient.

"You don't need to worry about it," Ryan told his Dad dismissively. "It's sorted."

"It's sorted is it? Ok so where are you working?"

"Here and there," Ryan snapped. "Why does it matter to you?"

"Is it in Straybeck?"

"Nope."

"Karasard?"

"Well if it's not Straybeck, then obviously yes."

"Which factory?"

"You wouldn't know it."

"Try me."

He'd had enough of the conversation. "I don't have to listen to this."

"If you're caught up in something, I need to know."

Ryan's stomach clenched up and he stopped halfway

across the kitchen. His immediate reaction was to tell his dad to go fuck himself. But Brynne had taught him to be smarter than that. Something about the whole conversation was prickling his suspicions. When had his dad ever shown an interest in what he was doing? And all this on the day that a stranger turns up at Brynne's chapel.

Ryan was certain now that it had been an undercover gunnerman and on the walk home he had replayed the scene, analysing exactly what Brynne said. The old man had been almost cruel in the way he dismissed Ryan. That wasn't like him at all. But maybe if he had known from the beginning that it was a gunnerman, then maybe he had done it to keep Ryan safe.

What if his dad had found out about Brynne? What if he had already informed and that was why the gunnerman had shown up. He searched his dad's face, looking for any sign of guilt.

"Come on Ryan. We both know something has changed in you. The way you act, the way you talk, the way you *think*."

"Trust me, you don't have a clue what I'm thinking."

His dad's eyes flared wider and Ryan knew his patience was wearing out. Years ago, he would have backed down, but now it made him want to push harder.

"It's not just you to think about. If you're caught up in something you shouldn't be, then it puts us all at risk. So I'll ask again, where do you go when you should be working?"

Ryan let out a bark of laughter. "Do you really think I'd tell you anything? You're a traitor. You sold out your best friends. Why would I share anything with you?"

His dad jumped up, sending his chair skidding backwards across the kitchen.

"Watch your mouth," he shouted but Ryan refused to back down.

"You want to know what I'm doing? It's everything you should have done if you hadn't been scared shitless."

His dad was around the table before Ryan could get up. He grabbed his neck and shoved his face against the tabletop.

"You think you've got it all worked out, don't you? You say all these clever speeches, spout off all this bullshit, but underneath it all you're just a scared, arrogant kid. You have no idea the trouble you're bringing down on us."

The grip at his neck grew tighter, but his dad's voice dropped to a whisper. "And your friend at the chapel. Believe me, his days are numbered."

Ryan froze. How had his dad found out about Brynne?

"Robb, let him go," his mum had come home and was running through the hallway towards them.

Ryan used the distraction to twist out of the grip and then shoved against his dad. "You don't know what you're talking about," he snarled, but the certainty had drained from his voice.

"Don't I?" He jabbed a finger at Ryan. "If *I* know about him, you can be sure the gunnermen do too."

Ryan didn't want to hear anymore and shouldered a path between his parents. As he pushed through, something clattered to the floor and shattered into dozens of tiny pieces. A frayed length of electrical wire dangled accusingly from Ryan's waist and they all stared in shock at the covert camera that was spread out before them.

"What's that?"

Ryan said nothing but went to his knees and gathered the pieces back into his coat pockets.

"Is that a camera?" his dad said. "Have you been recording us? Here?" He hauled Ryan to his feet. "Who's got you doing this?"

But he was tired of being pushed around. He shoved back with all his strength, sending his dad into the table and throwing the chairs into disarray.

"It's got nothing to do with you," he screamed and tore upstairs, kicking open the bedroom door where his brother reared up from the top bunk in fright.

Ignoring him, Ryan pulled the wreckage of the camera from his pockets, threw it to the lower bunk, and covered it all with the blankets. He wanted to hide it beneath the loose floorboard but couldn't let John see.

His younger brother was propped up on his stomach with an open notebook in front of him. As soon as Ryan had seen it, John quickly hid the book from sight beneath the blankets.

"What's that?"

"Nothing. I was just writing."

"Writing what?"

"Nothing."

"Nothing?" Ryan was instantly on guard. "Well it must be something or you wouldn't be trying to hide it."

John didn't answer and he wouldn't meet his brother's gaze. Seized by a sudden urge to kick down on someone weaker than him, he shoved John to one side and yanked the blankets from the bed. He grabbed at the notebook, but John was quick as a viper and snatched it back. They both held fast until Ryan twisted it away and found the page where John had been writing.

"*Dear Alia*," he read aloud. Of all the things he had expected to see, that had been the last. How did John even know Alia? It was outrageous. For a moment they just stared at each other and then he couldn't stop laughing.

"You're writing to Alia? Oh my God this is too funny."

John jumped down from the top bunk, but it was easy to fend him off. Ryan continued to read it aloud while pinning his brother to the bed with one hand.

"*Dear Alia. I've never been able to talk to girls the way I can talk to you. So why is it so hard to write this letter?*"

He felt an odd sense of satisfaction watching his brother's eyes glisten with tears and his face drain of colour. The next line of writing had been scribbled through, so he squinted closer to decipher the scrawl.

"*Since the first time I saw you in school, I haven't stopped thinking about you.*" Ryan gave him a patronising look. "Aw, you can't stop thinking about her?"

John threw a punch that caught him behind the jaw and rattled his teeth shut. It was never going to knock him over, but it stung enough to provoke a surge of anger from Ryan.

"You little shit," he growled and grabbed his brother by the head, pushing him to the carpet. They landed in an awkward tangle and Ryan quickly pinned him down and placed one knee across his chest. He still had the notebook in his hands and threw it down hard onto John's face.

"Never hit me again. Alright?"

The book landed on the floor and slowly flipped open, settling near to the front. There was a date written at the top from a few weeks ago and as Ryan scanned through the paragraphs beneath, his heart sank.

"*I followed Ryan to an underground station at the far side of the Worker District. He met the man from the chapel and then disappeared. The man pinned me against the wall and threatened to kill me."* Below that there was another entry dated a week later. Ryan stood up and spoke the words quietly as he read them. *"I followed Ryan to the chapel again and waited outside until he left. When I went inside, the man from the train tunnels was hiding in a secret room beneath the altar."*

"Ryan, stop." John scrambled up and grasped at the book.

"I hid behind one of the benches and then a gunnerman came in. He called the man Brynne. They went down to the secret room together."

Ryan crunched the notebook in one hand, eyes closed. It had all become startlingly clear. "How could you let him turn you," he murmured.

"I'm trying to help you," John pleaded.

"Help me?" he shouted. "How? By informing to that traitor downstairs?"

"No," John was almost crying now. "I haven't even shown it to Dad." Heavy footsteps sounded at the base of the stairs and John rushed to finish before they were interrupted. "He's bad Ryan. The man in the chapel. I know he is."

"I can't believe you'd do this to me," Ryan repeated but then their dad was in the doorway, red-faced and breathing hard.

"What the hell's going on?"

"Here he is," Ryan jeered, "dragging his leg behind him."

His dad gave a murderous look. "John. Leave us alone."

"Don't bother. I'm done with the lot of you. Keep your reports. Tell the gunnermen for all I care. I won't be back here again." Then he ran downstairs, slammed the front door and was gone.

CHAPTER 32

STRAYBECK WAS COLD but Ryan was too angry to feel it. He stalked the streets in a quiet rage, replaying the argument with his father and brother. He had been let down and betrayed too many times. He knew he couldn't live there anymore. It was no longer a home for him.

Ordinarily he would have migrated to the chapel, but he didn't even feel welcome there after Brynne had sent him away. For a moment he considered visiting Alia but dismissed it almost immediately.

Hi. I know we've only been out a couple of times, but can I stay at your house?

So instead, as the light faded and the temperature dropped, Ryan made for the train station in the Trade District. He flashed his card to the gunnerman at the gate, finding grim humour in the fact that the one time he finally had nothing to hide, he was able to slip through the checkpoint without even a question.

The platform was long and poorly lit and there were a handful of people already waiting. Two men in collars and ties were speaking in low voices and cast a nervous glance at Ryan as he waited nearby. Beyond them were two young women, waiting separately but both dressed in the typical mill-worker clothes.

The Straybeck mills and factories weren't due to shut for over an hour though and Ryan wondered why they should be heading for Karasard at this time.

He examined his own attire and realised they probably had the same thought about him. He'd left the house without his coat and was still in the clothes he'd tried to blend in with at the factories. After hiding behind the wall outside the chapel, one knee had gone through in his trousers and his sleeve was crusted with mud and brick dust. At least it added credibility to the cover story as an out of work factory-hand.

In fact, the only one who looked worse off than him was a journeyman nestled into one corner of the platform. He had a thick grey beard and was bundled into a collection of grimy blankets. Far from providing warmth, they looked more like a collection of ragged holes, ingrained with dirt. Ryan understood why the man had chosen to rest up here though. Screened by the high station walls, there was at least some shelter from the keen winds that tore through Straybeck.

The journeyman suddenly rolled into a sitting position, crying out in pain as he did so. The two white collars jumped at the sound and backed further away as the man propped himself on one elbow, hawked and spat onto the tracks. Ryan watched with growing amazement while the bundle of blankets was stripped away to reveal a tall, gangly man dressed in mismatched clothing. He was leaning against a bulging rucksack and curled beside him was a mangy dog with one blue eye and one cloudy.

In the distance, Ryan heard the quiet clatter of a train. It was timed so perfectly that he wondered if the journeyman had learned to rise and sleep with the arrival of each one. Ryan watched him loop a rope around his dog's neck and gather up his belongings. As it drew closer, the train checked its speed, issuing a series of squeals from its brakes. The five carriages grudgingly shunted and locked into place and then silence smothered the station.

Ryan climbed onto the empty central carriage while the journeyman went to the very last one. The other commuters boarded through various doors, all trying to separate themselves from each other.

Straybeck's Worker District was the final stop on the Karasard line. Or the first, depending on which direction you were heading. From there, the train took a sharp loop so that it could begin the return leg. Having completed the journey once already today, Ryan knew it would take over an hour to reach the big city. He pulled up the collar on his shirt and hunched down into the seat trying to get comfy. His thoughts fell upon the argument with John and he was surprised by the ache that it had left in his chest.

Ever since Brynne revealed the truth about Ryan's dad, he had been prepared for the inevitable betrayal. For it to have happened was neither a surprise nor a loss. But Ryan had always considered his brother's loyalty to be complete. The idea that things could be otherwise had never occurred to him. He wondered how their dad had persuaded him to do it.

I'm trying to help you Ryan.

There hadn't been even the hint of deceit on his face and Ryan wondered if it was genuine concern on his brother's part. He certainly wouldn't put it past his dad to twist John's emotions for his own ends.

Which just left the letter to Alia.

Ryan thought back to all their meetings. He had been so careful to check for people following. Yet on at least one of these occasions John must have seen him. And what had happened after that? Had John gone back to her house? Introduced himself?

Ryan shook his head. This was his twelve-year-old brother. There was no way he would have the courage to do that. Although an hour ago it wouldn't have occurred to him that John could inform on him.

Round and round the thoughts went until the train rattled clear of Straybeck and settled into a more sedate pace on its way towards Kirsk. It was twilight now and Ryan twisted in his seat to watch last of the city fall away. Finally, the sun sank below the hills and the moon glowed milky white overhead.

His thoughts returned to the Government agent who had appeared in the chapel. If Ryan had seen through his disguise, then surely Brynne would have too. His caution was almost an obsession. But if he had known all along that he worked for the Government, then why let him into the chapel at all? Whichever way he came at the question, Ryan could make no sense of it.

The train slowed and he saw the introduction of buildings in the open fields and up ahead were the glowing yellow lights of a small township. Several figures were standing on the platform and Ryan's heart sank when he recognised the sharp silhouettes of two gunnerman in amongst them. They boarded at the front of the train while the other commuters dispersed between the remaining carriages.

An older man passed by wearing a simple dark suit and found a seat on the bench opposite. Ryan didn't even make eye-contact and hunched further into his seat, keeping his head down.

As the train gathered speed and lurched forwards, one of the mill girls who had got on at Straybeck stepped through from the other carriage. Ryan raised his eyes and caught her staring at him. She was younger than he had first thought, maybe twenty. To his surprise, she gave him a coy smile as she stepped around his outstretched legs, using the roof rail for support. He managed a tight smile in return and she took a seat a couple of places down from him.

"These trains take so long," she said wearily and began un-braiding the weave of hair that she wore draped over one shoulder.

She had sharp clever features and her thick brown hair was swept back beneath a light blue bandana. Ryan could think of no reason why she would want to begin a conversation with him.

"My boss lets me finish early so I can catch this train. Still takes forever though."

Ryan nodded, unsure what to say. In his experience, people didn't just start conversations with complete strangers.

"You look like a factory man. Am I right?"

He seized upon the story that he and Brynne had so often rehearsed.

"I *was* working. But they don't need me anymore, so now I'm looking for work."

The girl stopped untangling her hair and looked at him sympathetically.

"I'm sorry," she said. "That's happened to me before. It's really hard, isn't it?"

Ryan shrugged.

"Where were you working?"

They'd rehearsed this too and he named one of the bigger factories in Karasard that Brynne said was well known for hiring and firing workers.

"Had you been there long?" the girl said idly as she plaited her hair once more.

Ryan felt his unease growing. "Where is it you work?" he said, ignoring her question.

"Graysons," she smiled. That was the busiest mill in Straybeck. It employed hundreds of women and men from the town. "They're alright really. Don't treat you too badly. Not like some of those ones in Karasard. I'm Emma by the way."

"Ryan."

"Nice to meet you," she leaned across to shake his hand. It was her charm that actually saved him. For in that moment he gave his real name rather than the one from the fake ID that was still with the wreckage of camera on his bed.

"So, do you live in the city Ryan? Or are you a Straybeck boy?"

Before he could answer, the door burst open and two dishevelled figures were propelled into the carriage. The first was a woman in her fifties with a face that was hollowed out at the cheeks. She fell to her knees with a shriek of pain and dashed her head against one of the upright poles. From there, she curled into a ball while the second figure, a man of similar age, rushed to her side. He too was malnourished and dressed in loose fitting rags. Ryan took them both for journeymen and probably dust addicts too.

"My head," the woman wailed. "My head. I think I'm going to be sick."

Her partner hooked a hand under each of her armpits and tried to haul her upright.

"Leave me. Let those bastards finish me off."

"Come on," he fussed. "Come on. It's just a knock."

"I'm going to be sick," she cried again, pressing her finger to the crown of her head. When they pulled away Ryan saw dabs of blood on her fingertips.

Two gunnermen moved into the carriage and looked over the scene. The first had a sneer on his face while the second appeared merely bored. He pulled on a pair of thick black leather gloves.

"Get up you pair of shit-heels."

"You're okay sir. You're okay. We're moving now." The old man bowed and scraped as he moved down the aisle, pushing the woman along as best he could.

Ryan saw Emma, the mill girl, look at them with utter disgust as she pulled her legs up onto the seat. He was astounded at how quickly a beautiful face could turn so sour.

"Any others?" the gunnerman said.

"Iris is with one in the end carriage. I'm not sure about this one," Emma pointed a finger at Ryan. "Says he's unemployed and looking for work at the factories."

The gunnermen closed in.

"Card."

Ryan knew he shouldn't have been surprised. He passed over his ID and they gave it a once over.

"Calloway? He a gypsy?"

Emma shrugged. "Didn't get that far. Said his first name was Ryan though."

The gunnermen double-checked the name and the

picture while Ryan looked at the girl with fresh eyes, making no attempt to hide his disgust.

"This is what you do?"

"Shut-up," she said dismissively.

The gunnermen were carrying the new portable radios and transmitted Ryan's details to the comms operator.

"Not known or wanted," came the reply. "If in company with Robb Calloway, stop and search."

"Who's Robb Calloway?"

"My dad."

"What's he done that's so special?"

"He's a traitor. I don't have anything to do with him."

"Why are you going to Karasard," the second gunnerman asked.

"No reason."

Which was a stupid answer because you were never free to act without reason.

"Where do you live?"

"Straybeck."

"Where in Straybeck?"

Ryan gave his address and the gunnerman scanned the card to check that they matched. Still not satisfied he radioed through a second time.

"Travel history for Calloway please?"

After a few seconds, the reply crackled through. "Nothing regular. This is the third trip between Karasard and Straybeck today though."

"That'll do for me," the gunnerman said to his mate and then gripped Ryan by the front of his jacket and dragged him from the bench.

"What are you doing?" Ryan protested.

"Kicking you off the train, what's it look like?"

"I've got clearance to travel."

"Not anymore. Premier doesn't want you lot dossing down here all night. You can sleep somewhere else."

Ryan was dragged between the benches and thrown towards the two dust addicts at the end of the carriage.

"I've done nothing wrong," Ryan turned to face the gunnermen, his anger boiling over.

The fist thumped into his cheek like a block of iron and knocked him to the floor. He scrambled up, but a heavy boot crashed into his ribs and he sank back to the floor. Suddenly the bony fingers of the dust addict gripped him by the arm and tugged him upright.

"Stay quiet lad," he hissed. "It's easier that way."

Ryan felt another shove at his back.

"Anything else you want to complain about?" one of the gunnerman goaded, but Ryan clutched his ribs and didn't look back.

The three of them were corralled down the train towards the end carriage. They passed the two businessmen who recoiled as though they could somehow be contaminated if they got too close. At the end of the train he saw the other mill girl, presumably the one called Iris. She was standing beside the prostrate body of the journeyman and his dog that Ryan had seen on the platform. He was nestled into a corner of the train nodding occasionally while Iris chatted to him. She was leaning against a railing and they seemed like old friends. Neither one was in the least fazed when Ryan's group arrived. The dog was resting its old grey muzzle onto her owner's lap while the journeyman stroked its ears affectionately.

"Time for us to go, old girl," he said.

And as if the train moved at his command, Ryan felt their speed falling away.

"Looks like a good haul for you today," he said to Iris. His voice was scratchy but had a warmth to it. He rolled to his knees and the dog gave a disgruntled whine of protest.

The gunnermen showed no intention of restraining the journeyman. The train checked its speed again and lights flickered past the windows. The lead gunnerman shouldered Ryan aside and gripped hold of the door release lever. He wrenched it downwards and the door slid open sending a rush of cold air into the carriage.

"Who's first then?"

He turned to them with a cruel smile. Through the open doors, Ryan saw a sloping embankment that rolled down into darkness. No one spoke and the only sound was the clattering of wheels on rails. Ryan saw the two dust addicts shrink towards the ground. The old journeyman seemed resigned to his situation and gave Ryan a wan smile.

The gunnerman grew tired of waiting. He grabbed the old woman by her hair and dragged her screaming to the door. Ryan wasn't sure if he'd have done anything if that old man not been staring at him. Whatever the reason, he jumped forward and grabbed the gloved hand of the gunnerman, twisting it free from the woman's hair. The look of shock on his face was quickly replaced by a snarl of anger.

"You little bastard."

The gunnerman slammed one palm into Ryan's throat, twisted to the side and hoisted him off his feet. Ryan's stomach lurched as he was thrown backwards. He had a brief glimpse of the wheels and coupling rods and for a moment was certain that the train would chew him up. Instead he landed heavily on the embankment, pushing all the air from his lungs. He tumbled and bounced down the slope and then his skull cracked against a rock and the world turned black.

CHAPTER 33

IN JOHN'S BACKYARD was an old outhouse that used to be the family toilet. All the workings had been removed years ago and now his dad used it to store stacks of bricks and wood. To John though it would always be the clubhouse where he and his brother had held their secret meetings.

Ryan had been the undisputed leader. His seat was way up on a shelf that used to hold the cistern, while John had to content himself with a makeshift bench. He could remember looking in awe at the carefree way his brother lounged on that shelf, throwing *luck stone* up and down.

Luck stone was something they'd found buried one day in the garden. A strange kind of quartz that glistened different colours depending on how the light reflected off its surface. Although John had been the one to find it, Ryan reasoned that he should keep it safe because he was older. So it rested on his shelf throughout their meetings, always on show, but always out of reach.

It had long since disappeared, but every so often John would climb up to his brother's shelf and take another look. As always, the only thing he found today was the lumpy remains of some candles they had burned years ago. On the wall behind them, the names *Ryan* and *John* were scratched into the red bricks. A shiver suddenly ran down his spine, but John knew he wasn't ready to go back in the house yet. That would only confirm what he already knew in his bones. Ryan wasn't coming home.

After the argument about Brynne and Alia, he was glad that Ryan had left. He was fed up with protecting him and trying to keep him safe. He could do whatever he wanted and deal with the consequences himself. That night though, John had lain awake on his bunk counting down the minutes until curfew. He still hadn't forgiven Ryan, but he couldn't shake the feeling that if the gunnermen arrested him, they'd take him to The Cathedral like his dad. Hours slipped slowly by while John prayed for the sound of their front door opening or the gentle creak of footsteps on the stairs.

His mum woke him at first light and John felt a moment of peace in his mind.

"Morning sweetheart," she soothed, and John smiled at her.

Then the worries of last night flooded back to him and he rolled over the edge of his bunk. Ryan's bed was empty and hadn't been slept in.

"I'm sorry love," his mum said, reading his thoughts.

John felt a stab of fear but masked his face and shuffled towards the ladder. "Is Dad still here?"

His mum shook her head, a sad smile on her face. "I've got work too. Will you be alright getting to school?"

He nodded but after she left, searched the house for any sign that Ryan had been home. He hoped that there would be a note or some secret indication that his brother was safe and everything was fine between them. There was nothing, either then or after his day at school.

The door of the outhouse pushed open and John looked up

hopefully. Instead of Ryan though he saw his mum's silhouette framed by the opening.

"Come on love. Come inside."

"I don't want to."

"He'll come back. I promise he will. But you won't change things sitting out here. Come on. Let's get warm and get some food."

"How can I? When he's out there without any food."

His mum's voice had an edge when she next spoke. "Your brother can look after himself. And he can always come home if he gets hungry."

She stepped to one side and unhappily John followed her across the back yard. Inside the kitchen, a big pot was bubbling noisily on the gas ring and he recognised the familiar smell of a potato stew. His stomach growled appreciatively.

"Go and change out of your school clothes," his mum said. "Tea won't be long."

John went upstairs and flopped onto his brother's bunk landing on something that was hidden beneath the blankets. Pulling them back he found a collection of broken plastic and wires. John sifted through the wreckage and found something that made his heart sink. It was a small camera and the sort of thing that Ryan had no business keeping in the house. He suddenly felt very lost, very sad and utterly alone.

"Your mother said you were up here."

He jolted upright to find his dad standing in the doorway. The camera was still strewn across the bed and there was no way to hide it.

"It's not mine," he said quickly. "I just found it."

His dad limped quietly into the room and sat beside John. A grimace of pain passed across his face as he did so.

"Seems you've got a knack for finding things you shouldn't," he said, gathering up the tangle of plastic and wires.

"What is it?" John asked.

"A covert camera. The kind you only need when you're doing something you shouldn't be."

"What was Ryan doing with it?"

"Something he shouldn't have been. You probably know better than I do what goes on in your brother's head." The forlorn expression on his dad's face was a mirror of John's own feelings. "Is there anything else hidden? I need you to be honest with me."

John felt a crippling indecision. The loyalty to his father ran almost as deep as it did to his brother. Slowly, he moved to the corner of the room and knelt beside the second to last floorboard which had split and worked loose from the joist.

"He thinks I don't know about this." John levered up the floorboard and revealed a shallow cavity maybe a foot deep which extended out of sight beneath the other boards. He lay on his side and swept the hidden space with one arm. His dad brought the camera over and knelt beside him, the gristle in his joints crunching angrily as he did so.

"Anything?"

John pulled out two pamphlets. They were like the ones he had found in the loft all those weeks ago. The first one had a tatty front cover with a grainy image of the gunnermen blockading a street. They had their rifles raised and aimed at a crowd of rioters. It looked more like a quarry village than somewhere in Karasard or Straybeck, but John couldn't be sure. He handed them over, noting the extra sag it caused in his dad's shoulders and worry lines on his face. His mum called from downstairs and the two of them turned quickly to the door.

"Let's put it all back in there for now," his dad said. "I'll get rid of it when I can. No one else can know about this stuff though John. You understand?"

"I know Dad. All they need is an excuse."

"This is much more than an excuse. If the gunnermen found these, we'd all be finished."

Together they placed the camera and the pamphlets into the hole and John slotted the floorboard back into place. "What will you do with it all?"

"I'm not sure. But it can't stay here. It's not safe."

He pushed off the floor, making his knees grind noisily again. In the doorway his dad hesitated as though there was something left to say. He put one hand on John's shoulder. It was an awkward gesture, but he didn't mind.

"I'm very proud of you, you know. The way you try to take care of everyone. You're so much like your mother."

"Does that mean Ryan's like you?"

His dad gave a humourless laugh. "More than he'll ever know."

"It really upset me when he laughed at my letter."

"What letter?"

"To Alia. You know, the girl from school."

A shadow of irritation flashed across his dad's face. "You mean the one that bought drugs?"

"Dad, I told you. She had no choice about that." They crossed the landing and headed downstairs.

"Okay, I'm sorry. So what did Ryan say?"

"He said that she'd never be interested in me because I'm just a boy."

"Well that's nonsense. Age doesn't matter. Your mother's a good twenty years older than me."

"I heard that," a voice called from downstairs.

His dad chuckled and then lowered his voice. "Ryan's just scared of the competition."

"Do you think I should finish the letter then?"

"Look at it this way. If you write it and she doesn't reply, what have you lost?"

John shrugged.

"There's your answer."

He watched his dad negotiate the rest of the steps, feeling very sad that he would never be able to walk normally.

"Are your legs alright?"

"They're fine. Just old and brittle like the rest of me." He paused on the bottom step. "Write the letter. If there's one thing you don't want in life, it's regrets."

That night John sat alone in his room with his knees tucked up like a pyramid beneath the blankets. Ryan still wasn't back and the room felt bleak without him. Pushing it from his mind though, he turned to a fresh page in his book and began to write. He had rehearsed it so many times in his head that the words flowed easily now.

Dear Alia

I've never been able to talk to girls the way that I can talk to you. Since the day we ran from the gunnermen, I haven't stopped thinking about you. I know there's an age gap between us, but if we really like each other, then it shouldn't make a difference, should it? I hope you feel the same way and we can see each other soon.

Love from

John

The next day at school, John left his final class with Alia's note gripped tightly in his hand. He raced down the corridor as fast as he dared, determined to reach the knife gates before the older students were released from lessons. He stopped momentarily at Mr Matthews' open doorway and peered inside. He was cleaning the blackboard with his back turned, so John took a chance and sprinted for the knife gates.

The queues were already forming and he pushed his way to the front, flashing his ID card to the bored looking school guard. Outside of the school, he climbed onto the wall and waited with keen eyes for Alia.

Packs of students gathered outside the gates and meandered past the Informer Station and towards town. John scanned each group as it passed him by, eventually spying Alia at the top of the steps frowning towards the overcast sky.

She was alone and John watched her plod behind a raucous group of second years. She had her rucksack looped over both shoulders and thumbs tucked beneath the straps. He jumped from the wall and into the schoolyard, moving against the tide of pupils until he was standing before her.

"John," she said, and a smile spread across her face.

He couldn't speak though and instead just passed her the folded letter.

"What's this?"

"It's for you. It's…" but suddenly afraid of what she might say, John ran through the crowd and out of sight.

CHAPTER 34

WHEN RYAN AWOKE it was morning and he found himself face down on the muddy railway embankment. A knife-like stab of pain slid neatly through his skull. He lifted his head and the skin on his face tightened and cracked as a freshly healed scab re-opened. Ryan rolled onto his back and opened his eyes to a pale blue sky and the fading twinkle of stars.

For a moment he had no idea where he was or how he'd got there. Then the confrontation on the train replayed itself and he felt once more the lurch in his stomach as he remembered falling from the carriage.

He rolled his head left to see dawn breaking over the nearby station. The early morning sun had chased black from the sky and a clean and vibrant blue was showing through. Songbirds chirped brightly along the railway embankment, chasing each other in a flurry of brown feathers.

Ryan propped himself up and felt his ribs groan in reply. Tenderly, he touched the side of his head where an egg-shaped lump protruded. He knelt and then rose fully before limping across the sloping embankment towards the station.

It was centred upon a collection of buildings that included

a ticket office, waiting room, toilets and guardroom. Running alongside the platform on either side of the tracks were open sided shelters so that the waiting passengers had some protection from the elements. The signs on the building declared this to be Obern Station.

Ryan knew that the town of Obern was at least twenty miles outside of Straybeck and maybe double that to the outskirts of Karasard. Thankfully, the station was empty and Ryan was able to shuffle into the public toilets. He was met by an enormous painting of Premier Talis staring at him from the wall opposite.

This station is monitored was written in stark white lettering across the Premier's chest. Ryan automatically scanned the roof space for cameras but could see nothing. It didn't guarantee they weren't there though.

He hunched over the porcelain sink and saw a battered and bruised figure reflected from the mirror. His clothes and face were coated with mud from the embankment. Awkwardly, he lifted his jacket and shirt to reveal deep bruises and a stripe of pain running from his armpit to his hip. Ryan dropped the clothing back into place and cradled his side where it was most tender. He guessed that something might be broken but hoped he'd be able to patch it up later.

More worrying was the lump that had risen from his head like a devil horn. The skin had split across the top of it and then scabbed over with dark blood. His hair, cheek and jawline were similarly stained crimson with blood and Ryan ran a slow trickle of water from the tap to wipe delicately at the cuts.

Just then, the toilet door dragged open and a guard stood silently beside the Premier's painting. Ryan nodded but the guard made no response.

"What time's the train for Straybeck?"

The guard was an old and formidable figure with bulging stomach, cropped white hair and a drooping white moustache. His uniform was crisp and every brass button rubbed to a shine.

"There is no train."

"No train? For how long?"

The guard twitched his moustache, straightening up.

"There's no train for you. At all."

"I've got clearance to travel," Ryan snapped, reaching for his ID card. His checked his trouser pockets and then tried his jacket. "Looking for this?" The guard held Ryan's ID just out of reach. "Two gunnermen gave it to me last night. Said you'd been bedding down on the trains and if I saw you, I should send you on your way."

He wondered if the guard was going to snap his ID right in front of him. It was an offence to do it, but who would believe Ryan? If he did, there was no way he could find his way back to Straybeck without the gunnermen picking him up at a checkpoint. If he didn't have his card, then they would arrest him. "Please," he said quietly. "I just want to get home."

And right then, he really meant it.

"Follow me," the guard said curtly.

Ryan closed his eyes as a sort of despair settled over him. Then he found a small kernel of resentment and drew strength from the anger. Steeling himself for whatever was coming, he left the toilet and moved out onto the platform. Instead of heading for the station house though, the guard moved in the opposite direction. He was a stout figure and carried himself with an almost military bearing, like a drill sergeant on the parade ground.

Ryan followed at a slow limp, the pain in his side making

it hard to breathe. They moved towards the train tracks and the grass slope where Ryan had woken earlier. The very last building on the platform was a small stone hut, slightly removed from the rest of the structures.

Outside were dozens of rusted railway sleepers stacked at waist height in a lattice shape. When he first went past, Ryan had presumed it was just an old storage. He couldn't understand why the guard was waiting for him there with the door wide open. He had no wish to go in, but the only other choice was to leave on foot without his ID. Which was no option at all.

"What's inside?"

The guard put one finger to his lips and then unexpectedly handed the ID back. Ryan clutched it tightly and considered making off on foot. After a moment's hesitation though he went through the door to find that the room within was furnished like a break room. There were two beaten-up armchairs with bulging foam cushions and between them was an old packing crate that was being utilised as a table. On top of it was a metal dish brimming with cigarette butts and a tea-stained mug.

The old guard settled himself on one of the chairs and gestured for Ryan to do likewise. Reluctantly he sat down and an uncomfortable silence hung between them.

"If you could ask me any question right now, what would it be?"

Ryan stared at him. There were so many to choose from, but very few he was prepared to say aloud to the man before him. He settled on a safe option.

"What do you want?"

The guard shook his head. "Wrong question lad. You see I could tell you any number of things. One of them may even be the truth. But it's not what you need to know. What you really need to know is whether or not you can trust me."

"And can I?"

"Well here's the thing. I could tell you yes, but what else am I going to say?"

"So I can't win either way."

"Now you're getting it," the guard grinned.

"Can I keep my card?"

"With my compliments. Although I really can't let you back on the trains."

"I wasn't doing anything wrong though."

"Doesn't matter. If those two jumped up pricks see you riding the trains today, they'll leave you with more than a few knocks and scrapes. They made that very clear."

"Knocks and scrapes? They threw me off a moving train!"

"They didn't shoot you though, did they?"

The old guard lifted a small metal flask that was standing beside his chair. As he unscrewed the top, a twist of steam escaped and condensation dripped from the underside of the lid. The guard poured a cup of copper-coloured tea and passed it to Ryan. Hesitantly he took it and sniffed over the top of the liquid.

The guard laughed. "It's tea lad, not poison."

As if to emphasise the point he poured a second mug and blew across the top before taking a long sip. Ryan realised how parched his throat was and took a gulp of the tea, closing his eyes as the heat ran down to his stomach. That momentary feeling of comfort jolted him to alertness and he snapped open his eyes expecting to find the guard advancing towards him. There he was though, unmoved and waiting straight-backed in the chair.

"Why have you brought me here?" Ryan placed the cup onto the wooden box that lay between them. "Why are you talking to me?"

The guard sighed. "I've brought you here because it's the only place in this station that I know for certain isn't watched. Not that I think they'd be particularly interested in listening to an old man like me. But if they are, I'd rather not be recorded talking to someone like you." He took another sip of tea. "No offence."

"Oh, none taken."

"And as for helping you? Well I guess I just remember a time when giving someone a hot drink and a place to sit for a while wasn't looked on as a crime."

Ryan doubted that anyone had so simple a motive for doing something nice. In his experience people were always running another angle. Greed. Revenge. Sometimes loyalty. But never kindness. Not anymore.

"I'm Gerren," the guard said.

"You already know my name," Ryan said churlishly. If the tone bothered him though, Gerren didn't show it.

"I certainly do. Ryan Calloway. Seventeen years old. From Straybeck." The guard smiled to himself. "I remember being seventeen years old. I bet you can't imagine that looking at me now."

Ryan shrugged. He couldn't imagine that Gerren was ever anything but this hulking man with a walrus moustache.

"Go on, guess how old I am."

He gave the guard an appraising stare, but it was like trying to guess the age of a sevener. Gerren had brawny shoulders and a powerful chest. Bigger even than Brynne, who he had always thought so strong. It was in the face though where the years were showing. The skin around his eyes was weathered and the jowls of his neck sagged over the starched white collar of his shirt. Ryan knew that his dad was fifty-one and guessed that Gerren must be a least ten years older than that.

"Sixty?" he said. "Sixty-five?"

"I'll be seventy-eight next month."

Ryan was astounded. People rarely lived that long in Karasard. And if they did, they were so worn down by years of labouring that they grew into hunch-backed old skeletons. He had certainly never seen anyone like the man sitting opposite.

"I used to be a gunnerman," Gerren said. "Three years as a cadet, then forty-one in the City Garrison. Until they put me out to pasture."

"Forty-one years?"

"That's right. I've fought in wars against the Gabblers, the Aftlanders, even the bloody exiles west of Willensbrough." His face took on thoughtful expression as he warmed to the conversation. "Do you know, I was the strongest man in the garrison. Maybe even the city. Gerren the Giant, they called me." He smiled, raising his huge right hand and curling the fingers into a fist. "I fought bare-knuckle with a sevener once."

Ryan wasn't sure which was more shocking. The sudden outpouring of memories from a complete stranger, or the fact that it was a gunnerman who was doing it. In spite of himself, he leaned forwards in his seat wanting more. Gerren lapsed into silence though, lost in his own thoughts.

"Did you win?" Ryan eventually prompted.

"What?"

"The fight? With the sevener?"

The guard's eyes cleared and he laughed.

"Against a sevener? Not likely. I tell you something though, he never knocked me down. Not once."

They finished the first cup of tea and talked their way through most of a second. Habit made Ryan deflect any questions that were too personal, but Gerren didn't seem to notice. In fact, he seemed more than happy to fill any gaps with reminisces from his own past. Ryan was happy just to be somewhere warm and comfortable. Eventually though, Gerren rose and drew a small silver fob watch from his pocket and squinted down his nose at the dial.

"Trains due in," he said. "Time for me to go."

"Me too, I guess."

Gerren gave him a pointed look.

"I know, I know. Don't worry. I won't try and get on the train."

"You know someone in Straybeck who can patch you up?"

Ryan was surprised that his first thought fell upon Alia. Again, he wondered if she would let him stay at her house for the night, but couldn't imagine having the courage to ask her. He wondered about Brynne and then dismissed it when he recalled how he had been sent away from the chapel.

"I'll find someone," he said to Gerren and then walked stiff-legged to the door. Each step sent a burst of pain through his ribs and when he touched the side of his head, the lump was as tender as ever.

Gerren left first, scanning the platform before waving Ryan out to join him. He pointed down the line to where a train was approaching at a steady pull.

"Follow the tracks," he said quickly. "But don't let the drivers see or they'll report you. It'll take a few hours, but you'll reach Straybeck."

Ryan held out his hand and the big man shook it. "I'll keep an eye out for you," he said. "If you're passing this way again. Take care."

He didn't have a watch, but the sun had soon reached its peak and begun a slow descent by the time he arrived at the outskirts of Straybeck. His feet were blistered and his whole body ached without let up. Ryan had lost count of the times he'd had to leave the tracks while the trains rumbled by in either direction. Mostly they were commuter links ferrying workers between Straybeck and Karasard. Sometimes though, one of the immense quarry trains thundered by, carrying ore and rock from the foundries at Insel. When he saw these, Ryan threw himself into the long grass and covered his ears as a quarter mile of freight shook the ground beneath him.

Eventually Ryan limped away from the tracks and found he could make better progress on the road. After another hour of walking he had reached the housing developments on the edge of Straybeck and was confronted by one of the fixed checkpoints that encircled the city.

The road had been blocked across the middle, leaving a gap barely wide enough for a gunnerman truck to pass though. Thick black railings and razor wire created a formidable barrier and beyond that was a metal shack the size of a railway carriage. As Ryan approached, he saw movement behind the large grimy window of the shack. A gunnerman stepped out, blocking the gateway to Straybeck and staring at Ryan as if he'd appeared from another world.

Ryan could only guess what he looked like, covered in the blood and bruises that came from being thrown out of a moving train. The gunnerman pointed at the swelling on the side of his head, which felt like it had expanded to cover most of his eye now.

"What happened to you?"

"Picked a fight with the wrong person."

"I can see that," he said unsympathetically. "One of my lot do that?"

"No."

"How'd you get it then?"

"I was at the Braziers last night. Someone didn't like my face I guess."

The Braziers was a notorious pub on this side of town. The gunnermen seemed at least partly satisfied by the answer.

"Card."

Ryan handed it over and the gunnerman walked it to the scanner in his booth.

"Are you wanted?"

"No."

The scan confirmed it, but the gunnerman waited at the screen. "Says you live on the other side of town. Why are you here?"

Ryan had already thought about his answer to this and knew it could get him in a lot of trouble. He'd already learned the hard way how dangerous it was to be homeless in Straybeck.

"I used to live there," he said. "My dad kicked me out yesterday."

"What for?"

"Said I owed him money," Ryan continued the lie. "I'm staying with a friend over here now."

"Where?"

Ryan paused for a moment. He thought back to some of the streets around Brynne's chapel.

"Overton Way." It was a long meandering road lined with clumps of terraced houses. It seemed sufficiently anonymous to prevent further questions.

"Which number?"

"I don't know. It's got a brown door."

"What's your friend called?"

"Jacob."

"Jacob what?"

"Don't know. I've only known him a few days."

The gunnerman sighed irritably. "You're full of shit."

"Honestly, it's the truth. It's about halfway up."

But the gunnerman raised his hand, over-talking Ryan's garbled explanation.

"You're full of shit and we both know you are. But quite honestly, I can't be bothered getting to the bottom of whatever it is you've done. Just piss off and don't come back this way."

"I won't," Ryan said quickly, retrieving his ID card on his way through the gate.

He suddenly felt drained of whatever energy had sustained him this far. His head was pounding and his legs could barely carry him down the street. Ryan realised that the only thing he'd eaten or drank in over a day was Gerren's cup of tea. He wanted to see Alia but guessed it would be at least another hour of walking and he knew he couldn't make it that far.

His only option was to go to the chapel and hope that Brynne was alone. The old man wouldn't turn him away again. Not if he saw the state he was in. With the decision now made, Ryan pushed on, clinging to the thought that he would soon have somewhere to rest.

The high arched windows of the chapel were reflecting the last of the afternoon sun as Ryan approached. The road was deserted and he limped wearily to the front door. He leant his shoulders against the heavy, oak door and it slid reluctantly over the flagstones. As usual, the inside of the chapel was dark and empty. Ryan moved up to the chancery and swept aside the tapestry that hid the secret staircase.

"Brynne?"

No answer.

"Brynne? It's me."

He allowed the thick material to fall back into place behind him and then lurched down the steps like a drunk. The dark and cold was soothing, but his mouth was parched and head still pulsed with pain.

"Brynne?" he hissed again, coughing as he did so.

Even with one hand tracing a path down the cool stone wall, Ryan missed his footing on the bottom step and stumbled into the cellar where he smacked his shoulder against the wall. He slid his hand along the lumpy stones and found a gas lamp and box of matches. Once lit, it brought a severe brightness to the empty living quarters.

Ryan searched through the cupboards where Brynne stored his meagre supplies and found some hard-baked bread and a wrap of cured meats. He set about devouring them immediately. There was a half-full bottle of wine there too and Ryan took a long slow drink from it. He had never tasted anything so sweet as that meal and once he was gorged, he slumped to the floor and slowly picked through the remaining scraps. For once he even ignored the dark black stain at the back of the cellar that disappeared into the secret room.

As he rested and the pain in his body eased, Ryan allowed

his mind to drift. Every so often though a sharp *drip* cut through his thoughts and pulled him back to the present. Lazily he turned his eyes across the cellar. The gas lamp suddenly flared, and Ryan felt the hairs on his arms stand up and his skin prickle. A terrible fear seized him, and the dripping grew louder, like fingers drumming on a tabletop.

The light flared again and this time a rush of gas blew through the filament and exploded the glass casing into hundreds of tiny shards. They flew across the cellar showering Ryan's face with sharp little needles. He yelled out but sat frozen in the darkness while his heart thumped.

The drip was a steady rhythm now, falling from above like rain and splashing off the stone floor. Ryan was pelted by the heavy droplets and fumbled through his pockets for a lighter. He thumbed the wheel until it struck against the flint. The small flame lit the cellar in a shaky half-light and as Ryan lifted it higher, a drop of liquid bounced off his knuckles.

Blood.

Slowly, Ryan tilted his head up to the source and with a cry of horror he saw a figure swinging from the ceiling like meat in a butcher's shop. It was the forger, Caylin, still alive and staring with one bright blue eye and one empty socket. A twist of black smoke breathed from the hole and he pointed his bony finger at Ryan accusingly.

He awoke with a scream, sweat-soaked and shivering on the cold floor of the cellar. The door to the chamber where Brynne had killed Caylin was still firmly closed and nothing else had changed. Even so, Ryan knew he couldn't settle there now. He found his feet and moved warily to the stairs. He was about to extinguish the lamp when he saw the metal dish in which Brynne collected his loose coins. Ryan swiped the handful of coppers and irons, just enough to feed him for a day or so, until he could get more from home. His old home. With a final glance at the back of the cellar, Ryan limped up the steps and away.

It was dusky dark on the streets, but full night had not yet arrived. The further he walked from the chapel, the better he felt and it wasn't long before he had found his way to the Slum District of Straybeck. A cloudless sky had opened overhead and a sharp wind whipped through Ryan's thin clothes, making the temperature bite even more cruelly.

He took a meandering route so that he could reach Alia's by only passing two checkpoints. At the first, he was asked about his injuries, but spared the interrogation he'd received at the outskirts. The next checkpoint was even easier, and he simply told the gunnerman that he was going to meet his girlfriend.

It felt strange to call her that, especially when the first time was to a gunnerman. Ryan mused over his past meetings with Alia. Was she his girlfriend? They hadn't even kissed yet. They probably would have if it hadn't been for the argument on Saintsday. The next time they had met was when she'd told him about her dad dying and how they were evicted from Old Straybeck. Kissing had felt like the last thing on their minds that day.

What about now? He was homeless, beaten up and wearing yesterday's torn and dirty clothes. He had a half empty belly and a handful of coins to his name. Hardly a catch. At the end of her front yard, Ryan wrinkled his nose against the smell of the metal skip but still gave it a tap for good luck. A light was flickering in the upstairs window and Ryan guessed Alia was using candles, so she didn't have to pay for the fuel. He gave three sharp raps on the door and waited.

A figure shadowed the glass panel and Ryan wondered if it was going to be her crazy mother again. He needn't have worried though, as a few moments later the door creaked open and Alia's face appeared. When she saw Ryan, she gave a genuine smile, but then quickly hid it away.

"Hi," she said quietly, her expression unreadable.

"Hey. Everything okay?"

As he stepped closer, she noticed the cuts and swelling to his face. "Oh my god, what happened?"

"It's a long story. If you've got time?"

She opened the door wider and surveyed the street like a wild animal. Without a word she retreated to the hallway and Ryan followed her in. It was desperately cold in the house, almost as bad as the street outside. Alia was wearing her coat fully buttoned.

"So what happened?"

"I got thrown off a train by the gunnermen."

"What? While it was moving?"

Ryan nodded.

"What for?"

"Nothing." He saw the doubt on her face and knew that he probably deserved that. "Honestly, they thought I was sleeping rough and wouldn't let me ride the train. They were going to throw an old woman off the carriage too and when I stopped them, they did this to me."

She inspected the lump on his head, moving close to see him in the darkness. Gently, she turned his face to the window and ran her fingers over his cheek. Ryan's breath quickened as he caught her scent. He wanted to press his face to hers, but instead held still, feeling a thrill at their closeness.

Alia gazed at him with a hungry expression. Her lips were parted, and her breath had drawn deeper than before.

"You came here the other day."

The change was so abrupt that Ryan needed a moment for his brain to catch up.

"The school uniform?" she prompted.

It was only three days ago but felt more like three years.

"Was it any good?" he asked.

Alia unfastened her coat to reveal a Straybeck Central jumper. "I've been wearing it all day. It smells like you," she said drawing the collar up over her nose and breathing deeply. She gave a momentary shy smile and then her melancholy expression returned. "When you were here…did you knock? Did you talk to anyone?"

Ryan thought back to the strange, almost wild figure who had answered the door that day. "I spoke to your mum, but she…" Ryan wasn't sure how to explain it. "It just seemed better to leave the clothes on the doorstep."

Alia's eyes glistened with tears. "She's not well Ryan. Things don't always make sense to her anymore." She wiped a thumb across her eyes. "You should probably just go."

"Go? Why?"

"Oh come on," she said, an edge of anger in her voice. "Why would you want to be with someone like me? Living in this filthy house with no money, no food and my crazy mother?"

"I don't care about any of that. It's you I've come to see. Not your house or your mother." He took out the fistful of coins from his pocket and held them out to her.

"That's all I've got in the world right now. And these clothes. And these bruises. We're not that different you know."

Alia studied him intently, searching for the lie. "Do you really mean that?"

"Yes," he said softly. "I thought you would be the one running a mile. Especially when you saw this great, daft lump on my head."

A smile flickered at the edge of her mouth and then she stared at his outstretched hand containing the meagre supply of coins.

"That's really everything you've got?"

"Technically, even this isn't mine. But yes."

Alia rummaged in her coat pocket and brought out two iron coins. She tipped them into Ryan's hand, a mischievous look on her face.

"Let's spend it."

CHAPTER 35

Half an hour later they were through the checkpoints and standing outside the notorious Braziers bar. Ryan knew it by reputation alone, but Alia hadn't even heard of it until tonight.

"It can get quite rough in here you know," Ryan said as the bar came into view.

"Sounds like fun."

The Braziers was at the heart of the loading yards where the River Stray circled the edge of the city. There was a single-track railway here too, so that goods and freight could be loaded on and off the flat-bottomed steamers that sailed the river connecting Straybeck to Karasard. It was also a slow but important link between the foundries at Insel and traders at Sail Bay and Cape Heritage.

The Braziers was a beacon of light in that bleak industrial landscape. Metal sconces jutted from the walls of the pub and the gas-lit flames flickered yellow and blue. As Ryan and Alia approached, three men ambled up from the waterside. Despite the cold, they wore no jackets and had their shirt sleeves rolled up to the elbows. They pushed open the thick wooden door and Ryan caught a glimpse of crowded bar within. "Sure?" he said.

Alia shrugged. "This is who I am now, right? I need to get used to it."

She looped her arm through Ryan's and together they crossed the cobbled road and entered the bar. It was hot inside and busy. At one end of the room were dozens of tables where people were sitting at simple wooden benches eating bowls of a thick stew. It smelled delicious and Ryan's stomach growled. He gambled that if they bought a bowl of food each, they might still be able to afford some drinks too.

"Stew?" he said.

"Definitely."

They found some empty seats at a table where a small group of mill girls were already eating. They were wearing the typical blue smocks and some still had the blue head scarves fastened over their long plaits. Instantly Ryan was reminded of Emma, the informant girl from the train. With sideways glances he searched each of their faces and was relieved to find that none of them were her.

"Do you think they'll come to us or do we have to go to the bar?" Alia said quietly.

Before he could answer, a young boy hurried past and deposited two bowls of the stew in front of them. They stared at it for a moment and then at each other. One of the mill girls broke away from her group, a bony-faced girl with pale skin.

"If you don't mind me saying, you look a bit lost."

"No, not lost," Alia said. "We just didn't order any food yet."

"Ordered? You've not been here before have you?"

Alia caught Ryan's eye for guidance, but finding none, just shook her head.

"Don't look so worried, we're a friendly lot," the girl

continued and then leaned over to the rest of her group. "Hey, it's their first time here."

"What?" One girl said, cocking her head to the side. She had a large mouth and a mess of curly blonde hair.

"It's their first time here," the bony-faced girl repeated, much to Ryan's annoyance.

The blonde looked shocked. "You've never been to the Braziers?"

They shook their heads.

"Never? What do you do every night?"

Ryan had never really considered it before and suddenly realised that he never spent any time with people his own age.

"I'm Gordi," the blonde said. She wiped her hands on the front of her smock before reaching across to shake with Ryan and Alia.

"Lexi," the bony-faced girl added.

"I'm Alia, this is Ryan."

The three other girls gave them a smile but then resumed their own conversation.

"So, what brings you to our wonderful pub tonight?" Gordi said while she and Lexi shuffled down the bench.

"I don't live far away," Alia said. "And we really needed a drink."

"That sounds like me every night," Gordi laughed. "Do you work at the railyard?"

Ryan shook his head and Brynne's cover story came automatically into his head. "I was at Tillersons, but they got rid of a load of us. I'm looking for work at the moment."

Lexi gave her friend a knowing look.

"What's up?" Ryan said quickly.

"Gordi's brother runs a crew on the railyard. One of his

guys left yesterday. He'll be wanting to hire someone now. We could put a good word in if you like."

"Err, thank you," Ryan said. He felt strangely touched by this unasked for kindness and momentarily forgot that he wasn't actually looking for work.

"Don't thank me yet. My brother's a complete bastard. But money's money, right?"

"How about you," Lexi said to Alia. "I've not seen you at Graysons." That was the main mill in Straybeck. Alia tried to swallow down a mouthful of stew and potatoes before answering.

"I'm still at school."

Lexi stopped untying her blue headscarf to look at Alia in disbelief. "School? How old are you?"

"Sixteen."

Gordi was impressed. "School at sixteen? Well you must be some kind of genius."

"Hardly."

"I was sent to the factories straight from primary. Poor old Lexi never even made it that far."

"You cheeky cow," the skinny girl aimed a kick at Gordi beneath the table.

Ryan knew that all the children of factory workers left school at eleven. Most of them even sooner. A child would have to be especially gifted for the school governors to sponsor them beyond that. He suddenly grasped how unfair it was that he should have had five more years of teaching simply because his father worked on the top corridor in the factories and his mother was a nurse. Thankfully, no one asked him how long he'd been out of school for, so he didn't have to lie.

The young serving boy returned to the table and swept

any morsels of food into his hand. Gordi and Lexi's empty bowls of stew were snatched away and he looked pointedly at Ryan's bowl that had barely been touched.

"Don't you want it?" he said curtly.

"Yes. I was just talking."

"Over there's for talking," the young lad said. "Here's for eating."

Gordi and Lexi gathered their jackets with a smile. "Better get it eaten, or he'll bump you. Don't like time wasters do you Siam."

"I've got a business to run," Siam puffed, full of his own importance.

"Bumped?"

"Moved to the main bar so someone else can sit down," Lexi said.

Faced with the threat of losing his food, Ryan set upon it with an enthusiasm that wasn't forced.

"Come find us when you're done," Gordi said. "We'll introduce you to everyone."

Then they were left alone on the table and as they ate in silence, Ryan tuned into the atmosphere around them. He really liked it here. The noise and vitality were refreshing and unlike everywhere else in Straybeck, there wasn't even a trace of the suspicion and fear that usually clouded ordinary conversations.

He was about to say something to Alia but saw that the confident and flirtatious girl from twenty minutes ago had been replaced by the sullen and fragile thing that had met him at the door.

"What's the matter?"

"I don't belong here," she said quietly. "You heard what

they said. They think I'm some scholarship kid. What do I have in common with anyone here?"

Ryan checked that they weren't overheard before he responded. "You've about as much in common with them as I do," he hissed. "Who cares if we stayed at school a few extra years? Doesn't mean we can't all get along. They're just people."

He finished the last of his stew, angry that she was bringing the mood down again. Alia took a small tablet from her pocket and slipped it into her mouth.

"My head's been pounding all day," she said quickly and then they sat in silence while Ryan scraped his spoon around the edge of his bowl.

"I'm sorry Ryan. I don't mean to be like this."

"It's okay."

"Do you want to know something amazing I've just figured out?"

"Go on?"

She leaned forwards with a shadow of her earlier humour. "I think the stew is *free*."

"No."

"Yes. Take a look. No one's actually ordering and no one's paying."

Ryan searched their end of the room and realised it was true.

"Why would they do that?"

"No idea. Maybe little Siam's not as good at business as he thinks he is."

"Well whatever the reason, I think I've found my new favourite bar." Ryan was pleased that Alia was mellowing again. "Come on. Let's just enjoy ourselves tonight."

They went through to the main bar and Ryan ordered drinks while Alia found a patch of wall to lean against. He returned with two beers, a handful of coins still in his hand and a massive grin on his face.

"I really, *really* like it here."

Alia smiled, although her change in mood was less to do with cheap beer and free food and more a result of the numbness that was creeping steadily through her body. The pill she'd taken at the table was already working hard to smooth the wrinkles from her mind. She sipped at the chilled beer contentedly then ran her fingers over the swelling at Ryan's temple.

"Does it still hurt?"

"Not so much. Does it look bad?"

She shrugged and then prodded it with her finger, laughing as Ryan flinched.

"Just checking."

Their conversation flowed easily and by the third drink he still had a weight of coin in his pocket and they had found a corner of the room to call their own. Raised up on a set of railway sleepers at the other end of the room was a large stage where the band was setting up. They were a three piece outfit, two men and a girl all in their twenties and all looking as though they'd stepped straight off the factory floor and simply found the instruments on stage.

The drummer tried a few snatches of rhythm, stopping every few bars to shuffle the floor toms into place or change the angle of his snare. The man on guitar was hunched over as though he could charm the music from the strings. He caressed each one with thick, unbending fingers listening to a sound only he could hear. Then, without warning, a series of rich bright chords sang from the strings.

Alia broke off their conversation to face the sound, nestling against Ryan as she turned. He placed one tentative hand on her waist, his palm resting on the curve of her hip. Alia's breath caught and with the bravery of drink and pills, she took hold of his fingers and pulled his arm all the way around her.

A tingle ran down the length of her back as his thumb rubbed gently upon her stomach. Without thinking she eased into him, both shocked and thrilled to feel him growing stiff against her. Little pulses of pleasure trembled in her legs and they stood in silence, neither one willing to break contact.

The girl on stage flicked open the latches of her tatty brown case and drew out a violin. There was no preamble, no testing of the strings, she simply raised the instrument, hooked it beneath her chin and set about a lively reel. The pub erupted with a roar of approval. Alia's heart lifted with the music and she half-turned towards Ryan. Their faces were inches apart and she could feel the heat from his body.

He dipped his face and their lips brushed together. Alia broke the touch for a moment to twist fully into his embrace. She had her hands pressed flat against his chest and they kissed again, more fiercely this time. Her tongue teased against his and she felt Ryan's strong arms holding her tightly

"Someone's having a good night," Gordi's face appeared beside them.

Alia and Ryan separated and despite the beer, her face flushed bright red with a mix of embarrassment and excitement. The music was loud and lively and Ryan scanned the room, finding every face sharing their exhilaration.

"What do you think of the place?" Lexi said as she

skipped up beside them. She was drinking form a pint glass that looked huge held in her tiny hand.

"It's great," Alia said, having to shout above the fiddler. "The music…everything."

"That's Amaline. She's from our mill."

"Absolutely hopeless on the looms," Gordi added, "but bugger me, she can play fiddle."

"She's amazing," Alia said.

"We've got a table over there. Why don't you come join us? My brother will be in later and you can ask him about the job."

Alia and Ryan crossed the bar and found a seat with the mill girls who had been at their table when they were eating. A group of four men had joined them who were not much older than Ryan. Everyone shuffled round the table to make room and Alia found herself wedged between Ryan on one side and Lexi on the other. The skinny girl was speaking much louder than when they had first met and moving her hands quickly as she introduced each of the group. It made Alia feel less self-conscious to know that she wasn't the only one getting drunk. She was slightly worried that the pill had given her a strange reaction though. Ever since she'd swallowed it, a giddy feeling had taken hold of her. As though she were standing at the edge of a precipice, only inches from falling. Lexi was still jabbering away so Alia took a deep breath and smiled as though she were paying attention.

"What do you think of the place?" It must have been the third time she'd asked the question.

"It's great. Everyone's been really nice."

From across the table, a great lump of a youth leaned towards them.

"It's amazing how friendly we are when you've a nice smile and pair of tits."

"Marlo!" Lexi shrieked indignantly.

"What? I was talking about me." Marlo cupped his own ample breasts, wobbling them up and down while Lexi coughed a mouthful of beer back into her glass.

"This is Marlo. He's a pig," Lexi said, leaning across the table to slap him about the head. He ducked and continued laughing.

"We try to ignore him, but he keeps coming back."

"Don't be like that. You know you love me really."

It turned out that Marlo, like most of the men in The Braziers, worked on the freight yards loading and unloading an unending supply of goods that passed between Straybeck and Karasard. Alia suspected that he wanted Lexi to be more than just a friend, but judging by the wearisome look she showed him it was a very one-sided dream.

While they bantered with one another across the table, Alia searched her jacket pockets for the reassuring touch of her tablets. She quickly found the smooth plastic bottle, but it was tangled within a scrap of folded paper. Curiously she took it out and saw that it was the note from John.

"What's that?" Ryan said as she unfolded the paper.

"It's a love letter." She smiled fondly, remembering John's face when he'd given it to her.

"A love letter? From who?"

"Don't worry," she said. "You're still my number one man. This one's a little young for me."

She handed Ryan the note and they read over it together. Alia had been touched by the soft words that must have taken so long to write. Each letter was perfectly formed and yet still so obviously written by a child.

"What does he mean here?" Ryan asked after he'd had time to read it. "About running from the gunnermen?"

"Haven't I told you? I was in a shootout."

Ryan listened attentively while she described meeting John at her new school. She went on to tell him about the day in the Trade District. In this telling of the story, Alia said the tablets were for her mother, but everything else was the truth. When the story was finished Ryan stared back with a stunned expression on his face.

"Are you okay?" she asked.

"Yeah, I mean I can't believe he did that. This John." Ryan scanned the bottom of the letter to check the name again.

"You're not mad, are you?"

"About the love letter?" Ryan frowned, folding the piece of paper and passing it back. "No I'm not. In fact, I think you should write back to him."

"Okay, I'm not sure you know how this boyfriend thing's supposed to work."

"Very funny. I don't mean like that. I just mean he sounds like a decent kid. Probably deserves to be told in person, don't you think?"

Alia gave a grumbling sigh. "I hate stuff like that."

"Like what?"

"You know, all that *letting you down gently* stuff. I never know what to say."

"What? I thought you girls are given lessons in it."

She took another mouthful of beer and leaned her head against his shoulder. They shifted to face the stage where

Amaline had set up a furious pace on the fiddle. A dozen or so girls were already dancing in the space between the tables.

Alia couldn't remember a happier time in her life. If anyone had told her a year ago that she would be laughing and joking with a group of workers, she would never have believed them. She thought of her father then and what the workers had done to him. A familiar flash of anger seized her, but Alia forced it from her mind. She would not let that govern her mood tonight. Not when everything was going so well. Ryan's arm was around her shoulder and she reached up to lace her fingers into his. It was the last clear images she had of the night.

Hours later The Braziers emptied its punters onto the cobbled square at the front of the bar. Everyone was reeling drunk and a carnival atmosphere was upon them. When Ryan and Alia eventually stepped into the cold air, she pirouetted in a circle around him. In truth, he was finding it hard to keep from stumbling as he walked but was determined not to show it to Alia.

He saw that Lexi had finally given in and paired off with Marlo. He couldn't imagine two people less well suited, but Lexi seemed happy enough as the big lad scooped her onto one shoulder and ran down the street with her. She shrieked with laughter as he invited people to smack her on the backside.

Ryan caught sight of Gordi too, leaning against the wall of the pub. She had her arms wrapped around a dark-haired worker and they were illuminated by one of the blue gas flames beside them. Oblivious to the tawdry cheer that erupted from those nearby, she allowed his hands to roam beneath her skirt as they kissed.

Somewhere amongst the crowds, a group of voices took

up the chorus to a song Amaline had been playing. It was a catchy song with bawdy lyrics about a young girl who seduced her factory boss and then stole all his money. More voices joined in and soon the refrain was reaching far into the night while people stumbled home.

That was when the flashing red lights of a patrol vehicle suddenly bounced between the buildings. A jeer erupted from some people in the crowd, but most seemed to instinctively quicken their pace across the cobbles. A large van stopped sharply at the end of the street and the side door slid open. Five gunnermen leapt out with their batons drawn and shoved anyone within striking range to clear an area around the van. Their sergeant stepped forward. He was tall and rangy with a shaved head and sour face.

"This area is now under curfew," he bellowed. "Go home or come with us. Your choice."

The revellers were momentarily subdued, staring mutely at the newcomers with a mix of resentment and incomprehension on their faces. From deep within the crowd a bottle sailed overhead and smashed against the van, showering broken glass and beer over the rear two gunnermen.

Their sergeant struck out immediately, driving a wedge into the crowd as he swung the long-handled baton. The cries of more sirens wailed up and down, drawing steadily closer. Ryan saw the driver of the van giving a series of updates into a radio before jumping onto the street and levelling his rifle.

CHAPTER 36

Two patrol cars arrived next, flooding the railyards in flashing red light. Ryan felt instantly sobered, realising this was a battle with no purpose and no chance of winning. It was simply sport for the gunnermen to show who was in control.

He gripped Alia's wrist. Together they ran deeper into the railyards and away from the fighting. They slowed and he pulled her into a doorway so that they could catch their breath while he checked that no one was following.

"Bastards," Ryan hissed, hawking a mouthful of spit into the road. "Are you okay?"

But Alia didn't answer and he found her staring vacantly at the wall.

"Alia?"

"Yes?"

Something in her voice wasn't right though. She slurred the word and as Ryan stepped closer, he saw that her eyes were swimming in and out of focus. Both pupils were the size of iron coins and despite the run, she was barely out of breath.

"What's the matter Alia?" At first he thought she hadn't heard him, but eventually she gave a slow shake of her head.

"I'm fine," she repeated in the same low drawl.

He knew they'd drunk a lot tonight, but she'd seemed okay when they were inside. Besides, this wasn't like any drunk he'd ever seen. Especially for it to happen so quickly. He checked his surroundings and judged that they weren't more than a mile or so from Alia's house.

"Come on," he said and pulled her arm around his shoulder so he could support her weight. Her legs were leaden and she stumbled as they walked, at times leaning entirely upon him and almost dragging them both into the gutter.

"Try and walk," he grumbled, struggling to keep upright.

Alia gave some incoherent reply, but all he could make out was the word *home*.

"It's okay," he said. "I'll get you home."

She straightened up at that, locking her body rigid.

"No," she said sternly. "No."

"Alia? What's the matter?" He pulled her forward. "We need to get you back. You need to sober up."

Alia's strength drained like water and she suddenly emitted a heartfelt sob. Ryan had no idea what caused it, but he had to get her off the street. It would only lead to more trouble if a patrol found them now.

Once he had got his bearing from the main road, it took almost an hour to retrace the journey that had taken just twenty minutes at the start of the night. It was a relief when they reached the familiar metal skip at the end of her path. He sat Alia on the low wall at the end of her drive and took a few moments to rest. Somewhere in the distance a gunnerman siren flared up. Ryan instinctively tensed, trying to discern its direction of travel. Satisfied it was moving away from them, he returned to Alia and lifted her face with both hands.

"Alia? Where's your key?"

She seemed more alert than before and managed to focus her eyes upon him. The sobs from before had faded, but Ryan's heart ached when he saw the melancholy expression that had settled upon her face. With a deep shuddering breath, she pulled a loop of string from around her neck. It had a key attached and she passed it to Ryan.

"Please," she slurred.

"Please what?"

But she said nothing more and when he took the key her head sank to her chest.

As he unlocked the door a wave of foul smells smashed into him. It was the unmistakable stench of human waste. Ryan guessed that the sewage pipes had backed up and held his breath as he guided Alia into the hallway. She took off her coat and draped it over the banister, but if she noticed the smell, she said nothing. Ryan led her into the dingy front room and cleared a pile of dirty clothes and crockery from the sofa so that she could sit down.

"It's cold in here," Ryan said. His breath was frosting as he spoke. "Do you want your jacket?"

"Just go," she murmured.

"What?"

"Just go. I don't want you here."

Ryan frowned. "I'm trying to help you."

Her eyes seemed to clear and she held him with a venomous look. "I don't want your help," she shouted. "Just leave me alone."

Ryan looked around him. At the house, the mess and then the angry drunken girl in front of him.

"You know what? I've got enough of my own shit to deal with without worrying about yours."

"Just get out," Alia yelled again.

Ryan went into the hallway but realised he still had her key in his hand. He stuffed it into her jacket pocket, intending to throw the whole lot at her before storming out. As he did so, his fingers unexpectedly closed around a small bottle. He stepped closer to the window to read the label.

"What have you got?" Alia said sharply from the lounge. "Give me my jacket now."

"Opiates?" Ryan murmured, reading the label. He'd heard enough from his mum to know that they were highly addictive and highly illegal. It suddenly became clear why her moods fluxed from deliriously happy to sombre and morose in the drawing of a breath.

"Why've you got these?" he said, returning to the lounge with the bottle in his hand.

"Give them back, I need them."

"Is this what you've been taking tonight? With everything you've been drinking?"

Alia snatched them out of his hand and stomped back to the sofa.

"I just need them."

"What? Because of this?" He gestured at the house. It was bad, but there were thousands of people living in exactly the same conditions or worse. They just had to get on with life. The difference was, they'd never lived a life of power and privilege like she had growing up. Once more Ryan pictured her magnificent house in Old Straybeck. A house that only a handful of people would have been admitted to, never mind been able to own.

He tossed the bottle on the floor and was about to give some clever parting line when a tremendous crash sounded from upstairs. It was followed by a long wailing sound, like a baby's cry, but deeper.

"What's that?" Ryan had assumed they were alone in the house.

"Just leave," Alia cried. She barged past him and bounced off the doorframe before sliding up the stairs with her shoulder propped against the wall.

Ryan could have left then. Probably should have. But there was still some part of him drawn to this sad, mercurial girl. Cautiously he followed her up the stairs placing one sleeve over his nose to block out the awful smell that was growing stronger with each step. The wailing had now become a high-pitched keening, like that of a trapped animal. Ryan crept onto the landing and followed the sound to one of the bedrooms. "Alia," he whispered, pushing the door open and creeping inside.

He could not have imagined a more awful sight than what met him on the other-side. Alia was kneeling beside the bed trying to restrain the man who was laying there. He was emaciated and his nightclothes were soiled and stinking. Although his legs were unmoving, he thrashed violently from side to side with his arms and body.

"Just let me help you," Alia was pleading as she hoisted him into a sitting position.

He lashed out, slapping her across the cheek, making Alia fall backwards. As she lost her grip on the man, he dropped to the wooden floorboards and his head cracked with loud thump. He set up an even louder wailing and Alia covered her ears, retreating to the corner of the room. Ryan rushed forwards and held her in his arms.

"You told me he was dead," he whispered, like it could make a difference.

Alia began to fight against him, but her strength quickly failed. "All you do is look for reasons to hate your father. It's just not fair."

Looking down at the pitiful sight before him, Ryan had to agree.

He tried to settle her in the other bedroom but found Alia's mother lying on the bed unconscious. Ryan checked that she was alive, but nothing more and then shut the door while he took Alia back onto the sofa.

"I'll be down soon. You stay here."

Then he returned to her father's room and cleaned him up as best as he could. When that was done, he lifted him onto the bed and found fresh pyjamas to dress him in. Within minutes, his hollow eyes had closed tight and his breathing, although shallow and rasping, found a steady rhythm. Ryan doubted if he was even aware of what had happened.

In the lounge, he knelt beside Alia and put his jacket around her shoulders. It was a small gesture, but it was at least something he could do. She opened her eyes and for the first time he understood the perpetual look of sadness that resided there. He stroked her face with one hand.

"How long has it been like this?"

"Forever." She sighed. "It's true what I told you though, about the riot in the factory. When the seveners cut him down he should have died. They got him to a hospital though and they promised mum they'd fix him as long as she kept paying.

I don't blame Mum. She'd never worked and had no clue how to manage the money. It took just over a year, but one way or another it went. Once that happened, the hospital put dad in asylum care."

Ryan shook his head. Even The Cathedral would be kinder than that.

"By the end of the first week, Mum used the last of her money to buy him out and get him home." She looked around the lounge in disgust. "Home."

"Who looks after your dad?"

"At first we paid for a nurse to come in every day. She changed the dressings and…cleaned him. After that, Mum tried to do it, but you've seen what all this has done to her."

"And now?"

Alia laughed although there was no humour to it.

"Now it's just me. Just me and my tablets."

"I'm sorry."

Neither of them spoke for a long time. Eventually Alia rolled her head to face him.

"If you want to end this…between us…I understand."

Ryan shook his head. "I don't want to do that."

Fresh tears came to her eyes although this time they were accompanied by a smile. She shuffled back on the sofa and Ryan crawled up alongside her so that they could hold each other.

"We'll work this out," he whispered and kissed the top of her head. "I promise."

CHAPTER 37

John had been miserable all morning at school. Now he was ghosting through the corridors, bouncing shoulders with the older kids. He had no appetite but like an automaton he trudged towards the dinner hall with his head down. After all, it might be the only food he ate for the rest of the day.

John lined up and tried his best to ignore Danny Saunders. They had fallen out a few days ago and now he had turned the rest of the class against him. He heard his voice carry from the front of the queue and everyone started laughing. John scowled but knew that it wasn't even the real reason he felt so miserable.

Ryan was still missing and hadn't been home in two nights. He had left without any clothes or money and John felt certain that he'd been picked up by the gunnermen. As awful as that was, he was ashamed to admit that it was only half the problem. Yesterday he had given Alia the letter and the anxiety around that was ever present in his mind. She had tried to talk to him at the time, but John had mumbled something barely articulate and practically run in the other direction while she unfolded the sheet of paper.

Without intending to, he had spent morning break

patrolling the places where she usually sat. A strange mix of excitement and fear seized him each time he caught an imagined glimpse of her. It was a slow and steady torture. Finally, he had given up. Either Alia wasn't at school or, worse still, she was avoiding him.

The dinner line shuffled forwards and John could smell boiled vegetables and rice, the staple diet at Straybeck Central. He caught himself staring at Danny Saunders and his new gang once more. He felt a twist of envy in his stomach and stepped out of line, suddenly wanting to be anywhere else but there. Immediately he collided with Alia, catching his forehead against her mouth. She stumbled backwards, clutching her lip and swearing.

"Oh God, Alia, I'm sorry. Are you okay?"

She dabbed at her mouth but it wasn't bleeding. "I'm fine. Just bit my tongue."

She looked anything but fine though. Her eyes were sunken and hollow, ringed by dark circles. Her skin was bone-white and even her posture was stooped as though she were too weak to stay upright.

"You look awful," John said. Then immediately wished he could drag the words back into his mouth.

"Thanks," Alia said wryly. "Just what I was hoping for."

"I'm sorry. I didn't mean…"

"It's okay. I do look awful. I'm not well today." She moved away from the lunch line and John followed. "I only came in to speak to you."

John's stomach flip-flopped. "Me? Why?"

"I read your note." She took an all too familiar piece of paper from her pocket and John's ears burned scarlet. "I thought we should talk about it."

"Okay."

"But not here."

John glanced around and saw that more than a few people from the line were taking an interest in their conversation.

"Okay."

"Meet me after school?" She asked.

"Okay. I could wait at the gates?"

Alia shook her head. "I'm not staying long. Not today. I could see you at the Trade District though? I'll be there later anyway. How about we meet outside the shop where you saw me last week?"

She could have asked him to meet her in Karasard and he'd still have found a way. "Great. Yes. Definitely."

The smile she gave was genuine, but even that seemed to cost her effort. She turned and John watched her shuffle out of the canteen leaving him alone in the middle of the tables.

"What's the matter Calloway?" a familiar voice jibed. It was Danny, carrying a large dish of steaming broth. "New girlfriend dumped you?" He laughed again and then bumped shoulders as he went past.

"She's not my girlfriend," John said quietly, although his whole body ached with the hope that maybe she could be.

What followed felt like the longest afternoon ever. When the school bell eventually sounded, John raced to the knife gates and squeezed through the crush of bodies to flash his ID at the school guard. It had been cold all day and the sun had barely filtered through the leaden grey sky. Now that it had finally surrendered and begun its steep descent, the temperature was quickly falling away. John pulled his thin coat tighter around his chest, mourning the loss of the thicker jacket that his dad had burned after the shooting in the Trade District last week.

John hadn't been back there since he and Alia ran from the gunnerman. He felt guilty that he was breaking the promise his dad had wrung from him not to return. There was nothing he could do though. He had to see Alia; right now that was the only thing he knew for certain.

The more he thought about it, the more he reasoned that his dad would understand the risk he was taking. With this in mind, he walked briskly across town until he came to the static checkpoint marking the boundary between districts. As it was, the gunnerman barely glanced at John's card and no alarms sounded from the scanner. Somehow, he kept the relief from his face and walked through the barrier.

The streets were busy with the trader traffic. Open-backed vans jostled down the cobbled streets and weaved slowly around the horse-drawn carts still used by the less prosperous traders. A military jeep moved slowly across the junction in front. The gunnermen were the only ones who could interrupt traffic without being subjected to torrents of abuse from the busy traders.

John nearly walked past the meeting place at first and it was only the shopkeeper that caught his attention. He instantly recognised that hawkish face, still showing the same sneering expression to anyone who dared pass by without purchasing his goods.

John waited on the pavement opposite, watching him with narrowed eyes. The man finished his cigarette, flicked the end into the road and ducked back into his shop. John waited in the alleyway where Alia had collapsed and remembered how scared she had looked that day. He followed his thoughts and remembered how he had placed one hand against her waist and helped her to stand up.

Suddenly, there were footsteps behind him and he felt a jolt of nervous excitement. It was Alia, still wearing her school clothes and looking little better than she had in the canteen. Her arms were wrapped tightly around her middle like she was in pain and every step took a force of will. She gave him a weak smile, but John wasn't fooled.

"Are you still feeling poorly?"

"I'm okay."

"Has it been like this all day? Do you need a doctor?"

"Honestly, I'm fine. And don't feel too sorry for me. It's mostly my own fault."

John didn't understand that, but looking at her sunken eyes and washed out skin, he knew something must be properly wrong.

"Is it like before? Do you need to sit down or something?" he lowered his voice. "Do you need me to get more pills?" He hoped that she wouldn't but also knew that he'd do it if she asked him to. Alia's face tightened up though and she didn't answer.

"Come on," she said eventually. "Let's walk."

The alleyway was narrow and Alia led him between the high buildings until they opened out onto a large square of shops and a public house. The benches outside were all empty and in spite of the cold, Alia took a seat at the first one. John sat beside her so that their legs were almost touching. He turned expectantly, but Alia stared into the distance chewing her lip.

"It's really cold, isn't it?" he said.

She nodded.

"I'm glad you came into school to see me today." He moved his leg an inch closer so that they pressed gently against one another.

"John I…"

"I meant what I said in the letter you know." Alia lowered her head, but he pressed on regardless. "I really haven't been able to stop thinking about you."

"John please."

"I know you're a couple of years older than me, but it doesn't matter. Not really."

"John, just wait," she snapped.

He froze, eyes wide at the rebuke.

"Why is this so hard?" she whispered before turning to face him. "Listen, I wanted to meet up today because I thought it was better to do this in person. And I didn't want to talk about it in school, because I didn't want you to get upset in front of your friends. I thought your letter was lovely," she said, taking it from her pocket. "And I think you're great. You make me laugh, you're really kind…"

"And they're good things," John blurted out. He felt like he was watching the tide go out all around him.

Alia sighed. "You'll make a girl very happy one day, I know you will. But that girl isn't me. Not in that way."

Tears gathered in the corner of his eyes and John bit hard into the side of his cheek to stop himself crying. "Is it because I'm younger?"

"No."

"Have you already got a boyfriend?"

"It's not about that either. I just wanted you to know…"

But John had heard enough. He snatched the letter from her hand and screwed it into a tight ball. His mouth began to pull down at the corners and his voice cracked when he tried to talk. He took a couple of steadying breaths, but Alia was staring at the ground embarrassed to hear anymore. Ashamed of himself, John threw the letter at her feet and ran.

He stopped on the main street, suddenly aware that people were staring at him as they went past. He wiped his eyes with one sleeve and then wandered aimlessly for some time, finding himself back at the checkpoint. The bulk of the school crowd were migrating across the Trade District now, mixed in amongst the everyday shoppers. John turned off the main street, refusing to let any of his friends see that he'd been crying.

He waited until most of them had moved on and replayed the conversation with Alia over and over in his mind. How could he have believed that she would ever like him? He was angry at himself for ever writing the letter and humiliated that he had cried and thrown it at her when he left.

A jolt of fear ran through him when he realised he'd left the letter lying on the ground. What if someone else read it? Anyone at school would know immediately who had written it. If Danny Saunders found out, he'd tell everyone.

Seized by a sudden urgency, John rushed onto the main street and retraced his steps to the centre of the Trade District. He convinced himself that his most embarrassing secrets had already been laid bare for everyone to see. Breathing hard, he reached the alleyway and tore along it towards the pub where he and Alia had been sitting.

A young couple stepped into view and he skidded to a stop to avoid bowling them over. It was Alia, still holding his letter, which was now spread flat so that she could show it to the man standing beside her. John looked at his face, seeing one that he knew as well as his own.

It was Ryan, one arm draped casually around Alia's shoulder. She at least had the grace to look embarrassed, but Ryan's face was a mask. Any joy at seeing him alive was quickly snuffed by a surge of anger. John reflected on all the worry and heartache both of them had caused him. All the sleep and tears he had lost only to find them here together, reading his letter.

That was when he finally grasped what they had done. He remembered how angry Ryan had been, the last time they spoke. How he had promised to get back at him for keeping a journal about Brynne. His brother had known about the love letter and persuaded Alia to meet up with him. John looked at the bench where they had been sitting earlier, slowly piecing it together. When she had first sat down it seemed an odd choice, but now he saw how it was overlooked from the front window of the pub. With a shake of his head, he imagined Ryan watching from the window. Laughing as it all played out. The betrayal made him want to cry, but he refused to shed another tear for either of them.

"Were you in there?" he said quietly, pointing at the window. "Did you see it all?"

"John please," Alia said. "It's not like that."

He snatched the letter from her hand and waved it in their faces.

"How about this? Did you both have a good laugh about it?"

For the first time he noticed the lumps and bruises on Ryan's face, but beneath those, it was the same mocking expression, just masked beneath a feigned look of confusion.

"John listen," he said, "it's not what you think."

"Ryan, just let me talk to him," Alia interrupted.

"Yeah Ryan, just let her talk," John parroted. "She's good at doing your dirty work. Dad was right about you. All this time I kept protecting you and sticking up for you, but now I finally see it."

"John, wait."

"No. I hate you. Both of you."

He shoved between them and ran through the square and towards the checkpoint. His mind searched for words deep enough or dark enough to say to them. When he couldn't find any, he turned his mind to revenge. They needed to be hurt as much as they had hurt him. They needed to know what it felt like to have something special twisted and turned against you. Then it came to him and with a new sense of purpose, John strode through the checkpoint and back towards school.

CHAPTER 38

BY THE TIME he saw the featureless walls of the Informer Station, John's anger was cold and controlled. Exactly what he needed for a task like this. He waited out of sight and planned what he would say to cause maximum effect. When the last of the post-school informers had drifted away, he moved around the outside of the building and entered through the large white door.

Inside was a grand atrium that housed an enormous plinth and copper figurehead of Premier Talis. Aside from that, the room was bare. The opposite wall and those on either side had each been partitioned into eight smaller cubicles though and all of the doors were standing open. John approached the closest one and took his first look at an informer booth.

As he stepped inside, the door closed quickly behind him and with a gentle click, the room was illuminated in a soft yellow light. John gave the door handle a gentle tug, but found it was fastened in place by a magnet along the top of the frame. On the opposite wall was another door, which he assumed led outside and to the rear of the building. He nudged it forwards and a small crack opened up. At least he wasn't trapped inside.

Beside him was a black telephone receiver hanging from a clip. The ribbed metal cord made a delicate loop and then disappeared into the wall like a rat's tail. With sweaty palms, John lifted the receiver and heard it whir against his ear. A line clicked open and an official sounding voice spoke to him.

"Informant's line."

"I've got information about someone," John said dropping his voice deeper. "He lives in a chapel in the Worker District in Straybeck."

The questions from the official came quickly and calmly as though he were reading off a script. *Why is he of interest? What has he done? Where exactly is the chapel?*

John answered as fully as he could but refused to say that his brother was involved. He might hate him, but he didn't want to see Ryan in The Cathedral. Besides, he knew it would be more satisfying to ruin his brother's plans by informing on Brynne and having the chapel shut down.

"I'm not sure what street it's on. It's near an old underground station though. From the outside it looks empty, but he lives underneath the chapel. There are stairs at the front near the altar. He has lots of people visiting."

"What kind of visitors?"

John explained how these visitors sometimes put up posters on the factory walls or delivered bags of stuff to houses in the Slum District. All the while he could hear keys tapping away on the other end of the phone as the official was typing it up. He smiled to himself, imagining how Ryan would feel when Brynne was arrested.

"What does he look like?" the official asked.

That was when the hairs prickled on John's neck. The call

was taking much longer than he had thought and it was the third time he had been asked that question.

"I've already said that. Listen, I need to go now. I've told you everything I can."

"Just a few more questions sir. It won't take long."

"I don't have time," John said, panic rising. The official's voice grew stern though and his questioning changed tack.

"What's your name?"

"Why do you need my name?"

"I don't really. I know you're in booth one at the Straybeck Central Informers Station. We've recorded the call and there are cameras throughout the building."

John looked up and saw a black box with a blinking red light attached to the ceiling. Behind him, a bolt clunked into place on the exit door.

"I want you to stay where you are," the official said. "I want you to wait for the gunnermen to arrive."

All they need is an excuse.

John dropped the receiver, leaving it to clatter and swing against the wall. He heaved his shoulder against the door, but it wouldn't shift. In a panic he whirled round and tried the one he had entered through. It creaked towards him a fraction, but the magnet held firm.

John wiped the sweat from his hands and steadied his foot on the doorframe before taking hold of the handle again. This time he heaved backwards with all his might and the door separated from the magnetic plate with a bang.

In an instant he was across the atrium and sprinting past the sculpture of Talis before bursting out into the school grounds. He had barely made it a dozen steps before a shout reached him. John stopped, certain to see a gunnerman waiting. Instead, he found Mr Matthews, briefcase in hand. He looked first at John and then at the Informer Station.

"Calloway?" he said. "What is it? What have you done?"

John didn't know how to answer.

"Tell me. Quick."

"I've informed on someone. A man that Ryan's been meeting."

Mr Matthews strode forward, dropping his briefcase and taking a knee before him. He grabbed John by the top of each arm, his grip painfully tight.

"Did you tell them Ryan's name?"

"No."

"Yours?"

"No."

"Then leave and don't tell anyone else what you did." When John didn't respond, he shook him to life. "Go."

"But they said I had to stay," John was close to tears. "And there was a camera in the ceiling."

"The cameras," Mr Matthews groaned, his jaw clenching tight. "Okay, leave that to me. Now run."

CHAPTER 39

Robb limped off the train, along the platform and out of the station. It had been a long day and his legs were throbbing by the time he reached the road. He grimaced and sucked in a great lungful of air, berating himself for being so frail. Even so, he checked his pace and took it slower than usual on the long walk home.

"Robb?"

The voice startled him more than it should have. He hadn't known anyone on the train and he was sure that none of the commuters had followed him from the station. He spun round too quickly and the movement sent an agonising cramp up his right leg. Robb gritted his teeth against the pain and found himself staring at the enormous figure of Kellie Downs. The sevener was in full uniform and closing fast, a troubled expression on his face.

"I need you to be straight with me Robb. What are you mixed up in?"

The question took him off guard and for a beat he had no answer. The sevener leaned closer and the next thing he said was almost a whisper.

"They're going to raid your house. Now. Do you understand what I'm saying?"

Robb thought about their last conversation on the town hall steps. The unspoken doubt that had lingered on from the past. "Have *you* done this?"

Kellie's face twitched. Robb had seen it many times, usually before the big man lost his temper and someone else lost their teeth.

"I'll let that one go," he said. "I don't know why they're coming for you, but the warrant came through an hour ago and they're keen to get it done. I've managed to tag one of mine along, but he can't help you if they find something."

Robb felt his chest constricting. He'd always been so careful to stay under the radar. Thirty-three years he'd played by the rules and all for nothing. An image of Ryan's room and the loose floorboard flashed into his mind.

"Shit." He spun round and lurched towards home.

"I'll do what I can to slow them down," Kellie shouted after him.

Robb gave a nod of thanks and then loped away. When he reached the static checkpoint, he was already breathing hard and a sheen of sweat had appeared upon his forehead. Luckily, the gunnerman was a regular and Robb gave him a pained smile.

"Always in a rush," he said conversationally.

The gunnerman made a snort of agreement and then passed his card back through the glass screen. Robb forced himself to walk calmly beyond the turn of the road, only then breaking into a jog once again.

He made it home in half the time it usually took and staggered to the door. His legs burned hot with lactic acid and felt as though they could buckle at any moment. Even so, he couldn't afford to rest for a moment. He burst through the front door, calling for Eliza with the last of his breath before collapsing in a fit of coughing.

"Oh my God," she said, rushing through from the kitchen. "What's happened?"

The sound of a diesel engine reached them from outside. Robb pushed her away and went into the lounge where he lifted the net curtains and glanced onto the street.

"Shit," he hissed.

"Robb? What is it? You're scaring me?"

"The gunnermen are here. It's a raid."

Eliza's hands trembled and she stared open-mouthed.

"Listen to me," Robb continued. "In the corner of Ryan's room there's a loose floorboard. You'll find pamphlets, magazines and a covert camera hidden there."

Two car doors slammed shut and he heard footsteps on the path.

"Go," he said. "I'll stall them."

"Okay," Eliza mumbled, then she dashed up the stairs.

A furious hammering set up at the front door, rattling through the house. Robb checked his appearance in the hall mirror and slowed his breathing. After a moments pause, the banging sounded up again and a low voice shouted through his letterbox. "It's the gunnermen. Open your door."

The unmistakable outline of a sevener drifted past the lounge window, presumably to guard the back door. At least Kellie had been true to his word. When the third bout of knocking shook the front door, Robb quickly untucked his shirt and loosened the belt on his trousers. He opened the door and then went through the charade of re-tucking himself in front of the gunnerman that was waiting there.

"Sorry, I was taking a leak."

He seemed oblivious to the explanation though and shouldered past Robb into the hallway. Before he shut the door, Robb caught sight of a jeep parked outside. There was a second gunnerman waiting in the driver's seat who seemed content to wait outside.

"What can I do for you?" he said obligingly.

"We've had a report that your son, Ryan Calloway, is involved in an anti-government group."

"That's ridiculous."

"Watch it," the gunnerman warned, his face only inches from Robb's. Despite the provocation, he kept his expression neutral, using every ounce of self-control to lock down the anger he felt rising in his gut. Eliza still needed time.

"Can I at least ask what he's supposed to have done?"

"No. You can take me to his room or get out of the way."

Robb made a note of the twin crosses on his epaulette. "Of course I will Sergeant. But don't I get to see a warrant if you want to search the house."

The gunnerman shoved his forearm into Robb's chest, bending his back the wrong way across the bannister.

"One more word and you're coming with me, you old bastard."

"It's alright Robb," a voice called from overhead. Eliza appeared at the landing and gave a charming smile to the gunnerman.

"Please Sergeant, he doesn't mean to be obstructive. We're just not used to having gunnermen here."

"Bollocks," the sergeant scoffed. "I've seen his pre-cons. He knows what's what."

Before the conversation deteriorated further, the front door slid open and an imposing figure ducked beneath the lintel. It was impossible not to be impressed by how huge he was in the confined space. Even the gunnermen momentarily checked his attitude.

"I'm going up," he said, shoving Robb as he stalked past. "You watch him."

The sevener raised one eyebrow at the command but said nothing. In a matter of seconds, the house was echoing to the sounds of a search. There were several bangs followed by an enormous thud that shook the ceiling, showering dust and flecks of plaster from around the lightbulb.

Unable to control himself, Robb strode towards the staircase until a large hand settled on his shoulder. He spun around angrily, but the sevener just gave a placid shake of his head.

"Kellie told me you had a temper." He pointed to the ceiling where the thuds and bangs had resumed. "If you start arguing though, that one'll lock you up and tear the house apart anyway. So just take a deep breath. They're only things."

Reluctantly he gave a nod of agreement and only then did the sevener remove the hand from his shoulder.

"So what's this about?" Robb said eventually. "Why are they here? Why now?"

The sevener shrugged his massive shoulders. "You're better off asking Kellie about that. He just asked me to keep the peace."

"And how's that going?" Robb said testily as another thud shook the ceiling.

"No one's been shot yet."

When the gunnerman clumped downstairs empty handed, Robb was waiting in the hallway. The sevener had been making small talk and trying to explain why the winter snows this year would be the worst for a generation.

All Robb's attention was on the gunnerman though and judging by the scowl on his face, he'd found nothing. For a moment he dared to hope that the worst was over. The ice had held beneath their feet one more day. That was until the door opened and Ryan came into the already crowded hallway.

CHAPTER 40

"What's going on?" Ryan said, his voice cold as winter.

It was the first time Robb had seen him in nearly three days and although his face was beaten up and clothes dishevelled, he'd lost none of that defiance in his eyes. It was exactly what the gunnerman was after. All they needed was an excuse.

"Are you Ryan Calloway?"

"What's going on?" Ryan repeated, looking only at his dad.

"Ryan, just talk to the sergeant and answer his question," Robb said quietly. "It'll be alright."

"Are you Ryan Calloway?" the gunnerman repeated.

"I don't have to tell you anything," Ryan snarled and then left the way he had come in.

The gunnerman was on him immediately, relishing the chance to vent some anger. He kicked the back of Ryan's knee which sent him sprawling to the concrete. Ryan leapt to his feet and squared up to the sergeant. A gloved fist thumped him hard and Ryan staggered backwards, clutching his jaw.

Robb limped outside and recognised all too well the expression of unthinking anger that had appeared on his son's face. The gunnerman saw it too and snatched the steel baton from his belt. In one quick arc he swung it down towards Ryan's skull.

Robb caught the metal rod and halted its fall. The gunnerman wheeled round to face him and delivered a solid head-butt to the edge of his cheekbone. Robb's face flashed with pain, but he never loosened his grip.

The sergeant tried to wrench it free, but Robb clung on so fiercely that his arm just shook up and down. With his left hand, the sergeant swung at Robb, hitting him once again on the cheek. The older man doubled over and at that moment Ryan ran forwards. Instantly Robb was up and thrust his free arm at his son, palm outwards.

"Stay back," he yelled.

If this was to end as he hoped, then Ryan had to hold his temper long enough for someone else to intervene. His son continued to rage though, and somewhere nearby Eliza screamed as the gunnerman threw a final punch. Robb braced himself for an impact, but it never came. Instead, a huge arm had hooked into the gunnerman's elbow, stopping the attack as easily as a teacher would settle a playground fight.

"Enough," the sevener boomed. "No officer of the Premier shall harm a citizen of these lands without due provocation."

The gunnerman was stunned. He untangled his arm from the bigger man and even released his hold on the baton.

"You can't do that," he sputtered. "I've got a sworn warrant for the boy."

"To search his room. Which you did and very thoroughly from what I heard. Did you find anything?"

The gunnerman's jaw worked silently for a few moments. "But the boy tried to escape lawful custody and then the old bastard helped him resist arrest."

"I didn't see that. The boy was never in lawful custody. So he couldn't have been escaping. And if he was never in lawful custody," the sevener reasoned calmly, "then there was no arrest to resist. As far as I'm aware, there's no law against a father stopping his son from getting a cracked skull."

In the silence that followed, Robb passed the steel baton to the sevener who in turn offered it to the gunnerman. It was snatched back and the gunnermen held them with a murderous expression, eyeballing first Robb and then Ryan.

"You'll see me again," he warned. "I won't forget what happened here."

"I sincerely hope not," the sevener smiled, still as water.

With a final curse, the gunnerman stomped back to his jeep and sped away.

"There goes my lift back," the sevener sighed. "I dare say there'll be repercussions for today. But what's done is done." He leaned closer to Robb, seeing the blood on his face. "You'll want to get that eye looked at. He's made a hell of a mess."

"I'll patch him up," Eliza said, stepping up to her husband and examining the injury. The entire right side of his face was swelling up and the skin around the eye had sliced open.

The sevener gazed upwards and smiled at the first white flakes that tumbled from the sky and settled on his deep blue tunic.

"At least I was right about the snows," he smiled. Then he placed one arm around Ryan's shoulders and stooped to whisper in his ear.

As the words were spoken Ryan turned to his father and for the briefest of moments Robb saw his son from five years ago. For those few seconds, all the confusion and all the fear and all the pain were laid bare in his eyes. Robb took a tentative step forward, but then the walls came up and Ryan backed away.

"I've just come for some clothes," he said quietly. "I won't be in your way for long."

Avoiding eye-contact, he returned to the house and went upstairs. Eliza stifled a sob and Robb drew her into an embrace, but when he turned back to thank the sevener, he had already disappeared.

CHAPTER 41

"What were they looking for?" Alia said.

"I don't know, but they absolutely trashed my room. My desk was overturned, the curtain rail ripped from the wall and the bed smashed into pieces. They even sliced open my mattress and pulled out the insides."

It was about an hour since Ryan had returned from his parents' house with a rucksack of belongings. He had hugged his mum before going, but nothing more had passed between him and his father.

"How was John?" Alia asked quietly. She'd been so upset after what happened in the Trade District that afternoon. Even more so when she'd realised that he and John were brothers.

"He wasn't there. He hasn't been home since…since you spoke to him." Ryan sighed deeply. "At least he didn't have to see the gunnermen."

"I suppose so. Although it would have been nice for you both to make up."

"We will. I'll go and see him this week. He'll understand."

While Ryan was out, Alia had made a token effort of cleaning the lounge and kitchen. The clothes were either folded or deposited into a wicker basket and a stack of crockery was standing on the kitchen side while another load soaked in the sink. They were lying on the sofa side-by-side, legs entwined, staring at the empty fireplace.

"I still don't get why they came. Why would they suddenly pick your house?"

Ryan had wrestled with the same thought since he'd seen that gunnerman jeep outside the house. He wondered if the two gunnermen from the train had reported him. But why would they give his card to Gerren? And why bother with a search warrant at all? Why not just arrest him for how he'd acted on the train?

Then his thoughts had turned to Gerren, wondering if the ex-gunnerman had turned him in. He replayed their conversation from the storage shed to check if he had let some detail slip, something that could have made the old guard suspicious.

Again, Ryan dismissed the idea. Why would he have shared the flask of tea and told him those old stories only to turn him in later. In fact, hadn't Gerren given away much more about himself than Ryan? He realised that Alia was still waiting for an answer.

"I'm not sure why they came," but as soon as he said it, Ryan's thoughts fell to his dad. Hadn't he been the one that betrayed his best friends all those years ago? The last time they spoke he had been furious about Ryan bringing a covert camera into the house.

Then he pictured the swelling and blood around his dad's face after he'd taken those punches for him. He remembered too what the sevener had whispered on the doorstep. Ryan shook his head as though disturbing a fly. There was just so much that didn't make sense.

In any case, he was more worried about all his stuff that had disappeared. The pamphlets that Brynne had lent him and the wreckage of the covert camera were missing. Worse still, his journal had gone too.

"Ryan? What are you involved in?"

He had known this question was coming, but even now was unsure how to answer.

"What do you mean?" he stalled.

Alia rolled around to face him and arched one eyebrow.

"You know what I mean," she said. "The first day we met, you were hiding from the gunnermen. You had those posters, remember? You don't go to school and you don't work, and yet somehow you're always busy."

He tried to think of an excuse. Something that would explain it all without letting his secrets go. He could almost hear Brynne's voice in his head.

Never tell outsiders. We can't trust them. We are alone in this.

Ryan was tired though. Tired of being alone and tired of keeping secrets.

"You're right," he said quietly. "I haven't been honest with you. I'm part of a group of people who are fighting against Premier Talis."

He nearly laughed out loud when he heard himself say it. To her credit though, Alia kept quiet and Ryan took that as a signal to continue. He always thought it would be more difficult to tell her. That he would end up hiding parts from her. Once he had started though, it was impossible to stop. He told her about Brynne and the work they did together. He told her about the forger and how Brynne had killed him for being an informer. Through it all, she listened without comment, only withdrawing when he spoke about his dad's past and how he had betrayed his friends to save his own life.

"How do you know all that?" she asked.

"I saw his confession on an old recording at Brynne's."

"I don't understand," Alia said. "Why would he show you that?"

"He didn't. I just kind of found it when he was out."

"Did you ask your dad about it?"

"No."

"Maybe you should."

Ryan laid his head back against the arm of the sofa. His breathing was slow and steady and his muscles relaxed. The weight of Alia's body was comforting and for the first time he could remember, he felt *free*. He gazed at the girl beside him, marvelling at what he had just unloaded on her and how unquestioning her loyalty seemed.

Alia's eyes flicked open and she raised her chin. Ryan angled his face until their lips met and they shared a slow, deep kiss. He drew back, resting his forehead against hers while a tremble of nerves rippled through his body.

"Thank you," he whispered.

In the dead of night, he lay awake on the sofa listening to Alia as she tried to comfort her father. He had woken the house with a dreadful howling and almost an hour later he was still whimpering like an animal whenever she tried to leave the room. Despite the curfew, her mother had left the house when the noise first started. Neither of them tried to stop her.

Eventually, Alia returned to the lounge where Ryan was lacing his boots. "Where are you going?" she said, a note of hurt in her voice.

"Don't worry, I'm coming back, I just need to see someone."

"Now? It's the middle of the night. There's a curfew."

Ryan gave what he hoped was a reassuring smile. "That's why I need to go now. It's the best chance I've got of seeing him."

"Is it because of my dad? Because he'll sleep now, I promise."

Ryan stood up and pulled her into his arms. They kissed, softly at first and then with more passion. He stroked his fingers through her hair and then over the smooth skin of her neck. "I'm coming back," he said quietly. "I just need to sort something out."

"Can't it wait until morning?"

He shook his head.

"I won't sleep now. Not until it's done. Besides, you need the rest more than I do right now."

Reluctantly Alia agreed and then allowed herself to be fussed over as she took Ryan's place on the sofa. He gently swaddled her in the threadbare blanket and kissed her forehead.

"Are you going to see Brynne?" she said quietly.

He nodded.

"Please don't go."

"I'm going to talk to him. That's all."

"Will you tell him that you're not going to do it anymore?"

Ryan's jaw clenched tight. He didn't want to lie, but he still wasn't sure what he was going to say to Brynne.

"I'll sort it out," he said. "Get some rest."

She closed her eyes and gave a contented murmur in

response. Ryan had no doubt that she would be asleep before he reached the end of the drive.

Even though the snow had been trying for hours, once outside he saw that only a light dusting showed on the side streets and the main roads were completely clear. Ryan was thankful for that, not wanting to leave a trail of footprints for the gunnermen to follow.

It was a strange kind of compulsion that made him want to find Brynne now. So much had happened since he had been sent from the chapel and Ryan felt compelled to find Brynne and report in. There was the fight with the gunnermen; the conversation with Gerren at Obern station; finding out that John had been following him and then of course the raid at his house. Ryan's head was spinning, and he needed the old man's counsel more than ever. As he approached in the darkness though, the chapel - that had once been so welcoming - cut a forbidding silhouette in the struggling moonlight.

Snow had gathered more easily here on the cold stonework of the slumbering building. Ryan pushed the heavy wooden door inwards and tensed as the swollen wood scraped over the flagstones. Moving inside he groped in the darkness with one hand until it rested on the back of the first wooden pew.

"Brynne," he hissed. "It's me."

Overhead a bird fluttered free of its rafter and sought sanctuary deeper in the church. Ryan crept forwards, waiting for his eyes to readjust to the near total darkness. From behind him came a scuffle of quick feet and then a hand clamped around Ryan's neck, throwing him down onto the bench. He struggled against the grip, but it was useless, and Ryan felt the pressure on his windpipe grow.

"You've some nerve Calloway," a voice growled above him.

"Brynne," Ryan gasped. "Stop. Please."

The old man kept him pinned though.

"I let you into my house. Took care of you. Dragged you away from that traitor of a father and for what? So you can sell me out, just like he did?"

Just as Ryan saw white spots dancing on the edge of his vision, the old man's grip loosened and he was able to slide out, clutching at his throat and gasping for breath.

"Why did you do it?" His voice was barely audible.

"I don't know what you're talking about Brynne. Honestly I don't."

The old man didn't respond straightaway, but instead rose slowly from the bench. The wood cracked and echoed like a gunshot through the empty chapel.

"Follow me."

They walked in silence towards the chancery and Ryan knew instantly that something was wrong. The tapestry that usually concealed the secret doorway was now lying in tatters on the stone floor.

"You first," Brynne said, standing aside.

Ryan paused at the top of the stone staircase, his heart hammering in his chest. He had never before felt afraid of the old man. Not really. Not even when he had shot Caylin for being a traitor. Yet with each step he took, he imagined the cold muzzle of a gun appearing at the base of his skull.

He reached the bottom step and fumbled for the gas lamp that was already burning on its lowest light. Ryan twisted the collar valve and light flooded the cellar, revealing the source of Brynne's anger. His quarters had been ransacked and all his belongings destroyed. The newspaper clippings, the rows of books and the stacks of film reels were either shredded or strewn across the floor. His bed, desk and bookshelves were upended and smashed and the room was barely recognisable as the home it had once been.

"Gunnermen came Ryan. Here. To the chapel."

"Brynne, they came for me too."

"Don't give me that. You think I don't know what's going on here? I've got an informant in the gunnermen comms station. They tell me if any of my lads are stopped or arrested. Wednesday night your card was scanned on the trains out of Straybeck, but you never got off at the other end. Then Thursday you're scanned again but on the outskirts this time. You disappear for a day and then your house gets raided and then a few hours later the gunnermen are kicking through my door too."

"You think I informed on you?"

"Didn't you?"

Ryan was shocked at the question. "Of course I didn't. Why would I?"

"I've known all sorts of people broken by the gunnermen. People just like you."

"I was never even arrested though."

Brynne said nothing as he slowly sifted through the debris. Suddenly his eyes lit upon a bottle of whisky, somehow unbroken amongst the wreckage. He un-stoppered the cork and took three long gulps.

"You saw the undercover gunnerman the other day, didn't you? Before I sent you away."

Ryan nodded.

"How did you know? Was it the car?"

"The earpiece."

"Smart lad." He took another mouthful of whisky and

then offered the bottle to Ryan. "Do you think I'm with them? Is that why you did it? You think I'm playing both sides?"

"Of course I don't."

"He was one of my sources Ryan. A young lad I recruited eight years ago from the Slum District. He tells me what's happening in Karasard and then passes my orders to the other cells I have there."

"Brynne, you've got to believe me. I haven't told them anything. Whoever sent the gunnermen to my house must be the ones that sent them after you."

Brynne gave a frustrated sigh and reached towards the back of his waistband. In one awful moment Ryan watched him produce a pistol and rest it against his leg.

"I want to believe you," he said quietly. "God knows I do. But I've been here before. Many, many times and it never ends well."

"Brynne," he swallowed hard, trying to work some saliva back into his mouth. "Please don't do this. I never told them anything. They never even asked me anything. On the train the other day they thought I was sleeping rough. That's why they checked my card."

He pointed at the purple bruises on his face.

"They threw me off the train while it was moving and I had to walk back to Straybeck. That was why they scanned me at the outskirts."

Ryan paused, trying to slow his breathing. He looked for some sign that Brynne believed him, but the old man's face was as unreadable as ever.

"I even came here. I was looking for you and..." Ryan frantically recalled the details of that day. "I ate some of your food, over here," he pointed to the far end of the cellar. "And then I borrowed some money. From the bowl."

He fished inside one pocket and brought out some irons that he had brought from his bedroom earlier that day. "You can have them back."

Still Brynne remained motionless, the gun never wavering. Ryan nervously stacked the coins into a neat pile on one of the shelves. "What did you tell the gunnermen at your house Ryan?"

"Nothing," he shouted. "I swear. There was only one gunnerman and one sevener. They'd already finished searching when I got there. He tried to arrest me but…" Ryan felt it would only make things worse to mention his Dad. "The sevener was with him and he said the arrest wasn't legal as they'd found nothing."

"So they never took you in?"

"No. I went back into the house, got some clothes and some money for you and then I went to Alia's. I had no idea they were coming for you too. I'd have warned you if I'd known."

Brynne tapped one finger against the barrel of the gun, contemplating all he had heard.

"I want to believe you," he said eventually. "I really do. But you've been so different lately. You hardly come round anymore and when you do, you're always questioning, always going against what I ask."

"I don't mean to be like that. I just…" Ryan chose his next words carefully. "I can't shake this feeling that I should be doing more. Doing something meaningful that makes people sit up and take notice."

Brynne took his time mulling over the words and

eventually flicked his head in the direction of the staircase. "Go on."

Ryan hesitated, not wanting to show his back to the older man. Brynne saw the delay for what it was and tucked the gun out of sight with a long sigh.

"I could never shoot you Ryan," and there was real sadness in his eyes when he strode past. He paused at the bottom step as though he had more to say, but then shook it off and moved out of sight. Ryan followed in a daze and climbed towards the main chapel. When they reached the top of the staircase though, instead of turning into the chancery, Brynne hooked his fingers into a groove at the corner of the wall. With a practised movement he felt up and down the slender gap that ran from floor to ceiling. On closer inspection, Ryan saw that the bricks of one wall had not been laid square with the other.

There followed a sharp click and to his amazement the entire wall slid forwards at an angle. Ryan saw that it was hinged like a door from the opposite corner and the supposedly ancient bricks were in fact just a replica less than two inches thick. It was too dark to see past the opening, but such unspoiled blackness suggested a large room within.

"What is this place?"

"It's the old priests' quarters," Brynne said, stepping inside. "Apparently the gunnermen aren't as good as they think when it comes to searching buildings."

He lit a match and Ryan heard the hiss of a gas lamp followed by a low *whoosh* as the flame took hold. He felt a flutter of nerves when the orange glow finally pushed back the shadows. On each wall, photographs had been fastened showing dozens of stern young faces. Alongside each one was a small newspaper clipping that had been preserved in glass. He scanned across the first few.

Simon Carter – arrested and executed for sedition.

Lawrence Ranil – executed for refusing allegiance to His Greatness, Premier Talis.

Nicholas Trevallin – executed for promoting sedition in the city of Karasard.

Ryan flicked from one face to the next, seeing both the photo and then the reflection of himself within the frame. Smoke from the dead match drifted in the air and then Brynne moved alongside him bringing the light towards their faces.

"I hadn't planned on showing you this yet," the old man said. "But I think it's something you need to see."

"Who are they?"

"They're my boys." Brynne said. "Each one of them brave beyond measure." He crossed the room and stared at three photos that seemed newer than the rest. "These were the latest. You saw the procession on Saintsday, right?"

Ryan's mind flicked back to those sombre young men and women who were paraded around the fire before being led to a quiet death.

"Three of those poor souls were in my group. These three men here."

The old man's voice was hollow, his eyes dead. He pulled a table from the sidewall and placed it in the centre of the room. There were two candles on top and he struck another match to light them. Lying between the candles was a leather-bound book, its surface decorated with ornate metal. He beckoned Ryan over to him and opened the book to reveal a ledger of names.

"A book of Martyrs," he said. The names had dates that went back years.

"You mean all of these," Ryan looped his hand in the air to indicate the photos. "You knew them all? They're all dead?"

"Each one of them was murdered for their beliefs. Either caught by the gunnermen or sentenced to death by Talis for refusing the oath." The oath of allegiance was publicly sworn by every citizen when they turned eighteen.

The old man took a pen from the table and began writing below the final entry. The words flowed in a smooth copperplate style that seemed impossible from those thick and callused hands. He wrote three names, one after another, while Ryan waited at his shoulder.

"There are so many," he said.

"They made the ultimate sacrifice. Like I told you, brave beyond measure."

The room suddenly felt very oppressive and Ryan wanted nothing more than to get out of there. Out of respect though, he stayed and searched the photos in silence. Eventually, Brynne blew out the candle on the desk and put a hand on his shoulder. They walked back into the chancery and Ryan waited for the old man to secure the room behind its false wall. Once it was done, the old man took a seat on the front pew and motioned for Ryan to join him.

"I know the path you're walking, and I know it's a lonely one. But it has to be that way. Don't you see that?"

"I don't," Ryan said, at last finding his voice. "I don't see why I can't meet the other people like me. We could have meetings, help each other plan, do protests, do….something."

Brynne lit a cigarette and the match pooled red and orange around his face. "Did I ever tell you what it was like when I first started this?" Although it was a question, he spoke as if Ryan wasn't even there. "It was all so different then. Grittier. More real somehow. There were four of us in the group, until I asked your father to join us."

Ryan was stunned. "My father?"

"We'd been working on the plan for months. I thought I'd taken every precaution, but I guess I wasn't as thorough back then as I am now. The night the gunnermen came I was late to the safehouse. I'd been followed across town by an agent and forced to double back to dodge the checkpoints. You know what it's like. By the time I reached them, it was all over and my friends were dead." Brynne's eyes suddenly hardened. "Except your father."

Ryan felt sick. "How did he do it?"

"The details? I don't know. It might not even have been him that tipped them off to begin with," he said. "It could have been *me* who missed something. All I know is that he was the only one left alive. A month after that, at least a dozen other activists were dead across Carlsgard and Kilvaren."

"How did you escape?"

"I got out of Karasard and spent the next six years bedding down in the gutters of Willensbrough and Priest. He half smiled again and flicked his eyes over the chapel. "I've really gone places since then." There was no humour in his voice.

"My whole life was torn away and scattered to the winds. Until that happens Ryan, you can't even try to understand how I felt. I hope you never will."

Everything was silent and Ryan felt as empty as the church around them. Brynne had slopped thirty years of guilt onto his shoulders.

"I don't blame you for what happened Ryan," he said.

"But that's why I keep you all at arm's length from each other. If any one person is caught, the rest of the group survives. You understand now?"

Ryan understood all too well and he was ashamed of the reason.

"Anyway," Brynne said, "we're out of time."

"You're throwing me out?"

"No way, today you're with me. You wanted to see more? Well that's what you're going to get."

"I can't. I have to get back."

"Your plans just changed. Today you're helping me in Karasard."

"Karasard?"

He nodded. "At the town square. You know what that means, right?"

"I think so."

"Then let's get moving."

Brynne reached beneath the bench and pulled out two identical canvass satchels. He passed one to Ryan and looped the other across his chest like a bandolier. It had a surprising weight to it and Ryan gave him a questioning look.

"Just something we'll need later. Come on."

He turned out the light and led Ryan onto the dark, Straybeck streets.

CHAPTER 42

It was three-thirty in the morning. Robb was awake and alone sitting at the kitchen table. Eliza had been called into the hospital and John had gone to bed hours ago. The boy had been heartbroken when he saw what the gunnermen did to his room. Almost as much as when he'd seen the bruises on his dad's face.

Robb had cleared the debris from the bedroom floor and made up a mattress in the space. When he finally turned off the bedroom light, John was still sobbing quietly.

Robb's head began to nod and he jolted awake. Part of him was still waiting fearfully for the gunnermen to return, while the other part was hoping it would be Ryan. He massaged the bridge of his nose and with a groan of effort pushed out of his chair and limped into the hallway. His knees cracked angrily and the bones in his left shin felt as though they were working against one another. He paused at the bottom step and slowly bent each leg at the knee so that the joints ground together like broken rocks. After an initial surge of pain, it gave him some relief and Robb turned to the mirror that was hanging on the opposite wall. A large bruise had swallowed his right eye socket and Eliza had stuck a piece of gauze over the split. He prodded at it gently and felt the skin tighten as he moved his mouth up and down.

With a deep breath, he unfastened the buttons on his shirt allowing it fall open. Immediately his eyes were drawn to the angry, red scars that coloured his chest and neck. For the first time in years, Robb studied his disfigured reflection, tracing his fingers over the bulging lines and melted skin. He closed his eyes and remembered the damp grey walls of The Cathedral. How they chained him to the archways in the upper cells and laughed at his screams.

Robb was swinging by the wrists from a thick knotted rope. As he swayed backwards, his body passed through the open archway and into the darkness above Lake Stretten. These brief moments were like a sweet wine. Then his pendulum swung back inside and Robb's body was driven against a glowing metal rod. Ashgate, the gaoler, was holding it between them like a swordsman. Robb had watched them turn that metal poker through the fire and now they were doing the same to him.

He tried to wriggle free of his ropes, praying that he would fall from the archway and smash his skull on the ground a hundred feet below. He flip-flopped like a speared fish while Ashgate smiled at the screams and tears. He waited patiently for Robb to wear himself out.

"Are you ready yet?" he asked gently. "Will you do it?"

Robb snivelled and choked on a mixture of phlegm and blood. He knew that Ashgate enjoyed these vague questions and so he was resolved not to engage. Punishment for an unsatisfactory answer was always swift and brutal.

"Come on Robb," Ashgate continued in a voice like

honey. "Think about why you're still here. Why would I be keeping you alive? Why would I still bother hurting you like this?"

Robb swayed back and forth, his head thick with pain. Blood trickled down the front of his mutilated chest and collected on the floor in the grooves between the large stone slabs.

"Why do you think you're here?" Ashgate returned the poker to the glowing coals and showed his empty hands in a placating manner. He gave an inviting smile and in spite of himself, Robb found he was compelled to give an answer. "To punish me?"

"Partly," he nodded. "It's partly that." He was standing to one side but swayed in time with Robb so that he could keep eye-contact. "Look at that face," he said like a proud parent. "Not a mark on it."

Robb instantly jolted back, expecting the gaoler to smash his teeth or gouge an eye, but Ashgate just smiled indulgently. "No Robbert. We won't be touching that face. Not now."

A chilling thought occurred to Robb and his mind groped for a timeline of his imprisonment. At first, he had been interrogated about the planned attack and the rest of his group. So far as he could guess, that had abruptly stopped maybe two days after his capture. Since then, Robb had been beaten and tortured but not questioned. Another memory clicked into place and Robb realised what the change had been.

They said you were dead. I didn't know Robb.

Ashgate smiled like a cat. "I think you've got it."

He guessed that Farren told them everything before they killed him. Robb had no energy left to be angry though. Farren had settled his own debt and right then it didn't seem like a bad trade off. Robb lifted his head to stare at Ashgate.

"Kill me," he murmured.

"What? Kill *you*? Oh no Robb. We need you. The Premier himself has deemed it. And that leaves me with only one unanswered question. Are you going to do it?"

"Do what?" Robb screamed, voice cracking. The repetition was maddening but Ashgate's smile never wavered.

"Unmask yourself as the double agent that you are. Tell the world how you chose to sell out your own side. Explain how you will work tirelessly to fight against the traitor Colonel Stephens until he is captured or killed."

Robb shook his head, pride hardening his glare. The idea of branding himself a traitor had dredged a reserve of strength he thought they'd knocked out of him.

"Don't be so hasty," Ashgate warned. "Think about the repercussions of your answer."

Robb inhaled the stench of his own burned flesh and looked down at the melted skin on his chest. Both legs were broken and bound in thick bandages which were soiled in blood and excrement. In that moment – naively as it turned out – Robb guessed there wasn't much else they could do to him. He stared at Ashgate, meeting him with unblinking eyes and tight lips.

The gaoler shook his head sadly. "I'm afraid you're not going to like what happens next."

CHAPTER 43

AFTER LEAVING THE Chapel, Brynne was even more cautious than usual and zigzagged across town towards the train station. The snow was heavier than an hour ago and wherever possible Ryan walked in the gutter where it hadn't fully settled.

"Save your shoes," Brynne said. "The snow will cover our tracks quickly enough."

They travelled the rest of the journey in silence and by good luck, or good planning, they stayed clear of any roaming checkpoints. Although the old man hadn't said, Ryan guessed what was waiting for them at Karasard. It was a new month and they were going to the town square. It could only be the oath ceremony. Before they reached the entrance to the Worker District Station, Brynne unzipped his coat and repositioned the canvas satchel he had brought with him. Ryan tried to conceal the contents as much as possible around his hips and stomach, but whatever was inside had an awkward feel to it and dug into his ribs as he walked.

"Which ID have you got?"

"Both."

"Use the real one. We can't risk those gunnermen catching you using a different name."

"What if they try to throw me off the train again?"

"I'll sort it."

Ryan doubted whether even Brynne would be able to talk his way past those two, but he said nothing. The journey took over an hour and his nerves rattled worse than the old carriages. He found himself wondering if Alia was still awake and if she was thinking about him. He doubted that she'd approve of what he was doing now, which only added to his worries. He tried to block them out when the factory lights of Karasard twinkled through the train windows. Their speed dropped to a crawl as they approached the station.

Despite the early hour, Karasard Central was already abuzz with activity. Platform attendants were sweeping the concourse, while small pockets of workers gathered on the cross-city platforms which led to the other underground stations.

"They're stokers," Brynne said. "Always first to arrive at the factories."

"What do they do?"

"If a furnace goes out it stops production for days. Their job is to make sure it never happens. Twelve-hour shifts stoking the flames. Poor bastards."

Ryan studied one group as he passed by. They were small and unremarkable men, waiting like stones, as though they refused to waste energy in conversation.

The snows hadn't reached Karasard yet, but under the yellow streetlights Ryan could see the occasional flake drifting past. Together, he and Brynne moved towards the heart of the city until the main square came into view. The old man gazed up at the clock tower.

"We've a bit of a wait," he said.

"What time will they get here?"

He shrugged. "Ceremony's always at eight. But the families arrive early. You ever seen one before?"

Ryan shook his head. He knew that the oaths of allegiance were taken at the top of the town hall steps. He'd been taught the words at school for as long as he could remember but had never actually seen the real ceremony take place.

"Well you're going to remember this day for the rest of your life then."

The town square was completely enclosed except for the checkpoints on each corner. The streets had been widened here to allow hundreds of military vehicles to drive in and out each year for the parade. Along each side of the square was an unbroken block of three-storey buildings. At first glance, they looked to Ryan like the grand houses he had seen in Old Straybeck. Maybe at one time the wealthy and important people of Karasard had lived here. Now they were inhabited by law firms and financiers.

They approached the southwest checkpoint and saw two gunnermen waiting at the booth. Brynne suddenly stopped and unhooked the heavy satchel from Ryan's shoulder, placing it around his own neck.

"I'll deal with this," he said quietly. "Wait a minute and then follow me through."

Ryan wondered what Brynne would do if he were searched but knew the old man could look after himself. He counted a slow sixty and then headed for the checkpoint. As he presented his card though, the gunnerman stepped out from the booth.

"Against the wall," he ordered sharply.

"My card's clear," Ryan said but it only earned him a swipe around the head to encourage his compliance. He was made to stand with his hands on the wall while one gunnerman patted him down. With a practised movement, he kicked Ryan's feet wider apart, knocking him off balance before going through his pockets and throwing anything he found to the floor.

"Take off your boots."

Ryan kicked them off and the gunnerman checked inside each one, pulling out the soles and banging them against the wall. Finally satisfied, he allowed Ryan to retrieve his belongings and pass through to the town square. By the time he had fastened his boots up, his socks were sodden and both feet like blocks of ice.

"What was that about?" he fumed.

"It's an oath day," Brynne said. "Sometimes there are people who don't agree with the Premier. And sometimes they bring weapons to make their point. Take it as a compliment. You must look like a dangerous man."

"They didn't search you though."

"Looks can be deceiving."

Inside the square, a metal barrier had been erected at the bottom of the town hall steps to create a cordon around the oath takers.

"Over here," Brynne led him to an alcove between two immense stone pillars and deposited one of the satchels into a nook he found there. "Wait here. I'll be back in a bit."

"Where are you going?"

Brynne pointed to a band of people that were waiting at the far checkpoint although Ryan couldn't make out their features from so far away. "His name's Arris. He's a good man. Everyone will see that today."

Then he stalked across the cobbles and Arris crossed the

square to meet him. As he drew closer, Ryan saw a young man with angular features and pale skin. In fact, everything about him seemed stooped and worn out. Arris removed his wire-rimmed glasses and cleaned them as he approached. He and Brynne shook hands stiffly and spoke a few words.

Behind them, a small group of people approached from the checkpoint and Arris introduced them to the old man. Ryan guessed they were his parents and maybe an uncle too. Saddest of all was the little girl who trailed behind, no older than six or seven.

Brynne offered a handshake to the first male, but it was pointedly ignored. More words were exchanged and then the uncle lunged forwards. Arris checked him with one arm and was able to restrain him until at last he broke free and stomped back to the checkpoint and out of the square.

Brynne gave Arris a pat on the shoulder and then returned to the steps. The younger man lingered behind to embrace his mother and then shake hands with his father. Ryan watched him put one knee on the wet ground and open his arms to the little girl. Instead of coming forwards though, she clung to her mother's legs, hiding her face from view. After his entreaties were ignored, Arris reluctantly stood and walked away.

He hadn't gone more than a few paces before the little girl let out a heartbreaking sob and ran after him. Arris caught her against the front of his legs, smoothing her blonde hair and trying to soothe her tears. She refused to unfasten her grip though and eventually the mother and father took an arm each and pulled her away so that the young man could leave.

When Arris arrived at the stone pillars he gave Ryan a hard stare. "Who's this?"

"It's a friend. He's okay."

"No friends today Brynne, just family."

Ryan didn't blame him for that, and he was almost glad to remove himself. After all, what do you say to a man with less than an hour to live?

"Don't go far," Brynne said flatly.

Before too long, a small crowd had gathered at the steps and Ryan stood beside them listening to each conversation in turn. The oath-takers themselves were kept in a separate area near to the pillars where Brynne had been waiting with Arris. Three gunnermen were standing beside them, chatting quietly while two more officials strutted around organising everyone.

Eventually, the oath-takers were herded into formation at the foot of the steps. Ryan searched for any sign of Brynne but couldn't see him. His eyes focused on Arris though and watched him fade down the line and take position at the very end. The others said nothing, and the officials seemed not to have noticed.

As the ceremony began, Ryan made his way back to the pillar and waited beside Brynne's satchel. The lead official called for attention and then began his speech.

"These twelve young citizens of Karasard are here today to confirm their loyalty to The Unified City States and our most Supreme Leader. Through his benevolent wisdom, they shall become full citizens of these kingdoms, with all the rights and all the expectations that follow from it."

Ryan's brow furrowed at the hypocrisy of it. There was no free choice here. Not when the only other option was pain and a slow death. He scanned the crowd and saw that most were listening with mute acceptance, just waiting for the ceremony to end.

One man was watching with such intensity however

that it drew Ryan's attention. It was Arris's father, his jawline set hard, one arm fastened around his wife's shoulders. She stood alongside him, barely watching the stage and clutching her daughter tightly. Silent tears slipped down both of their cheeks.

One by one, the oath-takers climbed the steps and waited at the wooden block to say the words. *"I declare myself a subject of The Unified City States under Premier Talis, the Supreme Leader. As a citizen of his lands, I will abide by his laws and subject myself to his judgements."*

The oath was read from a card, sometimes with passion, but mostly in a nervous mumble of words. That was until the gaunt and awkward figure of Arris ascended the steps and took his place before the crowd. The official handed him the oath card and then moved aside.

Arris glanced at the card, drawing a deep breath through his nose as he did so. He removed his glasses and folded them precisely before placing them inside his coat pocket.

Ryan felt nerves rise in his chest and glanced at the gunnermen nearby. They were either unaware or indifferent to what was happening on stage, but Ryan found he couldn't look away.

"I think my whole life has been counting down to this day," Arris said. His voice was soft and filled with melancholy, but he had a way of projecting it so that the words carried across the square. "I've often wondered what decision I'd make when I found myself standing here."

The official hurried forward, taking hold of his arm. "We don't want to hear any speeches thank you. Just read the…"

"Take your hands off me," Arris flared, his voice full of authority. "By the Premier's own laws, the laws you claim to uphold, I am afforded the right to speak on this day." He reached into his coat and drew out a small canvas bag. "And speak I shall."

It took Ryan a moment to recognise it, but then he saw that Arris was holding the same satchel that he had carried from Straybeck. Beside him the gunnermen were now on full alert, reaching for their rifles as Arris unzipped the top of the bag.

"Don't shoot," the official screamed, his eyes tracking from the small bag, along a coiled wire and finally to the detonator that Arris now held in his other hand.

A gasp of panic rippled through the crowd but as they tried to scatter, Arris spoke again. "I have no heart for violence. That much I have learned about myself. And this," he raised the bomb higher which provoked another frightened gasp from the crowd. "This is not the way to begin a dialogue, but I learned a long time ago that a powerless man is a desperate one."

He scanned the faces before him and Ryan wondered if it was Brynne he was searching for. The seconds lingered until eventually his shoulders slumped with resignation.

"Well it looks like I'm alone in this," he said wearily. "But that changes nothing. I refuse to swear an oath to this dictator we call Premier. I refuse to subjugate myself to his laws. I refuse to…"

A gunshot cracked sharp through the square and Arris was spun off his feet, landing heavily on the ground. The lead gunnerman had overcome his inertia and was running up the steps, gun zeroed on his target. He wrenched the detonator from Arris's hand and hurled it, satchel and all, into the empty space behind the crowd. People at the rear squashed forwards, waiting for an explosion that never came. Instead, two smooth lumps of scrap iron rolled out of the satchel and lay dormant on the ground. There had been no bomb. Just a naive young man with a big heart and a point to make.

On stage, the bullet had struck Arris in the chest and blood was soaking through his jacket. He was still conscious and had risen to one knee as he attempted to staunch the wound. The first gunnerman threw him down onto his chest, evoking a scream of pain, while the second reached for his handcuffs.

More gunnermen appeared and cleared a path through the crowd. They formed a protective cordon at the bottom step while Arris was dragged from the platform. Ryan climbed up the stone pillar to get a better vantage point, desperately searching for a way to help Arris. As he watched it all unfold though, he suddenly heard a sharp click and a sound like gears turning from the base of the pillar. He glanced down and found himself staring at the second satchel.

CHAPTER 44

AT STRAYBECK CENTRAL, John was waiting in line at the school gates, his eyes wide with fear. One corner of the Informer Station was charred black and the metal exterior warped by fire damage. A gunnerman patrol car was parked on the grass alongside it and beside that was an investigator's van. Everyone was gawping as they filed past until the headmistress, Mrs Reaton, appeared from the back of the burned-out building.

"Into class," she yelled. "Keep moving."

As always, she was viciously efficient in maintaining discipline at school and John could sense the anger dripping from her as he went past. Instead of registration that morning, an emergency assembly had been convened in the great hall. Over a thousand students took their chairs in narrow rows, their excitement occasionally bubbling up into a rush of whispered exchange, only to be snuffed each time Mrs Reaton strode past.

John thought he was going to throw up. He clutched his stomach tightly and swallowed down the excess saliva in his mouth. The events of the last day continued to plague him and he had felt so wretched when he got home that he barely slept all night. Even the anger he had once felt over Ryan and Alia had deserted him. When he arrived home and saw all the damage and his dad's injures, John knew it hadn't been worth it. Not even close.

Worst of all, the gunnermen must have tracked him to the school now. There was CCTV in the Informer Station and they'd have his face on camera. They were probably going to drag him on stage in front of the entire school and arrest him.

John remembered how he had run from the sirens when he left the school grounds. As one thought led to the next, he was overcome with a fresh wave of panic. He swivelled round in his chair searching the hall. Where was Mr Matthews? He suddenly felt like crying. What if they'd got him too? He would already be at The Cathedral telling them everything.

Just then the double doors at the far end of the room swung open and Mr Matthews stepped into the great hall. He strode purposefully down the corridor of space left between the chairs and stood next to Mrs Reaton. They spoke in hushed tones and the noise in the assembly hall dropped to an absolute whisper. This was bad. Very bad. If Mr Matthews hadn't been arrested, then he must have informed to the gunnermen already. How could he have believed that a teacher would stick to his promise and help? John knew he was finished. All he could do was wait for the gunnermen to arrive.

"I have assembled you here in light of the appalling crime that took place last night." Mrs Reaton liked to punctuate her speeches with long pauses, allowing time to cast her mistrustful gaze over the rows of students. It was her way of probing for weakness.

"I'm sure that you all saw the gunnermen at the main gate. They are here because some *criminal*," she practically shrieked the word, "set fire to the Informer Station. The station that is here to protect us all. And now it has been confirmed by the gunnermen that they suspect a student at this school as being the responsible party."

The hall erupted with excited chatter.

"Be quiet," Mr Matthews bellowed and a stunned silence returned. That was when the double doors creaked open a second time and someone with heavy footsteps moved slowly between the rows of children. Everyone, including John, turned to the sound and followed the gunnerman as he took position beside Mr Reaton.

"This is Gunnerman Dravis from the Straybeck Garrison," Mr Matthews announced. "He has a message for those people in the room who were responsible for last night's criminal activity."

Mrs Reaton and Mr Matthews stepped to the side leaving Dravis as the focus of everyone in the room. He was maybe fifty years old, with a crumpled appearance and tired expression.

"Last night," he began, "at the end of school, someone in this room went back to the Informer Station. This person contacted the authorities and gave us certain information."

John squirmed in his seat and his ears burned red. He didn't dare look up for fear he'd find all eyes turned upon him.

"After the call was terminated, we believe that this person - or persons known to them - returned to the station and set fire to it." A flutter of excited whispers passed through the assembly. Dravis waited for it to pass before continuing. "Those responsible should know that all informer stations are monitored by cameras that are constantly recording. The footage from last night is being recovered at this moment. Once the Investigation

Sector have reviewed the footage, it becomes a state level crime. I urge those responsible to come forward before it reaches that point. Far better to confess to me than wait until the Sector catches up with you. Far, far better."

John could stand it no longer. The urge to confess was swelling like a balloon in his chest. It was only a matter of time before they got the recording anyway and then it would be too late to put across his side of the story.

"I will be in school for one hour and then it's out of my hands," Dravis said. "Once again, I urge you to come forwards before it goes to The Sector. And if you have any information, speak to a teacher and let us know."

Dravis nodded to Mrs Reaton and then returned through the rows of students. The headmistress was quick to begin her prayer for the Premier's continued health and loyalty to the Unified City States.

John stared ahead, speaking the words automatically, numb to the excitement that gripped everyone else. When the prayer finished though, Mr Matthews moved himself into the space that John's gaze had been fixed upon. They locked eyes and John was shocked to see the hardest teacher in Straybeck with fear on his face. Like a mask had slipped, he suddenly appeared vulnerable as he gave an almost imperceptible shake of his head. It was only a small movement - barely noticeable - but to John the warning was stark.

Keep your mouth shut.

The next moment it was gone and the normal Mr Matthews had retuned. He harangued the students as they left the hall, daring them to disobey him. As John filed out in silence, he held the slenderest thread of hope that he and Mr Matthews were now bound by the same fate. And seeing him as he was now, John knew that a mouse like Gunnerman Dravis would never break him.

At lunch he kept moving between the upper and lower playgrounds, never waiting in one place long enough to draw attention. All his friends were discussing the damage to the Informer Station and he was too scared that he'd trip himself up in lies if they asked him about it.

"John," a voice called from behind.

He immediately recognised it and considered ignoring her. Instead he turned to see Alia closing the distance between them.

"What is it?" he said sullenly.

She looked at him with a weary expression and John couldn't help but stare at the dark circles that bruised her eyes. "I want you to know how sorry I am."

He could tell that she really meant it and after everything that had happened John didn't have it in him to stay angry anymore.

"Do you want to talk about yesterday?" she said

"I don't think so."

"Okay. But I really didn't know that Ryan was your brother. I promise."

John nodded silently and together they set off around the perimeter of the top yard. There were chain link fences marking the boundary line and from the far side it was possible to look down a grassy embankment to the school gates. Beyond that lay the Informer Station. The full damage could be seen better from up here and the pair of them stared down at the blackened metal hull.

"I heard that the gunnermen came to your house."

John's stomach lurched at the reminder, but he was careful to control his expression. "How did you know?"

"Ryan told me. I'm glad you weren't home when it happened."

John's guilt swelled so strongly that tears gathered in his eyes. He stared down at the Informer Station, unwilling to look at her.

"John?" she said, her voice no more than a whisper. "I think I figured out why they came."

He froze, hardly able to breath. "Why?"

She stood beside him and placed her fingers through the links in the metal fence.

"I think someone got hurt by the person they love the most. And I think that person got so angry that they made a very bad decision."

The first of John's tears rolled down his cheek.

"And if I know that person at all," Alia continued. "I think they'd take it all back, if they could."

John's voice cracked. "I think they would too. I think they want to more than anything."

Alia leaned back on the fence and the metal links sagged inwards to support her. John no longer tried to hide his face and to his surprise there was no laughter or mocking smile. Instead, Alia placed one hand upon his shoulder.

"I never had a brother," she said earnestly. "But if I did, I'd want him to be you. From now on, your secrets are my secrets."

By the end of school, no one from the Investigation Sector had come for him, so with a quick-beating heart, John scuttled down the corridors towards the knife gate. Once he had cleared the bottleneck of students, he felt a sudden euphoria. Maybe Mr Matthews had kept his promise and deleted the footage. Feeling better than he had for days, John found himself jogging across town, wanting to be home as quick as possible. He allowed himself to daydream that maybe he could persuade Ryan to come back too. Maybe they could all make amends. Maybe they could be a real family.

When he turned the corner of his street though the fragile sense of hope was suddenly shattered. Grouped around his front door were three gunnermen swinging a long metal ram against the hinges. With a final smack, the wood splintered and as one they ran over the broken planks and into the house.

CHAPTER 45

THE FIRST STRIKE shook the walls of the house and Robb ran to the hallway in time for the second blow to fall. The door buffeted inwards but held firm. On the third strike it flew open and a huge splinter of wood cartwheeled at Robb, smacking into his shoulder. The gunnermen were on him immediately, bellowing as they stormed forward.

A primitive anger seized Robb, an old and familiar friend. He met the lead gunnerman head on, ducked beneath the swinging punch and drove up with his shoulder. The gunnerman grunted as his feet left the ground and Robb pushed him into to the wall.

The second one was on him then, tackling Robb around the waist sending them both sprawling to the carpet. All three gunnermen surrounded him, landing solid kicks into his back and legs. Robb barely felt them though, so strongly did the fury have hold of him. He covered his head and waited. Waited for the gunnermen to grow tired so he could finish them one by one. He pictured hurting them, savouring the images with grim satisfaction. He sensed the moment approaching, felt the strength bunching in his muscles.

A sound broke through his rage though, quiet at first, but

insistent and strong. It was a voice, higher than the others. A female voice that he tried to block out. He knew instinctively it would cheat him of his strength. He felt the kicks from the gunnermen growing weaker, their sting fading. His moment was close, and Robb revelled in the anticipation that twitched in his muscles. But the woman's voice was at his ear now. Her cheek pressed against his. The kicks had stopped and only her voice remained.

"Don't Robb. Please. Just lie still. Please."

As the words chipped away at him, he felt his resolve failing. An almost crippling pain took its place but still the voice talked him closer.

"Don't do this," it whispered. "You're not that person anymore."

The anger deserted him and Robb was just a tired old man lying face down on the carpet. The voice was Eliza's and she was using her body as a shield against the gunnermen attack. His back and ribs sang with pain but as their kicks slowed he was able to roll away and prop himself against the stairs where he lay panting for breath. One of the gunnermen drew a sidearm and levelled it at Robb's head.

"It's not him," a voice said. It was the sergeant who had searched their house the day before. "It's just his fuck up of a father. One of you search upstairs, the other check down here. I'll keep an eye on this one."

The other two set about their orders while the sergeant leaned forwards, positioning his face just inches from Robb's.

"Told you I'd be back," he grinned. "And this time there aren't any seveners to get in the way."

Robb no longer had the energy to fight or even stand. He lay uncomfortably against the bottom three steps, not trusting himself to stay upright. "Where's your shit-heel of a son?" the sergeant said, nudging Robb with one boot.

"Leave him," Eliza snapped, which provoked a cruel laugh.

"She's got a bit of fight in her. More than you anyway."

Eliza put her palm against Robb's face, using the coolness of her skin to soothe him. "Just focus on me," she said. The sergeant gave a snort of disgust then nosed around the lounge waiting for the other gunnermen to return. There was a sudden yelp from outside and the sound of a struggle.

"Get off me," a voice yelled and then let out another squeal of pain.

The gunnerman who had been searching the back yard appeared at the kitchen doorway. In one brawny arm he was dragging a small figure who was flailing angrily in a bid to escape.

"This him Sarge? Found him sneaking around out back."

"John," Eliza yelled. She dragged him away from the gunnerman.

John looked shaken and close to tears but was otherwise unhurt. He sprang into his mother's arms though and then saw his dad crumpled on the floor.

"What's happening?" he cried.

"It's okay," he said as calmly as he could. He tried to stand, but the best he could manage was rolling onto one knee. The sergeant laughed again and pushed down on Robb's shoulder, forcing him back to the floor. Stepping between them he grabbed John under the jaw and stared at him.

"It's not him," Eliza snarled. "You can see he's too young."

Reluctantly the sergeant shook his head at the other gunnermen.

"Anyone upstairs?"

"Empty."

"So where is he?" he whipped round to face Robb.

"I don't know. I haven't seen him since you were here yesterday."

"Bullshit."

"It's the truth."

"You want us to take him?" one of the gunnermen offered, gesturing at Robb. "We'll find out how truthful he's being."

The sergeant considered it in silence and then shook his head. "No. Leave him. The old bastard's had his treatment." He gave Robb a twisted grin. "But know that your boy can't stay hidden forever. Sooner or later he'll show his face and then …well I don't have to tell you what happens next, do I?" He laughed and led the other two gunnermen from the house.

As soon as they were gone, John began to cry. He was trembling all over and Eliza led him to the kitchen table and made him sit down. She poured a glass of cold, cloudy water from the juddering taps.

"Drink it slowly," she said softly. "I'm going to see to your dad."

Robb was already on his feet though, leaning heavily against the doorway.

"I'll be fine," he said. The cut on his eye had opened up again and he looked like he might fall over at any moment. "There's something else I need you to do, Eliza. We need to know what Ryan's caught up in. This wasn't about yesterday. This was something new. Something serious."

"What can I do?"

"Go to Karasard and get a message to Kellie Downs."

"Kellie?" Suddenly the name snagged in her memory and Eliza stepped back. "The sevener? After what he…"

"I know what you're going to say," Robb cut in. "I haven't forgotten what he did. But right now, we need his help."

"You can't trust him."

She was probably right, but Robb knew he was out of choices.

CHAPTER 46

IN HIS FIRST few moments after the explosion, Ryan was blind and deaf to the world. His bones felt like metal pipes struck by a hammer. They quivered and shook while a high-pitched whine split his head. He felt the pressure build at the base of his skull and he thought the inside of his head was going to force its way out. There was a sudden crack from his right ear and a pop in his left as though someone had jammed a screwdriver deep inside.

Clutching his head, Ryan rolled to his knees, desperately trying to orientate himself against the muffled chaos. He could hear screams and each breath he took was a choking combination of smoke and powdered stone.

With the sleeve of his jacket, Ryan wiped a streak of blood from his eyes and staggered forwards. He was knocked aside by someone running in the opposite direction and then his feet stumbled over something on the ground. He fell heavily on the cobbles and his hands stopped on something warm and wet. Ryan had trouble recognising it as human, so disfigured was the gunnerman's corpse. He rolled away as the bile rose in his stomach only to find more bodies and limbs strewn around him. He staggered through the grisly scene until he was clear of the smoke and debris.

At each corner of the town square, workers and tradesmen were gathering at the checkpoints, drawn by the explosion. They were prevented from entering by the barriers, but dozens of white-collar workers were stumbling from the rear doors of the law firms and office blocks. They stood in packs, watching nervously as the scene played out. Ryan coughed the dust from his lungs and a man and woman wearing neat blue suits ran over.

"What's happened?" the woman said. Her face was framed by straight blonde hair and she placed one hand on Ryan's shoulder to steady him.

"I don't know," he coughed. He tried to think back to the explosion but couldn't escape the image of those dismembered bodies. He spat onto the cobbles and tried to shake loose whatever was blocking his ears.

"Did you see anyone?" the man said. He was more rattled than the woman had been. "Was there a bomb? Shit there might be others," he moved back towards the offices.

As they spoke, more gunnermen ran into the square from each checkpoint and even with his muffled hearing, Ryan could make out the discord of the sirens as more patrols responded.

Where was Brynne?

Against all his instincts and the protests of the woman with blonde hair, Ryan stumbled back the way he had come. Was the old man lying injured? Was he dead? Ryan steadied himself for the possibility that he might find his mangled remains amongst that awful collection of corpses.

Now the dust had mostly settled, he searched quickly but

still kept one sleeve over his mouth. Some of those he passed were conscious, gripping onto legs and arms that had been damaged in the blast. Others were still alive but crying out senselessly as they writhed on the floor. Then there were the bloody remains of those who had been closest to the blast.

Ryan steeled himself to search their faces, praying that he wouldn't see Brynne's cold blue eyes staring back at him. Suddenly he came upon a body that was smaller than the others. He tried not to look. Tried not to see the lifeless little girl with bright blonde hair now matted in blood. Arris's sister.

A nearby gunnerman blew a whistle and its shrill note pierced through Ryan's thoughts.

"Put a block on the checkpoints," he yelled, trying to bring order to the scene. "Nobody leaves without my say so. Get some medics to the wounded. Everyone else surrenders their cards."

Ryan stole one last look around him, praying for a glimpse of Brynne. As more gunnermen appeared though he knew he had tarried long enough. If they found him at the scene of a bombing there would be no coming back from that.

Ryan fled from the carnage, heading for the checkpoint he had passed through earlier. Hopefully there would still be time to escape the square before it was completely sealed off. He was only a few metres away when he saw three more gunnermen running towards him from the street. Worse still, the one at the checkpoint had kept his wits about him long enough to lower the metal gate and block the exit. With a curse, Ryan changed direction and made for the opposite corner of the square.

It was a vast space to cross and with all the life knocked out of him, Ryan was slow to cover the distance. By the time he reached the checkpoint he was hardly able to breathe. Two gunnermen were waiting there, locked in an argument with a bruised and battered man in his fifties. Ryan recognised him from the oath ceremony where he had been clapping proudly after one of the girls said her words. Now the smiles had vanished and he was screaming at the gunnermen and gesturing at the chaos around the town hall steps.

Ryan considered slipping through the gate while they were distracted, but then three more patrol cars drew up and he knew it would be impossible. His head was throbbing and he gently dabbed the front of his hairline finding blood on his fingertips. He stepped back from the checkpoint and cast around for another option. There had to be another way out.

That was when he spied the woman with blonde hair who had spoken to him a few minutes earlier. She was about to re-enter one of the office doors.

"Hey, wait a minute."

The woman was startled but to her credit waited in the doorway for Ryan to catch up. As he jogged over, he broke into another bout of coughing that took several seconds to pass.

"You need a doctor," she told him, a concerned expression on her face.

"I know, but I have to tell my family I'm safe first. Could I use your phone?"

"Your family have a phone?" the woman asked sceptically.

"Of course."

She gave his clothes an appraising look, obviously squaring it with the fact that he had been in the explosion.

"I shouldn't really let you in."

"Please. Just one quick phone call before this whole place is shut down. My mother will be so scared otherwise."

The woman relented and pushed open the door into her law firm, beckoning for Ryan to follow. Inside there were maybe a dozen people, all wearing the crisp white shirts and wide neckties of the professional class. The background chatter and ringing phones dulled slightly as Ryan entered and he saw most of the lawyers had ceased working and were staring from the windows over the square.

"Close the door Neriese," a man called, rushing forward suddenly. Ryan recognised him as the one who had been on the cobbles earlier. His fear was plain for all to see and obviously infecting those around him.

"Why have you brought him inside?" a woman said, staring at Ryan from behind her desk.

"He needs to use the phone," Neriese said defensively. "What was I supposed to do? Leave him out there?"

"Yes," the first man said. "We don't know anything about him. He could be one of the bloody bombers for all we know."

"Oh for heaven's sake Tillet. Look at him. He's more likely to drop dead than to harm one of us," she gave a quick glance to Ryan. "Sorry."

Once inside, he had hoped to talk his way through to the other end of the building and leave via the trading doors. He realised that Tillet and the others were never going to let that happen though.

"I'm going to be sick." He doubled over and clutched his stomach.

"Toilets," Neriese said sharply just as Tillet jumped away, covering his mouth.

"Oh God, how do we know there wasn't poison in that bomb. Get him out of here."

"Shut up," Neriese scalded and shepherded Ryan to the far side of the office. He rushed into the bathroom and slammed the door quickly behind him.

Inside was a toilet, a sink and a frosted glass pane overlooking the main street. Ryan turned the faucets, marvelling at the cool, clear water that collected in his hands. He took three deep gulps and instantly his head cleared. He wiped wet hands down his face and through his hair, cleaning away the worst of the blood.

The window beside him was set into the outer skin of the wall and created an alcove about a foot wide. There was a small mirror and some flowers arranged on the ledge which Ryan removed and placed quietly on the floor. He lifted the locking arm that fastened the window and gave it a solid push. It didn't budge. He leant harder, jamming the heel of his hand against the wood but still it held firm. Panic seized him and Ryan banged the frame, first with his hands and then by standing on the toilet lid, kicking at it with the bottom of his foot.

"Are you okay in there?" Neriese called through. Ryan saw the handle twist around.

"I'm fine," Ryan said. "I'll be out in a minute."

"What's all that banging?" He couldn't think of any excuse so said nothing. Neriese knocked again. "Hello?"

"I'm going for a gunnerman." Even with his muffled hearing, Ryan could hear Tillet's voice and knew he had to get out now. He scanned the small room, searching for something to smash the glass with. His eyes settled on the toilet cistern that was fixed to the wall overhead. It was an ancient contraption identical to the one they used to have in the family outhouse. Ryan clambered back onto the toilet and reached up to remove the heavy porcelain lid. It scraped out of its casing and he hefted it down.

With a quick back swing, he thrust it through the single pane of frosted glass and watched it shatter instantly. Neriese yelled something from the office but he ignored her and dragged the porcelain lid around the window frame, breaking off as much of the jagged glass as he could. He scraped the broken pieces from the alcove and carefully crouched onto the windowsill.

"He's climbing out the window."

Ryan froze, one foot dangling in mid-air above the street. He overbalanced and then fell onto the pavement where a splinter of glass gouged a slice into his back. Ignoring the pain, he jumped to his feet and fled.

CHAPTER 47

It was mid-morning when Alia awoke. She was still lying on the sofa where Ryan had left her in the small hours of the morning. As the memory of his confessions returned to her, Alia sprang up and made a bleary-eyed search of the room. It was empty and she hugged herself against the cold.

Through the cracked windowpane beside her, pale sunlight washed over the lounge. It held no comfort or warmth and Alia could feel a familiar weight of anxiety upon her chest.

She crept upstairs to retrieve the bottle of pills she had hidden in the bathroom. When a loose floorboard shifted noisily underfoot though, her father began to groan and shout from the next room. Alia placed her hands over her ears and scurried to the bathroom. Quickly, she shut the door and slid down to her knees with her eyes closed.

Her father continued his awful keening and Alia found that she was both ashamed and scared by it. She knew that he was hungry and hadn't eaten since yesterday afternoon. Even so, she couldn't muster the strength to fetch the bowl of porridge that she force-fed him twice a day.

"Alia," a shrill voice called. "Alia. Come to me now."

Her mother's footsteps pounded downstairs and – after a short silence – rushed back up and into the bedroom. Alia had grown to recognise these sudden bursts of activity as part of her mother's condition now. There were times when she would sit dormant for weeks, barely speaking unless it was to voice her unhappiness at life. At these times, Alia tried to coax and cajole her back to life but with little success.

The blanket of depression was occasionally lifted by brief and uncontrollable surges of energy. They might last an hour, or a few days and Alia quickly learned to fear these more than the dark days. Her mother could not be reasoned with when she got like that. Her thoughts would flit from one topic to the next and she would convince herself of ridiculous and often dangerous notions.

Last month, she had declared that gunnermen bullets could no longer hurt her. She left the house shouting threats and challenges, forcing Alia to drag her back like a screaming infant. When they got inside, her mother slapped her with such force that Alia's teeth rattled. Then she barricaded herself into the lounge where she grumbled and raged for hours.

Now as she sat alone in the bathroom, Alia recognised the imperious tone in her mother's voice. She tried to ignore it, hoping that she would think the house empty. A sudden banging rocked the door though and the handle flicked up and down.

"Alia? I know you're in there. Come out child, your mother needs you."

Alia dropped her head onto her knees and squeezed her eyes shut, forcing back tears. Her mother only paused for a moment.

"I've finally succeeded where those moronic doctors could

not. We can fix your father and rebuild the company and be back in our home by tomorrow."

Alia stayed quiet but twisted open the lid of the tablets and emptied one into her palm. Glumly she swallowed it down, all too aware that she was breaking her promise to Ryan. Her mother gave the door one final whack.

"Fine. If you're not going to help me, I'll fix him myself."

Alia went to the sink and tipped her head beneath the tap to wash down the chalky aftertaste. On the landing outside, her mother stomped away. Alia prepared herself for another haranguing but was surprised to hear only silence. She waited for a few moments and then realised that her father had also ceased his groaning for the first time in hours.

Frantically she unlocked the door, raced across the landing and into her dad's room. She found her mother standing over the bed with a pillow in her hands and a serene expression on her face. Her arms though were shaking with the effort it took to hold the pillow across her husband's thrashing face.

"Mum," Alia screamed, rushing forwards and pulling her away. She was able to remove the pillow just long enough for her dad to gasp a lungful of air.

"Let go of me, stupid child. I am curing him."

"You're killing him." She yelled, continuing to struggle. Despite her mother's small frame, she was surprisingly strong.

"He needs to stop breathing so he can learn to talk again," she grunted, freeing her hand and thrusting it back onto the pillow.

"Stop, just stop." Alia grabbed her mother around the waist and heaved her backwards. They fell in a tangle of limbs in the doorway.

"Alia?" Someone was running up the stairs and she craned her neck towards the voice.

"Ryan." A surge of relief ran though her. "Help me. She's trying to kill Dad."

"I'm saving him," her mother cried and wriggled like a cat as Ryan grabbed hold of her wrist. Together they dragged her into the other bedroom and restrained her on the bed.

"What happened?" Ryan said as he grappled with the older woman's arms. Alia was kneeling across her legs, breathing hard.

"She was trying to suffocate him with a pillow."

"I was helping him," her mother screamed, but her voice was hoarse and her kicks lacked any real power. They stayed with her like that for a long time, slowly releasing their grip as though she were a wild animal. Eventually they were able to retreat to the doorway and Alia's mother rolled over and chuntered quietly to herself while her eyelids grew heavy.

"It should be okay to leave her now," Alia whispered and stepped into the hallway. "My dad still needs feeding though. Will you watch her while I go and get the food?"

"Of course."

When she returned with a bowl of smooth brown porridge, he was standing outside the room with one ear pressed to the door. "I think she's asleep," he whispered. "She's stopped talking anyway."

"Thanks. I won't be long with this."

She suddenly became aware of Ryan's dishevelled appearance and the new collection of cuts on his face. Even his clothes were torn and stained with patches of dried blood.

"Oh my God, what's happened to you?" she said, pulling gently at his shirt and studying the fresh injuries. She felt a sudden irrational need to keep him in sight for fear that some new danger would claim him.

"It's okay. Go and sort your dad. We can talk after." Ryan gave her a calming smile. "I'll wait downstairs. Just call if you need me."

Forty minutes later, Alia returned with only a few scrapings of cold porridge left in the bowl. After feeding him, she had cleaned her father and changed his clothes. That was when she came to the sobering realisation that she felt neither revulsion nor pity when doing it.

In the lounge, Ryan was cornered in the sofa, his chin supported on one hand, eyes closed while he snored softly. At that moment he seemed so young to Alia. No more than a boy really. Feeling a sudden weariness deep in her bones, she eased herself up against him.

"I was just resting," he murmured, wiping at his mouth quickly.

"It's okay. We can rest together."

He gave a contented grunt, lifting his arm so that she could lean up against him and he didn't wake again for several hours. Alia had lain with him for part of that, but when her mother's footsteps tramped on the floorboards, she crept upstairs to keep a cautious eye on her.

She was treading a path across the landing carpet like a caged animal, back and forth from the bathroom without rest. Eventually she moved past Alia without even acknowledging her and headed for the front door. "Where are you going Mum?"

She made no reply and although Alia knew she should go after her, she just didn't have the energy. With any luck, the cold Straybeck air might restore balance to her troubled mind. She closed the front door and crept back to the lounge where she tidied quietly around Ryan as he slept.

He eventually drifted back to consciousness and Alia settled on the arm of the sofa. She wanted to hold him close but there was something she had to say first.

"How long have I been asleep?"

"All day."

"I'm sorry," he reached towards her, but Alia kept her hands clasped on her lap.

"What's wrong?"

"When you were here yesterday, you told me all about the things you do. The things you've been involved in."

"Yes." His tone was guarded.

"And I told you all about me."

"You did."

"And I hoped you'd understood what that meant to me."

Ryan frowned. "I'm sorry, have I done something wrong?"

"You said you'd only be a couple of hours," she blurted. "You said you were just going to talk to him." Without knowing why, Alia was on the verge of tears. Ryan straightened in his seat, suddenly defensive.

"What's the matter? Is it because I was away for longer than I said?"

"Look at your face," she half shouted. "Look at your clothes." She knew it wasn't making any sense, but it was all so overwhelming. "It's this Brynne. Why do you let him do it to you?"

"Brynne didn't do this," Ryan said. "There was a bomb. In Karasard."

He tried to tell her about the Town Hall and how he had watched someone refusing their oath, but it only made her more distressed. She waved away his words, trying to gather her own thoughts.

"What were you even doing in Karasard? You said you were going across Straybeck to find Brynne. You said you'd be back and then you weren't and then you turn up like this."

"I did go to find him. I went to his home, but it had been raided by the gunnermen. He thought I'd informed on him. I had to go to Karasard to prove it wasn't me."

"That makes no sense."

Ryan sighed, either at his own answers or her lack of understanding. "Don't you see, it was like a test"

"A test?"

"Of loyalty. I don't know, it's complicated."

"No it isn't Ryan. It's really simple. You just tell him that you don't want to be part of his insurrection or whatever he calls it. Then you walk away."

Ryan shook his head. "He's a hard man to walk away from."

He looked so miserable then that Alia felt the strength of her own anger evaporate. She slid from the arm of the sofa and landed on the cushion beside him. When she spoke, her voice was level again.

"What happened to the man with the bomb?"

"It was fake. The one he had." Ryan screwed up his eyes as he tried to remember. "There was another bag though," he said it slowly as though he was just discovering the memory. "It was on the ground next to me. Brynne had brought them both from the chapel and I carried one across town for him."

Alia's chest tightened. "You carried the bomb?"

"No," he said quickly. "Well yes, but not on purpose. Brynne just gave me a bag to carry. He had one too. He took them both through the checkpoint though and I think he gave one to Arris. It's all a bit muddled. There were bodies everywhere. I saw…" he closed his eyes again, pained by whatever image had come to mind. "I've not seen Brynne since."

"You think he's dead?"

Ryan found grim humour in the idea. "I seriously doubt it. I don't know what it would take to kill Brynne. I need to know he's okay though. I can't explain why." He seemed to read the expression on her face and tried to backtrack. "I just need some answers, that's all."

"You need, *you* need." Her voice rose again and she could feel the terrifying trembles of a panic attack. "It's not just about you anymore." Her legs were tingling and as her chest tightened, she struggled for each breath. When she tried to leave the room, her knees buckled and she collapsed to the floor.

"Alia," Ryan dashed to her side.

"You have to decide," she gulped air between the words.

"What's happening?" he said, but Alia ignored him.

"You have to choose," she gasped. "I won't keep…" she clutched at her throat and all the words stopped. The edges of her vision blurred and then blackness closed in around her.

CHAPTER 48

IT WAS LESS than a minute before she opened her eyes, but to Ryan it felt like a lifetime. He lifted her legs onto the sofa and slid a cushion under her head, his own expression clouded with worry.

"Are you okay?"

Alia took two long blinks like the words had been spoken in a different language. With a jerky movement she propped herself up onto one elbow before sinking back down to the floor again.

"What happened?"

"You couldn't breathe and then you passed out."

"It sometimes happens. It looks worse than it is."

"It looked pretty bad."

Alia shrugged. Ryan didn't know if she remembered what had caused it and he didn't know if he should bring it up again. Her words rolled over and over in his mind.

You have to choose.

"I can't fall in love and then lose you. I'm not strong enough." Her eyes were closed but Ryan saw tears pushing through her long eyelashes.

"You won't lose me," he said, stroking her face. "I'm right here. I'm not going anywhere."

"That's not enough. You can't keep one foot on both sides of the line. If we're together, you leave Brynne and all his world behind."

"That's what I'm trying to do."

"No you're not. He's still got you." She rolled away from him, balling her knees up to her chest.

"I need to know he's safe," Ryan said, hearing the desperation in his own words. "I owe him. He's always watched out for me. Always listened to me when my own dad didn't care." Even as he said them though, the words rang hollow.

"Where is he now?" Alia said sourly. "I don't see him tearing up the city to find you. What about when *your* house was raided? Where was he then? Or when you were thrown from the train? Or even this morning?"

Ryan stepped back, annoyed not just at her words, but at the truth he heard behind them.

"It's fine if you don't want to listen to me," Alia continued. "Or even your dad for that matter. But won't you at least listen to the one person who has only ever wanted the best for you?"

At first, he had no idea who she meant. Then John's face swam into focus. Instinctively he fought against the image, but it felt too right to be ignored. Everything that John had risked had been to keep Ryan safe. It was a painful truth to acknowledge though and Ryan was suddenly ashamed of how he had treated his brother.

"Go and see him," Alia said, quietly. "Make it up to him. He'll forgive you Ryan. Then ask him what he thinks you should do."

But he didn't need to ask because he already knew what John's answer would be. "I'll go tonight," he said quietly.

Since the explosion in Karasard, the gunnermen had driven round declaring a citywide curfew. Even so, Ryan felt confident he could dodge their checkpoints and set out in the early hours of the morning.

There had been no more snow in the night and, despite the cold, what little there had been was now melted in the gutters. Ryan ached all over as he limped slowly away from Alia's house and through the Slum District of Straybeck. She had patched up most of his injuries but the gash in his back was still snagging against his shirt as he walked.

He had been thinking about Brynne most of the day. No matter what Alia said, there was still a loyalty too deep to shake. Ryan had to know if he was okay and he had to tell him in person that he was leaving the insurrection. He owed him that much.

There were three drop-sites they had used in the past to get messages to each other. One was in Karasard, but there was no way he could reach that tonight. The second was at the park where he'd waited for Caylin. The third was the old underground station in the Manufacturing District. Ryan chose a route he had used before which took him through the rear yards of the shops in the Trade District and then out onto Friary Lane.

The streets here were wide, black and empty and Ryan was instinctively cautious. He waited on a high wall at the edge of the district for ten minutes, tuning into the sounds of the night. It was empty as winter.

As he descended into the underground world below Straybeck, the only sound was the thump of his heart and the quiet step of each foot. One solitary bulb was still lit partway down the platform and it struggled to hold back the shadows all around. Ryan quickly covered the length of the platform before his nerve could fail him. He found the bench where he had met Brynne all those weeks ago when he had collected the spray-cans. He ran his hand beneath it and all down the sides, checking for a note. There was nothing. Ryan unfolded one of the two scraps of paper he had taken from Alia's house and scribbled a short note.

Alive? Safe? Meet? R

He folded it into a square and positioned it beneath the bench leaving one edge poking out from a crack in the stone. He retreated up the platform, climbed the steps and crept back into the night. After leaving an identical note under the bench at Straybeck Park he jogged the last couple of miles onto the Victory Estate.

As he left the cover of the park, the wide streets and low walls of the estate felt like the most dangerous part of his journey. The moon was almost full and it was a crisp cloudless night. The bells from the church struck three times, their low chime carrying like a solemn warning over Straybeck.

Ryan crept ever closer to his house, moving off the roads so he could use the network of paths and alleyways. Eventually he found the wall with handholds that were familiar even in the darkness. He was over it in an instant and found himself crouching on the old brick outhouse where he and John had played as children. With light feet, he dropped down into his rear yard and surveyed their house.

He had expected it to be in darkness but to his surprise saw a candle casting a brave light over the kitchen. Sitting beside it and reading from a book was Ryan's dad. He had a half empty bottle of spirits beside him and a full tumbler in his hand. His head was resting on his knuckles as he scanned the pages of the book with weary eyes.

Ryan moved closer, scuffing his toes against something on the ground. It only made a slight sound, but his father was alert and at the back door before he could hide.

"Wait."

Reluctantly Ryan turned to face him. His dad was clearly drunk, or at least close to it. There was an edge of emotion in his voice that Ryan rarely heard.

"Come in. Out the cold," he gestured back to the kitchen. "Please."

Ryan nodded and followed him inside. When he reached the table it immediately became clear what had kept his dad up until the small hours. The book he'd been reading was Ryan's journal and for a moment he tried to fumble it out of sight. When he realised there was no longer any point though, he gently handed it back to Ryan.

Part of him wanted to shout at his dad. To demand an explanation for the invasion of his most private thoughts. From the look in his dad's eyes, he was waiting for that exact reaction too. It was a surprise for both of them when Ryan found he no longer had the energy.

"I didn't mean all of it."

His dad gave a tired smile. "Yes, you did."

They sat opposite each other at the table and Ryan said the only thing that seemed to matter anymore. "Tell me about The Cathedral."

CHAPTER 49

ROBB KNEW THAT death was close, but he wasn't afraid anymore. Ashgate had hurt him more than he ever imagined possible. He should have been proud of holding out for so long, but looking down at the ruin of his chest and legs, Robb wondered if the price had been too great.

It had been hours since Ashgate was last with him. Hours since he had last been questioned about the Colonel. They didn't know it, but Robb only had one thing left to tell. One last ember that he was shielding. He contemplated it now as he lay slumped in the corner of his cell. It was of no great worth anymore, but that had never really been the point.

The door moved silently open and Robb realised they hadn't even locked him in. For a brief moment, he imagined hiding himself behind the door or playing dead just beside it. When Ashgate bent down to inspect him he would grab him by the throat and squeeze the life from him. It was only a fleeting thought. He could barely make a fist, never mind overpower his sadistic gaoler.

Ashgate was wearing a curious smile as he entered the cell. Robb tried to prop himself upright but the gaoler waved away his effort.

"No, no," he said politely. "Don't get up."

Like a marionette with cut strings, he slumped back against the damp bricks.

"I have a surprise for you Robbert."

A feeling of unease settled in his stomach, but he stayed silent.

"I have met with Under Secretary Lascam. He was in a briefing with the Premier himself about our little situation. You'll be pleased to know that it is still Our Leader's wish that you come and work for us. At least in the eyes of the outside world."

Robb frowned. He had expected a move like this when he first arrived. The promise of a pardon and a new life if he turned against the group. But the offer never came and they had beaten every secret out of him anyway. All but one. It made no sense for them to make an offer now when he had nothing left to bargain. Ashgate read the confusion on his face and knelt beside him. Close, but not too close.

"We want you to denounce your former beliefs and say that you are helping the Government with their fight against the insurrectionists...people like your old friend Colonel Stephens."

"Why? Why not kill me?"

"Partly for the risk that you become a martyr. The Premier does not want a popular movement rallying behind the figureheads of an old warhorse like Stephens or the young bull Robbert Calloway. That could pave the way for another generation of misguided youngsters."

Robb snorted. "You give me too much credit."

"Maybe. Stranger things have happened," Ashgate smiled. "But the main reason he won't kill you is that it amuses him not to. We will see you shame yourself and slowly ruin the name of your group. You will become a pariah for the rest of your life, unloved and mistrusted by your friends, hounded and victimised by the gunnermen. Now isn't that more fun than a quick death?"

"I won't do it."

Ashgate was a patient man. "Yes you will. And whenever we say so, you will stand up in the town square and repeat your confession. You will betray the people in your group over and over again. And when you run out of people to name, we'll find new ones for you."

Robb shook his head, staring at the stone floor. "I'll kill myself first. You won't be able to stop me. Not forever."

"You know," Ashgate stood up and worked some blood back into his legs, "when you've worked in this profession for as long as I have, you develop an eye for reading people. I can tell immediately if a man will cry or scream or grit his teeth and think around the pain. I usually know who will vomit and who will shit themselves, who will faint and who will die."

He leaned over and gripped a handful of Robb's hair, pulling it up, exposing his throat. "It's not always the ones you expect either Robbert. There are men like your friend Farren, swaggering in here, full of bravado, fighting the guards. As you saw, it doesn't get them very far. Then there are the quieter ones, like yourself, who have that extra *something*."

"You were always a mixed bag. An enigma. Right from the beginning I thought we'd end up at this crossroads regardless of what I did to you physically. Still, you can't blame me for trying, ay?" Ashgate gave him a wink like they were old friends. He released Robb's head and then walked to the central fireplace where he absently turned a metal rod through the coals, stoking them back into life.

"So if there is someone who no longer cares for their own life, part of my job is to find out what they do care about." He turned to the doorway. "Bring her in."

Outside there was the sound of a struggle and moments later a young woman thumped to the ground at Ashgate's feet, landing heavily on her elbows and knees. It was Eliza. Shocked and pale and cradling the cheek where the guard had just punched her. Her mouth was covered by a length of filthy bandage which formed a makeshift gag.

Robb slithered across the floor towards her, but Ashgate quickly kicked down on his back. Eliza's eyes went wide as she screamed for him, the bandage muffling any sound she made. She lunged towards him, but the guard grabbed her shoulders and pitched her back against the heavy wooden door.

"So Robbert," Ashgate said calmly. "You can see where things are headed."

"You fucker. I'll kill you." The threat lacked conviction and they all knew it.

"If I were you Robb, I would start to show a little more caution. If not for yourself, do it for her." Ashgate grabbed Eliza at the back of her neck and dragged her closer.

Robb couldn't understand it. No one had known they were seeing each other. At least no one outside the group. He had been so careful to hide their relationship from even his closest friends. Inevitably, Farren had found out and tried to talk him out of seeing her. At first, he had complained that she was tying him down and stopping him from having fun. When that didn't work, he threatened to tell the Colonel, saying it was an unnecessary risk for their group.

After a month or so, Robb decided to tell the Colonel anyway. Far from forbidding the relationship though, he had asked just one question.

Do you love her?

It was the first time Robb had thought about it, but he knew that he did. Colonel Stephens patted him on the shoulder and wished him good luck.

For the following six months he had never been so happy. The night the gunnerman raided the safe house he had proposed to Eliza. Laughing and crying all at once, she had pulled him up off one knee and helped him to slip the ring on her finger.

No one else knew. Just Farren and the Colonel. And now, in an archway cell of The Cathedral, he watched blood trickle down from her beautiful face and knew it was all because of him. She stared back, eyes sharp with fear.

"If you hurt her," he said, "you'll get nothing from me."

Ashgate shrugged. "You're looking at it back to front. You see, you're not cooperating now are you Robbert? So if I hurt her…" he slid a knife from the table, "or *kill* her," the knife stroked a line across her cheek, "or slice off little pieces of her face, it would be of no consequence to me. Can the same be said for you?"

In one quick movement he hauled Eliza to her feet while Robb watched helplessly from the floor. "Hold her," he shouted, and the guard secured her with a vicious arm lock. The gag around her mouth worked loose and Eliza gave a terrified scream.

"Robb." Her eyes were on him, but he knew he couldn't save her. He couldn't save her *and* kill himself.

"Let her go," he said without thinking. "I'll do it. Whatever you want. Just let her go."

Ashgate smiled and once again scraped the knife down her face and across her neck. It was a feather touch, just enough to mark the skin. Eliza's chest was heaving up and down with fear. Ashgate deepened his pressure drawing a line of blood from her skin about six inches across.

"Stop it, please," Robb crawled forwards, dragging his broken legs behind him "I'll do it. I promise."

Ashgate's smile never fell from his face. "I believe you will. But let this moment forever remind you of what it is to keep a promise."

The guard switched his grip and held Eliza's wrist in both hands. In one deft movement Ashgate sliced off her finger to the second knuckle. Her mouth fell open in a silent scream and Robb saw the stump of her finger drop to the floor, the engagement ring still fixed tight.

CHAPTER 50

IN THE HOURS between night and morning, Ryan's dad finished the tale. It was a hollow time when past and present seemed close enough to touch. He was weary in a way he'd never felt before, although his mind was wrestling with the new information he'd learned.

"I never knew that was how Mum lost her finger. She told me it was an accident at work."

"We thought we were keeping you safe." He gave a quiet laugh. "All these secrets. They seem so pointless now."

Ryan found himself nodding too.

"You know, I loved your mother more than anything in the world. I still do. Maybe that excuses what I did. Maybe not. But at least it's the truth." He seemed embarrassed to be saying the words. Even so, Ryan could tell they were from the heart.

"I promise you I've paid for my sins a thousand times over. But this..." he lifted Ryan's journal from the table, testing its weight in the air. "This is not me. Not all of it anyway."

Ryan sat among the words, trying to find order in his own jumbled thought. "I believe you Dad," he said eventually. "At least I think I do."

"That's a start."

"I just," Ryan began, and for the first time found himself treading around his dad's feelings. "I just don't understand why you didn't lie."

"Lie?"

"I know what they did to Mum. I get that now. But after they let you go, why didn't you just say you'd told them everything you knew. Why keep on finding people for them?"

"Weren't you listening?" Robb snapped. "I didn't give anyone up. They just gave me the names and I said it was me who'd found them. It was Ashgate's way of sticking the knife in. Destroying any life I had left."

Ryan wanted to believe it, but he couldn't just forget what Brynne had told him either. His dad had been captured and then within a few weeks the whole group was destroyed.

"If there's something you need to ask," Robb said, "believe me, now's the time to do it."

"I heard," Ryan said slowly, "that because of what you said, your entire network was captured and killed." For the first time in years he felt no sense of satisfaction saying these truths.

"Who told you that? This man you meet up with? Brynne?"

"Dad, he knows all about it. He was the one leading the mission."

"I'm sorry Ryan, but that's utter bullshit. There were three of us in the safehouse that night. Alistair was shot by the gunnermen, Farren died in The Cathedral and I was left a cripple. Whoever this Brynne is pretending to be, he's lying."

Ryan marvelled that his dad could be so blind to the obvious. "Dad. Don't you think that…?"

"No, you're wrong. Colonel Stephens is dead." He shoved away from the table and paced across the kitchen. "I can't think straight in here," he hissed. "Why should I have to talk in whispers, cowering in my own home?"

He stalked through to the hallway and snatched his coat off the hook. Ryan was stunned by the outburst but followed him to the door.

"Fuck the curfew," his dad muttered and stepped out into the night.

All this talk of the past had dredged the canal of emotions Robb had sunk years before. The shame, guilt and anger he'd buried since The Cathedral now simmered dangerously close to the surface. He strode from the house, refusing to acknowledge the flashes of pain in his legs. When Ryan slid into step alongside him, he was barely even breathing hard.

"Where are we going?"

Robb hadn't thought that far ahead. He ran through all the possible places they could talk that were away from the patrol routes.

"We'll go to the city park. It should be empty this time of night."

The streetlights were out on most streets, but the moon was full and it showed them the way. Robb led his son on a looping route that circled around the static checkpoint. As he veered left onto Park Road, a hand gripped his shoulder.

"There's a roaming checkpoint," Ryan said in a low voice.

"Where?"

"The next street. I came this way earlier."

Robb didn't comment but felt a strange mix of both jealousy and pride that his son knew these streets better than him. He let Ryan lead the way, waiting until they'd passed the gunnermen before speaking again.

"It looks like you've a few more bruises since I last saw you," he said.

"I could say the same about you." Usually that would have ended the conversation, but this time Ryan continued without prompting. "I was there when the bomb went off in Karasard."

They were halfway up a steep, muddy embankment, and Robb almost slipped backwards when he stopped. "Bomb?" The news had reported a gas explosion at the town hall, but they said it was caused by a cracked pipe.

"It was the oath ceremony," Ryan said. "Someone planted a bomb."

Robb's chest tightened as he ran through the implications. They crested the hill and Robb found himself staring down towards the blackened remains of the Sainstsday bonfire. There had been so many fires on that spot that the earth was permanently scorched in a crooked circle.

"Are you sure it was a bomb? They said it was a gas leak on the radio."

"It was real, Dad. A man called Arris was refusing his oath. He had a replica bomb and while they were arresting him another one exploded."

"Are you okay?"

"I'll live."

"Are you involved?"

It was a simple enough question, but Ryan didn't answer straight away. Instead he moved away from the hilltop and sat upon a nearby bench. Robb didn't like the choice. It was more exposed than he would have liked. He turned around and saw that the tree line was close enough for them to run to if they needed a quick escape.

"Are you involved?" he said again.

"I think I might be. I think it was me who brought the bag to Karasard."

"Why would you do that?" Robb couldn't hide the anger from his voice.

"I didn't know what it was."

"Did anyone see you with it?"

Which was a stupid question and he knew it. Ryan would have crossed half a dozen checkpoints to get there, not to mention the underground stations. At least it explained why the gunnermen came to his house again.

"Who gave you the bag? Was it the boy taking the oath?"

"No. He was already there when we arrived."

"We?" Robb finally caught on, his heart sinking. "It was Brynne, wasn't it?"

Ryan's silence was all the answer he needed. He had to sort this once and for all.

"Where can I find him?"

"You can't"

"This isn't just about you anymore. He's brought the gunnermen to our house. They threatened Eliza and John too." That was one problem. There was also the fact that Brynne had claimed to be the Colonel, something that he couldn't just let go.

Robb remembered The Cathedral with Ashgate and his questions. How the gaoler had tried to study, slice and sever every secret in Robb's mind. Those secrets had been hoarded like precious stones and mined until the vein ran dry. Ashgate had been so sure of himself that he never suspected Robb had clung to just one. A secret that now threatened to swallow them all.

In his mind he was suddenly back on the cobbles after jumping from the safe house window.

Go. Just go.

We're not going anywhere, you dumb bastard.

Broken pieces of wood from the board that he had kicked through were lying in chunks all around his body and shattered legs.

Go. Just go.

They had never realised who he was shouting out that night. They hadn't known that Robb was focused on just one man, crouching beside the rear bumper of a gunnerman truck. Maybe a dozen years older than him, but with a face that was weathered by a life of fighting. Colonel Stephens wore a grim expression and had his pistol drawn, unable to accept what Robb already knew.

They were all fucked.

The pain in his legs had been almost unbearable, but Robb managed to call out one final warning. Even then, part of him didn't believe the Colonel would leave and it was with a profound sadness that he watched him lower his gun and creep away.

That had been the last time he saw the Colonel. Their shared secret became the slenderest thread of honour that Robb could hold onto. In the darkness of The Cathedral he had clutched to it like a drowning man. He could not let Brynne take that from him. Not without a fight.

"I can't tell you where he is Dad," Ryan said, "because I don't know. His home was raided like ours and then he disappeared at the town hall."

"How do you contact him then? There must be a dropbox or a safe house or something."

Ryan paused long enough for Robb to know he was lying. "No there's nothing like that. I always just meet him at the chapel."

Robb considered taking a look for himself, but there was no way of knowing if the gunnermen were surveilling it. Besides, Eliza had already brought a message from Kellie. The sevener was going to pay a visit this morning and would hopefully have news on Brynne. He might know a way to keep his son safe.

"Promise me something," Robb said. "I'm meeting with an old friend in a few hours. He's a sevener. Can you at least come home and lay low until we've met? Then together we can figure out what to do."

"I can't Dad, I promised Alia I'd go back and see her. I've already been gone too long."

"Alia? Isn't that the girl that John likes?"

For the first time in years Ryan laughed at something his dad said. "Yes. It's the girl that John likes." Then his expression turned solemn. "I really need to speak to him. Sort things out."

Far across the park, the black skies were losing their weight as first light approached. The factories were silent, traffic had stopped and Robb could hear the chirrups of birdsong all around. It brought him an unexpected warmth and peace.

"It's easy to forget that moments like this exist. Down there," he pointed at the sprawling town below, "it's all about Talis and the gunnermen and the factories. But there's still a good life to be had. So long as we don't let them take it from us."

He wasn't sure what he was trying to say, or if it was for Ryan's benefit or his own. It was just a vague wish for something better than what they had right now.

"Come on," he said. "Let's go home."

"Okay. I'll speak to John, but then I have to see Alia."

CHAPTER 51

JOHN WOKE IN darkness to find his brother standing beside him. Since the gunnerman had trashed their room, John was still sleeping on a mattress on the floor. He propped himself up and rubbed at his eyes sleepily.

"Hey John."

"What's wrong? Are you okay?"

"I'm fine," Ryan whispered, almost ghost-like in the darkness. "I came home to see you though. And Dad."

John smiled at that, eyes still half shut. "What time is it?"

"Still early. I can't stop long."

John took hold of his brother's leg protectively.

"Don't worry," Ryan laughed. "I'll be back again soon. I just wanted to talk to you first."

As John's eyes cleared, he noticed his brother's injuries. They looked even worse than when he had seen him with Alia. Had that been because of him? A sudden knot pulled tight in the pit of his stomach.

"What happened to your face?" he asked quietly.

"It's fine. Looks worse than it is." But John didn't believe him for a second.

"I actually came here to apologise," Ryan continued.

"Apologise? What for?"

"For what happened with Alia. I really didn't know that you liked her before we started seeing each other." Ryan sat down on the mattress. "Not until I read your letter. And even then, I promise I never told Alia we were brothers. You shouldn't be mad at her either. It was me who suggested she arranged to meet you the other day. Not to laugh though. I just thought it would be better than getting fobbed off in a note."

Seeing his brother safe, after so much worry, John knew that he would forgive him. He wasn't sure if he deserved the same understanding.

"I need to tell you something too. It's about what I did after I saw you and Alia." John kept his head down, not daring to look at his brother. He was so scared that he could barely speak, but neither could he hide the truth any longer. When he finally looked at Ryan though, there was no trace of anger on his face.

"It's okay John. I know what happened."

"You don't. I did something terrible and everyone got hurt and…"

"No," Ryan interrupted shaking his head. "None of what happened is your fault."

"But you don't know what I did."

"Yes I do. I know exactly what happened. And I understand why you did it." John was speechless. "Someone reminded me today of a truth I'd somehow forgotten. Do you know what that was?"

John shook his head.

"They showed me that the only person who has ever looked out for me, without any thought for themselves, is you. I've not been doing a very good job as a brother lately, but I promise that's going to change. From now on we're going to take care of each other. Okay?"

Jon nodded, unable to speak so great was his relief. He threw his arms around his brother and gave him a fierce hug. Ryan laughed and squeezed him back.

"But I really have got to go now."

"Where?"

"I'm going to see that man. Brynne." John saw that his brother was holding a scrap of paper in his hand.

"What's that?"

"A note. He left it for me at the park. He wants to meet up."

"You can't," John said quickly, panic rising in his voice. He took the note from Ryan and read it through.

"It's okay," Ryan said quickly. "It's not what you think. I'm telling him that I'm finished with all of that."

John's face must have shown how hard he found it to believe his brother.

"It's true. And next year, I'm going to take the oath."

"Why now? What made you change your mind?"

"I don't know," Ryan shrugged. "I think I just finally realised that there's too much here. Too much to keep…fucking up any longer."

John gave him a reproachful look. "You said a swear."

Ryan chuckled. "Shut up you goon."

"Are you going to come back home?"

"I think so."

"So are you and dad friends again?"

Ryan paused before answering. "We're not enemies. Which is a start. Now go back to sleep."

With one last hug, his brother left the room and John laid back on the pillow and fell into a long and peaceful sleep.

When he awoke - for the first time in days - John felt free of the awful weight of anxiety that had been slowly crushing him. He hardly dared acknowledge this new sensation in case it vanished completely. Cautiously he replayed the conversation with Ryan until at last he was satisfied that it had actually taken place. Then he read the note that he still held in one hand, giving concrete proof that the conversation had been no wishful dream.

With a deep and contented sigh, he rolled out of his blankets and sat on the cold wooden floor. Downstairs he could hear the breakfast places being set and wondered if Ryan had already met Brynne and come home. Hurriedly he dressed and then bounced down the stairs to find just his mum and dad at the table. Judging by the sympathetic smile his mum gave, his face must have shown how disappointed he was.

"He'll be back soon love."

John looked at his dad for confirmation.

"It's true. He's coming home this afternoon."

At least partially satisfied, John took his seat at the table and gnawed at the hunk of bread that was waiting. "Mum?" he spoke in his most agreeable of voices.

"Yes?" she said suspiciously.

"Is there any of last night's gravy left? Just to dunk my bread in."

His dad suddenly came alive and began nosing round the pans. "I like the sound of that. What do you say Lizzy?"

"I say you're a pair of animals," she grumbled, but lit the hob and began heating it through. His dad gave a conspiratorial wink as he took his seat. It was all so nice. Like it should be. Like it could be again.

"Before I forget," his dad said, "Ryan left you a present."

"A present? What is it?"

"Well I don't know, you'll have to go and see. He said it was in the club-hut?"

John grinned. "It's club *house* Dad. I'll go and have a look."

"Finish your breakfast first," his mum said.

At the prospect of a present from Ryan though, all interest in the gravy had vanished. John shoved the bread in his mouth and chewed furiously before scurrying past. Eliza rolled her eyes but didn't stop him opening the door.

It was a bright but bitterly cold morning. The sky was white enough for more snow to fall and John decided that he wouldn't mind that one bit. As he stepped towards the outhouse he heard footsteps on the narrow alleyway that ran across the end of their yard.

A colossal figure rolled into view with wild, shaggy hair and a thick, black beard. In one easy stride, he vaulted the wall and was in the yard moving towards John who stumbled backwards and landed on the ground with a smack. The man loomed closer and grabbed him by the front of his jumper with one shovel-sized hand.

"I need to see your father." He lifted him into the air and plonked him back on his feet while John just gawped in terror.

"What's wrong?" Eliza gasped. Before he could answer though, Kellie had stooped beneath the doorframe and filled the small kitchen. Robb quickly pushed up from the table.

"I wasn't expecting you until later." There was a familiar tightening of his chest and Robb glanced through the window checking for gunnermen.

"It's just me," Kellie said. "I thought you were starting to trust me by now."

Robb bluffed a smile. "Old habits die hard."

"They do."

Eliza ushered John out of the kitchen and then offered the sevener a drink.

"No thank you. It's better for all of us if I don't stay too long."

"What is it?" Eliza said, her voice tight. "Is Ryan okay?"

Kellie gave Robb a guarded look.

"She knows everything."

The sevener nodded. "No, it's not Ryan. At least not directly. It's about the man you had me track. This Brynne."

Robb forced himself to sit back at the table and gestured to the chair opposite. "Sit down. Talk to me."

Kellie checked his watch and reluctantly took a seat that suddenly seemed tiny beneath his huge frame. Robb had never seen him so tense, which did nothing to settle his own nerves.

"Tell me you're not mixed up with this man."

"Who is he?"

"Brynne? He's a no one. A ghost. There's no record of him in any of the official city registers and when I asked around, it seems that even talking about him makes people uneasy."

Robb tapped his fingers irritably on the tabletop and then lowered his voice as though there were spies at the window. "I've heard that he's behind the bombing at the town hall. He made Ryan carry one of the devices."

Eliza's body stiffened up and all the colour drained from

her face. "I only found out a few hours ago," Robb added quickly. "I promise."

Eliza seemed to crumble beside him, resting her forehead in one hand. She let out a shuddering sigh before collecting herself. "Kellie, what have you found out?"

"I spent the past two days trying to track down this Brynne and then I realised I'd been looking in the wrong place."

"What do you mean?"

"No one wakes up at fifty and suddenly begins a war on the Government. Whoever he is, he's got a past and that means arrest records and intel reports."

"Can you access those?"

The big man raised an eyebrow. "What do you think? There's a massive archive out in Carlsgard and yes - before you ask - I've just spent half the bloody night looking through them."

"And?" Robb leaned forwards, eager for any news.

"And…there are no records of a man called Brynne – or any variation on that name."

"So that's it. We've got nothing."

Kellie sighed. "Just shut up for a minute Calloway and let me finish. You ever hear of a man called Lascam?" Eliza shook her head, but Robb felt a chill slide down his back.

I have met with Undersecretary Lascam

"I've heard of him, but it was a long time ago. He worked for the Premier, didn't he?"

Kellie nodded. "A government man from a long way back. And depending on who you ask, the one behind Talis's most brutal crackdowns. Anyway, about thirty years ago he came up with a new plan and started putting sleeper agents into every anarchist group in the city states."

"That's nothing new. There were always informers."

"Not informers, Robb. These were different. They were told to incite violence *against* the Government."

"Against?" Eliza said. "Why would they do that?"

"Think about it. Talis needed justification for what he was doing across the City States. They were imposing curfews and setting up those bloody checkpoints in every city. Lascam wanted to make ID cards compulsory and probably thought a bit of anarchy would make it easier to swallow for everyone else. Why risk losing to a real opponent though? Not when he could manufacture his own and rig the fight at both ends?"

Robb's mind was racing. For thirty-three years Ashgate had made him a public traitor and convinced him it was all part of his punishment. Had it really always been that simple? Had he really just been a sideshow that allowed the real traitors to operate in the shadows?

"So what are you saying?" Eliza cut through the silence. "Brynne's one of these agents? He's working for the government?"

"I'm as sure as I can be," Kellie said. "But I doubt we'll ever know for certain."

"Why not?"

"Someone already got to the records before I did."

"A traitor in the seveners?"

Kellie let out a deep sigh. "I'll not be the one to say it. But the fact is, I found plenty of references to these agents, but almost every direct report had been removed from the index."

"*Almost?*"

Kellie gave a tight-lipped grin. "In the last few years, the government stopped covering their tracks."

"That doesn't make sense," Robb frowned. "If nothing else, this Government has always been thorough."

"True enough," Kellie said, "but the City States are a different place to what they were thirty years ago. The Premier's grip is near unshakeable. My guess is that if any of these agents are left alive, they're finding it harder and harder to stay useful."

"So what do the more recent reports say?"

"That someone is still radicalising the young men in Karasard and Straybeck. That he persuades them to sacrifice their own life in a make-believe struggle against the government."

Eliza stared hard at Robb. "That's him. That's the one who's got our boy."

"Then it looks like we have two choices," Kellie said. "We either make your boy disappear."

"Disappear?"

"New name, new card and a new life somewhere else. Or…" Kellie's face turned grim. "We make this Brynne disappear and hope no one comes looking."

Robb was searching hard for a third option, but knew it was hopeless. "Neither one will be easy."

"True. But the first, at least, I can help with. The second… that's on you."

Robb considered killing again. Then he imagined the alternative and weighed his son's life against that of a stranger, finding that it was not even a consideration.

"I'll take care of it," he said quietly. "There's one other thing though." The thought had been eating away at him most of the morning.

"Go on."

"These government agents. Could Colonel Stephens have been one? Could it be him that's behind this?"

Kellie shrugged his massive shoulder. "You knew him better than I did. Does it matter though?"

"It matters."

"Well let's go and find out."

CHAPTER 52

JOHN HAD LISTENED to the whole conversation from the hallway. Was his dad really going to kill someone? When the sevener had gone, he opened the door to find his mum and dad speaking in whispers.

"Can you give us a minute John," his dad said quickly.

It would have been very easy to walk away then, but he knew that Ryan needed him.

"Ryan's gone to find Brynne."

"What?"

"He told me this morning. Said he was going to meet Brynne so that he could leave the group."

His dad grabbed John by the shoulders. "Are you sure? What exactly did he say?"

John was seized by fear, but forced his mind back to that dream-like conversation. "He said he was going to meet the man from the chapel. Said he had too much to hang onto to risk it all now."

"Did he say where?"

John pulled the folded scrap of paper from his pocket and handed it to his dad. His mum was beside them in an instant and snatched it from them both so that she could read it aloud.

"*Safe. Need help. M station. 10. B,*" she turned to them, clearly angered by the cryptic note. "What does it mean?"

His dad scanned the note. "This isn't Ryan's handwriting."

"He said he got it at the park last night. It's from Brynne."

"He's arranging a meet up." His dad's jaw clenched tight. "*M Station.*"

"What does that even mean?" his mum snapped. "A police station? A train station? A fucking petrol station?" John had never heard her swear before, which made it all the more shocking.

"*M Station*," his dad repeated, threading the paper between his fingers. "It must be the Municipal Station. It has to be. It's the biggest one in Straybeck. Plenty of exits and big crowds too. If I go now, I can make the next train. Hopefully it'll get there before Ryan even turns up." He strode for the front door.

"I'm coming too," John said, already reaching for his coat. His dad looked ready to say no, but John's face must have relayed just how useless that would be.

"Wait." Eliza rushed to them and for a moment John wondered if she was going to kiss his dad. Instead she leaned in close and spoke in a whisper. "Do whatever it takes. No half measures."

His dad nodded solemnly. "No half measures."

Then they left the safety of their home and stepped out beneath heavy, white skies. The air had grown even colder and the occasional snowflake circled slowly to the ground. John was so full of nervous energy it was all he could do not to run ahead. Every few steps he had to check his pace and fall back in line with his dad who was breathing hard and taking long, uneven strides.

"How long until the next train?" John asked.

"A few minutes," his dad answered, checking his watch. They were at the bottom end of Station Road and as John squinted, he saw a figure at the station gates.

"Is that the sevener?"

"That's him." His dad said, focusing on the huge figure in the distance. He tried to break into a run, but after two awkward strides he dropped back and gave a shout of pain. "You go ahead," he grimaced. "Get him to stop."

John sprinted up the road, running parallel to the tracks where he could see that the train was already waiting. He showed his ID card to the gunnerman and passed through the barrier, only to be met by an empty platform. The sevener had disappeared.

Beside him, the noisy diesel engine growled into life as it prepared to leave and John stared back to the wall in a panic. His dad was still struggling towards the gates, but there was no way he would make it. Summoning his courage, John ran between the doors of the train as they slid shut. He would get to the station and warn Ryan himself.

Robb made it onto the platform as the final carriage trundled away towards the centre of Straybeck. He screamed in frustration before a fit of coughing wracked his body. Hunched double, one hand resting on the wall, he sucked in some air and faced the reality that once again he had failed his family.

"Robb?" a deep voice called.

Even though the platform had been deserted moments before, he snapped his head up to find Kellie standing over him.

"Thank God," Robb gasped.

The sevener glanced cautiously up and down the platform, but the gunnerman hadn't noticed and was still in his booth. "What's happened?"

Struggling for breath, Robb handed over the slip of paper

that Brynne had left for Ryan. As the sevener read it his face set hard.

"You know what this means, right?"

Robb was unable to hide the emotion behind his voice. "He's going to kill him, isn't he?"

The sevener gave a solemn nod. "Either that or hand him to the gunnermen. If your lad can tie him to the bombing, he's too much of a liability."

"There won't be another train for an hour and they're meeting in half that." He paced back and forth as the hopelessness of the situation hit him. "Oh God, John's on the train. He'll try and stop the meeting and then Brynne will take him too."

He rounded on the sevener. "If ever there was a time to help me Kellie, it's now. Please. I need to save my boys."

Kellie blew out his cheeks with a harsh exhale. "Robb, you don't know what you're asking me."

"I do. I need you to do anything in your power."

Robb waited anxiously while the snow fell between them. Then Kellie turned away and strode up the platform. Robb's heart sank. It had been the last hope he was clinging to. The last roll of the dice.

"Kellie," he shouted. "You still owe me."

The sevener stopped sharply, a hard look in his eyes. Then he dropped down onto the tracks and vanished.

CHAPTER 53

"Kellie?" Robb limped forwards. "Kellie?" He crouched at the edge of the platform and craned his neck above the track. Directly below him was the opening to a shaft that sank maybe twenty feet into darkness. There were metal rungs fastened down one wall and at the bottom he could see Kellie's shadowy outline.

"You coming?" he said, deep voice echoing upwards.

Robb lowered himself onto the track and then clambered carefully down the rusted metal rungs. As he reached the bottom, he realised that what he had first taken for a narrow maintenance shaft actually opened up into a long, wide tunnel. Kellie was standing nearby with a freshly lit gas-lamp in one hand. It cast a warm light through the space and Robb could see the arched ceiling leading off into shadows.

"What is this place?"

"You've heard the stories Robb."

Every kid in the City States had heard about the sevener tunnels. Then they grew up and assumed it was just make believe. "They really exist?"

Kellie ignored the question. "You need to understand something Robb. By doing this...by bringing you down here…I'm breaking a trust that my kind have kept for over a thousand years."

"Your kind? Kellie, what are you talking about?"

The sevener shook his head. "I've already said more than I should. Just know that bringing you here and walking these tunnels, it's no small thing. You can never breathe a word of this."

"On my children's lives."

"Good enough." Kellie moved swiftly down the tunnel taking the light with him. "There's a direct route to the Municipal station. If we hurry, we'll be there in time."

Robb lurched forwards struggling to keep up with the impossibly long strides but determined that he wouldn't be the one who slowed them down.

"What do I do if we see another sevener down here?"

"Look taller."

The train ride across Straybeck went quickly and it was with a mixed sense of relief and fear that John stepped onto the platform at Straybeck's Municipal Station. He checked the large yellow dial of the station clock and saw there were only fifteen minutes until the meet. As the sheer scale of the building hit him, John suddenly realised that he had no idea where he should start looking.

There were eight tracks terminating here and the platform from each one led onto a long, wide concourse. John joined the rest of the commuters and found himself in the busy waiting area beneath a vaulted atrium. Crowds of people pushed past him on either side and John fell into step so that he could walk a slow circuit of the entire area. As he went, he scanned the faces for any sign of Ryan or Brynne. His dad had said they'd want to meet somewhere public to blend in, so he stayed with the crowds.

As the minutes passed though, John grew more anxious. Something wasn't right. Whenever he had seen his brother meeting Brynne, it had always been dark and secret. He thought back to the derelict chapel and then to that abandoned station in the Manufacturing District.

M station.

He was at the wrong place.

John sprinted for the checkpoint at the end of the terminal and waited in line to show his card. Its progression was painfully slow, but as soon as the gunnerman waved him through, he hared up a short flight of steps and onto the road. Snow was falling quickly now, and a delivery wagon blared its horn, swerving to avoid him. The driver hung his head and shoulders out the window to bellow at him. John ignored the man and continued through the Trade District. Behind him, the station clock began the first of ten strikes.

Alia looked with sad eyes at her reflection in the grimy hallway mirror. There was no other word for it, she looked like a beggar. The only winter coat that still fit her was from her mother's wardrobe. It was old fashioned and obscenely expensive in its day. On top of Alia's mismatched clothing though, it just appeared cheap and tacky.

The front door was half open and she frowned uncertainly at the heavy flakes of snow that were drifting to earth. With a huff of annoyance, she flung the coat onto the stairs and stomped out into the cold. She had found an iron coin that morning just lying on the street. At first, she had marvelled at the idea that someone could lose an iron and not miss it.

Then she had marvelled at the person she'd become to have such thoughts. With the coin held tightly in her hand though, she was determined to make a fresh start with Ryan.

Since he had promised to leave his old life behind, for the first time in nearly two years Alia had felt – not hope - but the touch of what hope could be. She set off across Straybeck towards the markets in the Trade District. The main street was lined with the usual mix of newsagents, groceries and buyall stores. It ran parallel to Station Road and as she wondered what to cook her and Ryan that evening, she heard the station clock chiming for the hour. As usual, her eyes darted to the shop where that hateful man worked and she crossed the road so that they wouldn't meet.

People were hurrying from shop to shop trying to stay out of the snow. They were bundled up against the weather and more than one person cocked an eyebrow at Alia wearing only her thin school jumper and trousers.

She passed a butcher's window with a selection of animals hanging from hooks. She remembered the wholesome smell of beef stroganoff and the lip-smacking taste of veal cutlets in a thyme butter sauce. When she lived in Old Straybeck those dishes would arrive on the table at exactly the right time and temperature presented for the three of them and Alia never gave a moment's thought to where it had come from or how long it had taken to prepare. Those days were gone, but surely one iron could buy a cheap cut of meat and some vegetables for her to make a halfway decent meal.

With a decisive nod, Alia went to the shop doorway just as a figure sprinted around the corner of the road and clattered against her. The boy lost his footing in the snow and slid onto his backside.

"Are you okay?" Alia said, offering her hand. She couldn't believe it when she found John staring up at her. "What are you doing here?"

He was on his feet immediately. "Where's Ryan?"

"He said he was going to see you." She suddenly felt that familiar churning in her stomach. "What's happened?"

"He's in danger."

"What kind of danger?"

"They're going to kill him if I don't find him first." John had tears in his eyes as he spoke.

"I'm coming with you."

"No. I need you to wait for my dad. He's coming on the next train, but you need to tell him he got the code wrong."

"Code? John, you're not making any sense."

"M station. It's *Manufacturing*, not Municipal. Just tell him, he'll understand."

"I don't even know what your dad looks like though?"

"You've got to find him. Look for the man with the limp."

The station clocked made one last chime and then an ominous silence filled its space. "I've got to go," John said, turning away. "Just tell him. Please."

For a few moments, all Alia could do was watch him leave. Her body had seized up like rusted gears. Only with a conscious effort could she put one foot in front of the other and move through the shallow snow towards Municipal Station.

They're going to kill him.

The idea was stuck, blocking all rational thoughts. She showed her ID to the guard and drifted into the bustling concourse. A dozen platforms led to and from this main area and Alia searched the boards for one that passed through the Victory Estate. She walked the full length of the station, seeing the lines from the outer districts and those travelling even further to Carlsgard and Kilvaren.

There was a direct line to Karasard and then a commuter line that went to the mining camps at Insel. Not one of them showed the stations they were passing through though and Alia, who had never needed to travel by train, had no idea how to find out.

She glanced up at the huge yellow clock face and saw it was ten past ten. Her anxiety rose to an almost crippling level as she made a second loop of the station. Absently, she felt inside her pocket and grabbed the small bottle of tablets.

"Can I help you miss?" Alia spun around guiltily and pushed the pills out of sight. It was a short chubby man wearing a dark green porter's uniform. In one hand he was balancing a two-wheeled trolley. "You look a little lost, if you don't mind me saying."

He was a few years older than her and had a genuine smile that quickly disarmed her suspicions. "I need to know which platform the train from the Victory Estate will arrive at."

"Ooh, now," the porter mused, relishing the opportunity to demonstrate his knowledge. "That will probably be the outer circle line," he said as he dragged on a metal chain that draped between his waistcoat button and pocket. It produced a dull metal fob watch which he gazed at for a few seconds. It was the sort of thing Alia had seen her servants wear in Old Straybeck, although now it would have bought her food for a week.

"Now hang on," the porter said good-naturedly. "I'm letting time get away from me. The outer circle line came in just before ten, so the next one to go through the Victory Estate is the slow train from Willensbrough."

"Slow train?" Alia groaned. "When does that arrive?"

The young porter tapped on his watch as he counted out blocks of five in his head. "Should be through by about half past."

They're going to kill him.

Another twenty minutes of waiting. A fresh wave of panic consumed her while the porter prattled on at her side. "If it's a case of waiting around miss, I've just come on my break and could wait with you."

But Alia wasn't listening. At that moment, two people emerged from a shadowed corner at the rear of the station. One of them was so huge that he dwarfed those around him. The other was struggling to keep up as he limped towards the waiting area.

CHAPTER 54

THE SNOW LEADING to the Manufacturing Station was reassuringly clear of footprints. Ryan didn't doubt that Brynne could find a way inside undetected, but he hoped that a gunnermen patrol would leave more obvious signs of their presence.

As the clock from the Trade District finished its tenth strike, he skirted around the edge of the road trying to make his own trail as hidden as possible. Passing beneath the wrought iron archway was like stepping into a different world where the blizzard couldn't reach and the biting winds were barred entry. Ryan descended into the gloom and shadows, halting on the last step to listen for the slightest sign of danger. As before, only one of the overhead lights was working on the disused platform. Ryan waited for ten slow breaths before moving forwards with soft steps.

When his eyes had adjusted to the light, he was able to see a figure sitting on the bench at the far end of the platform. He was slumped at an angle, his head resting on his chest, eyes closed.

"Brynne?" his voice clanged around the empty space and the figure stirred. Two lifeless eyes stared out from a slack face. "What's happened?" Ryan said, rushing forwards.

"Ryan?" the old man croaked. He tried to straighten up, but the pain it caused him was written large on his face. "I've been so worried about you. Since the town square."

"I was looking for you after the explosion, but then they closed the square and I ran." Ryan dropped to one knee in front of his mentor, checking his clothes for bloodstains.

"You did well to get out," Brynne hunched forwards and a bout of coughing rocked him. "How did you stay clear of the gunnermen?"

"I kept moving for a while and then I went to Alia's."

Brynne nodded slowly, dragging in a deep breath. "I thought you might. I couldn't find her house to check for you though. You never did say where she lived." Ryan could find no obvious injury, but the old man seemed to be drifting in and out of consciousness. He had to keep him talking until he could figure out what to do.

"You gave Arris the bomb, didn't you?" Ryan said. Brynne opened his eyes and he watched them swim into focus. "They were in the bags we carried across town, weren't they?"

"Standard operating procedure," the old man nodded. "The primary device brings shock and awe while the secondary one takes out any first responders." He let out another hacking cough, clutching his ribs tightly. "That damn fool Arris botched the timings though. The first device was never primed and the second one detonated too soon." His face shone with a sudden intensity. "We're going to rebuild though. You and I together."

Ryan had waited years for those words and yet now they had been spoken, it brought only sadness. "Brynne, I…"

"I know I shut you out before," he spoke quickly. "But this time it'll be different. There's something special about you

Ryan. I see that now. You're a survivor, like me. And if we're ever going to defeat this Government, we need survivors."

"Brynne, wait please. I need to tell you something."

"There'll be time for all that soon. I promise. I'm ready to listen to your ideas now. With my experience, we can guide a new generation of fighters. Only this time they'll have all the fire and passion that drives you. I see it now. Together we can truly be the spark."

Ryan was dumbstruck. He had sworn to Alia that he was leaving all this. He'd promised the same to John and his father. Yet hadn't this been the dream he's chased for years? To fight the Government with Brynne, but do it how *he* wanted? Ryan allowed himself to dream what it could be like. The good they could do together. And when he looked at Brynne he saw his own starry-eyed expression reflected back.

"You see it, don't you? You've always had vision Ryan. I should have trusted your instincts much sooner." The old man smiled weakly. "Better late than never, ay?"

"Brynne, we need to get you patched up."

"Later, later." He stood up, still unsteady on his feet. "What I need first from you is a list of names."

"Names?"

"Recruits. We need a strong team around us. A fresh team full of young men like you. And I can think of no one better than you to put in charge of recruitment."

"Recruitment? I wouldn't know where to start. But it isn't just that. It's the whole thing. I'm…" Ryan took a deep breath. He was standing on the edge of a precipice. "I'm out. I can't be involved in this anymore."

Brynne went silent. His eyes narrowed, face on a tilt. "What did you say?"

The cracks split through Ryan's confidence. All his well-rehearsed explanations were stripped away beneath the old man's gaze. He wanted to live, something that should have been easy to articulate. But Brynne wasn't letting it run like that.

"I just…I'm not going to be a part of this anymore"

The old man's grip never left his shoulder or the threat from his eyes. All trace of injury seemed to have left him. "I'm sorry Ryan, but it's not that simple anymore. This isn't a youth club where you can come and go as you please. I've put too much work into this. Into you."

Then he shook his head and with a quick laugh all the charm and smiles returned to his face. "It's fine," he said. "Just nerves. I'd be surprised if you didn't have them. All you have to do is give me a list of names. Just a few at first. The ones that could rise to the challenge. Then take a few days for yourself. Spend some time with your girl. You'll soon appreciate what it is we're fighting for."

He tapped the side of his head with one finger. "You've let them get to you, that's all. It's just those little voices of doubt that we all have." Ryan noticed that the grip on his shoulder had not loosened any.

"Just give me some names and I'll make contact and get things started. Then when you're ready, we'll hit the ground running. The two of us together."

Before Ryan could answer though, there was a sound at the end of the platform and two gunnermen appeared.

CHAPTER 55

By the time they emerged from the sevener tunnel at Municipal station, Robb was ready to drop. He had been forced to jog the entire way just to trail behind Kellie's massive strides.

"I've got to stop," he gasped.

"No you don't," the sevener replied, thrusting his huge hand into Robb's back, urging him forwards. The station was heaving with thousands of people all rushing to their destinations or taking a few moments to stamp the snow from their boots. Kellie was searching the crowds as they passed by.

"Where is he?"

"I'm tall, not bloody clairvoyant."

Suddenly, a girl blocked their path staring straight at Robb. She was maybe fifteen years old, pale and thin, wearing a Straybeck Central jumper that was soaked through. Robb assumed that she wanted money and tried to move around her.

"Are you Ryan's dad?"

That got even the sevener's attention.

"Who are you?" he growled.

Far from being intimidated though, the girl stared at

him with big solemn eyes, like a schoolteacher staring at an unruly child. She didn't answer his question and turned back to Robb.

"Are you? Ryan's dad?"

"You must be Alia," he said, instinctively pleased with the choice that both his sons had made. He held out one hand and saw the worry on her face relent for just one moment.

"John told me to wait for you," she said.

"John? Is he here?"

"No, but he gave me a message." Alia closed her eyes for a moment as though she were making certain of the wording. "He said that you got the code wrong. That the meet up isn't here, it's at the Manufacturing station."

"Manufacturing?" Robb glared at Kellie. "But that closed decades ago. Are you sure?" He searched Alia's eyes.

"That's what John said. He said they were going to kill him." Just repeating the words seemed to break whatever composure she had left. She covered her face with one hand, but Robb knew there was no time to comfort her.

"Come on," he said to Kellie and set off for the station doors. Kellie grabbed his arm and held him in place.

"There's a quicker way," he nodded back to the shadows.

"Take me with you," Alia cut in.

"Not a chance." The sevener marched away.

"Go west on Market Street and into the old Manufacturing District," Robb said quickly. "When you reach a crossroads, go right and then follow that road for another half mile. You can't miss it."

Then, despite the burning protests from his legs, he lurched after Kellie and soon found himself back inside the sevener tunnels. The ground was rough and Robb was taken on a dizzying series of turns and twisting steps. Only when he had lost all sense of direction did they seem to settle on a long, straight tunnel that cut deep into the shadows.

The pace was quick and Robb soon fell back, only able to navigate by following the distant glow from Kellie's lantern. The sevener however moved with a sureness of step that was incredible to see, somehow reading the tunnels in spite of the perpetual gloom.

After a few minutes, the light grew brighter and Robb guessed that Kellie was waiting for him. With a grunt of effort, he pushed forwards and found the sevener halted at a sliding door made from old, rusted metal.

"We're almost there. This door brings us out a few hundred yards from the platform. "

Robb's lungs were on fire as he dragged in deep breaths. His back and face were drenched with sweat and he nodded quickly, knowing that he couldn't speak.

"I don't know for certain what we'll find there, but you'd better take this." Kellie handed him a heavy black pistol. "You remember how to use one?"

He turned it over and studied its shape in the lamp light, feeling the weight in his hand. Then with one deft movement he snapped back the chamber to check it was loaded and released the magazine of bullets before sliding it back into place.

"Let's go then."

The sevener jammed his boot against the bricks and heaved back on the metal door. It grated against the runners but eventually gave way beneath the policeman's greater strength. It revealed a tunnel barely ten feet across and Robb was surprised to see a set of rails running above the base layer of stone and gravel. The uneven ground made it hard to walk so Robb moved onto the wooden sleepers using them like stepping-stones.

After another minute of walking, Robb reached out to get Kellie's attention, but the big man had already stopped. They collided and the sevener clicked his teeth irritably.

"Are we there?" Robb whispered, but Kellie made no answer. He slowly knelt and placed one hand on the metal rail that ran beside them.

As Robb waited too, he became aware of a hissing sound just on the edge of hearing. It was barely a whisper at first, like a quiet threat from the darkness. Within seconds though it had grown to an insistent chattering and Kellie turned back, wide-eyed.

"Move," he boomed, grabbing Robb by the scruff of his jacket and dragging him to his feet.

"You said this line was abandoned."

"To passengers," Kellie shouted over the growing noise. "But that's not people. It's a thousand tonnes of fucking quarry train."

Dead ahead and closing fast, Robb saw the twin beams from a diesel locomotive bearing down upon them. On his left, the tunnel wall gave way to a dimly lit platform, but in his heart, Robb knew that he couldn't make it. He was too old and too late.

CHAPTER 56

Ryan watched with growing alarm as the gunnermen strode confidently towards him. Their uniforms were covered in snow and Ryan guessed they had been waiting on the surface for some time.

"What do we do?" he hissed.

When Brynne answered there was no panic in his voice, just mild irritation. All trace of his earlier injuries had vanished and he stood straight and tall before the gunnermen.

"I left instructions to stay on the street. I said to wait until I brought him up."

"Well as you can see, it's not really the weather for waiting around Besides, I don't take orders from you." That was the lead gunnerman. He had a solid square stitched into his epaulette marking him as a second lieutenant. Like all gunnermen officers, his surname was written below the insignia. This one was called Lannon.

"I must confess, no one really believed you'd show today," he continued. "Not after that mess at the town hall."

"I always produce," Brynne said. "They should know that by now."

"Is that what you did?" Lannon smiled.

"I gave them what they wanted. And I'll continue to do that, unless I'm told otherwise." Brynne finally turned his attention to Ryan. "Although I'm guessing you won't be giving me those names now?"

Ryan closed his eyes, finally seeing what a fool he had been. "Arris never botched those explosives, did he?"

Brynne shook his head. "They needed a crime and they needed a face. Yours or his was fine by me."

"And the raid on your chapel? That was faked too?"

He nodded. "You were beginning to doubt me and I still needed time. I've got to say, I was almost proud when they didn't find anything at your house."

The second gunnerman - a private - unhooked his handcuffs and advanced slowly like he was trapping a skittish animal. Ryan's shoulders slumped, the inevitably of his situation sinking in.

As the gunnerman took hold of his wrist though, a strange sound reached them from deep within the tunnels. Ryan turned towards the darkness and a wave of displaced air breathed against his face. "Was any of it real?" he said weakly as the noise of an approaching train grew louder. "All our talks? All your advice?"

"Don't make this difficult Ryan. You're a good kid, but I work for people who want results. If it's a choice between my life or Arris's, or even yours...well I'm always going to be the one left standing."

An enormous locomotive thundered into view and its yellow lights crashed against the shadows. The gunnerman was momentarily disorientated and took a step away from the track, releasing Ryan's wrist as he did so. In that moment of confusion, a figure sprinted into view, screaming above the sound of the freight train.

It was John.

Like waking from a dream, Ryan found he could move again. He knocked Brynne's hand off his shoulder before hurling him against the wall. John hadn't slowed for a moment and barged into the Lieutenant's back at full speed, sending him sprawling to the floor. The second gunnerman dropped his handcuffs but before he could level his rifle, Ryan pushed against him with all his strength. He stumbled backwards, dashing his head against one of the wagons as it thundered past. His skull sliced open and his body was whipped into the air. His legs were caught by a second wagon and his body bounced and dragged down the platform.

Ryan grabbed his brother by the wrist and together they sprinted for the staircase and the world above. They were three steps up when the first of two gunshots ripped through the chaos. Together they tumbled forwards, smashing into the cold hard stone. Ryan cried out, but his mouth wouldn't move properly. There were shouts behind him and people running closer. When he tried to stand, pain ripped through his body and he fell back to the steps.

CHAPTER 57

EVERY MUSCLE IN Robb's body burned with effort as he ran toward the oncoming train. Death was moments away, he knew that, but he refused to give up. A few strides ahead of him, Kellie had already leapt clear of the track and was crouching on the platform. He hung one arm over the rails while staring at the bright lights that were almost upon them.

"Come on you slow bastard," he yelled and with a final kick, Robb leapt forwards feeling strong fingers lock around his wrist.

The train shrieked past, clipping his rear foot and knocking his legs together. Kellie had dragged him clear of the wheels and they were both laying on tiled floor panting for breath. Suddenly, above the din of the train, Rob heard shouting and saw a group of people fighting at the far end of the platform. He tossed the gun to Kellie.

"Go. Save them."

The sevener was up in an instant, his huge legs eating up the distance with each stride. Robb pushed off the floor but found his right foot could no longer support his weight. He shuffled forwards just as gunshots split the air, their echoes bouncing round the tunnel. He watched two figures flop forwards and felt his heart break.

"Lower your guns," Kellie boomed. He cut a terrifying figure as the train flashed by in the background. He hadn't even levelled the pistol, but such was his command that the lieutenant slowly placed his rifle on the ground.

There was another man crouching near the stairs with his hands raised, but Robb barely saw him. He scrambled up the steps on his hands and knees to find both his sons lying motionless. A narrow line of blood was pooling by Ryan's legs.

He rolled his eldest onto one side and saw that he'd smashed his lower teeth on the steps and probably broken his jaw.

"Dad?" Ryan mumbled. He reached for his mouth with one hand, but Robb stopped him from feeling the damage. Better he not know, than risk going into shock. Blood was seeping from a gunshot wound on his leg too, so Robb placed his hand firmly over it. Ryan gave a cry of pain, but that was a good sign.

"Keep pressure on it son. You've got to keep pressure on it."

Frantically he yanked open his belt and looped it above the bullet hole in a makeshift tourniquet. Then he moved up a step where John was lying face down. As gently as possible, Robb helped him roll over and saw two fearful eyes blinking back.

They stared at each other. John's breathing was quick and shallow and he had one hand held protectively over his chest.

"Let me look," Robb whispered.

He eased John's hand away and a sob caught in his throat. The second bullet had struck in his back leaving an exit wound in his chest the size of a copper coin. Blood welled up in the centre of his chest until Robb covered the hole with both hands. Ryan climbed up beside him and watched in horror as his brother's face drained to a pale grey.

"Kellie," Robb yelled, voice trembling.

The sevener recognised the urgency in his friend's tone and rounded on the gunnerman. "Keys. Now." The freight train had vanished and Robb was able to hear the lieutenant's answer.

"My partner had them," he said coolly. "The one they threw beneath the train."

Before anyone could reply, another voice spoke out.

"Robb."

It was so quiet, so softly spoken, that it barely registered at first.

"Robb."

It came again, an almost mocking tone with something so familiar in its cadence.

"Turn around."

Robb did as he was told and found himself gazing at the man called Brynne. He hadn't known what to expect when they finally met. He'd imagined someone much taller, more remarkable, but here was an ordinary man not so different from himself.

They stared at one another and Robb gradually felt a prickle of recognition. Cold blue eyes, sharp as hooks, glared back at him and he knew that he'd seen them before. But it was only when Brynne flashed that familiar cocky grin that Robb finally understood and saw Farren standing before him.

"Hello friend."

In a flash of rage Robb lunged at him. Farren jumped away,

but too slowly and Robb's hands closed around his throat. He smashed his fist again and again into his face until a trailing leg sent them both sprawling to the ground. Robb was on him immediately, unable to control the fury even if he'd wanted to.

Farren struck back, but his blows were nothing. Robb swatted them aside or absorbed them on his chest and arms. His own fists were like granite blocks dropping onto Farren's face. He felt his nose and cheekbones give way beneath the beating and rejoiced with each impact.

A thick arm suddenly hooked around Robb's chest, dragging him away from the senseless figure lying on the floor. Robb spun round and threw a huge right hook that caught Kellie square on the jaw, rocking him backwards. The response was an open palm sent crashing into his face, making the teeth rattle in Robb's head.

"Enough," the sevener shouted. "See to your sons."

That knocked the anger out of him more than the slap had done. In an instant he was back on the steps beside John trying to rouse him. Farren was unconscious, or dead and Kellie quickly searched his clothing for keys. When he found nothing, he rounded on the lieutenant and ripped one epaulette off his shoulder.

"I've got your name now. If you follow us, I'll kill you. If you report us, I'll kill you."

He scooped John from the floor and bounded up the steps towards the surface. Robb followed with Ryan's arm draped over his shoulder, both helping the other to limp towards daylight. As they stepped beneath the curved metal archway of the Manufacturing Station, a blizzard of snow hit them. The wind had grown fiercer and it whipped the snow around them, forcing Robb to guard his eyes with one hand as he searched for Kellie.

The sevener was partway down the street standing beside a gunnerman jeep. He had already gained entry by smashing one of the windows and laid John across the back seats. Robb watched him dash around the car and wrench open the driver's door before he hunched below the steering column and tore at the bundle of wires fastened there. He slid into the back seat while Ryan struggled into the front and in seconds the engine roared into life.

The wound on his son's chest was no longer bleeding and his skin felt cold to touch.

"Stay with us John," Robb whispered. "We'll get you fixed up. We're going to a hospital."

He clutched John's hands tightly in his own while Kellie wrestled the jeep around corners, fighting for grip on the white roads. John's eyes were closed but he called out in a small voice. Robb was afraid to listen though, somehow knowing that if he let John speak, it would be for the last time.

"Dad," he said again, barely a whisper.

In spite of himself, Robb leaned closer, tilting one ear to John's mouth. "I'm here. Go on."

"Is Ryan okay?"

Robb clenched his jaw tight as tears fell from both eyes.

"I'm fine," Ryan said, reaching between the seats to hold his hand. "We got away. You saved me."

John gave the flicker of a smile before releasing a deep sigh.

"How long Kellie?" Robb shouted.

"We're here," he replied, almost losing control of the car as it slid through the hospital gate. They stopped outside the emergency doors and together lifted John from the vehicle while Ryan dogged their steps. Two doctors ran out with a trolley, but John's breathing had already stopped, and his once bright eyes were cold and vacant. Robb let them take him and stood numbly in the hospital entrance, utterly lost.

CHAPTER 58

Ryan was home, sitting on a plank of wood in the old outhouse. It was the seat that John had made for himself years ago and he'd never appreciated until now just how uncomfortable it was. He looked up at the high shelf that had been his perch and wished he had allowed John to sit there. Just once.

Ryan was holding *luck stone*, turning it over in his hands, rubbing his fingers over the jagged quartz. He had left it there as a present for John. That was before the train station. Before…

His jaw ached dreadfully, and he could barely swallow or speak. They'd removed the roots of two teeth and patched up the hole in his leg too. Ryan was in constant pain, but he knew it would never be enough.

His thoughts were always of John. Especially here where they had played before the city got its hooks into them. He bowed his head and felt grief once more pulling at his heart. He squeezed both arms across his chest and clenched his teeth, able to force down the feelings once again. It hurt more to contain them like this, but he couldn't cry. Crying brought forgiveness and he didn't deserve that.

Through the wall of the outhouse, he heard the back

door open and footsteps sound in the yard. "So how are you holding up?"

He recognised Kellie's deep voice and then there was a grunt of effort as his dad stepped out of the house too. Ryan moved to a gap in the bricks and watched him cross the yard. His dad was limping worse than ever and didn't answer the sevener's question, except with a non-committal shrug.

Kellie said nothing, passing the time in companionable silence while staring at the white skies. The snows had stalled for now, but the clouds still weighed heavy over Straybeck. Eventually Ryan's dad spoke.

"Did you find the gunnerman?"

Kellie nodded.

"And?"

"It's taken care of."

Ryan wasn't sure what that meant but he hoped it was a slow and painful.

"What about Farren? What happened to him?"

"It's taken care of."

Even to Ryan, the answer was unsatisfactory.

"Kellie. Just tell me. Did he talk? Did he say why?"

"It won't bring him back."

Robb tried to answer, but his voice cracked on the first word. He covered his eyes with one hand. "I need to know why."

Kellie put one hand on his shoulder. "They broke him Robb. It's as simple as that. They broke him and then they used him to recruit the next generation."

Ryan remembered a room with dozens of pictures and a ledger of names.

"All those young men," his dad said. "Those boys."

But Ryan knew that he wasn't thinking about them. All his thoughts were for John. His dad turned away from the sevener, not realising that he was now showing his gaunt and grief-worn face to Ryan.

"It's funny," he said, rubbing the tears from his eyes. "Years ago, when Eliza miscarried, I cried for a few hours. I thought I knew real sadness back then. God I was so young." He gave an unhappy laugh.

"But now? Now there's not a moment goes by when I'm not thinking about him. It's anchored me here and I can't stop the sorrow creeping in. It swells from my stomach and it's in my head and it's in *here,*" he grabbed at the front of his chest.

"I can't get it out. I can't…" he broke off, trying to compose himself. "To outlive your child. It shouldn't be allowed, it just…" The rest of the words were lost and for the first time ever, Ryan watched his dad weep. Even then, his own tears wouldn't come.

CHAPTER 59

Two days later, on a wintery afternoon in Straybeck, Ryan and Alia drifted through the gates to the hospital cemetery. They walked behind his parents making a slow procession between the headstones. Overhead, the graveyard-birds were circling and crying out in their reedy voices, fighting for branches at the top of a bare tree. The minister was already at the graveside, anxious to get started. Burying the body of a traitor was a risk, even when it was a child. Alia had no doubt that it had cost Robb plenty to get him here.

The plain wooden casket was hanging over the open grave, strapped tightly to a metal frame. Alia's stomach dropped when she saw it and her vision swam from focus. She tapped the bottle of tablets in her pocket knowing that they were the only reason she could face this day.

Ryan was beside her, leaning on a wooden cane they'd given him at the hospital. His face was bone white but, unlike her, he refused to look away from the grave. They had barely spoken since it happened, and he ignored any attempt to talk about John. Even now, the few inches that separated them might as well have been a brick wall.

To her left, Eliza was heartbroken and crying quietly.

Robb held her close and eventually she pressed her face into his shoulder, muffling the sound of each sob. Alia heard him speaking softly into her hair, his soothing voice at odds with the pain that was etched on his own face.

"I should go," she whispered to Ryan, feeling once more like an intruder in their grief. To her surprise, he grabbed her wrist though and held her in place.

"Please don't," the words passed clumsily from his swollen mouth and his eyes never left the ground. He loosened his grip and she took a half step closer so that their arms were touching.

The minister began his eulogy, the words drifting between them like music. He spoke in a soft and lilting voice, but the words were empty, holding no weight of the sacrifice that a twelve-year-old boy made for those he loved most. It struck Alia that four people huddled by a graveside was very poor payment for all he had done.

After a short prayer the priest closed his book and approached the family.

"I'm deeply sorry," he said, shaking hands with Robb and quickly pocketing the bag of coins that he passed over.

"So what happens now?"

"Now?" the priest frowned, although it was painfully clear what Robb had meant.

"With my son?" They all stared at the coffin suspended above an empty grave. "With the burial?"

The priest blustered for a moment looking more and more uncomfortable. "It's risk enough for me to be here. To involve the groundsmen…well they just couldn't be trusted. It would cost too much."

Alia thought Robb was going to attack him right there.

Instead he detached himself from Eliza and dragged the priest by one arm to the very edge of the grave.

"I need to bury my son," he growled.

"I could say another prayer if you like. While you and your family..." he at least had the good sense to leave the sentence unfinished.

While you and your family pick up those shovels and bury him yourself.

"Fuck your prayers," Robb snarled, shoving him away. The priest lost his footing on the uneven ground and fell forwards on his hands and knees. He scrambled up and ran back into the hospital.

Alia didn't know what to say. They all looked so worn out and broken. It was Robb who moved first, stooping beside the coffin to loosen the straps. Ryan eventually roused himself and limped to the other side. Suddenly a deep voice called out.

"Wait."

Behind them, a dozen seveners filed through the gates forming a circle around the grave. Kellie Downs placed one hand on Robb's shoulder and led him back to Eliza, while two more of the giants lowered John's coffin into the ground. With tears falling down her cheeks, Alia recoiled at the sound of each clod of earth as it slipped from the seveners' shovels and onto the wooden lid.

It was only when the hole was level that Ryan turned away. He gave a sidelong glance to Alia, and she fell into step beside him. Robb and Eliza followed behind, but no one spoke or touched, or even drew breath too sharply.

They passed through the gate and onto the road which circled the hospital. Alia matched her pace to Ryan's, seeing that he limped worse than his father now. They drifted along in silence until Alia glanced back and saw that Robb and Eliza were no longer with them. "Ryan."

He followed her gaze and sighed wearily at the sight of his mother standing alone like a lost child. In the distance his father was back at the grave, his silhouette stark against the white skies.

"Shall I get her?" Alia said.

"No."

He retraced his steps and stood before his mother. After a few words, she held him close although Alia saw how he waited straight-backed throughout the embrace. He broke away and beckoned her towards them.

"Will you wait?" It clearly hurt him to speak. "While I get my dad?"

Alia nodded. "Of course."

He moved slowly, each step taking its toll, but eventually he was standing at the grave with his father. Alia watched them for a long time, not knowing if they spoke or simply waited in silence. In the failing light she saw Robb's hand move up to rest on Ryan's shoulder and to her surprise he didn't flinch. That was when she dared to hope - as only John had been courageous enough to do - that maybe they could survive the fear and violence. Maybe they could re-build their lives and create a monument truly worthy of John's sacrifice. Maybe life, one day, could be worth the living.

EPILOGUE

Kellie waited in the alcove, shrouded by shadows. The sun wasn't up yet, but he had always preferred darkness. Besides, it was the only unguarded view he ever got of the two men who were now waiting on the station platform. Six weeks ago, their lives had been destroyed and Kellie thought there was no way back for them.

As he watched though, he saw tendrils of life clinging on and taking root. It was only a short exchange of words or a softening of body language, but it was enough to give the sevener some hope. Maybe this father and son could rebuild their lives. Maybe they would seek justice for the son and brother that was taken too soon. If that could happen Kellie mused, then maybe it was time for him to step out of the darkness.

For now though, he clambered down the hidden ladder at the back of the alcove and dropped into the tunnels beneath Straybeck. He had forgotten when this particular one was built, but then he'd lived a very long life and that was to be expected. It hardly mattered anyway. The tunnels served a purpose and right now that was to conceal a dark secret. He chose his path instinctively, a left then a right, sometimes sloshing through water and sometimes stooping below a partially collapsed roof. Inevitably the direction was down.

The temperature had already risen by a couple of degrees and Kellie loosened the top button of his tunic. He had worn many uniforms over the years, but the gold and blue of the seveners gave him the most pride. He stowed that feeling though, aware that it had no place here today. There was nothing honourable about him being in the tunnels. Just a cold, calculated necessity.

Kellie paused before a metal door that was rusted orange in places. Thick bolts held even thicker hinges in place and these were sunk deep into a stone archway. A central bar ran down the door with a large wheel connected in the middle. Even the sevener gave a grunt of effort as he spun the wheel and released the creaking locks. Then, with the weight of his shoulder, Kellie inched it open to reveal a small, dark cell. Instantly he balked at the overpowering stench of sweat and faeces.

Orange light painted the walls within and fell upon a wretched figure in the far corner. The prisoner's clothes were dishevelled and his face a jigsaw of broken bones. As he shrank away from the light, Kellie noted that those blue eyes had lost none of their sharpness.

The sevener moved further into the cell and watched Farren roll into a low crouch. His eyes flickered to the doorway, no doubt wondering how quick he could be.

Kellie scoffed. "If it's another broken nose you're after, by all means have a go."

The prisoner had reached the same conclusion and slumped against the wall. "What's this then?" His voice was dry and gravelly from lack of use. "You going to turn me over to the Government?" He found that amusing. "I'm sure they're very worried about me."

Kellie said nothing. He knew how oppressive a silence

could be and he let this one drag out, all the while staring at those blue eyes. Farren was unfazed and spent the time studying his cell now that he had light. His saw a bucket that was hanging from a spike on the wall.

"Ah that's where you put it. I'm afraid I've been improvising until now," he pointed at a large pile of shit in the opposite corner. Again, Kellie said nothing and eventually a grin spread across Farren's face.

"Something about this you find funny?" the sevener asked.

"Just you."

Kellie bristled but said nothing.

"You've got me tucked away in your little dungeon," Farren continued, "and now you don't have the faintest clue what to do with me."

Kellie crouched down in front of him so that their faces were only inches apart. "The mistake you've made," he said quietly. "Is thinking that I have to do anything. I can keep you here until the flesh rots from your bones and not a soul would know about it." Somewhere outside the cell there was the scuttling of tiny feet and a tunnel rat slunk past the doorway.

"But it's not going to come to that. Do you know why? Because one day you'll ask…no… you'll *beg* for me to let you help." The sevener turned away and moved back through the doorway and into the tunnel.

"And why would I ever want to help you?" Farren shouted, his voice betraying the fear he felt.

"Because of Robb Calloway," Kellie said quietly. "And the fact that right now, I'm the only one holding him back."

The squeal of the hinges silenced his screams as the door sealed shut.

If you want to learn more about the
Calloway Blood series,
please visit my website -
www.michaeljameslynch.com

Lightning Source UK Ltd.
Milton Keynes UK
UKHW020216290721
387904UK00009B/288